A Matter of Time

Lane Cohen

2020, TWB Press
www.twbpress.com

A Matter of Time
Copyright © 2020 by Lane Cohen

Edited by Terry Wright

Cover Art by Terry Wright
Images licensed from Shutterstock

ISBN: 978-1-944045-70-8

Inspired by Benji, Dexter, and my best friend Ollie.
If I could go back in time, just once...

What would happen if history could be rewritten as casually as erasing a blackboard? Our past would be like the shifting sands at the seashore, constantly blown this way or that by the slightest breeze. History would be constantly changing every time someone spun the dial of a time machine and blundered his or her way into the past. History, as we know it, would be impossible. It would cease to exist. **Michio Kaku - *Hyperspace***

Chapter 1: Lebanon, Ohio
Summer - 2019

Jessie Warren rounded a bend on the trail at an easy jog. The sun was sinking behind a cluster of purple clouds; a summer storm was about to break.

That was fine. She liked running in the warm rain, unless electricity crackled across the sky. Lightning bolts rarely struck people, but not rarely enough for her to risk her life. Her love of the outdoors aside, if the heavens started crashing, she would take cover inside the farmhouse and jog on her treadmill, as boring as that might have been.

Since middle-school, fitness had been a constant in her life. Back then, for an extra push when she trained with the cross-country team, she would picture old-fashioned movie slashers chasing her. It didn't really make her run any faster, but it took her mind from the relentless pain in her belly, especially when the team climbed steep hills, and her imagination made the monotonous running way more fun.

When she turned thirty a few years ago, she'd started a new running program, right after her parents passed away and she had healed sufficiently from hip surgery. Though she had been promoted on the Cincinnati police force, and physical exertion was usually less needed as a detective than as a patrol officer, she noticed the young female recruits who joined the department always seemed to be in terrific shape. She used the newbies as motivation to accelerate her own workout program; no *rookie* was ever going to outrun her on the track, or out-lift her in the gym, not if she could help it. Besides, hard running was good for her hip rehab. And the pain in her joints served as an adequate distraction from the rest of her life, at least some of the time.

The rain sprinkled and she paced through it. The droplets felt cool against her face, bare arms and legs. Running in the rain was at least one way to feel closer to nature. She smiled through the gathering shower and powered forward. Her hip barely hurt, her legs were strong and still had a lot left this evening. *Let's see how fast I can go.*

Lights glinted from inside a few farmhouses as she strode over the dirt trail across the rear boundary of her neighborhood. Much of this section had been overbuilt in the last twenty years, but many of the original farmhouses still stood untouched, and the *Mayberry*-like feel remained in a few spots. It was nice, in this world of relentless renovation, some things from her childhood still had not changed.

She rounded the final corner of the trail before the path leading to the back of her property branched off to her right.

An incredible boom shattered the air.

She jerked to a halt and shot her arms up to cover her head. *Christ, that was loud.*

The lightning had exploded right above her. She needed to find shelter, started ahead through an abrupt downpour but halted again. Something darted onto the trail in front of her. She wiped the rain from her eyes. It was *a* dog, a small black-and-white mutt. Probably lived in one of the houses close by and got stuck outside in the weather, just like she had.

She took one step closer. "Here, boy."

The dog stopped, turned to her.

Jessie's breath caught in her throat. Poor thing was missing one back leg. She moved closer.

The dog stood on the path and glanced from side to side, again and again.

Without thinking about the dog being vicious, she approached, got a foot from the dog then bent her knees to the ground. "What happened to you, boy?" She gingerly reached over and touched his shoulder.

The dog stretched out and shook the water from his short fur. After steadying himself, he gazed at her with puppy-dog-brown eyes. He inched forward and pushed the top of his head against her hip.

A sudden burst of tears streamed down her cheeks and mixed with the rain as she gathered the black-and-white dog into her arms and pulled the little guy as close to her pounding chest as she possibly could. "Doc? Doc! It can't be..."

The dog licked her face and wagged his tail as if he'd just found a long-lost friend.

Time travel used to be thought of as just science fiction, but Einstein's general theory of relativity allows for the possibility that we could warp space-time so much that you could go off in a rocket and return before you set out. **Stephen Hawking**

Chapter 2: Mt. Adams, Ohio
Three Weeks Later
Present Day

Jessie squinted through the morning sunlight, tightened her grip on the dog leash, and stepped off the curb into the narrow Mt. Adams cobblestone street. She angled toward the sidewalk patio of *Evangeline's Tea House* where the man she'd been searching for was purported to hang out on Sunday mornings. It was already 70 degrees, but a persistent shiver tingled in her hip and down her leg. She took a deep breath and forged ahead.

She'd just parked her battered Jeep that she normally hated navigating up the steep hill from the valley to Mt. Adams. There was almost never anywhere to park, and she resented the aura of chic trendiness this once quiet and unassuming residential community had become. Its lofty perch that overlooked the Ohio River had something to do with the inevitable upscale changes. At least parking hadn't been an issue today, as many of the fashionable clothing and jewelry shops that dotted the rehabbed urban landscape had yet to open.

Walking in this hilly, sequestered community, with the little black-and-white dog at her side, felt quite pleasant, except for the familiar twinge she felt now and then around her right hip. She used her free hand to re-adjust the holster and pistol under the left arm of her jacket to make sure it was secure, and continued forward. She passed only a few joggers on her way toward the tea café.

A Matter of Time

As she caught sight of a man across the street, she slowed her pace. He sat at a table behind a wrought iron fence that separated *Evangeline's* patio from the sidewalk. She felt a sudden pressure in her chest.

The man was quietly handsome. He wore a gray Fedora and sat at a small bistro table. He perused a newspaper, probably the Sunday edition of The Cincinnati Enquirer, folded in his hands. A ceramic teacup rested in a saucer on the table. His appearance was exactly as he had been described, even though her source had last seen him more than five years ago.

She halted at the fence. "Doc, sit." The dog sat at her heel. She had no idea how to start a conversation with the man whose eyes just rolled up at her.

Mistake. This is a mistake. There's no real reason to believe this stranger might have the answer to my questions.

After all the hours she had considered approaching him, she had planned what to say, but no words formed in her mind, and she simply stood there, her mouth halfway open. The melody of a song from the 60s, a ballad by The Beatles, distracted her as it echoed softly in the background.

"Curious," the man said. His eyes were sharp, sky blue, and they studied her from behind a pair of wire eyeglasses.

"Hello," she managed.

"Miss." He stood and removed his Fedora.

She saw he broke the six-foot mark.

The man rested his newspaper atop two others stacked on the table. "You are *not* an acolyte, not a follower of my books."

"I'm not?"

"No."

She took a breath. "I've read both."

"But you carry neither with you...for my signature on the title page."

"I have a Kindle, and I've never been much into author autographs."

He blinked. "You are *not* an investigative journalist."

"Oh? How do you know?"

"Journalists carry recording equipment, or perhaps a writing tablet at the very least. You hold nothing this fine morning, except for the canine leash."

She glanced down at the dog by her side. "Curious. You said curious."

"Have I unwittingly run afoul of law enforcement?"

"No. Oh, no. Why?"

"Could this be an official visit?"

She studied him. "Have you seen me before?"

"Never."

"You must know I'm a cop. That's what you meant."

He gestured with one open palm at an empty chair. "Please. Join me."

She blinked several times, and then stepped through a gate in the fence. The small three-legged dog followed at her side. as John Lennon's soft melodic voice accompanied them. Seated in the proffered chair, she gazed at the man standing on the other side of the table. He had short-cut dark brown hair highlighted by a few touches of gray at the temples. Clean-shaven and properly neat, he wore pressed tan dress slacks, brown tie shoes, a long-sleeved white shirt buttoned all the way up, no tie, and a tweedy vest.

"Pardon me for barging in on you like this."

"I welcome pleasant conversation."

She glanced around and adjusted her position on the chair. "It's nice here, as if this place were lifted from a quaint English village."

He sat and placed his Fedora atop the newspapers. "I visit this lovely establishment each Sunday."

She nodded. "Thank you for, well, for *talking* with me. I wasn't sure how you might react."

"It is, as they say, no problem."

"Your accent...that's Scottish."

"Yes."

She folded her hands in her lap and squeezed them together; they pulsed with an insistent tremble. The small dog stretched up and rested his front paws on her thigh. His nose sniffed at the tabletop.

"No, Doc." She patted his side. "Down."

The dog glanced at her with those puppy-dog browns.

"Sorry. Not for dogs."

His paws slid from her thigh and he curled up on the

concrete beside her chair.

"Cute fellow," the man said. "Intelligent."

She nodded. "We've become friends."

A different song began from hidden speakers. This time it was *Because I Love You*, by The Dave Clark 5.

"May I order tea for you, or perhaps a scone, Miss...Miss..?

"Oh. Sorry. Warren. Jessie Warren."

He extended his hand across the table. "I am pleased to meet you, Miss Warren."

She took his hand. His fingers gripped hers with a gentle strength.

"And I, and as you must know, am Wallace Brewster."

"Yes."

"Miss Warren, I have two questions."

"Uh, all right."

"How did you manage to locate me?"

She cleared her throat. "I started with the usual online searches...but nothing popped up."

A server in her early 20s appeared tableside with a ceramic teapot. She had a blond ponytail and sported a black apron with *Evangeline's* embroidered across the front. "Mr. Brewster? More hot water?"

"Please."

The waitress carefully poured steaming water into the small teacup. She completed her refill and faced Jessie. "May I bring you something?"

"Lady Grey, please." Jessie noticed the man gaze at her as if he were studying a scientific formula on an old-fashioned chalkboard.

The waitress smiled. "Certainly."

"And a dish of water for my dog, please."

The waitress nodded and glided away.

"Of course," Jessie said to Brewster, "my search was stymied when I was looking for Alice Victoria Carroll."

"My sobriquet."

She squinted at him. "A man who writes under a *female* pen name is not unheard of, but still odd."

"Precautions to protect my privacy."

"Obviously."

"But *obviously* my precautions had some flaws."

She chuckled. "The authors of blogs about you never believed Alice Victoria Carroll was your real name. The speculation was you pieced that name together, the Alice from *Alice in Wonderland*, and Carroll from, well, the author."

"Alice found herself tumbling down a rabbit hole."

"That story gave me the creeps when my mother read it to me. I don't know why it's thought of as a classic for kids."

"Falling down a rabbit hole has taken on metaphorical implications for many authors who followed Mr. Carroll. The metaphor serves as the inspirational focus for many stories, transport to another world, and unintentional involvement in circumstances beyond control of the protagonist."

"And *Victoria*?"

"My mother's name."

"I see."

"And so, your search..?"

"The only real clue I had was your publisher. I figured somebody at Putnam must know how to contact you."

"I receive an occasional email from them. They ask if I'm writing another novel." He smiled. "And direct deposit is a marvelous invention."

"Are you writing another book?"

"An idea is germinating."

The song, *This Diamond Ring*, by Gary Lewis and the Playboys began to play.

"So, I drove to New York."

He gazed at her.

"Found your editor's office, flashed my badge, and gave him my best steely-eyed stare. Sometimes that works better than my badge. I stretched the truth a bit and told him I was investigating a murder." She pushed a few strands of her auburn hair from across her forehead. "And eventually—"

"He told you my name. And location."

"He said he met you once, about five years ago, but remembered enough to give me a pretty good description. He told me of your real name, Brewster, your strong accent, and said he thought you lived around here and frequented this tea café on Sunday mornings, though he couldn't be sure you still lived in

Mt. Adams. It had been so long ago."

He nodded. "I suppose all secrets find their way to the surface, given enough time and a beautiful pair of eyes, if you will pardon me for saying so."

Jessie was struck silent by the unexpected compliment. She composed herself and leaned slightly forward on her elbows. "You knew I was a cop."

"Yes."

"From the moment you saw me."

"Yes."

"Am I that transparent?"

"Efficient observation."

She blinked. "You are not as I expected."

"What did you expect?"

"A pale recluse, rumpled, overweight."

"Why?"

She shrugged. "From the movies, maybe, a genius writer, hidden away, shunning public acknowledgement." She stopped and studied his expression. "But you look nothing like that at all. Nothing."

"Are you disappointed?"

"I learned something else about you...when I was online."

"The internet is truly amazing."

"When I searched for Wallace Brewster, one sleepless night about a week ago, I uncovered many men of Scottish descent named Wallace, or Brewster, but none were you."

"Your conclusion?"

She grinned. "Who is probably the most famous Scotsman in all history?"

"Please tell me."

"William Wallace. *Braveheart*."

A smile started at the corners of his mouth.

"And I discovered that David Brewster, in the 1800s, was probably the most famous scientist from Scotland. Invented the stereoscope, one of the first successful attempts at viewing objects in 3D."

"I am familiar with Sir David's accomplishments."

"And so, just as you cobbled together your pen name, you did the same with the name you are using now, which, I imagine, cannot be your real name either."

He raised his teacup to his lips, took one sip then carefully placed the cup back on the saucer. "Sound reasoning, indeed."

"You don't seem upset that I found you."

"I feel something *important* has brought you here today."

"Yes."

"And that, Miss Warren, is my *second* question."

She gazed at him while reaching to the back pocket of her pants and pulled out her phone. After she pressed at the screen several times, she turned the screen so he could see it. "I took this picture yesterday."

Brewster studied the glowing image. "A lovely home."

"*My* home."

"A rural area, I see. A farmhouse?"

"Lebanon. Thirty-five miles north of here."

"A historic inn is there."

She froze. "The...*Golden Lamb?*"

He seemed taken by the surprise on her face. "Are you all right, Miss Warren?"

She gathered herself. "Yes."

"As I was about to say, I have dined at *The Golden Lamb*. The food is excellent, and the inn's surroundings seem untouched by time."

She set the phone face-up on the table. "This farmhouse is the only place I've ever lived, Mr. Brewster. My grandparents built it when they were in their 20s. The farm has always been known as *The Warren Place* by everybody in the community."

Wallace Brewster didn't say anything.

Jessie reached inside her blazer. She pulled out a small square of crinkled photographic paper and placed it face-down on the table. The back of the paper was yellowed with age. "Look at this. Tell me I'm not crazy, Mr. Brewster."

She leaned back in her chair and waited as Brewster gazed at her questioningly.

"Please look at it."

He edged his hand forward, pinched the corner of the paper, and flipped it over. One glance at the photo shot him instantly to his feet. His chair scraped backward across the concrete patio floor. "Good God."

"I know." She took a long breath. "That is my place, Mr. Brewster. My farmhouse. And those two people on the front porch rockers are my grandparents when they were young."

A man and woman sat beside each other in rocking chairs on what appeared to be the same farmhouse porch as the one on the screen of Jessie's phone. The two of them smiled at whomever was behind the camera.

Brewster lowered himself back onto his chair as he gazed down at the sepia photo.

"Paul and Nancy Warren," Jessie said. "As I told you, they built that house and lived in it the rest of their lives. My parents bought it from the estate."

Brewster brought his eyes up from the photo. "The image on this paper is *remarkable*." He shifted his eyes from the old photograph to the image on the phone. "I have no doubt this is the same house, but this old picture must've been taken at least fifty years ago."

"It sat unframed on the farmhouse mantle when I grew up. My parents kept it there as a tribute to my grandparents. Look at it very closely."

"Yes. The *extraordinary* factor is what *else* is in this photograph."

She bit her bottom lip and waited for him to make the connection.

"And that extraordinary factor is what has inspired you to find me."

"I don't know if it's possible, Mr. Brewster, but I need to know what you think."

He shifted his focus back to the photo on the table, at a young farming couple, smiling, apparently happy, reclining in their rockers. And between them sat a dog.

A black-and-white dog.

The same three-legged dog that was at this moment lying on the concrete floor at Jessie Warren's feet.

Time travel offends our sense of cause and effect – but maybe the universe doesn't insist on cause and effect. **Edward M. Lerner**

Chapter 3: Mt. Adams, Ohio
Present Day

B rewster studied the young woman at the teahouse table. Her iridescent blue eyes brimmed with sudden tears. She had been silent for the last thirty seconds as she collected her composure.

"Miss Warren?" He reached into a vest pocket and pulled out a handkerchief decorated in a muted paisley design. "Please." He held out the handkerchief to her.

She waved it away. "I couldn't stop crying. The rain pounded down on both of us, but it didn't matter. Don't you see? His coloring...and three legs, I *recognized* him right away."

Brewster stood, took a money clip from his pants pocket and dropped a twenty-dollar bill on the table. He folded his handkerchief back into his vest pocket and reached for a black cane with a silver head that leaned against an empty chair. "Time to go."

She sniffled. "Go?"

He extended his free hand to her. "Please."

She took his hand and stood. "Where are we going?"

"*My* home. A brief walk."

The waitress appeared with a tray and a metal dish filled with water. "Mr. Brewster?"

"Please pardon our abrupt exit, Britney. We must leave."

She smiled at him. "Next Sunday then?"

"That remains to be seen, Britney." He glanced at Jessie. "That remains to be seen."

***

A Matter of Time

Brewster's condominium was nestled between two renovated brick structures on the edge of a hillside. He unlocked and opened the front door. A little wire-haired dog scampered to greet him.

"You have a dog," Jessie said.

"Won't you and Doc come in?"

Brewster waited at the door as Jessie and Doc stepped inside. The dogs sniffed at each other. Brewster pulled the door closed. "This is Scooter. He is quite friendly, although he does practically nothing I ask for him to do. I sometimes bring him with me to *Evangeline's*, but his manners there have not been the best."

"Is it okay if I let Doc off his leash?"

"Certainly."

Jessie unclipped the red nylon strap, and Doc trotted out of sight, his nails clicking on the hardwood floor. Scooter followed right behind, as if eager to give his new houseguest a tour.

Jessie gazed around the room. Dark area rugs spread in small rectangles and ovals across the wood floor. Bookcases covered several walls, and the shelves were crammed with hardcover books. Furniture was sparse, with only a dark leather sofa, one high-back chair and ottoman, and a few floor lamps. A wooden roll-top desk sat near the back of the room beside a huge window overlooking the hillside and the Ohio River below. Jessie noticed a pipe stand lined with pipes, a humidor, and an old-fashioned typewriter on the desk. A laptop computer sat beside the typewriter. "Nice." She pointed to an oil painting on the wall near the bookshelves. "Scotland?"

Brewster took small steps assisted by his cane and stopped at her side. "Edinburgh. Where *I* was born and raised."

"And two Polly Bell prints." She sighed. "I had a Polly Bell print on the wall of my college dorm. The look in that girl's eyes haunted me all four years I lived in that room." She studied the paint and gasped. "These aren't prints. Are they? My God. Two Polly Bell *original oils*." She glanced at Brewster.

His lips were drawn tight.

"You okay?"

"I am fine, Miss Warren."

She looked away from him and eyed rows of CD cases.

"Van Morrison. I like him."

"His voice somehow speaks to me."

"Simon and Garfunkel, Beatles, The Who."

He gazed at his collection. "For a brief time I lodged with an older lady, a widow. She listened to popular music from the 1960s. I suppose it seeped under my skin."

Jessie chuckled as she examined the CDs. "And Merle Haggard? Johnny Paycheck?"

"She had eclectic tastes in music. Do you know those singers?"

"I know their names."

Brewster nodded. "Their songs speak to me as well, with melodies of lovers long gone, heartache. Songs of being lost."

She gazed at him questioningly. "I suppose."

He leaned his cane against the chair and sat then gestured to the sofa. "Please, Miss Warren."

She raised one eyebrow at him and wandered to the sofa. Across the room, Doc parked himself by the picture window and stared outside. Scooter plopped down on an area rug beside his new friend.

Brewster pulled a pipe from inside his vest. "Do you mind if I smoke?"

Jessie shook her head.

"A pipe can help the concentration." He struck a long, wooden match. His fingers trembled as he held the small flame to the bowl of his meerschaum pipe.

"Are you sure you're okay?" Jessie asked. "Your hand—"

"Your photographs pose an amazing story, Miss Warren."

She squinted at him. "It's true."

He exhaled a swirl of fragrant smoke. "I do not doubt it."

"Good."

"Would you allow a third question?"

"You want to know why I've gone to all this trouble to find you and tell this story. Right?"

"I would like to *hear* the answer from you."

She swallowed. "There's no doubt this dog here with us on this summer morning in 2019 is the very same dog from the photo of my grandparents' porch."

"That appears to be the case."

"Let me show you."

She whistled. "Doc." The little dog trotted to her, with Scooter by his side. "Take a look at his collar, Mr. Brewster."

Brewster set his pipe on a side-table, bent to the black-and-white dog and took the worn leather collar in the fingers of one hand. A tin tag hung from the collar. "Doc," he read.

"My parents told me Grandpa Paul found the little mutt in the woods, caught in a hunter's trap. Grandpa saved him and rushed him to the local vet in town who had no choice but to amputate his leg. Grandpa decided to adopt the injured guy, and named him *Doc*, in honor of Doc Holliday, my grandpa Paul's favorite western hero."

Brewster leaned back on the edge of his chair. "The collar and tag are made of old materials."

"The collar and the dog's appearance leads to only one conclusion."

Brewster waited.

"I'm afraid to say the words." Her voice cracked. "If I *say the words*, it makes all of this real."

Brewster nodded. "The photograph of your grandparents' front porch is the single most exciting thing I've experienced in the last five years."

"It proves something, doesn't it?"

"Perhaps."

"Could it prove the extraordinary theories of time travel from your books might be closer to the truth than most readers could understand?"

He shook his head, stood, and took a few steps across the room where he sat on the sofa beside her. "No, my dear. No. That's not it at all."

"Uh oh."

"Your meaning, Miss Warren?"

"You're a man of *many* secrets, it appears."

He retrieved his pipe from the table. "Perhaps it would help you understand if I explained a bit of my life in Edinburgh."

She squinted at him. "I'm all ears."

Brewster puffed on his pipe and wondered the best way to begin.

What if tomorrow vanished in a storm? What if time stood still? And yesterday, if once we lost our way, blundered in the storm, would we find yesterday ahead of us, where we had thought tomorrow's sun would rise? **Robert Nathan - Portrait of Jennie**

Chapter 4: Dundee Lunatic Asylum
Summer - 1892

B rody MacKay dropped a dirty blanket over one shoulder and stood beside the concrete archway as Dr. Bell took one step into the room.

Bell nodded to him.

MacKay pulled the thick wooden door closed, inserted the large key with his left hand, and clicked the lock then turned and stood with his back to the door. He watched the doctor walk across the rough cement floor and sit in the chair across from Irene Lithgow, a young woman who put the shivers to his spine if she even tossed him a casual glance.

"Brody," Dr. Bell said. "Please give the blanket to Mrs. Lithgow."

MacKay edged forward, locked eyes with Dr. Bell, and draped the stained coverlet across the back of Irene Lithgow's slumped shoulders.

"Thank you, Brody," Bell said.

MacKay didn't say anything, returned to his post at the door, and gazed at the woman in the chair. She looked the same as she always did when Dr. Bell came to visit, about every three days or so, but the very sight of her again, with those fiendish eyes just *staring* into the air, was always the worst part of MacKay's week. She was barefoot, and under the blanket she wore a light green smock. Her skin was so thin he could almost see her veins pulsing just below the pale, cold surface. But it was the *insanity* he sensed behind her wide green *eyes* more than anything else that made him bite his bottom lip until he nearly drew blood. Instead of standing guard at the door, making sure Irene Lithgow did not jump up and escape into the Dundee countryside, he wished he could be miles away, as far as he could get from this Devil-spawn.

He crossed his arms on his chest and tried to think of something other than this slip-of-a-woman in the center of the room, empty except for the two chairs and a weathered brick column with old metal horse-hitch rings nailed into it. The column was one of the last remnants of the old building, before they started all those improvements a few months ago. The bricks ran from the floor to the ceiling, and probably were too expensive to remove. Or the builder just wanted to let them stay as a reminder of olden times.

MacKay gazed at her and shivered.

...Several weeks ago...he was leading Irene Lithgow from her cell to the talking room when she gripped his forearm and halted. He stopped with her and stared down as she rasped: "I'll see you suffer before you die, Mr. MacKay. You will beg me to end your life long before your last breath escapes your lungs."

Since that day, MacKay felt ice in the air whenever he and Irene Lithgow were in the same room. For the moment, he tried to calm himself as he remained silent by the door.

"Mrs. Lithgow," Bell said. "Does the blanket warm you?"

"There is no heat in my room."

"I am sorry, but there is no heat in any of the rooms."

"Yesterday, several of the attendants submerged my body in freezing water. *Freezing*. After ten minutes, I thought my bones might shatter."

"I will speak to them for you, Mrs. Lithgow. In my opinion, the benefits upon mental stability by submersion in cold water are quite suspect."

"I appreciate that kindness. And thank you at least for the blanket."

"You are quite welcome. Shall we start?"

She stared at Bell and cleared her throat. "It is all a matter of perspective, wouldn't you say so, Dr. Bell?" Her voice lifted soft and hoarse, as if she had just awakened.

Bell studied the young woman. She sat still and collected; her head was slightly tilted to one side, and her eyes aimed straight at him. "Odd way to begin a conversation, Mrs. Lithgow."

She chuckled. "*Mr.* Lithgow disappeared from this world, Dr. Bell, *our* world. I think it is long past time we drop the *Mrs.* title. My name is Irene. Irene Thayer Tennyson. Lithgow is no longer part of my life. No reason not to return to my birth name."

"If you wish. *Irene*, then."

"I asked you last time."

"I know."

She sighed. "Things can be different, depending upon *who's looking*, Dr. Bell, as I was saying about *perspective*."

Bell stared down at a closed leather-bound journal he held in one hand. He held a gold-tipped fountain pen in his other hand. He needed to decide whether to open the journal and inscribe a few notes or wait until he was out of the room. He left the journal closed. "How are you feeling today, Irene?"

"You do not refer to my physical well-being."

"Physically as well."

"Ship-shape, Dr. Bell, as the mariners say, other than for the brutal cold in this place. Mr. Lithgow was a mariner."

"Oh?"

"Gone to the sea for ages, and would reappear with no warning, on my doorstep like Marley's ghost."

Dr. Bell sat stone-faced. "And emotionally, Irene. Today. Talk to me about that."

She shifted on the chair, and repositioned her hands in her lap, her wrists bound in leather cuffs. "In France, they used the guillotine to execute criminals, until not that long ago. *The guillotine*, Dr. Bell. Somewhat barbaric, wouldn't you say? *Chopping off heads*. Some heads missed the basket and rolled into the dirt. *Grisly*. But in France, for hundreds of years, execution by guillotine was generally accepted, from the perspective of *that* society." She shook her head. "But not here. Not among we more *civilized* folk. Our society is much more *civilized* about executions. Here, we *hang* the guilty, hang them until their necks are broken, or until the very life is *choked* out of them. Or both. It is meant to be quick but can last some minutes.

Somewhat torturous, and if you consider it, if you really study the way the body would react to either method, I believe death by guillotine might be considered more humane, if the word *humane* could be used in either circumstance. Death by guillotine would be instantaneous, after all. If we assume the blade is sharp enough."

"Interesting," Dr. Bell said.

"*Thou Shalt Not Kill*, Joseph." She squinted at him. "You don't mind if I call you *Joseph*?"

"Not at all."

"*Our* ethics, *our* morals start from the Bible, the Old-Testament Bible."

"You've mentioned this before."

"But even though the Old-Testament God instructed the people back then not to kill, even *that* society saw ways to carve out exceptions to *that* Commandment, which seems fairly clear-cut upon first reading."

"Exceptions?"

"Self-defense. It is *permissible* to kill, as long as it is in *self-defense*."

"I see."

"And in war as well, although I suppose war can be a different method of self-defense. But there are no exceptions to *committing adultery*, Joseph. No exceptions carved out for *that* Commandment."

"You've given this a great deal of thought."

"I have nothing but time. I'm *alone* in here, Joseph."

He took a breath.

She smiled at him. "What strikes me, Joseph, is how in our society today, from *our* perspective, we have carved out yet another exception to *Thou Shalt Not Kill*. We have decided it is permissible to *kill a criminal*, a man or woman who has been captured, convicted, but who poses no threat to anyone or anything. Certainly, killing a helpless captive cannot be considered self-defense."

"Most likely not."

"So, this and many societies have concluded that *killing is fine*, despite the Commandment, if certain circumstances are met. Do you follow me?"

"I believe so."

"A sin deserves punishment, back then, in the Bible, and today as well."

He sat forward. "It is basic philosophy, Irene. Morals, ethics, are invented and constructed by those in each of our societies around the globe. Some condone slavery. Some do not. Some punish by stoning, or by dismemberment. A *thief* in Arabia might have a hand amputated by sword as a justifiable punishment. We would never consider such action here. Yes, Irene, I understand your point."

"Good. That's good, Joseph. I knew you would." She stared at him. "You are the smartest man I have ever met."

"Thank you."

"Your intelligence is attractive to me."

"Irene—"

"Quite attractive, indeed."

Thunder crashed from all around.

She waited for the echoed booms to stop. "I am thirty-one years of age, Joseph. And I am spending what should be some of the most fruitful moments of my life imprisoned in this *establishment*." She took a breath. "I am thirty-one. And you are..?"

"I will turn forty next week."

"You are married, Joseph, are you not?"

"Yes."

"Her name?"

"Irene, we are here to talk about *you*, not to—"

"We *are* here to talk, to converse, to *discuss*. I have shared *intimate details* about myself with you, Joseph. That intimacy should be *shared* if we are to continue *properly*. I believe it appropriate we learn a bit more about each other."

He stared at her. "Elizabeth."

She smiled. "A lovely name. How long have you been married to Elizabeth?"

"Twelve years." He paused for a breath. "Seems as if the wedding were yesterday."

She studied him. "I cannot imagine Dr. Joseph Bell being unfaithful to his wife, to Elizabeth, in all your twelve years of marriage."

A Matter of Time

"Irene—"

"Is Elizabeth *worthy* of your love, Joseph?"

"I don't..."

She nodded. "I suppose she *must* be. Otherwise..."

"Irene, perhaps we should—"

"Children? Do you and Elizabeth have children?"

"One. Polly."

"What a perfect name for a little girl. *Polly*."

Bell remained silent.

"And your cane?" Irene said.

"Pardon?"

"Were you somehow injured?"

Bell remained silent and stared at her as jagged images instantly reoccurred from the back of his brain.

***

My boots and Polly's shoes were soaked from the night's heavy showers as my daughter and I walked hand-in-hand toward the edge of the stream. Our beagle, Malcolm, trotted beside us, his long ears damp from the raindrops that had settled atop the grass. It was early, and the sun was just breaking through the last of the remaining clouds.

Twice a month or so, I looked forward to my Saturday morning walks with Polly and Malcolm to the stream and then beyond to the pond that rested a short walk away, just behind our home in the rural outskirts of Edinburgh. I carried our fishing poles. This morning, as always, Polly insisted upon stretching a strap over one shoulder and toting the canvas sack that contained our hooks, lures, and the garden trowel we used to dig for worms. And in one hand she also carried a small basket with breakfast sandwiches of bread and strawberry jam Elizabeth had made for us just before she retired the night before. Polly took great pride being the custodian of our supplies, and she stepped along with a wide smile across her face.

We fished together for nearly an hour and caught nothing, as usual, with barely one nibble at the end of our lines. I left Polly and Malcolm by the water's edge and stepped back a few yards to the fire-pit dug into the earth and bordered by rocks from the stream. I set about building a small fire around which

Polly and I would sit, warm ourselves by the flames, and enjoy the treats from our picnic basket. I had been working for only a few minutes when heard Polly's screams.

I jumped up.

Polly screamed again: "Poppa. Poppa."

I sprinted toward the sound of Polly's voice and found her in seconds by the stream. When I bent to her, she sobbed and pointed to the rushing water.

"Poppa. Malcolm. Malcolm."

I straightened up and focused. Malcolm was being swept downstream by the currents that had risen rapidly due to last evening's heavy storm. I bent to Polly again. "You stay right here. Understand?"

Polly said nothing.

I took her by her shoulders. "Polly. Understand?"

She nodded through sudden tears. "Malcolm, Poppa. Malcolm."

I released her and broke into a run beside the stream. In a few seconds, I spotted Malcolm. The beagle's head was still above water, but the little dog was obviously struggling. I ran faster; if only I could rush in front of the dog before the current propelled him into the rocks that awaited downstream.

Without another thought, I kept Malcolm in my sights and leaped into the water as far as I could. My feet instantly hit bottom, and I was startled to learn the stream was only about three feet deep. I twisted around just as Malcolm rushed against me, into my arms. I lifted the beagle and clutched him to my chest.

"Got you." I laughed aloud and smiled at the dog. Malcolm focused his brown eyes on me, and then rested his chin atop my shoulder.

"Poppa," Polly called. "Poppa you saved him."

I chuckled to myself. Polly had not obeyed my instructions to stay where she was. I chuckled again. She was strong-willed, just like her mother.

I inched my feet through the water until I reached the edge of the rocky embankment that bordered the stream. I held Malcolm under his front legs, stretched out, and gently placed him on the grass at Polly's feet. The little dog shook his entire body, and water droplets sprinkled everywhere. Polly folded her legs underneath her and sat in the grass. She wrapped the dog with both her arms and hugged him closely.

I smiled at the sight of my daughter's reunion with her water-logged friend then lifted my left foot from the water and planted it atop the mud by the edge of the stream. At the same moment, my right boot slipped from atop a moss-covered rock and sank sharply downward. My boot got stuck between rocks. I tried to move my foot, but it would not budge. And any slight movement I attempted shot a sharp pain through my foot and around my ankle.

"Poppa?" Polly cried.

"I'll be right there."

"Poppa, your face has turned pale, like a nightmare ghost."

A sharp pain shot up my leg. "You stay right there, Polly, no matter what. Understand me?"

The fading image of Polly nodding at me was the last thing I saw before immense pain invaded my skull, my eyes fluttered, and I started to fall awkwardly forward onto the muddy embankment.

***

"Joseph?" Irene said.

"Yes. Yes, Irene?"

"You seemed far away for a moment." Thunder exploded again from high above. "I love the thunder, Joseph. Summer storms nurture my soul."

Bell shook away the image of Polly and Malcolm at the water's edge. "Storms are unpredictable. I do not favor unpredictable."

She tilted her head and smiled. "Mr. Lithgow *deserved* punishment for his sins. But our Scottish *society* would *not* have punished him." She grinned. "Whoring with any woman who has breath in her lungs may still be a sin in church, but what is an honorable, *proper* woman to do with a husband like that, a man who promised before God to be faithful?"

Dr. Joseph Bell flinched as another crash of thunder exploded and echoed again and again from inside the bare concrete walls.

Time is not a line but a dimension, like the dimensions of space. If you can bend space, you can bend time also, and if you knew enough and could move faster than light, you could travel backward in time and exist in two places at once. **Margaret Atwood - *Cat's Eye***

Chapter 5: Mt. Adams, Ohio
Present Day

T he little dogs jumped up on the sofa and settled between Jessie and Brewster. "Scooter, please. Off the sofa," he said. "God bless America, Scooter. Get down."

The dog did not move.

Jessie said, "You're a psychiatrist in real life?" She was still trying to process the story Wallace Brewster had just told her. "Or maybe a *former* life?"

"A medical doctor." He shook his head and rested his hand on Scooter's neck. "A surgeon. And while in Edinburgh I took on the responsibility of performing a rotation at Dundee Lunatic Asylum, as I just explained."

"*Lunatic*? Things must be way different in Scotland. If we used the word *lunatic* here, a wave of political correctness would crash over us like a tsunami. Here, people with mental difficulties are *emotionally challenged.*"

He nodded. "Times have changed."

Jessie glanced around the room. "Exactly what did you do at Dundee?"

"I monitored the patients and informed the local constabulary whether or not someone was ready to rejoin society. I decided if they were *cured.*" He shook his head. "The problem with medicine and psychiatry back then, was, unfortunately, we understood little about the workings of the human mind, and we had so few medications at our disposal."

"Back when?"

"We will get to that."

She blinked at him. "Am I to conclude, then, your real name is Joseph Bell? Dr. Joseph Bell?"

"Yes."

"I am surprised you feel you can trust me with that information, since you have gone to great efforts to conceal it. I am a stranger, after all."

"If you knew all the facts, it would be less surprising."

She nodded. "This *Irene Lithgow* seems like quite a character. From your tone, I take it you believe she killed her husband, and somehow disposed of the body?"

Bell gazed at her. "The Yard detective requested I inspect her residence. I assisted the Yard from time to time, with cases they found perplexing. I found no clue at the Lithgow residence to incriminate Irene or anyone else. No sign of a struggle, not a speckle of blood. In point of fact, the home was almost *too* perfect, every item sparkling clean, neatly in its place, as if no person had ever lived there."

"You helped the cops?"

"It was infrequent, but matters little, now."

She frowned at him. "You searched, inspected, and found nothing there?"

"Irene Lithgow is both brilliant and meticulous."

"You infer she hinted she might have done it. Why would she do that?"

He took a breath. "It became a *game* to her. I believe she enjoyed it. She knew I was her gateway to the outside, she knew she had to convince me not only of her *sanity*, but of her *ability to function in our society*, and yet she danced within our conversations, giving me everything, and giving nothing at the same time. I was not meeting with her to judge guilt or innocence, since she was charged with no crime. In our sessions, if nothing else I suppose she wanted to convince me of her advanced intelligence. In her mind, if I believed she was brilliant, then the law stated she must be released. And while I did not doubt her intellect, I also did not doubt her barely concealed true nature. Yes, Irene Lithgow is quite a character."

"Why tell me about her, this one patient? You must have

seen hundreds."

He took a breath, looked down at the floor, and then brought his eyes up to Jessie. "For reasons which you will find vital to our common purpose, once I provide you with all the facts. It is important you understand who she really is."

"Common purpose?"

Bell settled back on the sofa cushions. "Irene was first married to Dr. Thomas Utterson who maintained a medical practice on the outskirts of Whitechapel, England. He often helped patients who had little means to pay. I met Thomas, perhaps twice. He was a fine doctor."

"I've never been to England. But Whitechapel sounds familiar."

He puffed on his pipe and tilted his to face her. "It is familiar to you for the only reason Whitechapel is familiar to anyone today."

Her eyes widened.

Bell said, "In the autumn of 1888, a maniac who has still never been officially identified, used a sharp appliance with surgical precision until the streets of Whitechapel ran scarlet with the blood of eviscerated women, some of them prostitutes."

"The Ripper? *Jack the Ripper?*"

He nodded.

"I watched a documentary about him for about ten minutes a few months ago on another weekend at home by myself with nothing else to do. That ten minutes was enough. Gave me the creeps. Didn't need to know anything else." She chuckled. "I switched the channel to an old *Friends* episode."

"Irene was married to Thomas Utterson for little over a year," Bell continued. "She joined several ladies' groups and lived quite a social life. One evening, Irene returned home early from a meeting she attended with wives of other doctors. They had gathered to arrange one benefit or another. As she exited a Hansom cab from across the street, Irene was surprised to spy a tall young woman in a lavender dress exit Irene's Fleet Street residence, walking swiftly from around the rear of the house. It took Irene less than two seconds to realize what she had just witnessed."

"Which was..?"

"Dr. Utterson apparently considered his marriage vows slightly less than binding."

Jessie nodded.

"As she later told the investigating detective, she came home from her meeting and found Dr. Utterson in a sea of blood on the kitchen floor. He had been stabbed thirty-six times. And his manhood had been, well, his manhood was missing."

She grimaced. "You think Irene Lithgow, uh, Irene *Utterson* murdered her first husband, too?"

"The medical examiner concluded the wounds had been made with an extremely sharp surgical instrument. And yet the murder weapon was not discovered. Irene was found weeping in her kitchen, with nothing staining her skin or garments besides the tears that ran from her eyes, and a story about a tall woman in a lavender dress who the Yard could not locate."

She squinted at him. "What does this have to do with that Ripper guy from the 1880s?"

Bell scratched the heads of both dogs, one after the other. "Warren, before we go any further, may I make some tea for you? We left *Evangeline's* before you could have a proper cup."

She gazed out the picture window. "My first sergeant called me *Warren*. He referred to all the rookies by their last names. My captain does the same thing now."

"I do not have Lady Grey. May I offer you *Earl* Grey?"

She turned to him. "You knew why I came to find you as soon as you saw that photo."

He blinked. "As I said before, I had indeed arrived at that conclusion."

"Which is?"

"Please pardon me. I shall return presently."

She turned her back to him. "Sure."

Bell stood, straightened his vest, and stepped away with a slight limp. Jessie waited until he was out of view and she heard the clatter of dishware before she pulled out her phone and pressed at images on the screen.

The bottom line is that time travel is allowed by the laws of physics. **Brian Greene**

Chapter 6: Dundee Lunatic Asylum
Summer - 1892

I rene Lithgow tilted her head toward the ceiling and let the winds swirl around her.

The rare breezes were just about the only contact she had with the outside world these last two months, except for the occasional sunlight that filtered in through the small window high on the back wall of her cell. She supposed they reasoned she would likely attempt escape should the window be lower and within her reach. She supposed they reasoned she might jump up and lunge at skinny Brody MacKay, the godless bastard-child who stood guard at the door of this makeshift examination room, and that was why she must be shackled.

And they were right.

They were absolutely right.

Someone should reveal to them Brody MacKay was not actually standing guard. Brody MacKay was there in his seemingly emotionless and upright position so he could gape at her. He watched but pretended *not* to watch, pretended not to leer at her with perverse intention and picture her body beneath the filthy garment they threw at her when she first arrived. Wearing finery was her custom when she was on the outside. *Outside.*

Outside the asylum.

Dr. Joseph Bell arrived with clockwork precision every three days. He would sit as a proper person and they would have a proper discussion here in this stark asylum room. The cold from the cement floor stung her bare feet, but they took her shoes from her and all her jewelry. She was not permitted even a

A Matter of Time

belt for her waist or a ribbon-tie for her hair, now uncombed and stringy without the pleasure of washing, away from the sunlight of the *outside* world for the past two months. She kept account by scratching on her wall with what was left of her fingernails, but it might as well have been two years. It *felt* like two years.

Dr. Bell, the *eminent* Dr. Joseph Bell from Edinburgh, made notes in his journal, *her* journal. As always. She wondered what he might be writing. She wondered if he were writing anything at all. She wondered if anyone other than Dr. Bell would ever read the words he wrote in his journal. *Her* journal. She wondered if she could ever convince Dr. Bell to release her into the outside world, the world of clean air, of sunlight and nice things.

She tried to impress Dr. Bell with her intelligent conversation, and she knew she had succeeded many times. He knew she was intelligent. She knew he admired her intelligence, and he had to realize she was worthy. *He had to.* But Bell also knew beyond question what she had done to her husband, Adrian Lithgow, even though her husband's body was never recovered, and even though the county magistrate said over and over the evidence was just not there. No blood. No body. No dead Mr. Adrian Lithgow. Only the three witnesses who saw Mr. Adrian Lithgow leave his fishing boat when it docked in Edinburgh after two weeks at sea, and who then saw Mr. Adrian Lithgow rush with his salt-of-the-earth shipmates to Kelly's Pub, just a few paces from the dock, to drink to each other's health after a safe and profitable journey. And then these same witnesses, these *mariners*, now having drunk themselves three-sheets windward, said they saw their sea-friend set forth from the pub toward the modest residence he shared with his beautiful wife, Irene.

That was the last anyone saw of Mr. Adrian Lithgow.

The magistrate must have sensed something disquieting in her testimony or he would not have banished her to medical observation, under the specific care of Dr. Bell at the asylum in the Dundee farmland. She still was not sure what might have concerned the magistrate. He must have decided even though he could not find her or *anyone* responsible for the murder of Adrian Lithgow, since any number of possibilities might explain Mr. Lithgow's absence from the community, the magistrate must have felt Irene needed medical observation prior to closing the case and allowing her to be discharged and to roam free. Outside. In the sunlight.

The problem she faced, though, the very real problem, was Dr. Joseph Bell was indeed the smartest man she had ever met. He seemed to know all about her, things about which he had *no business knowing*, just *from watching* and exchanging a few sentences. And she knew Dr. Bell somehow deduced she had welcomed home her seafaring husband, had cooked him a delicious supper, and while he was savoring a heaping spoonful of fish stew she had crept up from behind and slashed the fisherman's throat. To be fair about it, perhaps she had presented Dr. Bell with a small fact or two which might have assisted in his arrival at that conclusion.

She spoke quietly to Mr. Lithgow as he slumped in his chair. Brilliant blood pulsed from the slice to his neck. She wrapped a towel around him to catch most of the blood, and asked aloud how she had failed him, why he needed to take feminine solace at every stop on his sea journeys. It was a small village, after all, and tongues became loose after several mugs of dark ale. And the tales told by his fishing comrades reeked with story after story of female conquests, as if betrayal of wedding vows was something men were supposed to be proud of and crow about.

She asked Mr. Lithgow why he betrayed her, in clear, direct sentences. But her beloved husband did not answer. She supposed he didn't really have the time. His life gushed away as she explained why the betrayal of wedding vows deserved punishment, sure and swift.

Dr. Joseph Bell stared at her now, his sky-blue eyes bored into her, examined her appearance, he listened to her voice, her words, watched her posture, the position of her arms, the tilt of her head. The doctor observed all; nothing escaped his notice. And she was sure *he knew*, even though he never spoke the words. *He knew* with some certainty she had dealt justice to Adrian Lithgow, her philandering husband of one year. Mr. Adrian Lithgow decided to forego the dictates of a proper society and seek the comfort of women all throughout Scotland and beyond. But she had set things right.

She certainly set things right.

She needed to convince the doctor she was *right in the head*, as the magistrate had spoken. For two months she had met with Dr. Bell. For two months they spoke with each other as if old friends, as if students in a classroom discussing topics of great importance. But she was still here. Imprisoned. Dr. Joseph Bell was not yet convinced.

She desperately needed to persuade him that she was worthy...

The first thing she would do after he released her is return home and take the longest, hottest bath of her life. Then she would arrange her hair, dab small spots of perfume on her wrists and at the base of her neck, put on her best dress and jewelry, and strut down the main street of Edinburgh, outside, ready to rejoin an appropriate society, and fully able to relate to Joseph Bell as a well-bred lady should. Perhaps after a few afternoon teas and pleasant conversation, Dr. Joseph Bell would see her as she truly is, and without the distraction of filthy rags instead of clothes, and the cold concrete walls surrounding them.

The wind overhead screeched with a vicious intensity.

Dr. Bell angled his head up at the ceiling.

Irene said, "One of those Scottish summer storms, a particularly bad one."

Bell closed his journal and stood. "We should stop now. I shall return later, after the squall passes."

She pulled the blanket closer around her shoulders. "It could be different, Joseph."

"Pardon?"

"If things were different, I wouldn't hate you."

"You have little reason to hate me, Irene."

"But I *do* hate you, Joseph. I hate you with a passion that simmers beneath my skin each second I am trapped in this horrid place."

"I am sorry you hate me."

She grinned. "I do not believe that is true."

Bell studied her closely. "Irene, if I might, please consider. I believe the Bard once said, hate and love are but a thread apart."

Her eyes narrowed at him.

He raised his voice over the wind. "We are making progress."

"Progress?"

"I report to the magistrate in two weeks. You and I will meet four times before then. Let us see what happens."

"I will not survive another two weeks trapped in here, held down under freezing water by your grimy attendants." She glared across the room at MacKay.

As Bell considered what to say, a crash of thunder rattled them. MacKay's knees buckled. Bell stumbled a step back from Irene Lithgow as the last of the deafening explosion pounded against his temples.

Time travel used to be thought of as just science fiction, but Einstein's general theory of relativity allows for the possibility that we could warp space-time so much that you could go off in a rocket and return before you set out. **Stephen Hawking.**

Chapter 7: Mt. Adams, Ohio
Present Day

Bell shuffled back from the kitchen. He held a teacup and saucer with fingers that trembled slightly then halted a few paces from the sofa, stared at Jessie, and took a breath. "Now you understand."

Jessie gazed up at him. "You *knew*."

"Yes."

"You *knew* I would use my phone as soon as you left the room."

"I surmised."

"You *wanted* me to look you up."

"Please have some tea."

"Why didn't you just tell me?"

"Would you have believed?"

"Maybe."

"Tea?"

"Not now." She shook her head. "Polly Bell. Dr. Joseph Bell..."

Bell carefully set the teacup and saucer on a side table. He eased back into his chair across from her. "Ask your questions."

"Questions?"

"You have many."

She leaned forward. "Is this, you traveling here from 1892, even possible?"

"You have already concluded that it is."

"I suppose so. You are here, after all." She took a breath.

"Am I the first person to know the truth about your true identity?"

"No." He cleared his throat. "Your next question?"

She squinted at him, scooped up her little dog from the sofa, and held him close against her chest. Scooter remained sacked out against the cushions. "No?"

"No."

She took a breath. "Once I read the first *Google* hit about Dr. Joseph Bell, well, *you*, suddenly everything made more sense."

"A composed response, Warren. Solid thinking."

"Is it true, then, what I read about Conan Doyle?"

"I was, indeed, his surgical professor, and that is the sole reason I should appear in any historical records. My life was unremarkable, but for that happenstance."

Jessie pushed off the sofa and stood then bent and released Doc onto the floor. He parked by her side and wagged his tail. "I see the Holmes books, right beside the sci-fi novels." She pointed at a bookshelf.

"Most of these Holmes stories were written, well, after."

"After?"

"Yes. After."

She stared at him. "Then should I call you Dr. Joseph Bell?"

"*Bell* is acceptable. I found it agreeable to address my students by their last names, and for them to address me as such."

"I'm your *student* now?"

"Perhaps we can teach each other."

"Bell. Just *Bell*?"

"If you are comfortable with that, Warren."

She looked up at the wall. "Those paintings. Polly Bell?"

He followed her eyes. "My daughter."

"Jesus." It dawned on her. "She was looking *for you*. You are the lost father Polly searched for in all her paintings."

"Yes."

She swallowed. "Would this be the right time for you to explain how you, well, got here?"

He huffed. "The *right time*, indeed. Almost poetic."

A Matter of Time

"You have my full attention."

"I traveled through time, Warren. I am *The Time Traveller*, as Wells named his protagonist. To grasp the validity of my method of time travel you need look no farther than to the little dog at your feet."

Jessie Warren glanced down at the black-and-white dog. His tail wagged against her leg.

"This little canine," Bell said, "exploded into your life in the midst of a massive *electrical storm*. He was *instantly there*, he is *here with us now*, even though it is seemingly impossible, once we conclude he is the same dog who lived with your grandparents many decades ago."

"I agree."

"You are an officer of the law, used to dealing with facts, accustomed to a known reality. You are self-sufficient; you live alone and support yourself, as do many women in this society. You exist in a world of order, normalcy, with all things in their place. You have no current romantic entanglements or close family members that might distract your focus. With that background, while spending hours in your home garden, or with rigorous strength training while trying to mend your damaged right hip, your mind gathered all the known facts and catalogued any reasons that would or might explain the little dog's sudden appearance near your home, the same home occupied by your grandparents." He gazed into her eyes. "You *reasoned it through*; even though it was seemingly *impossible*, somehow, and in some way, the dog must have traveled through time, since nothing else could serve as any sort of plausible explanation."

She squinted at him. "No romantic entanglements?"

He shook his head. "*That* is what you picked up on?"

"I'm not sure what could have given that sad detail away." A few tears appeared in her eyes.

"Warren? Focus."

Jessie cleared her throat. "Grandpa Paul was never the same after Doc disappeared."

"Please elaborate."

"He died much too early. Grandma Nancy told me one evening as we sat together on the same front porch she shared with her husband so many years before, how Doc did not come home one evening after a bad lightning storm. She remembered the *exact date* it happened. Grandpa searched the countryside for weeks but found no trace. Grandma said he was so crushed by the loss of his dog he turned to heavy drink. And he died a young man because of it."

Bell nodded. "Once you determined traveling though time was the only explanation that fit the facts, you researched the science of time travel."

"Yes."

"Einstein. Hawking."

"Yes."

"String theory. Black holes."

"Those concepts provided no practical answers."

"You then turned to the writers of fiction."

"I read either the entire books or just summaries of about ten well-received time-travel novels, and some short stories."

"I imagine I have read those same works."

"At every turn, *your* name, well, Alice Victoria Carroll, was spoken of almost *reverently*, as the author of what some reviewers, and many fans say, is the penultimate time-travel story, *Borrowed Time*."

"I see."

"They say your understanding and explanation of the various theories are the most believable. And your characters are so heroic, and *sympathetic* at the same time, heroes lost in time, just trying to get home, with no desire to change anything, not to travel into the past to get rich or to alter future events. None of that usual stuff." She took a breath. "I am somewhat embarrassed to tell you I cried at the end of *Borrowed Time*."

"It was an emotional period in my life. I'm afraid some of that emotion translated to the page."

"Okay. I get it. My grandpa's dog is a time traveler. But exactly *how* did he time travel? And how did a surgeon, Dr. Joseph Bell of 1800s Edinburgh, Scotland, come to be living in a Cincinnati condominium in 2019, and just when did he have the time, no pun intended, to write award-winning sci-fi novels?"

A smile crossed his lips. "Allow me to retrieve a few items. Then we can go."

"Go?"

Bell stood. "To your home. To Lebanon."

She stood and faced him. "You want to go there with me?"

"Please allow a few moments. We can speak in your vehicle while on our journey."

She watched Dr. Joseph Bell step away with a slight limp. The black-and-white dog at her side gazed up at her. Jessie turned and stared out the picture window at the river below as a thousand confusing thoughts jittered inside her head.

Once confined to fantasy and science fiction, time travel is now simply an engineering problem. **Michio Kaku - Wired Magazine, August 2003**

Chapter 8: Dundee Lunatic Asylum
Summer - 1892

A pounding like an oncoming locomotive rushed in. Bell crashed back against the door as the full force of the blast struck him; his pen and journal flew from his fingers. He squinted through the driven whorls of dust and dirt; Brody MacKay was sprawled flat, facedown, his cap flipped away by the tempest. He was not a big man and had to use all his strength to fight the wind, inch his body to the brick column, and grip a metal hitch rail with one hand.

Irene Lithgow tilted her head up at the sky through the shredded ceiling. Her chair toppled backward. She hit the floor, her arms shot out and she grasped a metal horse-hitch attached to the brick column.

Bell heard her laughing from somewhere within the swirling cloud of gray debris. He squeezed his eyes shut and blindly felt for anything to grasp on the door, but he found nothing as his feet lifted into the air. He experienced a nightmarish vision of a bizarre city landscape with buildings that reached far into the heavens, of low and sleek four-wheeled vehicles speeding along wide artificial roadways, of numbers and letters spinning in a chaotic dance, of otherworldly metal shapes soaring across the sky.

These visions all at once pummeled his brain at the very back of his eyes. He held his breath and desperately searched for some trace of sanity as his familiar world slowly blurred and faded into nothingness.

People assume that time is a strict progression of cause to effect, but from a non-linear, non-subjective viewpoint – it is more like a big ball of wibbly wobbly...time-y wimey...stuff.
Steven Moffat

Chapter 9: Dundee Lunatic Asylum
Summer – 1892

Nobody could make her take one step closer.

They were *wrong*, all of them. They *must* be.

She refused to budge. Mama looked down at her for a few seconds and nodded once as if she understood. Mama let go of her hand and started forward again by herself through a steady drizzle.

The little girl remained still and watched as Mama stopped a few paces from the rubble. Mama pulled the hood of her cloak up over her dark red hair and stared at the broken stone walls of the main asylum building. A few seconds later, Mama covered her face in her hands and began to cry.

The child was confused; the only time she had ever seen Mama cry was one evening when Malcolm didn't come in for supper, and it wasn't until near midnight when he finally decided it was time to return home. Mama cried again when she saw Malcolm appear outside the front door; those were *happy* tears.

The little girl blinked warm raindrops from her eyes.

Mama didn't know, didn't understand. Papa was *fine*. He *had* to be. Papa was so strong, the strongest man she ever saw. He often tossed her high into the air, so high the top of her head nearly touched the stars in the night sky. Even when Papa hurt his leg down by the stream, Papa was still strong enough to pull himself up, lift her into his arms, and carry her all the way home.

She thought quickly. Maybe when the storm came and knocked down the walls, maybe Papa got lost in the wind.

Maybe Papa figured out what had happened later, where he was, and had already started along the forest path on his way back to their home. That must be the answer. All those men across the way, lifting the gray rocks and broken walls were for no use; they would never find Papa up there.

Her hands closed into tight fists. She looked down at Malcolm who sat calmly on the wet grass at her feet. "Come on. Come with me, Malcolm. We must run home to greet Papa when he gets there. And if he hasn't gotten home yet, you can use your hound nose to track him down. He *saved* you once, remember? You surely know what he smells like. He hugs you and scratches your neck so much."

Malcolm stood, stretched up, and rested his front paws on the little girl's pale blue dress. As she turned back around, he dropped his paws to the ground and started after the girl with a happy trot.

If you see an antimatter version of yourself running towards you, think twice before embracing. **J. Richard Gott III - Time Travel in Einstein's Universe: The Physical Possibilities of Travel Through Time**

Chapter 10: Hartwell, Ohio
Summer – 2009

Her garden had never looked better, and she wished Lester Brooks were alive to see it.

She shifted her legs atop the square foam kneepads she used nearly every day this time of year, and bent forward with her trowel, closer to the carefully arranged rows of peppers. That *Instaflex* supplement she'd ordered from one of those TV ads last month must have been working; she barely noticed the arthritis that had cursed her fingers ever since her Social Security started five years ago.

Back in April she decided to expand her garden for this spring and hired Addie Grayson's grandson Brandon to wrangle the gas-powered tiller she'd rented from the Home Depot in Tri-County and churn a few additional garden plots. She had extra space in the back, nearly a quarter of an acre, one of the largest yards on the street. Maybe it was time to make better use of it. She gazed across the plentiful green sprigs that sprouted up everywhere. If she could manage a relatively inexpensive way to fence out the deer, perhaps this year's vegetable harvest would be a good one.

Her eye caught her little mutt Scooter as he dug like crazy in the corner of her yard near the fence line.

"God bless America, Scooter. Scooter, no."

The little wire-haired dog halted, stared at her for a moment, and then resumed his important task.

"Scooter, come on."

The dog ignored her. The mutt was the sweetest little guy, and for the last two weeks he'd been a perfect companion to help ease the loneliness of the big house with Lester gone, but the mutt listened to absolutely nothing she asked him to do. The folks at the pound said he was well-trained, and she shouldn't have any trouble. But after having Scooter home for a couple days, she suspected *shouldn't-have-any-trouble* was probably what those folks at the pound told *everybody* who came by looking for a new friend.

She stretched her back, took the wide-brim of her tattered straw hat, pulled it off, and let the early afternoon sun warm her face. Cincinnati winters were horrid; she hated them with a true passion. Four months of gray, cold misery had been nearly enough to convince her to flee to Florida, as many of her friends had done once they reached their retirement age. Autumn here was not much better, even though some felt the changing colors of the leaves were beautiful to behold, but she turned her nose up at the fall in Cincinnati, as well; for her, the changing leaves were an omen of the demise of warm sunrises, the end to birds happily raising new families right outside her bedroom window, and the final breaths of long, graceful afternoons out back on the covered deck while listening to the Reds on the radio with reassuringly cold bottles of *Schoenling* or *Weidemann's* or *Hudepohl* beer that lasted long into the evening.

A raspy cough rattled from her throat, and she pulled out a handkerchief stained with small red dots. She patted the kerchief to her mouth. Damn cough. It had disappeared for a while but had come back last week as if it missed her and could not bear to part. She stuffed the kerchief into a back pocket of her shorts.

She exhaled and gazed over her shoulder at the three-story Victorian home she and Lester lived in together since they first married in 1971. The house had been built around 1900, was made of heavy wood, and had stood the test of time. Other than repainting the outside once or twice, and fixing some occasional hail damage to the roof, the house had served her and Lester well.

She pushed to her feet, stretched her back again, and shuffled to the covered wooden deck Lester had spent two months constructing. He had made it one of his home projects after retirement, wanted help from nobody, and took great pride in his accomplishment three summers ago when he drove the last nail into a long oak plank.

She took her ceramic souvenir Reds mug from the 1990 World Series, wire-to-wire that year, and for her money, a better team than the much-heralded Big Red Machine of the 70s, and dipped the mug into a bowl of ice she had placed on a side-table fifteen minutes ago. She poured her Arnold Palmer mixture of lemonade and iced-tea into the mug, and then unscrewed the top on a one-shot bottle of Smirnoff vodka. She chuckled to herself as she tilted the vodka bottle against the rim of the mug. Lester would not have approved, and it was *ironic* that Lester would not have approved. After working the line at the Dekuyper cordials plant in Carthage for twenty-five years, Lester had never touched a drop, either on the clock or off. *The hard stuff killed my father*, Lester often said, and that had been enough to swear him off liquor for life.

She eased back into an Adirondack chair Lester had built to match the deck and rested her feet atop the ottoman. She pushed the tips of her toes against her heels, and her scuffed garden shoes dropped to the deck floor. A soft breeze cooled the fine sheen of sweat that had just sprouted on her forehead. She smiled. Scooter was still working on his deconstruction project at the end of the yard. She closed her eyes and listened to the song that had just started on her radio: *Boys of Summer*, by Don Henley. She typically liked The Eagles, Don Henley, but not this song. *Boys of Summer* made her terribly sad for some reason. If it were up to her, she would change the station on this radio from *Kool 105*, Lester's favorite station that played nothing but rock and pop oldies. She much preferred country music, and not the new stuff that sounded like all the other pop songs with just a twangy slide guitar added, but rather the *classic* singers like Patsy Cline, Tammy Wynette. The problem was she could not bring herself to change the radio station; just as she had not yet changed Lester's message on her home voicemail, she had not the strength to move the tuner on the radio even a fraction of an inch. After all, Lester had tuned the radio last, and she wouldn't do a single thing to remove Lester from her life any more than he already was.

Thunder rumbled from overhead. She blinked. The heavens were completely clear, the sun bright and strong through a cloudless sky.

Something flashed across her vision, fell from above, and landed with a solid thump in the center of one of her garden plots a hundred feet away. She sat up and stared. Her jaw dropped. The irregular shape was not moving. Scooter yapped twice and hopped over to the center of the garden.

She set her glass on a side-table and tilted her bare feet onto the deck planks. She could not take her eyes from the large brownish object that had dropped out of the sky. She stood and took a few small steps forward.

When Lester used to bring home copies of the *National Enquirer*, she hadn't liked to admit it to her husband, but she often enjoyed the far-fetched stories of two-headed goats, ETs discovered wandering in the deserts of Nevada, and UFOs spotted constantly in the New Mexico night skies. This thing in her garden looked like no ET. It was probably some piece of errant baggage accidentally dropped from a passing plane, or perhaps a chunk of space debris from one of those NASA satellites that break up in the atmosphere.

But as she held her breath and inched closer, she realized the large shape, stretched out crookedly atop her neat rows of peppers, was as far from satellite debris as anything could possibly be.

People like us, who believe in physics, know that the distinction between past, present and future is only a stubbornly persistent illusion. **Albert Einstein**

Chapter 11: I-75 North of Cincinnati
Present Day

Bell gazed through the vehicle window as the countryside passed by. The verdant green farms and ranches off the roadside reminded him of the paths he, Polly, and Elizabeth would hike together back in Scotland. Many of the fenced properties here were populated with horses, goats, sheep, and long-necked animals that were either llamas, alpacas, or perhaps both. They were quite a distance away, and he was unsure which species he might be seeing.

The speed he was traveling was unsettling, and something he had yet to grow accustomed despite many rides in hired vehicles of various shapes and sizes over the past number of years, even though his companion drove her vehicle in the far-right lane, with her hands firmly planted on her steering wheel, and her eyes fixed straight ahead. She guided her vehicle at a pace much greater than the speed limit signs alongside the roadway. What disquieted him most was how this young woman was able to trust the other drivers on the road to properly control their own vehicles. At such high speed, a single miscalculation of steering or braking might very well result in a crash of nearly unimaginable consequences. He had observed the results of many of these collisions on the television news programs he watched every so often before retiring. He was glad he did not venture forth in this manner very often.

He relaxed back in the seat of Jessie Warren's vehicle, an older Jeep Wrangler, as she had explained. Scooter was curled in his lap, and Doc was sprawled in a dog bed in the back seat.

Warren glanced over at them and smiled. Bell considered: The sudden appearance of the little black-and-white dog did not quite formulate into such motivation for this intelligent young woman to drop everything and search for his identity and whereabouts. Some facts had remained unspoken, and he hoped she would present her version of those facts to him when she felt comfortable enough to do so.

***

Jessie sat on a rocker on her front porch and waited for Dr. Joseph Bell to join her. She had walked with him around the farm and showed him the spot behind the house where Doc had appeared in the rain. She then led him throughout the farmhouse, and finally to a spare bedroom upstairs. He thanked her politely for her hospitality and began to remove a few overnight items from a small travel case. She nodded at him, smiled, and left the room.

The early afternoon insects clicked and buzzed all around as she gazed out at the same front lawn that had captivated her grandparents and her parents alike. She remembered playing on this porch as a little girl. Back then it became her one peaceful place where everything felt just right with the world. It was quiet and serene all these years later, and she still loved to unwind out here. She often thought that by sitting on this porch, in the same spot once shared by her family, maybe she was just a bit closer to them, even after all this time.

Bell appeared on the porch and stopped beside her. "May I join you?" He tilted his head at the second rocker.

She noticed he held what appeared to be a small scrapbook in his other hand. "Sure. Can I get you something?"

Bell sat and rested his cane against a wicker table beside him. "Nothing, Warren. Thank you." He noticed Doc stretched out on his side; his front paws hung in the air over the edge of the porch. Scooter sat a few yards away and sniffed at the air, apparently fascinated with his new surroundings.

"Let me know," Jessie said. "I have tea. Hot or iced."

He tapped the armrest. "Once again, I thank you for permitting me to temporarily lodge here with you. I thought it might serve as a better location for us to discuss. And to think."

"It's calm here..." She chuckled. "When there isn't a storm." She eyed his cane. It was jet black with a large silver head formed into the shape of a spaceship. "Your cane; it's The Enterprise, from the original series, am I right?"

"Series?"

"*Star Trek*. The one with Kirk."

"A gift from a close friend."

She decided not to ask anything else about the cane. "The gardening."

"Pardon?"

"You commented before, back at your condo, about my gardening, among other things."

"Ah, yes."

She held out one hand. "The dirt under my nails, the kind of dirt almost impossible to clean?"

"Such discoloration most likely comes from serious work with the earth."

"Uh huh. What I thought. You live up to your reputation."

"Oh?"

"Or, at least how Conan Doyle described you."

He took a breath. "Holmes possessed a portion of my personality, but the rest are exaggerations, as with most fictional characters. In most respects, Holmes and I bear little resemblance of personality to each other."

"If you say so."

He shifted his rocker in her direction. "Holmes is portrayed as all brain, consumed with observation, analysis, and reasoning, with little room left for any heart or emotion. I certainly hope that description fits only Conan Doyle's creation, and not me."

She stared at him.

"Well then, let's start, Warren, with what we know."

"Okay."

He pulled his pipe from a side jacket pocket. "Is it permissible to smoke on your veranda?"

"Of course."

Bell's hands trembled as he struck a match, held it to the pipe's bowl, and puffed blue-white smoke into the air. He rested back in the chair. "It is my belief the lightning, combined with sudden tornadic winds, ripped through a weakened seam in the time-space continuum." He gestured at Doc. "The little dog was propelled from his time, many decades ago, to 2019. He must have been in the exact epicenter of the convergence of the two energies. And it is my further belief his transference, from his present into *your* present, occurred *instantaneously*. Since his journey happened with such sudden and instant speed, the dog appeared in the same spot in your present, or nearly the same spot relative to his own perspective, as he had occupied in *his* present."

"Okay. I get it. But I don't know what point you are trying to make. *Of course* he appeared here. That's a given, isn't it?"

Bell took another puff from the pipe. "You read *Borrowed Time*?"

"Yes, I told you."

"Remember how Elise McFrey analyzed the facts and arrived at a radical conclusion?"

Jessie blinked. "I do. Now I do. But..?"

"We cannot be sure if this little dog, Doc, was transported to *exactly* the same geographical spot in space *here* as he occupied decades earlier, at least from our perspective. But, we can assume from the facts we do know, the dog must have been *in the vicinity* of his eventual landing spot back then, before he was transported here, and his transference must have been nearly instantaneous. The fold of the black hole must have been nearly complete." Bell waited a moment for Jessie to think.

"Black hole?"

"We can discuss the inner-workings of the science of it later. But for now, consider this: as compared to the dog, I was situated in the Dundee Lunatic Asylum, in *Scotland* mind you, and the completion of my journey landed me about twenty feet above the center of a residential garden plot in Hartwell, Ohio, thousands of miles from where my trip began, at least from *my* perspective."

"Hartwell? That's north of the city, at the Galbraith Road exit off I-75."

"Yes."

"My God, of course. *Borrowed Time*."

"Remember, Warren, I've had years to read and analyze every time-travel theory." He chuckled. "Not so much a theory any longer, is it?"

"Guess not."

He steadied his hands, rested his elbows on his knees and leaned forward. "The major problem with most authors of time travel, Mr. Wells included, is they focus on the *fiction* part of the adventure and ignore much of the *science*." He examined his pipe, took a puff. "We start with this proposition. Most of our literary time travelers are said to be moving through time, only time, *and not through space*. We are then left with an astounding conundrum, and a conundrum pushed to the wayside by most writers and filmmakers."

Jessie nodded. "Right. *Borrowed Time*. The problem with the other stories is they completely ignore the fact the *world* is always moving, spinning around on its axis once every twenty-four hours."

"Correct."

"And the Earth itself is spinning around our sun, constantly in motion."

He nodded. "And our solar system, our very galaxy, is in motion as well. So, as you and I sit beside each other at this moment, the Earth spins on its axis, the Earth itself spins around the sun, and our solar system is also spinning; at least three separate movements."

She pursed her lips. "Go on."

"What conclusions do we draw from this constant motion, as far as time travel is concerned?"

She breathed in, then: "If the time travel is incredibly fast, almost instantaneous, then the traveler will move to nearly the same spot from which he or she left, relative to his own perspective. But if the traveler is not propelled through time with enough speed, then due to the Earth's rotation, gravitational fields and all the rest, the traveler might reappear in a spot completely different, again, from the *traveler's* perspective. Like in *Borrowed Time*, I remember one of your travelers, Agatha, started her journey in Scotland, and when her trip through time was finished, she found herself in midair. She fell fifty feet into the center of the Ohio River and nearly drowned."

He scoffed. "Wells had it wrong. He forgets or ignores the fact that, since the Earth is constantly moving, his machine must be moving, too. The machine is not at a fixed point in space, nor should the machine be considered as a fixed object. Although the time machine in Wells' story does remain, well, *unmoving* relative to the laboratory, and to the Earth in general, *the machine is moving through space*, as you and I are, Warren, right at this very moment."

She took a breath. "I remember when I read that explanation in *Borrowed Time*, and how startled I was at all the incredible scientific flaws, and outright inconsistencies in some of my favorite movies."

He puffed a few swirls of pipe smoke into the air. "It also demonstrates a real danger of *haphazard* trips through time. Without a fixed point that remains constant relative to the objects around it, that is, to serve as a *spatial anchor* for the traveler, if you will, what is to prevent the traveler from reappearing inside a solid object, or deep under the sea?"

"20,000 leagues?"

He smiled. "Yes. 20,000 leagues."

She gazed at him. "Hartwell?"

"July 18, 2009, to be exact."

"2009? You've been here, I mean, you traveled from Scotland, I'm sorry, from what year?"

"1892."

She looked at her fingers. "1892. You've been here, in my time, for ten years, then."

"Almost exactly."

"Must have been quite an eye-opening experience for you, one second in Scotland, and the next..?"

"It was, Warren. It certainly was."

Time travel, by its very nature, was invented in all periods of history simultaneously. **Douglas Adams**

Chapter 12: Hartwell, Ohio
Summer - 2009

Bell cracked his eyes open to a blur.

"Your spectacles are on the table, right there," a female voice said.

Bell reached to one side and fumbled on a tabletop. He found his wire glasses and rested them on his nose and over his ears.

"Those are the kind John Lennon used to wear," the woman said. "Lester loved The Beatles, but I could take them or leave them. And I never could get by the thing John said about The Beatles being more popular than Jesus. That just didn't sit well with me."

A small dog licked at his face as Bell squinted up and blinked fog from his eyes. The woman who sat in a chair with her legs crossed at her ankles was about 70, he surmised, from the expanse of gray in her long hair, pulled straight back, and the crinkling of skin around her eyes. But her apparent physical strength greatly exceeded any 70-year-old woman he had ever observed. Short-pants hardly covered much of her legs, odd for a woman of any age to wear in public. She was barefoot, bright red color was on her toenails, and she wore a sleeveless blouse. Her lean, muscular arms were fully exposed. A faded tattoo on her left shoulder was the letter "L" in script, encircled by the outline of a heart. The skin on her face and arms was burnished a deep brown, as if the bulk of her days were spent working outside, perhaps on a farm. Freckles peppered her nose and cheeks. She never took her eyes from him as she lifted a cup to her lips. The words *Wire to Wire* were painted in red lettering on one side of the cup. He had no idea what that phrase could mean.

"Down, Scooter," the woman said to the dog. "God bless America, buddy."

Scooter pressed his face against Bell's chest.

"Ah, Scooter." The woman lifted the little dog. "Sorry. He isn't very well trained. I'm going to have a talk with some nice folks down at the pound."

Bell just stared.

"Would you like some iced tea?"

"Iced..?"

"Tea. Iced tea. I have some mixed with a little lemonade, out back."

"Pardon?"

"On the deck."

"Uh, no, thank you."

"How are you feeling?" the woman asked.

Bell took a breath, glanced from side to side and realized he was flat on his back atop a sofa of some kind. He edged himself up to a sitting position. "I have the worst headache of my life."

"Not surprising."

"But for the rest, I can identify no other complaints."

She chuckled. "You can *identify no other complaints*?"

"Correct."

"What is that accent?"

"Accent?"

"You sound a little like Scotty, the *Star Trek* guy."

He shifted himself a bit more upright and glanced about the room. He was in a parlor. Books and framed photographs filled two walls of shelving. The furniture appeared normal enough, if somewhat unfamiliar. A painting of a man wearing a red hat of some kind, with a black club gripped in both hands, was affixed unframed to one wall. The numbers "4192" were written in black under the painting. He also caught sight of a large dark rectangle elevated from a wooden platform by metal legs of some kind.

"You hit your head," she said.

He raised one hand to his forehead. His fingers felt a bandage or wound dressing. "Here?"

"Fell onto a stick where I mark the peppers. You've got a

nasty scrape there. Cleaned it up best I could. Put some Neosporin on it. Don't expect you need stitches. You were about half out of it, but I managed to get you to your feet and help you inside."

He studied her. "Are you a nurse, ma'am?"

She smiled at him. "Just a mother's battlefield training, you know, after raising a boy and living with a husband who couldn't help the occasional tumble to the ground or a hammer onto a finger and such."

He considered her words, edged his legs from the sofa and touched his feet to the carpet. He looked down. Someone had removed his shoes, but his thick argyle socks remained. He tried to push himself from the sofa and stand, but his vision faded and he collapsed back onto the sofa.

"Here now..." The woman stepped to the sofa and sat beside him. "Better take it easy at first."

He settled back and glanced around the room again.

The woman set Scooter on the floor. "I looked in your pockets for I.D. Found this little change-purse." She produced the small object which had the design of an old tapestry embroidered in the cloth. "My mama had one of these. I remember searching in her purse, finding her little pouch with its hidden treasure of coins, and playing with them on top of my bed."

"Yes. That is mine."

"And excuse me for noticing, not that I would have looked down there otherwise, but your pants have no zipper. You know, in front. Just buttons. Is that a new thing now, going to the way people dressed back in the day?"

"I don't..."

She waited for him to finish but it was obvious he could not find the words.

"I looked inside your change purse. It has change in it all right, but no change from around here."

"Around..?"

"You traveling from Europe or somewhere? You need these kind of coins for the bus, or maybe the subway?"

He took the change-purse from her and let his hand rest in his lap. "I am sorry, ma'am, but I am at a loss."

"Oh. Pardon my rudeness. My name is Nadine, Nadine Brooks. Most call me *Hattie*."

He studied her. "I am Joseph Bell." He rubbed the sides of his temples. "At least, I am fairly certain I am Joseph Bell."

"Huh. Well, not sure what you mean by that, except to say one can get pretty shaken up after a conking on the head."

"That is true, ma'am."

"Hattie."

"Yes. Hattie."

"Look, is there somebody I should call, somebody who could come get you?"

"Call?"

"Call. Yes." She pulled out a device from a side pocket of her shorts. "On my cell phone."

Bell gazed at the object and didn't have a clue what she meant.

"I don't mind if you stay here a while, Joseph, but at some point..?"

"Hattie, Miss Brooks, I am appreciative of your kindness, but I think perhaps I should leave. It is unseemly for a 39-year-old married man, a stranger as well, to be alone in your parlor with you, un-chaperoned. We are alone here, are we not?"

She chuckled. "I think Lester would have liked you. You sure sound like Scotty. You know, Lester was a real *Trekkie* until his dying day. He even bought a cane with the *Enterprise* on it at one of those conventions. He thought that cane was just the coolest thing."

"Lester?"

"My late husband. And you are right, Joseph. No chaperones here."

He tried to balance himself and push off the sofa. He made it only a few inches, glanced around quickly, and then eased back down. "I have a cane as well. Have you seen it?"

She shook her head. "Maybe I should get you to the hospital. Could be you've got some head concussion, and those can be serious. I'm going to call my neighbor Susie to come over. She can help me get you into my car. Don't think we need to bother with an ambulance, all that expense and such. Jewish Hospital in Kenwood isn't that far." She gazed at him. "And while we wait to see if my good friend Susie is still sober enough to walk over here from two houses away even though it's barely 2:00, why don't you work on telling me how you came outta nowhere and showed up in my garden?"

Dr. Joseph Bell stared as Hattie Brooks pressed her fingers to the surface of a glowing rectangle in her hand, and he knew the windstorm in Dundee was farther away from him now than it might be possible to ever imagine.

When time travel is eventually doable technologically, yesterday was a dead man who is going to be born tomorrow.
Toba Beta

Chapter 13: Lebanon, Ohio
Present Day

“I stopped her,” Bell said. “Hattie Brooks. I said I needed rest and asked if I could spend a few hours on her sofa, to regain my strength, get my legs back under me.”

“Bet it took longer than a few hours.”

He nodded.

“And this was ten years ago?”

“It happened just before my birthday, and that is next week, July 24.”

She studied him. Her eyebrows furrowed. “I've always thought I was a pretty good judge of age.”

“Oh?” He took a tighter hold of the scrapbook on his lap.

“Yes.”

“Say what is on your mind.”

She nodded. “You have a touch a gray, and a full head of hair. You are fit, as though you take the time to care for yourself, but a *young* fit, you know? There's usually a noticeable fitness difference between somebody who works out, and somebody who is just *young*.” She paused and stared at him. “You have a hint of a few wrinkles. I don't know. If I just walked up and saw you for the first time, sitting alone at a village tea house, for example, I might have thought you were between 35 and 40.” She smiled. “Just as I thought when I first saw you this morning.”

He nodded. “And now?”

“You told Hattie Brooks you were 39, you've been, well, *here*, for ten years, and your birthday is a week away.”

"Your conclusion?"

She shook her head. "The math doesn't add up. And the math always has to add up."

"Is this coming from your work as a police officer?"

She pulled her legs under her and leaned back against the sofa cushions. "Mostly as a detective. Being a street officer takes deductive reasoning sometimes, but not that often. If a motorist is speeding, I pull him over and give him a ticket. Not much reasoning needed. But, as a detective I've spent long nights trying to make sense of the math, *the logic* involved in a case. Sometimes that process is more exhausting than running a half-marathon, which I have done four times, by the way."

"Even while still recovering from your broken hip?"

She tweaked a brow. "You knew that because of the way I walk. Right?"

"Mathematics may prove to be important in this little play in which we find ourselves involved. Although, Warren, I feel it might be unfortunate for you to be inadvertently caught in a dangerous web of deception, which seems to have followed me across the ages."

"Oh?"

He glanced down at the scrapbook.

Doc got to his feet and padded over to Jessie. He stood on his one rear leg and placed his front paws atop her knees. Jessie rubbed the little dog's neck. "You've had that McGuffin in your hands for the last twenty minutes without mentioning it."

He tilted his head at her. "McGuffin?"

"It's what Hitchcock referred to as the thing in the movie everyone was after, like *The Maltese Falcon*. It didn't matter what the Falcon really was, or what was hidden inside, but only that the *plot was motivated* by trying to obtain that little statue. The McGuffin."

Bell considered. "I must say I have watched my fair share of movies since my arrival in this century. I will reveal my list of ten favorite films with you some other time. In any event, I have not watched this *Falcon* film. But Hitchcock is a favorite."

"That's something I didn't expect to hear."

"I have seen several of Sir Alfred's works. The first I saw was *Psycho*, his most popular, I believe."

"My God, I can't imagine what you must have..."

"My favorite was *Vertigo*, however. The psychological underpinnings of *that* story are in some respects more disquieting than any knife-wielding killer."

"If you say so. I still lock my bathroom door when I take a shower."

He chuckled. "As you say, Warren, the math must add up. 1 and 1 must equal 2. The result *must be* 2 so our lives can maintain some sense of recognizable order. But in my case..?" He shifted the scrapbook on his lap. "You are correct. I am apparently almost 40 years of age as I sit here on your farmhouse porch on this fine summer day. The problem? I was nearly 40 years of age when I dropped from the sky into Hattie Brooks' vegetable garden."

"You were..?"

"Some ten years ago."

She remained silent.

Bell touched his fingers to the cover of the scrapbook. "And that, Warren, is one of the problems we will have with the mathematical formula I have struggled with for the past decade."

Jessie held her breath as Dr. Joseph Bell pinched the edge of the brown leather scrapbook cover. His fingers trembled. He gazed at Jessie. "It's late." He took his fingers from the cover.

"Late?"

"May I prepare a meal for us?"

She shook her head. "You want to cook?"

"I have grown quite proficient, living alone and observing many programs on your Food Network."

"The Food Network. You?"

"I am drawn to *Chopped*. I find the elements of speed and split-second decisions fascinating."

"Well, sure. I suppose if you can find anything in my kitchen you are welcome to cook it."

"Excellent."

"But why now? Why cook before showing me..?" She pointed at the book in his hands.

He smiled. "I am not feeling my best, Warren. Let us share a meal together. We will then be refreshed. Besides..."

"Besides what?"

"I think it important we become better acquainted before we reveal our closest secrets and innermost thoughts with each other."

She grimaced in thought. "Can we talk about why your hands shake?"

"Eventually."

She nodded. "I have Mondays off, so we can talk all day tomorrow, if you like." She gazed at him.

He remained silent.

"Okay?"

Bell stood from his rocker and stepped back into the house.

The properties of quantum particles are fuzzy or uncertain to start with. This gives them enough wiggle room to avoid inconsistent time travel situations. **Brian Greene**

Chapter 14: Oak Ridge, Tennessee
June 14, 1944

Traffic was non-existent on the dirt and gravel road that led to the facility this morning.

Huh. *The facility.* That's what they all called it from the beginning, as if afraid to use its real name in public. *The facility* might describe a hospital, water works, school, an electrical plant, or a thousand other things. With that name, a person could jump to his own conclusion what the place was really about.

Maybe that was the point.

Ebb Cade flexed his right hand as he gripped the big steering wheel of the Chevy construction truck. The wrist felt pretty good. It was nearly healed after it broke in a smash-up back in January when some shirtless youngster jumped his Ford coupe through the stop as if his head was on fire and he had to find a bucket of water fast. The crash bent his wrist back, cracked a bone in his leg, and smashed the side of his head into the bare metal doorframe.

He blinked into the morning sun. Headaches lasted a couple weeks, but never came back. Pretty good thing he was in this truck. Would take an army tank to do any real damage to it.

He spied the parking area in the distance. No other vehicles had arrived yet. He was the first one to the job site this morning, but that wasn't unusual. Being one of the bosses, it was expected; that was something he'd learned from his pa. Nobody was around this early except for the MPs at the doors and walking the perimeter.

A Matter of Time

The MPs were always around.

His wife Ida hated this place, wanted to get out, maybe drive back to Georgia. She gave him a good *what for* about it this morning. Didn't even cook him breakfast before he left. His momma back in Macon always cooked his pa a decent breakfast before he started his work for the day at Macon County Elementary where he was boss janitor. Two other janitors worked for him. His pa was proud he had a good job and provided a roof over his wife and four kids. Must have been tough for his pa back then in Georgia, when coloreds were lucky to find a job of any kind, but he never showed any anger about it. He liked running the cleaning operation for that school. For *that* facility. Made him feel like he was worth something.

In the evenings, his pa would come home, sit on the front porch and smoke a pipe, with three of his kids beside him. The youngest, Wilhelmina, was usually asleep by then, and too young to sit outside anyway. His pa, Carl Frederick Cade, the *Frederick* after Frederick Douglas, would then start one of his tall tales about cowboys, great hunters and explorers, and spin his stories until the sun finally set over the western horizon. Momma would watch through a window from inside the house and smile. She always said how lucky she was to have a family this close to each other, and to have a strong, working husband who cared for his family more than for his own life. When Ebb thought about it, he could still smell the fragrance of the pipe smoke, and it warmed his heart to imagine his pa still surrounded by his kids on that front porch. He was sure those were the happiest moments of his pa's life.

The sunlight nearly blinded him as he rounded the last curve into the compound. It was so bright he didn't see the *pale thing* that jumped into the center of the gravel just a second before he stomped both feet onto the brake and swerved the big truck into a gully that ran along the side of the road.

***

Irene glided high in the air, but that was, of course, impossible. Even if the monstrous winds had freed her from confinement, it shouldn't feel like this, almost dreamlike. She tried to focus through clouds of heavenly sparkles, as if the stars themselves had descended to the ground. Her body lifted and fell on invisible waves. She spun slowly, again and again. Her eyes searched for something, anything recognizable as her body floated just above what appeared to be a hard gray slab.

Other visions appeared and faded, some familiar, some not. She drifted just above ground. Perhaps she *was* dreaming, still in the asylum, her wrists shackled with leather restraints. A huge rectangular construct with a painting across its face hovered high in the air over her. The words on the surface of the construct read: *Mike Sweeney Cincinnati Chevrolet Chevy Malibu Two Zero One Nine.*

Two zero one nine. What could that mean? Who was Mike Sweeney; an Irish lord? And what did the words *Chevy Malibu* mean? Perhaps the words and numbers referred to a deep blue portrait of an object with black wheels in the middle of the rectangle. This must be a vehicle of some kind.

Must be a vehicle...

Her vision faded again, all turned to black. The air instantly cooled and then warmed again. She was falling, but that couldn't be, still falling...

***

She felt the sharp pinch of stones pressed into the right side of her face. She opened her eyes and tried to make sense of it. Her body was flat, facedown. And the front of her head thumped with the thunder of a vicious summer storm.

A storm...

She groaned and shifted her body until she sat up. It was difficult since her wrists were still bound together. She took a breath and tried to settle. She heard a sudden noise, a terrible whining from behind. She turned...

Her eyes popped wide. A huge, fantastic vehicle sped right at her. She tried to stand but crumpled back down. The vehicle suddenly lost speed and angled away into the grass at the very last second.

She nodded and chuckled to herself. If she had been killed in that storm at the Dundee asylum, and if the Devil himself had already snatched her soul and pulled her straight down to his godless, evil domain, perhaps she had somehow also managed to bring some of her Earthly luck down here with her.

***

Brody MacKay spit dirt from his lips and started to move. Pain shot through his back and ribs. Felt like he had just been thrown from a horse. He shook his head; he was a boy when he had last been tossed to the ground by one of his family's horses. His daddy would never even ask if he was hurt when that happened. Instead, the big man with flaming red hair would make him brush the dust from his clothes and mount up again, right away, *no time to waste, boyo*, as his daddy often said. His daddy called him *runt of the litter*, right in front of his three older brothers, and was extra hard on him, maybe trying to show him a way to gain a little confidence and stick up for himself.

He pushed up to his knees and looked around. He was off to the side of a gravel path. A huge brick building loomed about three hundred paces away. He managed to stand.

The bright morning sun struck him as he struggled to focus. The front of his head stabbed at him with a relentless sharp sting. He squinted at large words drawn with red paint on a square perched on two wooden legs: *What you see here, What you do here, What you hear here, When you leave here, Let it stay here.* Three small monkeys were drawn over these words.

Nonsense.

He steadied his balance as he watched ten or so men spill outside of the brick building through a metal door and scramble in his direction. They were all in green, wore some kind of helmets, and carried long guns. His head was still painful and foggy, and he had no idea who these men might be or why they were rushing toward him.

The men ran closer, pointed their weapons, and as he heard their stern, excited voices yell at him to get his hands in the air over his head, Brody MacKay squeezed his eyes shut and prayed to God he wasn't fatally injured and slowly dying. Or maybe worse.

Maybe he was already dead.

The Grandfather Paradox [where you go back in time and kill your grandfather] is not an issue. In a sense, time travel means that you're travelling both in time and into other universes. If you go back into the past, you'll go into another universe. As soon as you arrive at the past, you're making a choice and they'll be a split. Our universe will not be affected by what you do in your visit to the past. **Ronald Mallett**

Chapter 15: Oak Ridge, Tennessee
June 14, 1944

"Jesus, Ebb."

"Get me a wash cloth and warm water, Ida. And that sharp kitchen knife."

The big man carried his limp bundle through the front door of his one-bedroom *hutment*. Ida Cade followed him into their living room and watched him lower the small woman onto the sofa, right beside their table with the radio.

"Ebb, what's happened? Who is that?"

Ebb pulled a comforter over the woman's smudged bare feet and covered the stained, plain smock she wore. The woman's eyelids blinked at him, once, twice, as if she was trying to awaken.

Ebb said, "And heat some of that soup we had last night."

Ida took a breath. "I'm not taking one step until you—"

He spun around. "Found her in the road. One second she wasn't there, and the next..."

"What road?"

"Just outside the facility. Almost ran over the poor girl with the truck. Lucky I was fast to the brakes."

Her jaw dropped. "What in heaven's name they doing in that place, Ebb?"

"Ida—"

"Haven't they done enough to everybody, to you? *To us?*"

He glared at her. "Careful with that kinda talk."

She placed her hands on her hips. "I *been* careful, Ebb. I *been* careful. Look where it's got us."

"First thing first. Let's see if we can get her up and around. See if she needs the base doctor." He took a breath. "Now, see about that knife."

"What you doing with a knife?"

Ebb took the woman's bound wrists so Ida could see.

"Good God, Ebb. Is she a criminal?"

"Please get the knife, Ida."

She scowled at him, dropped her hands from her hips, and stepped away.

Ebb stood beside the woman he had rescued from the road and studied her. Her face and hair were streaked with dirt. She had sickly pale skin, and short hair which might clean up to be a shiny black. Her red-rimmed eyes shifted to him and squinted.

"Holy Christ," she said.

"Miss, how you feeling?"

"My head..."

"You hit your head?"

"I didn't imagine it to be this way."

"Miss?"

"A coal-black giant with gray hair standing guard at the gates of Hell."

"I ain't guarding nothing, Miss. Just found you hurt in the road is all." He tilted his head. "The way you talk...is that British?"

She nodded. "And yours?"

"My..?"

"Accent."

"I'm from Georgia, Miss. Least I was born there."

"Georgia. In America?"

"That's right."

Ida appeared behind the sofa and held out a knife.

Ebb took it. "Hold up your wrists, Miss. Let's get those straps off."

The woman on the sofa blinked at him again, stared at her own hands as if seeing them for the first time, and then nodded.

Ebb covered both of her wrists with one hand and sliced through the cuffs. He dropped the weathered leather bindings to the floor.

"Thank you." The woman uncurled her clenched fingers and stared at the gold fountain pen in her hand. She set the pen atop the comforter and rubbed both her wrists.

"You're welcome."

She shifted her arms behind her and sat up. "Who are you, then?"

"Name's Ebb Cade."

"Ebb Cade."

"Right."

She glanced around. "Then please tell me, Ebb Cade. Just where do I happen to be?"

"In my house, Miss. Miss..?"

The corners of her mouth turned up. "Irene, Mr. Cade. My name is Irene Thayer Tennyson."

The basic idea if you're very, very optimistic is that if you fiddle with the wormhole openings, you can make it not only a shortcut from a point in space to another point in space, but a shortcut from one moment in time to another moment in time.
Brian Green

Chapter 16: Lebanon, Ohio
Present Day

Jessie cleared the breakfast dishes from her kitchen table.

Wallace Brewster, or Dr. Joseph Bell, had cooked a delicious omelet with a *Southwestern flair*, Bell had explained. He told her he remembered the recipe from a TV show where everyday cooks challenged Bobby Flay, a Food Network chef. Jessie placed the last dish in the sink and turned to her coffee mug on the counter near the gas range. She took the mug and raised it to her lips.

It didn't sink in how terribly odd her circumstances were until she got into bed last night and stared at the cracks in the ceiling plaster that spread like tiny river deltas over her head. A doctor from 1892 was in the bedroom down the hall. Just the thought of that idea was enough to make her dizzy. A terribly handsome man from more than *a century* ago, a man who may be a *genius* if she were any judge, was going to help her find the answer to a problem so insane she might have trouble saying the words aloud.

She pulled the crinkled photo from her back pocket and stared at her grandparents, smiling and happy on their front porch.

It was *her* front porch now.

"May I assist in the cleaning?" Bell said as he stepped into the room.

"No. Oh, no. All done."

"Good. Then I suggest we walk."

"Walk?"

"It is the morning of a lovely summer day. We can stroll together. Exercise energizes the blood and encourages deep thinking."

She set the photo on the windowsill behind her sink. "Then, let's go."

***

They stopped behind the farmhouse on a small rise that overlooked the downtown streets of Lebanon, less than a half mile distant. A bench of weathered wood planks sat at the edge of the hill. Bell stretched his arms over his head, took a long breath, and let it out. "It is fascinating, Warren, how much this countryside recalls memories of Edinburgh."

Jessie glanced at him and then at the vista of the town on the horizon. "I've never traveled to Scotland. It's on my bucket list."

"Bucket list?"

"You know, your list of things to do before you die."

"Well, obviously, Warren, if you have a list of *things to do*, then you would *have to do them* before you die."

She studied his face. "I can't tell if you're joking."

He smiled.

"Anyway, I imagined something last night as lay in bed, wide awake, as usual."

"What did you imagine?"

"I wondered what might have impressed you most, or *startled* you most, about being whisked more than a hundred years into the future."

"Perhaps not what you suspect." He removed his spectacles with trembling fingers and began to wipe the lenses with the bottom of his untucked white shirt. "It is time we were honest with each other. Can you be honest with me?"

"I have no idea what you are getting at."

He gestured at the bench. "Shall we?"

She smiled. "Grandpa Paul made this bench. I often imagine he and Grandma Nancy sitting out here, watching the sunrise or sharing a lunch basket together." A few tears came to her eyes.

Bell pulled a handkerchief from the pocket of his casual khaki slacks. "Here, Warren."

She took the handkerchief from him. "Seems I've developed a habit of crying since I've met you."

"Crying is a normal part of life."

"Yeah, well, it's not normal for me."

She wiped her eyes as she stepped through the thick grass and sat on the bench. Doc jumped onto her lap. His damp paws darkened her cream-colored shorts. She rubbed the small dog's neck. Scooter pounced after several grasshoppers. Bell remained standing and looked out into the morning haze that hovered over the valley.

"So, Mr. Bell, Dr. Bell..."

"Just Bell."

"You asked if I could be honest." She cleared her throat. "I think I'm an honest person. Wasn't the kind of kid who lied to her parents. And since I became a cop, I've managed to avoid anything even remotely out of line. No bribes. Nothing irregular." She gazed at him. "Good enough?"

He sat, crossed his legs, and rested his cane against the front of the bench then folded his hands atop one knee. "What about being honest to *yourself?*"

"Meaning?"

"Why did you decide to search for me, Warren? What did you believe would happen should you find me?"

"I'm not sure."

"You had determined this little black-and-white dog was a time-traveler long before you began to look for me."

"There was really no other answer."

He turned his head to her. "*You knew,* Warren. You gathered the facts at your disposal and had already arrived at that conclusion, impossible as it must have seemed to you."

She nodded. "I suppose."

"As you told me, you researched time-travel theories from renowned scientists, you read time-travel stories, and *then* decided to find me."

"True."

"For what purpose?"

Lane Cohen

She stared at the ground. "Maybe just to understand?"

"You understood already. You were looking for more."

She squinted at his face, which displayed an air of quiet authority. "How did you know I was a cop?"

"The confidence in your manner, the way your eyes studied me, gathering information as if I were a criminal suspect."

"Really?"

"I also noticed the bulge of the weapon under your jacket. As you sat down with me, your jacket pulled back and revealed the *full-sized*, semi-automatic pistol in the holster under your arm. It is not uncommon in this time for a woman traveling alone to possess a firearm for protection, but typically that firearm would be a small revolver, perfect for concealment and ease of use. Your weapon was worn in a tactical holster. The gun was, again, full-sized and typical of a law enforcement service pistol."

She locked eyes with his. "It's easy when you explain it that way."

"Efficient observation."

"Uh huh. And my hip surgery?

He glanced down at her legs. "The muscles in your legs are over-developed, as a runner's legs would be. But your lower leg muscles, your calves, are *larger* in your left leg, out of proportion, typical of someone who favors the opposite leg. Also, there is a distinct clicking from your right side when you sit or bend in a certain manner. That sound comes directly from your hip."

She blinked. "Nobody has ever noticed my *hip insect* clicking. That's what I call it. Sometimes it clicks softly, and sometimes loud, as if I'd suddenly aged fifty years."

"So, Warren, my question?"

She stared at him. "I just kept thinking..." She wrapped both arms around the black-and-white dog. "To some people, dogs are just animals. Nothing more. But to Grandpa Paul—"

"This little fellow meant a great deal to him." Bell reached over and scratched Doc's head.

"Doc disappeared the evening of August 17, 1962. 8:30. Grandma Nancy was quite certain. She said she could never forget that date and time. After Doc disappeared, Grandpa waited out on the porch that night, every night, in the dark, in the rain, the cold. After weeks of searching the forests and backcountry, he still had not given up. He hoped beyond hope his friend would come home. And he wanted to be out there to greet him when he returned."

Bell took a breath. "Our family had a beagle. Polly named him Malcolm. He was our gift on her fifth birthday, but he seemed to bond with Elizabeth, my wife, more than anyone else. Elizabeth's eyes would light up with joy when Malcolm would come padding into the room and inevitably jump into her lap. And now, of course, I have Scooter. We have grown to depend upon each other over the years. He depends upon me for food and shelter, and, well, he has nurtured my soul in ways I thought not possible. Scooter and I have had long discussions, indeed."

"You understand, then."

"Warren, I understand you are extremely intelligent. To what conclusion does that intelligence lead you, considering you and I are sitting here on this fine morning in 2019 having an illuminating conversation?"

"If you could have figured a way to go back to 1892, to your wife, your family, well, you would have already done so. And—"

"And I would not be here now."

"Yes."

"The mechanism of traveling through time is not so complicated as it might seem at first. But it is important to remember at this juncture, regardless if I could uncover the means to convey myself back to my own natural time, one obstacle yet remains. The past cannot be changed."

She tilted her head at him. "Cannot?"

"Do you understand the principle?"

She took a breath but didn't say anything.

Bell stood, left his cane leaning against the bench, and began to pace. "Our predicaments are quite different. While I do not wish to time travel for the purpose of *changing* the past, you..."

She stared and waited for him to continue.

He stopped and faced her. "If I could devise the proper manner to time travel in reverse, if I could locate and harness sufficient energy to *power* that journey, what do you expect I would do?"

"I suppose you would return home."

"Correct."

"To your wife and daughter. Elizabeth and Polly. And to Malcolm."

"Yes."

She edged forward. "You would devise a method to travel back to about an hour after you left, to allow for the winds to subside. In that way, you could simply resume your life from nearly the exact point you left it behind."

He raised one pointed finger. "And you?"

"Bell, in the short time we have known each other, you have grown predictable. You have a distinct tendency to ask questions to which you already know the answer."

He nodded. "Perhaps it is the *professor* part of my personality. The real question here, Warren, is not if I know the answer, but whether or not *you* admit the answer to yourself."

"To my..?"

"Your self-imposed purpose here."

"Purpose, how?"

"I will ask once again. What did you expect to achieve when you sought me out?"

She patted Doc. "I suppose that should have been obvious from the beginning."

"Your grandfather."

"Yes."

"You believe if you can find a way to return the dog to your grandfather, return Doc to just after he left, as if the dog had never gone missing, your grandfather would have lived a much longer and happier life."

Tears started in her eyes. "Of course."

"But if you are completely honest with me, Warren, if you are completely honest with *yourself*, for you it is and always has been more than this dog. Once you realized time travel was a distinct probability, it became much more than finding a way to send your grandfather's dog back to nearly the exact point he began his journey."

Tears streamed down her face. "Just go ahead and say it, Bell."

A Matter of Time

He brought his voice down to just over a whisper. "You wish to prevent the vehicle accident from several years ago, the one in which you were driving home from dinner at *The Golden Lamb*, the one which left you with a broken hip."

She wiped tears from her face. "Finish."

"You wish to go back and alter the past, to change events so the accident does not occur, so that your hip does not break, and your parents do not perish in that same accident."

Paradoxes are just the scar tissue. Time and space heal themselves up around them and people simply remember a version of events which makes as much sense as they require it to make. **Douglas Adams**

Chapter 17: Hartwell, Ohio
Summer - 2009

Bell took the tuna fish sandwich and glass Hattie Brooks had given him a few moments before and stepped out his host's front door and onto her porch. He held his breath as a metal vehicle whispered by on the street just beyond a thick green lawn. If it were not for that vehicle, and many other similar contraptions stationed by the sides of the roadway on this quiet street, he may not have noticed much out of the ordinary without more careful observation. But when he heard a distant roar in the sky, and as he tilted his eyes up and watched in fascination as a winged object soared across the heavens, Bell realized he had found himself in a place that was as far from ordinary as ever could be.

His stomach rumbled and he took a bite of the sandwich. It was delicious. He sipped from the glass of tea mixed with lemonade as Hattie had explained, a concoction so sweet that Scottish children would no doubt love it.

He sat against a wooden rail on Hattie's front porch and attempted to take measure of himself and his situation. The front of his head pulsed with an insistent throb. Perhaps the pain was because he had struck his head on the ground when he fell.

Fell?

When I fell from where?

The Dundee asylum flashed into the front of his brain, the terrible dust clouds, the shrieking winds overhead, and Irene Lithgow.

A Matter of Time

He took another bite of the tuna sandwich and studied the scene around him. He spotted what appeared to be a folded daily on a cement walkway leading from the street to Hattie's front door. He considered retrieving the daily, interested to note the date of today's edition. He shook his head. He need not see the date to confirm what he had already concluded. But it would be of great interest to confirm how far into the future the atmospheric disturbance had propelled him.

He had moved forward through the ages.

He had time-traveled and was perhaps the first man ever to have done so. There really was no other possible answer, and he was amazed how calmly he accepted this conclusion.

Another metal carriage wheeled past the house, this conveyance noisier than the first. It was much larger than the machine that had moved by before, and larger than those parked along the street. The words *Mayflower Moving* were painted on the side of the contraption, along with a white painting of a three-mast sailing vessel, perhaps meant to represent the ship used by the first settlers when they reached the shores of North America. He had seen wheeled vehicles with motors mentioned in the dailies for the last few years, inventions of a Mr. Benz and a Mr. Maybach, powered by electric or steam. He nodded. Those were certainly the start of it. And through the passage of time, science advanced their design and function. It made perfect sense.

The object in the air made perfect sense as well. Crude attempts at flying machines were often found in print and spoken of. He remembered a story from about a year ago, in which a gentleman designed an odd-shaped motorized contraption that traveled almost a hundred feet in the air before Earth's gravity won the day. While startling when he first caught sight of the thing in the air a few moments ago, the scientific advancement of flying vehicles was to be expected.

What surprised him most was how the topography of the land here had little to no resemblance to the Dundee countryside. The land near and around Hattie Brooks' home was flat, while the Dundee asylum was surrounded by small streams and rolling hills. None of that seemed to be here. If he had indeed traveled through time, he had apparently also traveled to some place on

Earth that was not Dundee, Scotland.

The door squeaked open behind him. He turned his head and watched Hattie Brooks join him on the porch. He noticed she held a small handkerchief dotted with red speckles as she sat back on the rail beside him.

"Feeling better?" she said.

"Yes. Thank you. I believe the food has settled me."

"Good."

"I would like to ask, though, why did you describe this sandwich as tuna *fish*?"

"What?"

"Well, the name of the fish is simply *tuna*. Not tuna *fish*. It would be the same as making a sandwich from salmon and calling it salmon *fish*. You would not do that, would you?"

She shook her head at him. "I have no idea what you're talking about." She coughed and raised the handkerchief to her lips. She wiped her mouth. "Damn it."

"Miss Brooks?"

"*Hattie*. Please." She touched the brim of her straw hat with her fingertips. "Cause of the hats I always wore when I was a kid. My daddy started calling me *Hattie*, and it stuck."

"Hattie, then. That cough worries me."

She cleared her throat. "It's been my companion off and on for nearly a year. It gets worse when I bend over too much."

Bell gazed at her. "With a cough that deep, perhaps..."

She squinted at him. "Perhaps what?"

"Nothing. I apologize. We have barely met."

"Nonsense. We've exchanged our names, I've patched up a cut on your head, and made you a sandwich, a *tuna fish* sandwich, all without a chaperone. That's closer than many people are."

"Yes, well, you may be correct."

She nodded. "And now that we're friends and all, let's talk about how you fell out of your invisible time machine from somewhere in 1892, and landed right smack dab into the middle of my 2009 garden."

His breath caught in his throat. "2009?"

"I *Googled* your name before I came out here. You may not think it to look at me, but I know my way around a computer.

Lester and I were heavy into *eBay*."

He stared at her. "Sorry? Computer?"

She chuckled. "Yeah. You wouldn't know."

Bell set his glass on the smooth surface of the porch railing. "I do know when a person is in need of medical attention."

She stared at him. "Sure. Wikipedia said you were a doctor. A surgeon."

"Wiki..?"

She stood and extended one hand. "Come with me, Dr. Bell. "I'm sure we both have questions we would like answered."

He blinked at her, took her hand, and followed inside her neatly manicured Victorian home.

An object traveling at high speeds ages more slowly than a stationary object. This means that if you were to travel into outer space and return, moving close to light speed, you could travel thousands of years into the Earth's future. **Clifford A. Pickover**

Chapter 18: Lebanon, Ohio
Spring - 2017

Her dad grinned across the table at her as if she were three years old, and his little girl had just managed to print her name for the first time.

The warmth in her dad's smile had been there ever since her first memory of him. Not once in her 29 years had he ever spoken a harsh word to her. Whatever she did, whatever choices she made, her dad had been right beside her, holding her hand, giving his unconditional support. He was always there as the one she could fall back on.

Her mom grinned at her, as well, but she had been a bit different over the years, a little less forgiving when the rules of the house were broken, and much more the disciplinarian than her dad. But her mom had also been right there, supporting her with love, in good times and bad.

She had been amazingly lucky. Her parents' marriage had lasted nearly a decade longer than any other marriage of her friends' parents. Most of those ended in divorce long ago. She gazed at her mom and dad across the table of *The Golden Lamb* and grinned back at them.

The waitress brought their desserts, apple pie alamode, the house specialty, and perfect for the end of their celebratory meal. *The Golden Lamb* was a cool place even to just come and visit, if only for its historical importance. Presidents and other important folk have dined and stayed at the inn's lodgings since 1803 when the inn was established. The food was plentiful and favored home-cooked meals of turkey and dressing, sliced country ham, and other dishes of traditional American fare. She really had no room for even one bite of pie, but when one dines at *The Golden Lamb*, it is heresy not to finish the meal with the inn's signature dessert.

Her promotion to detective came out of the blue, and at first, she thought her captain was joking around. But after the shock wore off, and she heard the applause from her supporters in the squad room, a tremendous sense of satisfaction settled in, and she almost couldn't believe that anything in this world was real anymore.

The Cincinnati force had plenty of female officers, but up until recently, just one female detective. As of a few days ago, that number had doubled. Her dad used her promotion as an excuse to take their family out for a special meal, as he had often done before. This time, even Billy Conger, her steady boyfriend of more than six months, was invited along. It seemed whatever her victory or accomplishment, winning a soccer game, getting a good grade on an exam, being accepted into the police academy, or her promotion to detective, her dad inevitably led the family parade to *The Golden Lamb* for yet another celebration.

She gazed at her parents across the table and small tears started in her eyes. She was, and always had been, blessed to have parents like these.

The most useful form of time travel would be to go back a year or two and rectify the mistakes we made. **Matt Lucas**

Chapter 19: Lebanon, Ohio
Present Day

Jessie's phone jumped in her back pocket. She wiped tears from her eyes, grabbed the phone, and held it to her ear. "Warren." She cleared her throat and listened. "I'm okay."

Bell studied his new companion.

"Right. Fountain Square. Leaving now." She slipped the phone into a back pocket of her shorts and turned to Bell. "I have to change clothes and go."

"I understand."

She stood. "We can continue later."

"That is fine."

She didn't move and gazed at him.

Bell said, "Is there something more?"

"Do you, uh, want to come with me?"

"To where on Fountain Square are you going?"

"Fifth Third Bank."

"Why should I come with you?"

"Because *I just found you*, Bell. I don't want you disappearing, slipping away on some cosmic breeze."

He smiled again. "Now who is joking?"

"Okay. We can talk more time-travel in the car."

"Certainly."

Bell stood and they both walked toward the farmhouse, with Scooter and Doc at their heels.

In General Relativity, you can do it in principle. It's to do with building these things called wormholes; shortcuts through time and space. **Brian Cox**

Chapter 20: Downtown Cincinnati, Ohio
Present Day

Fifth Third was the largest local bank in the Cincinnati metro area, and its main branch was the ultra-modern building downtown on Fountain Square, the urban epicenter of the city.

Bell had visited the square on many occasions. He recalled the last time he traveled downtown by taxicab to attend the *Oktoberfest* celebration, which for unknown reasons was held during the month of September. He enjoyed meandering out in public, and being part of the *beer and bratwurst* festivities, even though he walked alone and shared the experience with no other soul. Being among crowds of people who were taking part in a celebration kept basically the same since the 1800s made him feel almost a part of a familiar society again.

He strode, assisted by his cane, beside Jessie Warren now with a brisk step toward the entry door of the bank. He glanced at the police tape, blaringly yellow, stretched across the threshold. His new companion of less than two days, now fully immersed in her law enforcement mode and attitude as if an electrical switch had been thrown, nodded at a uniformed officer at the door. The young man nodded back and immediately moved to one side to allow them to pass.

The expansive bank lobby was all marble and glass. Many uniformed police officers milled about, talking with each other, some with cameras, some with electronic pads of one kind or another. Jessie and Bell walked toward a middle-aged African-American man with short, graying hair. He was dressed in a neatly pressed brown suit.

"Warren, sorry to call you in," the man said. He stopped in the middle of the lobby and blinked in Bell's direction.

Jessie shook her head and glanced around the lobby. "No problem, Captain. You know that."

"Introductions?"

Jessie thought quickly. "This is my cousin, Wallace Brewster. Wallace, this is Captain Gavin."

Gavin noticed the man wore a gray Fedora, angled down on his forehead. Gavin nodded at Bell. "Sir."

Bell tilted his head at him. "Sir."

Neither man extended his hand.

"Wallace is the last living member of my extended family," Jessie said, "and is a criminologist from Scotland, visiting with me for the next month or so."

"Scotland?"

"Yes," Bell said.

"I thought you wouldn't mind, Captain, if he tagged along with me, at least for today."

Gavin shook his head. "Criminologist?"

Bell smiled. "Of a sort."

"Good. I have a feeling we can use all the help we can get with this one."

Jessie glanced around. "This is not a robbery."

"We're fairly certain it is not." He squinted at her. "How did you know?"

"Nothing out of order here in the lobby. No mess, nobody getting prints, or taking pictures of any teller stations, no tape except at the door, no scuff marks, no shell casings, no odor of cordite. Anyway, you probably would not have called me on my day off if this were just a robbery."

Gavin nodded.

"And I saw the M.E.'s van outside on the square."

"The M.E. is still here."

"Who?"

"Dalmore."

Bell flinched.

Jessie touched his forearm. "Uh, you all right, cousin?"

He nodded at her.

Jessie blinked and turned to Gavin. "Where is she?"

"In the secondary vault, the safety deposit boxes."

She looked at the two large doors behind the teller area. "I thought this wasn't a robbery."

"Follow me," Gavin said.

***

They stepped through the open, metal doorway into the vault, and a few paces forward into the safety deposit box area. The walls were lined with small numbered rectangles, each with slots for the insertion of keys. A clear plastic evidence bag was on top of a large metal table set in the center of the room. A woman who wore a tan lab coat was bent over a body on the floor on the other side of the table. The body was twisted facedown, and was obviously male, thin, and probably short in stature. He was dressed in dark slacks and a long-sleeved shirt with patches of the bank's emblem sewn into the shoulders. The man's official bank cap, with that same bank emblem on the front, was upside-down beside him. The body was nearly encircled by blood; it looked to have streamed from the victim's head and spread into a large pool.

"Fallon," Jessie said.

The woman stood. She was about thirty-four, almost a head taller than Jessie, with deep red hair pulled back in a ponytail. "Jessie." Fallon Dalmore glanced at Bell as she pulled off a latex glove from each hand. "Captain."

"What have we got?" Gavin asked.

Dalmore stared at Bell. "And who—?"

"My cousin Wallace," Jessie said.

"Wallace?"

Bell straightened his shoulders. "Brewster, Miss. Wallace Brewster."

Dalmore squinted at him. "I'm Fallon Dalmore." She extended her hand to him.

Bell took her hand and gripped it solidly. His face showed no expression.

"Jessie..." Dalmore said, without taking her eyes from Bell, "is this Take-Your-Cousin-to-Work Day?"

"Dalmore," Gavin barked. "What have you got?"

She swiveled her eyes away from Bell and studied the electronic pad she held in one hand. "Detective Keaton interviewed a bank officer in here just a few minutes ago. I overheard, our victim is Timothy Timmons."

"Where is Buster?" Jessie asked.

"Looking at that video again, upstairs."

Jessie crooked a brow. "Video?"

"Go on," Gavin said to Dalmore.

"He's a bank employee known to co-workers as *Little Timmy*. Bank guy identified the body."

"He sure?" Gavin asked.

Dalmore nodded. "No question. Victim's ID confirms. The bank V.P., one Dudley Edward McGrath, told Keaton that Timmons had worked for the bank since he graduated from U.C. about six, seven years ago. Ran track for the Bearcats, distance running I believe. Was head of day-to-day security at this branch for the last two years."

"Was he stabbed?" Gavin asked.

"Punctured his left temple. He bled out. There is also a massive contusion to the back of his skull."

Gavin cleared his throat. "Time?"

"No longer than two hours ago."

She placed her hands on her hips. "And then, of course, we have the time-stamped video to think about."

Jessie asked Gavin, "What's on the video?"

Gavin gestured outside the vault. "A camera catches them both entering and leaving the vault area."

"Them...both?" She blinked. "Them who?"

"It is *incredible*," Dalmore said. "I've watched it three times. It makes my head hurt to think about it."

Jessie squinted at Gavin. "Captain?"

Gavin took a breath. "You see, Warren, that's the reason I called you down here. I wanted someone besides Dalmore and Keaton, someone else who I respect and trust to tell me that after twenty years of police work, I haven't suddenly gone completely insane. If *three* people tell me that, well then, maybe I don't need to see the shrink."

Bell tilted his head forward and took a step toward the table. He focused on the evidence bag. "Captain? May I have a look at this parcel?"

"Be my guest, Bell."

Bell edged closer to the plastic bag. He tilted his head down, studied the bag and its contents, and then moved a step back. "Thank you."

"What do you make of the pen in the bag?"

"Not the murder weapon."

"No?"

"The blow to the skull probably killed the man instantly. The stab wound from the pen was performed after."

Gavin frowned. "The pen was found on the floor beside the body. But why kill the man and then stab him with an old fountain pen? Why murder a man in a bank vault, take nothing, leave the pen in plain view, and then disappear?"

Bell took a breath. "I would like to see this video you've mentioned, if you do not mind."

Gavin shrugged. "It's our next stop." He turned around, halted, and then turned back again to face Bell. "Keep a *different* question in mind, Mr. Brewster, when you see the video. Not the *why* of it, but the *how*. Exactly *how* was the impossible accomplished?"

Gavin turned on his heel and stepped out of the vault.

Cosmic strings are either infinite or they're in loops, with no ends. So they are either like spaghetti or Spaghetti Os. The approach of two such {loop} strings parallel to each other, will bend space-time so vigorously and in such a particular configuration that [it] might make time travel possible – in theory. **J. Richard Gott**

Chapter 21: Oak Ridge, Tennessee
June 14, 1944

"**M**ister, this will go a lot easier if you cooperate."

The short, skinny man handcuffed to the table was sure the soldier in the green clothing seated across from him could not be real. It was not possible. *This room* was not possible, the strange lamps, all the soldiers with black shiny boots, the sleek rifles slung over their shoulders. The wind at Dundee must have lifted him into the air, spun his body into the clouds, and deposited him in some sort of middle ground between heaven and Earth where the angels decide what direction he would be traveling.

Eventually.

But *now,* this man who said his name was Sergeant Gleason, barrel-chested with extremely short black hair, spoke to him in words that made no sense. The accent he spoke made no sense either.

The man looked down at his hands. His wrists had metal bracelets around them and were connected to a rung on the table. He was hungry and terribly thirsty. And the front of his head pounded like someone was driving a pickaxe against his skull.

"I checked with the hospital downtown," Sergeant Gleason said. "No missing patients."

"I *work* in the asylum, sir, these are my *work* clothes, and it ain't no *hospital*, even though the coppers like to think it so.

A Matter of Time

Folks call the place the *Eighth Gate to Hell*, but I never thought it so bad, not being no patient. I *work* there to make a little extra when the docks ain't busy. Happens sometimes, yeah?"

Gleason squinted at him. The prisoner's face was streaked with dirt and fresh scratches. "That a Scottish accent, boy?"

"Full-blooded, sir, born and bred."

"Whereabouts?"

"Islay. Grand country it is. But the asylum is square in the Dundee hills."

Gleason said, "My grandparents were from Glen Ord."

"A seafaring town, sir. Know it well."

Gleason stared at him. "How'd you make it within the perimeter?"

"Peri..?"

"And so close to the laboratories?"

"If I didn't know better, Sergeant, I'd take a double bet that *witch* cursed me."

Gleason stared at him. "Witch?"

"A *sorceress* the likes me mum warned me."

Gleason studied the man handcuffed to the table. "Go on."

He scooted his chair back and stood, his wrists still fastened to the table. "My mum told me stories afore bed, stories of goblins, elfs. And banshees. Those stories scared me plenty. I ain't *never believed them*, sir. Never truly. But when I looked into the *witch* eyes of Irene Lithgow, well, all that changed."

Gleason shook his head. "Son, witches and goblins aside, you got on some peculiar clothes, your pockets were empty. Not so much as a scrap of paper on you. So, let's at least start with this: What's your name?"

"I might not know *where* I am, sir, but I do truly still know my name. Brody MacKay, sir. Brody Amos MacKay, son of *Angus William* MacKay, the grandest father a boy could ever have. But holy Christ, there ain't no brushing aside that *witch*, sir, that *triple-crossed banshee*. Cause if it's possible to *see* evil, then I've seen it in the darkness settled at the back of Irene Lithgow's eyes. She *hated* me and Dr. Bell both. And this is her *revenge*, sir, what she's done to me, how she's sent me to you."

"Irene Lithgow sent you here?"

"She called down the winds, I opened my eyes and I was

right outside here on the ground."

Gleason thought about it. "Mr. MacKay, Brody, you're saying this Irene sent you here from..?"

"Dundee, sir. Dundee."

"Okay. Dundee." He chuckled to himself. "Funny you mention an asylum. My pa used to tell me nightmare tales of the Dundee asylum. He said the place and the grounds were abandoned long ago, but the crumbled building remains and is still haunted by the spirits of countless souls who took their last breaths within those walls."

"The asylum ain't haunted. But an *ugly* place it is, sir, quite an *ugly* place."

Gleason nodded. "Let's say I believe the asylum, and about Irene the witch. Why would she, this Irene, *abracadabra* you out of Dundee and drop you into my lap here in Tennessee?"

MacKay thought about it. "Tennessee?"

"Why would she do it?"

MacKay's eyes widened. "*Revenge*, sir, plain and simple. For *bloody revenge*, to get even for guarding her, keeping her locked up tight, away from any of the other patients. And now she's found a way..." Brody MacKay gritted his teeth. "To make sure I suffer for all eternity."

In Einstein's equation, time is a river. It speeds up, meanders, and slows down. The new wrinkle is that it can have whirlpools, and fork into two rivers. **Michio Kaku**

Chapter 22: Oak Ridge, Tennessee
June 14, 1944

The miraculous hot downpour streamed over her naked skin. She decided if she had been spirited off to the underworld by the fierce winds of Hell, those winds would certainly not have taken her to a waterfall of such *pleasure*. Hell would never be like *this*. The water was so luxurious, the *opposite* might even be true; this could be *Heaven*.

The woman, Ida Cade, had led her to this palace of white tile. When Ida saw her obvious confusion, the small Negro woman explained the meaning and use of the knobs in the magnificent white tub. "H" meant hot. "C" meant cold. Of course they did. Ida started the magical flow of water and stepped out, closing the door behind her. She now had privacy, and endless water from above. She needed it to be as hot as she could bear, to scald every remnant of the Dundee asylum from her tender skin.

She had dropped her asylum smock to the floor and stepped over the high wall of the tub. The water streamed down, and she tilted her head back in the utter joy of it. She closed her eyes and tilted her face under the steady flow. *Heaven*. This felt like *heaven*. If this were Hell, Lucifer had one strange sense of humor.

After ten minutes, Irene twisted both knobs and the flow of water stopped. She took a thick towel from a bar at the back of the enclosure and began to rub it through her hair. She pushed aside a white curtain with yellow flowers on it and stepped over the tub onto the tile floor. She spotted the clothes Ida Cade had placed for her atop the closed seat of the commode, another miracle she had employed earlier.

She took her time and slowly dried her body with the thick towel. She smiled as she discovered each water droplet left behind. The dirt and decay of Dundee now seemed gone. No more locked rooms. No never-ending days without companionship, save the guards at the asylum.

And Dr. Joseph Bell.

Irene dropped the towel over the edge of the tub, touched the bundle of clothes left for her and pushed her arms through the sleeves of a plain white blouse. It was a bit too large, but comfortable nonetheless. She took her time with each button, starting from the top of the blouse and then to the bottom. She found a plain gray skirt and pulled it up to her waist. Again, this was too large, but better too big than too small. She separated a pair of white ankle socks and halted before she could pull them on when she noticed something that sent instant chills across her spine.

A periodical, *The Saturday Evening Post*, it said, lay flat on the counter beside the sink. The cover displayed a painting in brilliant colors of a boy in a physician's office. The physician held the end of a stethoscope to the boy's chest. From the expression on the boy's face, the metal disc must have been cold.

But it was not only the painting that caught her attention. It was the *date* of the periodical that shocked her, that instantly knocked the air from her body: *March 17, 1944.*

Irene sat on the closed lid of the commode and tried to gather her thoughts. This was not Hell. The Devil had no hand in this. Somehow, and perhaps only a scientist could explain *exactly* how, the storm winds of Dundee had split the skies and *carried her forward through time itself.* She chuckled. The world had moved on more than fifty years in two blinks of an eye. That would explain the strange sights. At least, that would explain some of them.

She recalled the words and numbers that had spun inside her brain from what seemed to be moments before: *Mike Sweeney Cincinnati Chevrolet 2 0 1 9 Malibu.* The numbers must have meant a year, 2019. But if so, why had she landed in 1944?

A Matter of Time

Her stomach growled. She realized she was hungry and suffered from a deep thirst. She finished pulling on her socks, stood and regarded her reflection in the wall mirror behind the sink. Her eyes were bright, her skin clean and sparkling. She smiled at herself, took a breath, and reached for the doorknob. Instead of being trapped inside the shadowed Dundee asylum for time without end, nature had presented her with the chance for a *new* life, free from the accursed stare of Brody MacKay. But also sadly without the all-observing eyes of the great, omnipotent Dr. Joseph Bell.

She turned the doorknob and stepped out onto the hallway.

Our heirs, whatever or whoever they may be, will explore space and time to degrees we cannot currently fathom. They will create new melodies in the music of time. There are infinite harmonies to be explored. **Clifford Pickover**

Chapter 23: Hartwell, Ohio
Summer - 2009

B ell sat beside Hattie Brooks at a small wooden desk in her parlor and stared at a glowing rectangle.

The colorful images were so startling he barely could think of words to describe them. If the swift, motorized vehicles he had just seen outside were to be expected within the natural progression of events, given the passage of enough time, this *Mac*, as Hattie called it, wasn't to have been expected or *even imagined* in all his wildest dreams.

"Would you like me to show you?" Hattie asked.

Bell tilted his head at the object on the desk. "You mean to say you can produce information on this device?"

She smiled. "Think of it like an electronic encyclopedia."

"And you said information about, well, information about *me* is in there?"

"I can't explain the workings of it. I dare say few could. But the world runs on these things now, or maybe I should say *these things run the world*. They are connected to our telephone systems, our water and electrical plants. They control our cars and aircraft. Practically nothing anymore works without some kind of *computer* connected to it."

Bell took a breath. "Show me." He sat frozen and watched Hattie's fingertips touch an arrangement of letters and numbers on a futuristic typewriter of mad design, and in two seconds an image filled the glowing rectangle. Bell stood; he could not tear his eyes from the pictures that floated in the air.

"That...*that is me*. The photograph was taken at the university, just a few months ago."

"It surely appears to be you," Hattie said. "But I ain't sure *a few months ago* is accurate anymore."

Bell lowered himself to the chair. "It mentions Conan Doyle. And Holmes."

"Not surprising."

"It says I disappeared in 1892. The last I was seen was...*at the Dundee asylum during a terrible storm. It is suspected I vanished in the storm's rage, along with several others.*"

"That true?"

Bell's wide eyes scanned the screen. "My wife and daughter. It mentions Elizabeth and Polly in these *blue* letters."

Hattie nodded. "Not much here about your wife, except her name, Elizabeth Dalmore from Edinburgh. But as for Polly..." Hattie pressed on an oblong object on the desk. Bell heard a click. "I thought her name sounded familiar."

The bright images on the rectangle changed.

Bell's jaw dropped. "My God."

"Polly Marie Bell," Hattie said. "Says she's about age twenty-six in this picture."

Tears started to pool on Bell's eyelids. He remained frozen in place, unsure if he should keep looking or run screaming from the room.

"My *Polly*..."

"She's surely a beautiful child."

Bell choked back a sob and pulled a handkerchief from his pants pocket. He touched the handkerchief to his eyes. "She is the image of her mother."

"Looks like."

"She was eight years old, last I saw Polly. *Eight years old.* She grew into a lovely woman, and I..."

Hattie touched his forearm. "You missed it. You missed her growing up."

Bell sniffled. "I lost most of my daughter's life. That is a terrible punishment for any father."

"Let me show you something any father would be *proud* of."

Paintings appeared. One painting showed a sad young girl

with wide eyes. A small beagle stood with her on a path in a shadowed wood. Tears glistened on the girl's face. A different painting displayed the same young girl, the same wide eyes and lines of tears, together with the same beagle. This time the two were walking close together on a darkened city street.

Bell cleared his throat. "These paintings are quite good."

"I know."

"The girl in the paintings *looks like* my Polly."

"Yes. And Polly had a beagle, didn't she?"

Bell inhaled. "Polly *painted* these?"

Hattie studied the text on the screen. "The paintings by Polly Marie Bell are apparently quite valuable."

"My God."

Hattie read: "Polly Bell first began painting when she was ten and always painted images of herself and her dog Malcolm, searching for her lost father in the darkness, the woods, city streets, sometimes on the beaches near Edinburgh. The face of this sad young girl is reproduced even today, as a symbol of a daughter's devotion to and love for her father."

Bell stared into the air as Hattie continued to read.

"Polly Bell spent many years searching for any sign of her father, the distinguished surgeon Joseph Bell, Sir Arthur Conan Doyle's original inspiration for Sherlock Holmes. Her father vanished one day in the midst of a suspected tornado that devastated a good part of the asylum at Dundee, Scotland, in the summer of 1892."

Hattie pressed a few buttons and the lights on the glowing rectangle faded to darkness.

Bell sat back and shook his head. He wiped away a few more tears with the tips of his fingers.

"You all right, Joseph?"

Bell cleared his throat. "I am not."

"You want a drink? I've got a cupboard full of vodka."

"Thank you, no."

"Look, you up for a ride?"

"Ride?

"You're probably curious to see the world I live in. It's *your* world now, unless you know of a way to shoot yourself back to 1892."

"Only if traveling through the eons of time is a normal course of events in 2009. I have not the power necessary, nor the mechanical expertise to transport myself through time."

She smiled. "Yeah, well, neither do I." She blinked at him. "Maybe it would be a good thing to get you outside. Some distractions. I know how feelings of loss can get to you."

"I thank you for your kindness, Hattie."

She coughed once and touched a red-speckled cloth to her mouth. She patted his knee. "Come on, then. We're going for a drive up to Eden Park."

"Eden..?"

"The city art museum is there. They have a few paintings I think you would like to see...in person."

He stared at her. "Polly?"

"Yep. They have two, according to their website."

"I'm sorry, but *website*?"

"Trust me."

He stood. "I would truly like to see the paintings."

"Come on back inside first. Need to change out of my gardening clothes." She studied him. "My neighbor Susie says I'm a little nuts, but I never got around to giving Lester's clothes to the Goodwill. Let's go upstairs and see if we can find a few things that fit you. These clothes you got on might raise a few unnecessary questions, if you follow me."

"I do. I do indeed."

"Well, come on then."

"And Hattie?"

"Yeah?"

"About that vodka..."

***

Bell thought he was ready to see more of the world of 2009, but nothing could have prepared him for the absolute mayhem he witnessed through the glass of Hattie Brooks' moving vehicle. He tightened the belt that ran across his torso, gripped the inside handle on the vehicle's door, and watched in amazement as the wonders of the 21st century sped by. Wheeled vehicles of every size and shape motored at fantastic velocity along a seemingly endless slab of concrete.

"What do you think?" Hattie asked.

"So many people, all speeding along. Where are they going?"

"Work. Play. Anywhere and everywhere. The traffic on I-75 never stops."

"I-75?"

"Name of this road. It travels generally north-south."

"For what distance?"

"All the way south to Florida, and north to, Detroit, maybe farther. More than a thousand miles, I know that."

"A monumental engineering achievement."

"You don't know the half of it. This is only one of many roads just like it."

"What is that offensive odor? I must say, this miasma is overwhelming."

"Miasma?"

"Traces of sulfur and organic decay. It is as if the atmosphere of Hell permeated up from the center of the Earth."

"We call it smog. Not sure what that word really means. Guess I'm used to it."

"And the great *size* of some of these vehicles that pass by. We are but *insects* to them in comparison." He studied a nearby truck. "What is *Coors*?"

"A beer from Colorado."

"The American west."

"Yeah."

"What is *McDonald's*?"

"McDonald's?"

"I saw a painting on the side of the road. *McDonald's*. It pictured food; a *Big Mac*. Does the *Big Mac* somehow relate to the machine on your desk?"

"Uh, no. Different things. Different Macs. McDonald's is a fast food restaurant."

"Fast?"

"I'll explain later."

"I have not asked, but *exactly* where are we?"

"City of Cincinnati, state of Ohio. We are presently passing through Norwood, which is a community north of the city's downtown. Where I grew up."

He rubbed the side of his neck. "Cincinnati. Situated on the edge of the Ohio River, across from the American state of Kentucky. The city's name is taken from Cincinnatus, an aristocrat from ancient Rome as I recall, best known for his integrity and civic virtue. I believe Cincinnatus lived somewhere in the 400s, B.C."

She smiled. "That's right. Pretty good. Most people who *live here* never bother to learn that fact. Lester was proud he knew all about Cincinnatus. He often brought it up, even though nobody seemed to be interested."

"World geography is one of my hobbies. I find it quite peaceful and calming." Bell let a moment pass. "Hattie, if you don't mind, what happened to Lester?"

"No, it's all right. Lester got the *lung* cancer. It didn't take them long to figure out what it was, and once they did, he passed in less than two months."

"I am sorry."

"It was the thirty years of unfiltered Pall Malls."

"Pall Malls?"

"Cigarettes."

"You mean to say the years of smoking somehow instigated his cancer?"

She nodded. "They proved that connection decades ago. And yet people keep on puffing, even now." She took a breath and let it out. "I smoked a pack a day, every day, until I stopped maybe five years ago, right when Lester was diagnosed. But, as I'm sure you've guessed, Dr. Bell, I waited a bit too long before I quit."

He studied her. "What has your physician told you?"

She shook her head. "Music?"

"Pardon?"

"Would you like some music?"

Bell's mouth opened but he didn't say anything.

"What would a doctor from 1892 like to listen to?"

She touched a button and music instantly blasted all around. Bell pressed back against his seat.

Help! I need somebody. Help! Not just anybody.

"My good God."

She yelled, "It's The Beatles."

"B...Beatles?"

She turned a knob and the volume of the music lessened.

"I know. Not my favorite either. But Lester last tuned the car CD player, and well, I'm a woman who is slow to change."

Bell felt the low register of the music pulse throughout his body as his new world of 2009 continued to flash by his window at impossible speeds.

The only reason for time is so that everything doesn't happen at once. **Albert Einstein**

Chapter 24: Cincinnati, Ohio
Present Day

Bell, Jessie, and Captain Gavin stood beside a desk and watched detective A.J. "Buster" Keaton press at buttons on a digital recorder.

"Almost got it cued." Keaton glanced at Jessie and pressed at more buttons. "Hi, Jessie."

"Hey, Buster."

Jessie gave him a quick smile. Keaton was about thirty, tall and gangly, and wore a plain black suit, white shirt, and thin black tie. He reminded Jessie of Dan Aykroyd in *The Blues Brothers.*

Keaton said, "Ready to have your mind blown?"

"As ready as I can be," Jessie said.

"Who's this?"

"Oh, Buster, this is my cousin, Wallace Brewster."

Keaton tilted his head toward Bell. "Hey."

Bell nodded at him.

"So, Jessie, I don't know where *the books* are, I mean the books from that old saying? But this one, this video, is *one for the books.*"

"What I keep hearing."

"Okay. Got it. Ready, Captain."

"Warren," Gavin said, "the lady you will see with gray hair in the wheelchair came to the bank first thing this morning. She was outside the main door waiting for the bank to open."

Jessie nodded.

"The lady steered her motorized chair to the manager's office, identified herself, and said she was interested in renting a box. The manager reported this same lady was here at the bank about three weeks ago, asking about the boxes. After the manager answered a few questions and introduced Timmins to her, the lady said she would be back later."

"Okay," Jessie said.

"Today, she asked to see the room which held the boxes. The manager, Dudley McGrath, called for Timmons to escort her again. McGrath said when Timmons was on duty, part of his job was to escort bank customers, or potential customers, down to the boxes."

"Here you go," Keaton said.

The video began.

Jessie focused on the dim image; the lighting in that area of the vault was quite low. The camera from outside the safety deposit box room captured a gray-haired female in a wheelchair, and a short, skinny male, both from behind; their faces were completely obscured from view. The female guided her wheelchair into the vault and into the adjoining safety deposit box room. The male walked beside her and was dressed in the uniform of a bank security guard. He appeared to be Timothy, *Little Timmy* Timmons who at this moment was dead on the floor of the safety deposit box section of the vault. As the two neared the entrance to the deposit box room, the male angled his head at the woman in the wheelchair and said something to her. At that moment his face was clearly in view. There was no doubt; the guard in the video was definitely *Little Timmy* Timmons, the ranking head of security at this main branch of Fifth Third Bank. The camera captured Timmons as he inserted a key into the lock of the gated door that separated the safety deposit room from the main vault area. Timmons pulled open the door, and both he and the female in the wheelchair edged out of the camera's view and into the next room. The video's time-stamp at that moment was 9:36am.

"That's Timmons, our body," Jessie said. "Who is the old woman?"

Keaton said, "She signed a visitor's card. Catherine Eddowes. You can see her face later. But, Jessie?"

"Yeah?"

He pressed a button and the video stopped. "You ever read

one of those locked room mysteries?"

"Locked room?"

"You know, like Agatha Christie, Sherlock Holmes?"

Her eyes remained fixed on Keaton. "I suppose."

"Watch the rest. Then we can walk over to Arnold's, sit at the bar, nurse a double Jack Daniels, and talk about it."

"Buster, this is weird, even for you."

"You don't know the half of it."

"Play the rest, Detective," Gavin said.

Keaton pressed the button, and Jessie waited for the ultimate surprise Keaton was anxious for her to see.

The bad news is time flies. The good news is you're the pilot. **Michael Althsuler**

Chapter 25: Oak Ridge, Tennessee
June 15, 1944

Robert Oppenheimer perched on the front edge of his office desk, took a small sip of Kentucky bourbon, and stared across the dingy room at Albert Einstein and Enrico Fermi.

They stared back at him.

Einstein was settled on a simple chair, his black tie pulled down, his grey suit jacket unbuttoned and rumpled. Fermi stood motionless on a threadbare area rug. He wore a stark white shirt, perfectly pressed dark slacks, and a gray Fedora.

Other than an occasional glass of red wine, Oppenheimer had never been much of a drinker of alcohol beverages. Nevertheless, he raised his glass to his lips and took a generous swallow of *Marker's Mark*. The whisky burned his throat and into his gut, all the way down.

"Gentlemen." Oppenheimer cleared his throat, set down his glass, and retrieved a lighted cigarette from an ashtray.

Fermi took a sip of whisky from his own glass. "This room smells as if it has not been aired out in two years, Roberto, and I suppose that's about right."

"Your voice," Oppenheimer whispered. "Quiet."

Fermi nodded. "Of course."

"We are endlessly spied upon here, more and more lately. You know that."

"Yes."

Einstein took another puff of his cigarette and remained silent.

Oppenheimer said, "To the matter at hand, we probably

have less than one year, and therefore, are running out of time."

"No pun intended, I'm sure," Fermi whispered.

Oppenheimer stared at him. "It is not funny, Enrico."

Fermi shrugged. "It is difficult to ignore the irony."

Oppenheimer fixed his eyes on Einstein. "The calculations?"

Einstein nodded. "Completed," he said in his German accent. He raised his glass under his nose and sniffed at the dark amber liquid inside. "I have wired the device accordingly. And..."

"Yes?"

"The power source is now placed within the lead-lined container, which is much smaller than I expected the final version to be. But *insertion* into the device was quite complicated, as you might expect."

Oppenheimer's lips pulled tight. "Are we ready?"

"I will require a week or so to adjust the chronometer. The dials must be set exactly, for *precise* accuracy. At this point, there is still unacceptable play in the mechanism."

"Then...soon?"

"I believe the device will contain sufficient plutonian power for certainly two, and perhaps three journeys. But no more."

"Two should be enough for our purpose," Oppenheimer said. "Once there, and once to return."

Einstein said, "We will still need valid testing."

"We've discussed this."

"The calculations and the theories behind the calculations are undoubtedly correct."

"They are your *own theories*, Albert." He crushed the stub of his cigarette into the glass ashtray.

Einstein took a swallow of *Maker's Mark*. "No matter the soundness of any theory, nothing can be *proven* until the theory has survived a practical application, after multiple and *thorough* tests. If not, the traveler could appear far off target."

Oppenheimer squinted at him. "You mean a different time?"

"Different time, different place, at least from the traveler's perspective."

Fermi took a long breath and let it out slowly. "It is pointless to go over this again, gentlemen. *Pointless*. Even if we could find someone who we could absolutely *trust*, even if we could find someone who would volunteer for what might be a suicide mission, due to the need for absolute secrecy there is no person we *could* absolutely trust."

Oppenheimer nodded. "But for we three."

"Yes," Fermi whispered. "Since, then, it is one of *us* who will take that dangerous adventure in any case. I see no reason to waste the incredible power and energy we need on a purposeless test." He waited until they locked eyes with him. "We might be able to mount only one successful attempt. And one of us would proceed with the plan and still attempt it, regardless of a failed test, if enough plutonian energy remained to power the device for a *second* try, and of that we cannot be certain. The stakes are that high, gentlemen, as the three of us have discussed over *and over*."

Einstein reached out and placed his empty glass on a side table. He bent forward and retrieved a simple brown-paper grocery bag from the floor. He reached inside the bag and pulled out a heavy metal rectangle about the size of a cigar box. He gripped it with both hands and set it carefully on one knee. "I have settled upon the particular gravimetric anchor."

Oppenheimer blinked at the box. "Are you certain?"

"The swing bracing is solid and metal."

Fermi's eyes widened at the box Einstein balanced on his knee. "Swing?"

"The soldiers constructed a children's play area behind the church, *The Chapel on the Hill*. It was built two years ago and is still there today, solidly in place."

"Two years," Fermi said. "Reasonable."

Einstein smiled. "A child's plaything. There is your *real* irony."

Fermi nodded but did not smile.

"They have several swings," Einstein said. "The metal poles are set into concrete. They are unlikely to ever move to any significant distance, unless purposely unearthed, which, as we know, has not happened. And the steel used is a perfect conductor." Einstein opened the lid on the box. "The controls are simple, but as I said, I need to find a way to adjust the controls more particularly, so that our traveler arrives perhaps two months after the original completion of the swings. Once finished, all one need do is ensure no other living thing is within the machine's three-foot range, tightly grip the box, and push one electrical button that will engage the power supply. After the task is accomplished, *reverse* the date to one second from the moment you left, and push the button again. The rest..."

Oppenheimer swallowed. "Then I suppose we have just one more item to decide."

None of the three men spoke for a few moments.

Fermi nodded. "*I* will do it. And it must be *you*, Robert. I'm sorry, but it must be."

Oppenheimer stared at him.

Fermi said, "Without any *one* of us, the project would probably fail. But I am positive the one truly *irreplaceable* member of our unholy triad is *you*, Roberto. Without you, none of this would have even a chance of success." He paused for a reaction, got none. "If you could call our goal a *success*, using any sane definition of that word."

Oppenheimer jumped in. "Albert, what about the dangers of the paradox we spoke about?"

Einstein squeezed his eyes shut. He rubbed his temples and forehead with both hands. "They are entirely unknown, to any reasonable degree of scientific analysis. But if we were faced with the question of a paradox, the answer to that question is probably staring us all in the face at this very moment."

Oppenheimer squinted at him. "You mean..?"

"If Enrico goes back and is successful, it has *already happened*, and Robert, you should not be sitting here with us now."

"Then it didn't work. Or, it *doesn't* work?"

Einstein sighed. "I have studied this eventuality and have no real answers. One possibility? If Enrico succeeds, then, theoretically the three of us would not be here in this room right now. We might never have even met, and one of us could actually be, well, gone." He paused to examine a thought. "Absent the reality of concurrent and parallel universes, a recent popular topic among physicists, by the way, perhaps altering the past has a *different* influence upon future events than we might suspect. Remember this axiom, gentlemen: History cannot be changed, because history in our reality, our universe, by definition, *has already happened*. But the sudden realization of a practical method of traveling through time, through gravitational dilation, might actually serve to *change* that old axiom."

Oppenheimer shook his head. "We have to try. Don't we? We must. I simply cannot let the project proceed in this manner. I positively will not be known by future generations as *the destroyer of worlds*. I cannot abide such a monstrous legacy. None of us should."

Fermi nodded. "Then let's decide...when is the opportune time for me to go?"

Einstein smiled. "Dr. Fermi, it really matters not whether you go back tonight or next week, or next *month*, for that matter. Remember the character, *The Traveller* in the Wells' story? He journeyed forward through time for ages, lived among the Eloi, people who would exist in his far future, but when he returned to his own time, *he appeared at the same dinner party moments from whence he left*. To the other dinner guests, The Traveller had been gone for only minutes, at least from their perspective. So, Dr. Fermi, you can leave here at any moment we choose, and as long as you come back to just an instant after you originally left, and you efficiently employ the gravimetric anchor, you should be fine. Of course, I would suggest leaving sooner rather than later, for if we allow this Oak Ridge project to progress to its ultimate conclusion, it might just be too late, and heaven knows if once exploded, our mischief could be reversed."

Einstein stood and took two small steps to the front of Oppenheimer's desk. He carefully set the heavy box on the edge of the desk and placed a small vase of daisies on top of the box. "On your desk, beneath a display of lovely flowers. *Irony* again, Robert."

"Inspired," Oppenheimer said.

Einstein stepped back to his chair.

Oppenheimer stood and turned to the wall behind his desk. He took the edge of a large oil painting of Manhattan Island, New York City and pulled the painting toward him. The wall behind the painting revealed a metal safe with a combination lock. Oppenheimer turned the combination and opened the safe.

"Your device will be more secure in here, Albert," Oppenheimer said, "although I can appreciate the irony of leaving it in plain sight under a flower arrangement."

He removed the flowers and lifted the metal box. He carefully hefted it into the safe, closed the door, spun the dial, and swung the painting back into place. He turned back to his companions, locked eyes with Einstein for a moment, and then reached behind to a bundle of rags on a side table. He unwrapped the rags and exposed the barrel, the cylinder, and the grip of a thick revolver. He held the pistol out to Fermi. "Come to the lab tonight. Albert and I will be there to wish you a successful journey, and a hearty...good luck." He waited for a response, got none. "At least, I believe I *should* be there with Albert. And take this pistol with you tonight, Enrico. Find somewhere you can practice without bullets in the chamber. You might have but one chance, and you should be familiar with the weapon." Oppenheimer bit his bottom lip. "Try *speaking* with me first. Attempt to convince me to either abandon or to sabotage the project. Remember to speak my dog's name, *Petrov*, from when I was a boy. I have not spoken to anyone in my entire adult life about *Petrov*. He was a large, light-brown Viszla. The mention of his name should serve to convince me."

"A Viszla," Fermi said. "I remember."

"But, even should that fail, and I assume it might, you will have but one other choice. Wait until I am not looking, put the gun to my head..."

Fermi stared at him.

"And fire."

"Roberto—"

"May God almighty help all mankind if you should miss your target."

***

Ebb knew they would shoot him dead in less than two seconds if they found him listening to these three important men from the other side of the wall, within the secret passage. But at this point, he really didn't care much, after what they already did to him. Most of his teeth had fallen out over the last couple months, and his fingers had gone real shaky. They told him he was helping to win the war. After all, everybody was giving what they had to defeat the Nazis, and those sneaky Japs who snuck up on Pearl Harbor and bombed thousands of sailors. So, after his wreck in the truck when they told him all he had to do was sit in the doctor's chair and roll up his sleeve, well, it didn't seem too bad.

Then the stuff they put into his veins burned with the unholy fires of Hell and hurt much worse than his broken wrist and leg. For the first few days after they pushed the yellow liquid into his veins, he thought he was truly going to die from the pain. But eventually all that went away, and he felt pretty good later, except for when his teeth started getting loose and dropped out two, three at a time.

It wasn't all bad stuff. Weeks later, and for reasons nobody ever explained, his eyes got much, much better in the dark. He could see things in his bedroom closet with the door shut. He thought maybe they had shot him full of some juice they made from *cat* blood, or something, even though they told him it was a solution made from *pluto*nium. And then, of course, he accidentally found out he could *walk through walls*. Quite a surprise, when he rolled out of bed two months later and found himself in the backyard in the middle of the night. The next morning, after he thought about it some, he tried pushing one hand through the wall of his bathroom. It worked, but the very sight of his hand disappearing up to his forearm put the fear of God right in him. That surprise came with a price as well, and it was something he hadn't tried again for months after.

The men were finished talking, and Ebb heard them walk out of Dr. Oppenheimer's office. Ebb could hear everything they said with his ear pressed to the wall behind the scientist's desk. Ebb not only knew all about the secret passage but helped to build it two years ago during the original construction. The army asked the passage to be put in as an emergency escape route for Dr. Oppenheimer, if the enemy ever invaded this compound. So far, nothing like that had ever happened, and Ebb thought everybody had probably all but forgotten the passageway was even there.

Ebb found his way back to the interior hallway and exited

the building in the dark. He crouched low and angled back toward his truck he had parked a few hundred yards down the entry road. He dropped into the driver's seat and started the engine.

Time travel. Those three men had been talking about *time travel.*

When he was a boy in Macon, his daddy made sure all his kids knew how to read. He brought books back from the Macon library. Jules Verne and H.G. Wells wrote Ebb's favorite stories. At first, reading was slow for Ebb, but he caught on fast. After all, he needed to find out what happened to the heroes who dove far under the sea, flew to the moon, or traveled far into Earth's future. Ebb was scared of the gray-skinned Morlocks, and there were many nights he hugged his pillow to his chest and hoped a crazy Morlock wouldn't come from under the ground and snatch him from his bed.

But what he heard tonight was different. This was *real.* If he understood what Dr. Oppenheimer and the other scientists were saying, they were planning a trip to the past. Fermi would hold onto the playground swings behind the big white church, push a button on some machine, and take off, back two years. If that Fermi guy couldn't persuade Dr. Oppenheimer to give up being the lead scientist on the project, Fermi had agreed to kill him with a pistol.

Ebb decided to keep this to himself. No good could come of spilling the beans, even if anyone believed him. Besides, if Oppenheimer and the others thought stopping the whole business here in Oak Ridge was a good idea, well then, it was probably the right thing to do. He had heard talk that these were the three smartest men in the world, and Ebb wasn't about to argue with them.

However, it felt strange that the army and everyone was here for years, trying to build something to end the war, and now Oppenheimer and his friends meant to stop it. Ebb wished he could talk this out with someone, perhaps Ida, but Ida would get mad and tell him to mind his own business.

Ebb put his mind to some serious thought as he guided his truck home, headlights off, down the Tennessee gravel road.

Nothing is as far away as one minute ago. **Jim Bishop**

Chapter 26: Oak Ridge, Tennessee
June 15, 1944

I da tried to be polite and not stare at the stranger who sat on the other side of her kitchen table. The woman looked cleaned up but still edgy and confused. Ida's momma taught her that manners were nearly *everything* in life, just as important as most Bible passages, both Old and New Testaments. It was easy to see when somebody had been brought up proper, her momma instructed, and that was by giving a good look-see to their manners; *you could tell most all you needed to know.* Because of that, Ida refused to stare at the spindly woman with shiny black hair, and she kept most of her thoughts to herself.

But it was difficult *not* to stare since this woman *slurped* spoonful after spoonful of her special lima bean soup with extra chunks of country ham. The woman was skinny as a beanpole and gulped this soup as if she had not had a bite in a month of Sundays. Or, maybe she ate as though she had just been served her last meal before being marched to the gallows.

"Do you, uh, like the soup, Miss Tennyson?" Ida asked.

Irene nodded as she swallowed. "Yes, Mrs. Cade. Yes. I cannot tell you how much. It feels as though I have not eaten in a month of Sundays."

Ebb cut in. "Let the woman eat in peace, Ida."

Ida glanced at Ebb who was sitting at the table. "That way you talk, Miss Tennyson...are you from England?"

Irene glanced at her. "The way I talk?"

"Child, I'm from Georgia, and folks here in Tennessee had trouble understanding *my* words, *and* Ebb's, for the longest time when we first got to this place, since we both talk at you with a strong, southern Georgia accent."

A Matter of Time

Irene set her soup spoon on the edge of her bowl, dabbed lightly at the corners of her mouth with a cloth napkin with red roosters painted on it, and sat back in her chair. She smiled at Ida. "You are a marvelous cook, Mrs. Cade. I believe that might be the finest soup I have tasted in all my years, although—"

"My momma's recipe." Ida smiled. "Learned most everything important from my momma, rest her soul."

"Although, Mrs. Cade, I seem to have serious gaps in my memory. I wonder at this moment how I can even honestly tell you anything about the soup I've had or not had in my lifetime."

"Please call me Ida."

"Gaps?" Ebb said. "What kind of gaps?"

"I know my name. At least, I *think* I know my name. I know my forehead throbs as if I just survived a kick from a sturdy boot."

"And that's all you remember?" Ida frowned. "Your name?"

A few tears came to Irene's eyes. "I'm afraid so." She inspected her soup bowl as if hoping it wasn't empty. "I know this may seem an odd question, but, well, the year of our Lord is not two zero one nine, is it?"

"Two zero..?"

"Never mind."

Ida squinted at her. "What are you getting at, Miss Tennyson?"

"I mean, the calendar year today is 1944, is it not?"

"Of course."

Ebb watched her closely. "After you have a rest, Miss Tennyson, your memory will straighten. Maybe you need some *lights out*. Does wonders for me."

"No need to be formal, Ebb. Calling me *Irene* is fine."

Ebb nodded. "Did the soup settle you some?"

"It did. And your marvelous bathing room did wonders. But the front of my head still pounds with an unfamiliar ferocity."

Ebb stood. "Let's get you back to the sofa, close your eyes for a couple hours. Then, we'll see."

Irene found her feet, teetered a bit, and smiled at him. "My sincere thanks to you, Ebb, and to you, Ida. Without your help..."

She shivered and wrapped her arms around her middle. Tears trickled down her cheeks.

Ebb stepped to her and took her arm. "Come with me, Miss." He led her to the next room and helped her ease down onto the sofa. Ida watched from across the room and wondered what the *real* story was of the frail stranger her husband had found outside on the ground a few hours ago. Ida always had a good sense about people; this *Irene's* story about losing her memory did not ring exactly true and was all too convenient. Losing your memory relieves a person of answering questions, *important* questions, like how does some ghostly woman wearing nothing but a filthy smock end up unnoticed inside the boundary of one of the most guarded locations on God's green Earth? Well, *unnoticed* may be the wrong word. Her husband Ebb had certainly *noticed* her.

Ida cleared the dishes from the table as she watched Ebb pull a comforter over this Miss Irene Tennyson on the sofa.

History will be kind to me for I intend to write it. **Winston Churchill**

Chapter 27: Oak Ridge, Tennessee
June 15, 1944

The solid wood door to his room creaked open, and a stooped-over man with wild silver hair and a matching thick moustache stepped inside. He wore a faded gray suit and carried a small metal stool in one hand. "Hello," the man said.

Someone on the other side of the door pulled it closed.

"Uh, hello." MacKay backed against the wall.

"Do you mind if I sit?"

"You're joking with me, yeah?"

The old man set the stool on the tile floor. "Why would you think I am joking?"

MacKay huffed. "No reason. No reason. Go ahead and sit, if it makes any difference. I got no say in nothing. Go on and sit. Sit all day and night if it suits you."

The man sat. "I understand your name is Brody MacKay."

"I been telling everybody who will listen, and it ain't made no difference."

"Pleased to meet you, Brody. My name is Albert."

"Welcome to *Hell*, Albert." MacKay slid his back down the wall and sat on the floor.

"Hell?" Einstein said.

"I can't reason to any other explanation."

Einstein shrugged and glanced around the room. "This used to be a school for the teenagers. It is sad how the importance of a good education for children is sometimes replaced by a search for better and more efficient ways to kill people."

"If you say so."

Einstein shrugged. "Brody, Sergeant Gleason tells me you hail from Dundee, Scotland."

"No, sir. I *work* in Dundee, when the docks is slow, but I hail from Islay."

"The docks?"

"I may not look it, sir, but I've got more than my fair share of muscle on these bones. My pa even taught me the tricks of fist-brawling, the way he tells it, *cause the runt of the litter better know how to take care of himself in a scrap.* Cause of that, I can hold my own, if I need to."

Einstein rested his palms on his knees and leaned forward. "Do you know where you are, Brody?"

MacKay stared at him. "The way you talk...where're *you* from?"

"Germany. I was born in Germany. I lived there until about ten years ago."

"Ten years. Lived most of your life there, did you? Why'd you leave?"

Einstein chuckled. "I came to ask *you* questions, Brody."

MacKay turned his head away. "Just forget it. Ain't nothing makes sense anyways."

"I left Germany after a madman rose to power. I think many of my countrymen turned mad as well. I quickly knew there was no longer a place for me there. He bowed his head. "The story becomes monstrous after that...and impossible to believe."

MacKay turned to him. "Yeah, well, that's tough, leaving your homeland. Sorry for you."

"Thank you. So, tell me, do you know where you are now?"

"Sergeant Gleason said this place is *Tennessee.* I suppose that's in America. And let me tell you something, Albert, I wouldn't want to pick no fight with America. You should see the soldiers and fancy rifles they got."

Einstein looked at his fingernails. "Now, Brody, please explain to me how you came to be in Tennessee."

"Don't know how she done it, Albert, but it was surely that *witch*, Irene Lithgow."

"A witch."

"Told Gleason about this, too. They're *real*, Albert, the witches. Me being here *proves* it."

He considered. "Where were you before you arrived here?"

"In Dundee, at the asylum, where Dr. Bell was talking with Irene. Then she called down the winds."

"Who is Dr. Bell?"

"Joseph Bell. He talks to the prisoners, the *patients*. He decides if they get so right in the head they can be turned loose. He's a stand-up guy. Treats me with respect."

"Dr. Bell is a psychiatrist?"

"Don't know nothing about that."

Einstein straightened his back. "Brody, the day you left Dundee, after Irene called down the winds, as you said, specifically where were you in the asylum?"

"In the *talking* room, like we called it, where Dr. Bell would sit with the patients."

"Please describe that room for me."

"Describe it? How?"

"Tell me about the walls, the floor, the door, all you can remember."

"Why the bloody Hell you need to know that?"

Einstein smiled. "Please, Brody."

"Yeah, sure. It got four walls, like most rooms, yeah? The floor was part concrete, half dirt. They was fixing up the place, and hadn't finished the floors. Same old wood door with a lock probably made before my *pa* was born. Roof was mostly done, but parts was still not all covered. Sometimes we would get some rain inside, if the wind blew it just right. And there was a column of bricks from floor to ceiling right in the center of the room, still had horse-hitches fastened to the bricks with rusty nails. I grabbed onto one of those hitches. Kept me from flying up and out, like the winds took Dr. Bell. I do think those bricks was part of the building when it was first put up. But I got to tell you, my hands slipped off that hitch right after Dr. Bell disappeared out the roof, and I felt my body lifting into the air, too."

Einstein cupped his chin. "Go on."

"Don't remember much but looking down from high above and seeing that witch Irene still on the ground, cackling away as if she was having the time of her life. Then I started with the visions, yeah? A roadway was filled with the most fantastic carriages. A city got built up into the clouds. I remember a painting as big as a house with the words: *Mike Sweeney, Mah-Li-Bu Two Zero One Nine*. Nothing after that. I blacked out, like I'd been kicked in the front of my head by a horse. Next time I saw anything, I was outside here, spread out in the gravel."

Einstein scowled. "Two Zero One Nine?"

"Figured I'd gone mad for a few seconds."

Einstein stood. "Thank you, Brody. I appreciate the conversation."

"You *appreciate*..? Mister, I would *appreciate* getting on the next steamer back to Islay."

Einstein gripped his metal stool in one hand and looked MacKay straight in the eye. "I must leave, brew some strong tea, and consider your predicament. But I promise you, Brody, I will return. Then we will see about putting you on that steamer."

"Truly?"

Einstein rested one hand on MacKay's shoulder. "I promise." He twitched his mustache. "Once more, you say the doctor's name was Joseph Bell?"

"It was."

"And the witch, as you call her...Irene who?"

"Lithgow. Irene Lithgow."

Einstein nodded. "Brody, if you don't mind, and to clear up something for me, do you know today's date?"

"Was never too good with dates. Sorry. Just know it's the middle of July, or thereabout."

"Fine. Fine. The middle of July, but in what year?"

"What do you mean?"

"What is the year, Brody?"

"That might be the silliest question you or that Sergeant Gleason has asked me."

"Humor me, Brody."

MacKay stared at him. "1892. It's 1892. Yeah?"

Einstein turned and rapped at the door. A few seconds later, the door swung open, and he shuffled through the opening and into the shadows.

***

A Matter of Time

Einstein developed a severe tremble in his hands as he left the compound and started across the lawn toward his laboratory. He told Sergeant Gleason he would come back later and inform him of his findings.

His findings.

One answer alone sufficiently solved this riddle: Brody MacKay was most assuredly a time traveler. Einstein nearly giggled at the thought. *A man who traveled through time.* Somehow, on a day in 1892, the severe winds, probably a tornado, ripped through a thinning plane of a worm hole and pushed Brody MacKay through that opening.

The morning sun warmed his face as he neared the unassuming brick building constructed specifically for himself and his associates, his *collaborators*. The fold of the black hole must have been variable in depth along its surface. Then, depending upon the exact location, and the particular force of the tornadic winds, MacKay could have broken the time barrier and completed his nearly instantaneous trip in one of many possible terminal locations since he had lost his grip on the gravimetric anchor attached to the brick column. That would explain MacKay's vision of *Two Zero One Nine*. This could have no other meaning than the *year* 2019. MacKay was swept along the time stream, guided by the exact fold of the black hole, and landed in 1944, even though he glimpsed another time period before coming to rest here.

Einstein smiled and stuffed his hands into his pants pockets. No *need* for any test before Fermi departed on his journey. The theories he had formulated had been proven correct. The only thing left was to finish his adjustments, and fully explain the workings of the box to Enrico at the end of the week. Hopefully the mission would be a success. The idea of being responsible for the deaths of thousands of civilians was unimaginable.

But before then, he had a promise to keep, and deciding what to do about Brody MacKay was not an easy problem to solve, even for someone whose entire life was a constant voyage of solving problems. He would speak to Gleason about it. And the name of Dr. Joseph Bell stirred a memory in one dusty corner of his brain. He would ask Dr. Dexter Braddock, his research assistant, to do a little digging in that direction.

He stepped slowly across the lawn, which was riddled with brown dry patches. Hopefully, he could find a few moments to add a nap to his morning. The very thought of slipping off his shoes and falling asleep in his big leather chair made a grin spread across his face.

Time is the most undefinable yet paradoxical of things; the past is gone, the future is not come, and the present becomes the past even while we attempt to define it, and, like the flash of lightning, at once exists and expires. **Charles Caleb Colton**

Chapter 28: Downtown Cincinnati, Ohio
Present Day

Bell could not tear his eyes from the video, even though he knew exactly what he was going to see. From the moment he spotted the fountain pen in the vault, it all became clear to him, without any chance of mistake or deviation. A sudden, throbbing pain pressed at the center of his chest as he watched wide-eyed and attempted to calm his rising panic. The old woman and the bank guard entered the vault. A few moments later, the woman and the guard exited the room of security boxes. Bell stared as he studied the guard turn his key in the lock of the door, test the door to confirm it was secure, and then both he and the woman moved out of range of the camera. The time-stamp on the video showed only 90 seconds had passed since the two of them had entered the vault.

Keaton said, "And there it is."

Jessie inhaled. "Jesus."

Gavin said, "I suppose you can see why I called on your day off."

Keaton shook his head. "I half expected Rod Serling to appear at the end of the video and welcome us to *The Twilight Zone.*"

Jessie glanced at Bell, saw him lean on his cane, stuff his other hand in his pocket, and tilt his head at the floor. "Cousin?"

"Mr. Brewster," Gavin said. "Any thoughts? I've watched this thing six times and I'm not closer to an answer that makes sense. I'd be thankful for anything you might contribute with your fresh pair of eyes."

Bell took a breath, pursed his lips, and glanced at Jessie. "Captain, my cousin is an excellent investigator. Her mind works in a precise and organized fashion. I am certain she can fit together the pieces of this puzzle without my assistance. And I believe she is *ready* to explain these seemingly impossible circumstances to you. Now, if you would excuse me..."

He turned and stepped out of the vault.

***

Bell walked straight to a restroom he'd spotted in the bank lobby. He stepped to the sink, switched on the faucet, cupped his hands, and splashed cold water on his face. He straightened and regarded his refection in the mirror. Water droplets trickled down his skin and darkened his blue oxford-cloth shirt.

Rarely was he taken by surprise, but Irene Lithgow managed to accomplish that feat today. It took all his strength to not burst out and yell. The woman's hair was gray, and the wrinkles around her eyes appeared real enough. A surgical mask often worn to prevent contact with airborne germs and viruses obscured the rest of her face. His best deduction was the woman he saw in the wheelchair was either wearing a disguise of aging makeup or was about seventy years old. But that was impossible; Irene time-jumped at nearly the same instant *he* jumped, and she was around thirty when that happened.

The mathematics do not add up.

And then there was Fallon Dalmore. Recognizing Irene Lithgow as the woman in the wheelchair was not Bell's first shock of the day.

Maybe a discussion with Warren would help. He was right about his new companion; she was intelligent, intuitive, and had a good heart.

It was time he entrusted the young woman with what appeared to be his darkest fears coming true.

***

Keaton chuckled. "Your cousin sounds like Scotty."

Gavin said to Jessie, "He has a lot of confidence in your

abilities."

Jessie scoffed. "Apparently."

"So? Give me *something*, Warren. And let's leave out the supernatural, if you don't mind." He shifted his eyes to Keaton. "That solution has already been suggested and discounted."

"Sure. Sure. Buster, play that thing again."

Keaton shrugged and turned back to the video controls. The image on the screen started. The gray-haired woman, her legs covered by a plaid blanket in the wheelchair, and the bank guard entered the picture and moved toward the gated door that separated the main vault from the room that contained the safety deposit boxes. The guard unlocked the door and opened it. They disappeared inside. When they exited, the guard locked the door, and they moved out of the frame.

Jessie waited until Keaton and Gavin fixed their eyes on her. "Let's start with this...what can the answer *not* be?"

Keaton cleared his throat. "That Timmons the guard could not be dead in the vault, all locked up, but also walk away from the vault, *not* dead, both at the same time."

"Correct."

"We know that, Warren," Gavin said.

"When I first saw Timmons on the floor, I noticed his uniform and his shoes. Did you see them, Captain?"

He furrowed his brow. "I saw them."

"The uniform was clean, pressed, and even his shoes were polished a shiny black. Apparently, Mr. Timmons took some pride in the way he dressed for work."

"So?"

"But if you play back the video again, you will see when they *exit* the vault, the guard's *shoes* are *not* polished a shiny black, but rather are streaked with something, probably mud. In fact, they are a different type of shoe or boot altogether."

Keaton stared at her.

"Also, you can see a taser on Timmins' belt when they enter the vault. The taser is clipped to the *right* side of his belt. But when they exit the vault, the taser has switched positions, and is clipped to the guard's *left* side."

Gavin said, "Holy crap. Didn't notice."

"And one more thing. When they enter the safety deposit

room, the guard in the video holds the key to unlock the door in his *right* hand. But when they exit, the guard locks the door behind them with his *left* hand."

Gavin nodded. "Of course."

"Nobody uses his non-dominant hand to insert a key and turn the lock."

"We were watching two different guards." Gavin chuckled. "That *had* to be the answer. But it was so *well executed*, the most obvious solution did not occur to me."

"The first guard is certainly Timmons. The second guard we saw, the one who *exits* the room, was somehow hidden under the covered section of the wheelchair. When the old woman with the surgical mask rolled the chair inside, the hidden guard extricated himself while Timmons was turned away, sneaked up behind Timmons, smashed him on the back of his head, drove the pen into his temple, and then took his place. He and the old woman exited the vault as calmly as can be."

Gavin grinned. "I see my recommendation for your promotion was a correct one."

"Unbelievable, Jessie," Keaton said. "I watched that thing over and over and didn't pick up on it. Good work."

Gavin took out a pad of paper and made a note with a cheap Bic pen. "But why, Warren? Why arrange this display? There was no robbery, at least that we know of. Certainly, if someone wanted Timmons dead, there would be many ways to do it much less complicated than this. Imagine the necessary planning, the bank vault, the wheelchair, the uniform, arranging for a doppelganger the same size and general appearance of Timmons, if we accept your theory as being true."

Jessie took a breath. "I'm working on that, Captain."

"You do that."

"But there's something else. "Whoever planned this escapade is obviously quite smart."

"Sure."

"Then why go to the trouble of all the timing, the double for the guard, and all the other precise details, but somehow overlook the shoes, the taser, and the door lock?"

"Meaning?"

"I think those discrepancies were purposeful."

"But *why?*"

"Working on that, too, Captain."

"Good."

"Look, since you don't need me anymore down here, I'd like to take my cousin home. I'll check in with you guys later?"

"Go," Gavin said. "Just come in tomorrow. We need you. *I* need you."

She turned and walked out.

***

Jessie glanced at Bell in the front seat next to her as she guided her Jeep off Fountain Square onto Walnut Street. "So, I suppose I should thank you."

Bell kept his eyes trained forward. "No need."

"Uh huh." She turned the wheel, and the Jeep rolled onward down 3rd toward the ramp to I-75. "You knew the answer in about ten seconds."

"Sooner."

"But you didn't want to grandstand it, take credit, and draw attention to yourself."

"I left the analysis to you."

"You wanted *me* to get the credit. Right?"

"I was sure you would arrive at the proper conclusions."

"You couldn't have known I would figure it out at all, or so quickly."

"I am usually a good judge of character."

"Right." She changed lanes and accelerated north across broken sections of pavement. "Tell me what you spotted first that tipped you off."

"The pen."

She eased off the gas. "In the evidence bag."

"Yes."

"I don't get the business about the pen."

"There is no reason you *should* know."

"I assume you will tell me at some point in our near future. No time-travel reference intended."

"Yes."

"Do you agree the differences we spotted in the guard were not mistakes by our murderer?"

"Murderess."

"Really. The woman in the wheelchair?"

"The pawns and other pieces in the game were revealed to me, along with the motivation behind the murder. The *mechanism* of the murder was inconsequential."

"Pawns?"

"Nothing more. Pawns are often sacrificed."

"And Fallon Dalmore?"

He swallowed. "Was it that obvious?"

"You said I was an excellent investigator."

"I did."

"You either recognized her, or she reminded you of someone. In either case, you were startled when you saw her."

"Fallon Dalmore is quite attractive, Warren."

"It was more than that, Bell."

He gazed at her for a moment and nodded. "Soon."

"When?"

"When we arrive at your home."

"Why there?"

"I believe the proper time has come to show you some images in my photograph album."

"The McGuffin?"

"Yes, Warren. The McGuffin."

'Closed time-like curve' is the jargon for time travel. It means you go out, come back and meet yourself in the past. **Kip Thorne**

Chapter 29: Hartwell, Ohio
February - 2018

Susie Palmisano lit her first unfiltered cigarette of the morning and dropped the Wednesday edition of the Cincinnati Enquirer onto her kitchen table. The whole paper weighed no more than a couple ounces. Ever since people started getting their news from the internet and other places, the morning paper had shrunk smaller and smaller, but the price kept getting higher and higher.

She chuckled. Had her husband Tony *The Cleaner* Palmisano lived long enough to see this, he probably would have put his foot down and quit the paper long ago, except for maybe the Sunday edition; he could not have survived without Sunday reporters screaming and complaining about the sad state of affairs with both the Bengals...and his beloved Reds.

The elderly woman chuckled when she caught sight of the date at the top of the Gardening Section: February 22, 2018. She sighed as she thought about it and tapped ashes on the edge of her Skyline Chili ashtray. *Nine years.* It had been more than nine years since her friend Hattie Brooks had passed. Poor Hattie. Lived a long life, never said a cross word about anybody or anything, had already suffered enough, losing her husband, and their only child years before that. But even *she* was not immune to the ravages of the cancer. If anybody should have been spared, it should have been Hattie. It was probably a good example of how the people God created were not expected to understand God's ways, or his plan for all of us.

Susie's own Tony had been stricken with the emphysema

after three decades of breathing in the fumes and chemicals from his dry-cleaning store on Vine near Empress Chili. *Tony's Cleaners* was empty now; nobody had rented the building since *Tony's* closed nearly twelve years ago, but *Tony's* sign remained there, like a ghost-ship on those *Famous Mysteries* TV shows. The building's owner still maintained the property, trimmed the grass, picked up any loose trash, so the place still looked as though it could open for business at any time, but the sign was never lit up like before. Susie liked the sign, and she smiled whenever she walked by it on one of her now infrequent strolls around one of the few safe blocks of Hartwell.

Susie eased her kitchen chair back, stood, and shuffled across the room to a collection of boxes stacked around her computer on her dining room table. She sat at the table, pushed a half-empty bottle of *Three Olives* vodka aside, and opened the box of Don Amigo cigars her Tony had enjoyed practically every day. She shook her head. The cigars had probably not helped the emphysema either. She peered into the box and studied the pile of photos she had taken over the years. She shuffled through a few and pulled out one of them then grinned at the person in the photo. Small tears started on her eyelids. There was Hattie, smiling, no, *beaming* at the camera. Her arm was wrapped around the waist of her friend Wallace, a man she met at a church social who had moved here from Scotland. Even though this Wallace was decades younger than Hattie, that hadn't mattered to her at all. Besides, it was obvious before he moved in with her that they were just the best of friends and nothing more. Susie thought at the time it was nice that Hattie had somebody to share her remaining days with, and to kind of look after her, even though no romance was included in the deal.

Susie sighed. Sometimes romance was overrated, anyway.

She reached over to her computer, wanting to scan this photo and post it to *Facebook*. She liked *Facebook*, since sometimes it was practically her only way of staying in touch with people. Her son and daughter moved away to Texas years ago, and she might see them and their kids on Thanksgiving, maybe, if she was lucky. So, *Facebook* pictures of her family and what was left of her friends was usually the best way. Besides, she wanted to *celebrate* Hattie's life. It was time somebody on this planet appreciated her friend, and the good and the mostly happy time she led on this Earth.

Susie smiled about her plan. She decided scanning the picture was too complicated, and positioned the photo of Hattie and her friend Wallace on the table. She aimed her phone, and pressed the camera button.

Lane Cohen

My colleagues and I recently showed that you can think of time travel, the process of going from the future into the past, as a kind of teleportation of information from now to back then. Moreover, we were actually able to use a simple quantum computer to demonstrate this effect. **Seth Lloyd**

Chapter 30: Hartwell, Ohio
Summer - 2009

The first few joyful weeks with Joseph sped by.

Hattie's normal routine of waking at 6:00, taking Scooter for his morning constitutional, which was more like Scooter taking *her* for *a walk*, coming home and brewing her first cup of Maxwell House Traditional Blend, which just meant Maxwell House was still making the same old coffee they had advertised in the 1950s, then plopping down on the sofa with Scooter at her side and watching The Weather Channel, taking small bites from two slices of Sara Lee cinnamon raison bread; all that had not changed since Joseph moved in with her. What *had* changed? Joseph was with her most all the time, on every walk, through their pieces of toast, although Joseph preferred English muffins, and despite the obvious changes involved with having a young man around all the time, Hattie enjoyed every minute with Dr. Joseph Bell, surgeon from Scotland, as he shared her household. Her life was unexpectedly freed from an unspoken loneliness, and was instead, filled with sudden possibilities.

While Joseph was a man of obvious great intelligence and highly educated, his face lit up like a small child's whenever she showed him more of the wonders of 2009. The first time she took him to the movies was glorious. They went to the Showcase Cinemas where they showed a classic film each Thursday evening. The large tub of popcorn drenched in butter-like oil was a huge hit with Joseph, right away. When the two of them walked out of *Lawrence of Arabia*, Joseph could not even speak, and Hattie thought he might have been struck permanently silent. He was completely overcome with the more than three-hour spectacle they had just witnessed. Joseph even commented that even though he was thunderstruck, yes, that was the word he used, *thunderstruck* by the magnificent images on the screen and the manner the movie told its story and enraptured its audience, it was the majesty of the *music* that most thrilled him.

On her third day with him, Hattie drove Joseph to the Cincinnati airport. Her new companion found it odd the airport was physically located in Kentucky but was named for a city twenty miles away and not even in the same state. Hattie shrugged at that one, since she had no idea how to answer.

But the name of the airport mattered little once Joseph began to watch the aircraft land and take off from the windows on the top floor of the main terminal. To him, the science behind these huge flying vehicles was intellectually amazing. Joseph never quizzed Hattie about the wonders he observed for the first time. He would just nod and smile, as if it all made sense to him already.

Joseph settled in easily at Hattie's home and helped with all the household chores. Since Joseph wore many of Lester's clothes for the first couple weeks, Hattie was sometimes startled when Joseph would appear around a corner, as if a younger version of Lester had suddenly materialized. At the end of August, Hattie took Joseph to the *J.S. Bank* store in Kenwood for some new clothes. Joseph protested about Hattie spending her own money for his clothes, but after she explained how he had no money of his own and really had no other choice, Joseph didn't say anything else about it.

Hattie smiled every time Joseph parked himself in front of the TV and watched *Jeopardy!* It was amazing how Joseph could beat the contestants to their answers, even though they had at least 125 years of history in their memory banks that Joe didn't and couldn't have. He was occasionally surprised when he missed a question, but then he discovered certain countries and cities had changed their names since his time. She was totally amazed at how unbelievably quick-witted her new houseguest really was. It was no wonder Conan Doyle selected Joseph as his inspiration for Sherlock Holmes.

From the beginning, Scooter followed Joseph around, and eventually never left his side. It seemed Scooter and Joseph had developed a thing for each another. It turned out Joseph was quite adept at knitting, and he put together a four-legged navy-blue sweater for his new little friend. As the weather turned colder, Hattie was sure that Scooter really appreciated it.

Nearly every Saturday morning, Hattie and Joseph walked to the Frisch's Restaurant a short distance away on Vine, where they ordered the breakfast buffet. While Joseph ate sparingly most all the time, the Frisch's buffet was his one exception. He craved the sausage links and scrambled eggs with cheese mixed in, and he piled his plate full. Hattie and Joseph used their Saturday morning time together to tell each other of their lives before the two of them met. Hattie loved hearing about Scotland and Joseph's family, and Joseph listened to everything Hattie had to say about her life growing up in an orphanage, later working at the DeKuyper factory, and her long relationship with Lester, who she met when they were in the same high school class together in Norwood.

Lester had been brought up as a regular churchgoer, and every Sunday, she and Lester spent all morning in the church pews. Before Lester came into her life, Hattie had never been religious, but Lester's momma was a stickler, and it rubbed off on him. Hattie took Joseph to the big Presbyterian church she had attended with Lester for more than three decades, and she made it a rule to take Joseph to services every Sunday. While Hattie could tell Joseph wasn't that interested in this, or probably any church, Joseph gladly went with her and sat politely with the hymnal in his hands. He even joined in, most of the time, with his clear, pleasant singing voice. Hattie suspected Joseph had never heard most of these hymns but managed to pick them up practically the second time he ever heard one.

Hattie knew that Joseph could not remain anonymous forever, a man with no provable identity, so she drove him to her old friend Nick *Fingers* Nicolas, who she met while they devoured ice cream in the parking lot of the United Dairy Farmers right up the street after they both came home separately from a horrible Bengals loss, and were trying to drown their respective sorrows in ice cream. Nick was a fixture in the neighborhood and could often be spotted trudging his 300-pound frame on two bad knees down the Hartwell sidewalks toward the UDF. She and Nick shared ice cream and a few words together about twice a month when they ran onto each other, and to this day she was unsure if Nick's parents named the man Nicolas Nicolas, or Nicolas was his last name, and people just called him Nick. She thought about asking him but decided to just leave it alone. Not knowing the answer was probably better than the answer itself.

Nick worked nights as a bartender at the Century Inn, a few miles down the Pike, but he also had a particular talent for magically providing various forms of identification. It was kind of a hobby, and fun for him. All Nick wanted in return, that is, if you were a friend of his, were gift cards to UDF. He was totally addicted to mass quantities of cookies-and-cream.

Joseph posed for three I.D. photos in Nick's basement studio, and in less than 30 minutes, *Wallace Brewster* left Nick's home with what appeared to be an Ohio driver's license, a Hamilton County library card, a zoo membership, a season pass to the community swimming pool, a Social Security number, and a copy of Wallace Brewster's birth certificate, which listed Terra Haute, Indiana as his birthplace.

Today was Wednesday. Hattie, Joseph, and Scooter had already returned from their walk around the tree-lined neighborhood streets when Joseph settled into a chair on Hattie's front porch. As usual, Scooter jumped onto Joseph's lap. Hattie appeared on the porch and handed Joseph a frosty cold can of soda.

"What is this, Hattie?"

"Soda. Diet-Cherry Dr. Pepper."

He examined the can. "Diet..?"

"It's good."

"This Dr. Pepper sells soda?"

"It's fun to watch your expression the first time you experience anything new."

Bell lifted the can to his lips. "Bubbles."

"It's called carbonation."

"Delicious." He took another swallow. "Thank you, Hattie. Will you join me?"

She shook her head as a cough struck pain in the center of her chest. She took a Kleenex from a shorts pocket and touched it to her mouth. "Maybe later, Joseph. Think I'll go stretch out for an hour or so. Will you be okay for a while?"

He studied her tissue. "Yes. Scooter will stay with me."

"Don't throw any switches or blow up anything."

"I will try not to."

She shuffled away, the blood-stained Kleenex still held against her mouth.

Man can go up against gravitation in a balloon, and why should he not hope that ultimately he may be able to accelerate his drift along the Time-Dimension, or even turn about and travel the other way. **H.G. Wells**

Chapter 31: Oak Ridge, Tennessee
June 16, 1944

Ebb had been married to Ida long enough to know when she was upset, even if she didn't say anything about it.

And this time, from the way she wouldn't look him in the eye as she pushed the door closed behind him, he could tell Ida *strongly* disapproved. But Ebb was both curious and concerned about Irene Tennyson, felt bad he had nearly run her down, and wanted to save her the crowds of soldiers and the hundreds of questions which would follow if he told anybody about finding Irene, who just appeared in the road, inside the main Oak Ridge complex, as if magically transported there by Harry Houdini himself.

He glanced at Irene as he guided the Chevy truck through the streets of his neighborhood. She sat upright, apparently surprised, and maybe *frightened* of being in his truck at all.

"You okay, Miss Tennyson?"

"Irene. Please."

"You look troubled."

"I shall be fine, Ebb. I need to get used to new things."

"New things?"

She turned and smiled at him. "Tell me about these streets, Ebb. And where are we going?"

He turned the wheel and decelerated as they neared a stop sign. "This here is what they built, mostly for us workers. Called *hutments*. Lots of us workers in Oak Ridge moved here and needed places to live."

She nodded. "Oak Ridge?"

"Name of the town."

"I see."

"I'm taking us up the hill, away from here. Thought we could sit outside near one of the churches and talk for a spell. Should nobody be over there this time of day."

She looked straight out the pockmarked windshield. "That sounds fine, Ebb."

The truck rolled to a stop a few minutes later in a small, gravel parking area beside a wooden church painted a bright white. A sandy children's play area spread out just behind the church near a huge tree. Ebb stepped out of the truck and swung his door closed. Irene still faced forward and sat without moving at all. He wondered if she was nervous about getting out, or maybe she was just waiting for him to open her door. He shrugged, strode to the other side of the truck, and opened her door.

Irene turned her head to him and smiled. "It is nice to know gentlemen still exist in this time."

He offered his hand.

She took it and gingerly stepped down the good distance from the truck to the ground. "Thank you, Ebb."

"No need to thank me."

She strolled to the grass. "It is lovely here."

"There's a bench under that big oak." He gestured at the tree, about ten yards from them at the edge of the playground. "Figured we could sit. Nice shade there."

Irene slipped off the shoes and ankle socks she had borrowed from Ida Cade, left them beside the truck, and walked barefoot through the grass toward the bench. "I love the feel of summer grass on my bare feet."

He watched her walk away, and then started after her.

She sat on the white slats of the bench and patted the empty space beside her. "Come sit, Ebb."

He eased down to the bench. It gave him an eerie feeling to see the pretty, white woman in Ida's clothes, which were far too big for her. It made her look like a little girl. And the way she gazed at him, with something in her eyes he could not figure, did not sit well. She seemed to like him, even though she might just be grateful for his help, but that wasn't the end of it. And his reaction to her, which he could not deny, was something he couldn't explain either.

"You feeling okay, Irene?"

"The pain in the front of my head is nearly gone."

"Miss Irene, if you don't mind, I'm curious about those leather cuffs I cut off you."

She glanced at her wrists. "I don't recall anything about them."

"Were you, well, being kept against your will?"

"Well, I'm sure if I were being held captive, it would have been against my will. But..."

"Yeah?"

"I told you. My memory seems erased, as if it were nothing more than faded letters on a chalkboard."

"Maybe it would help get your memory straight if you could think of the last thing you *can* remember before I found you."

"May I ask *you* something first, Ebb?"

"Sure."

"Can you tell me what *Mike Sweeney Cincinnati Chevrolet* means to you?"

He stared at her. "Cincinnati is a city on the river between Ohio and Kentucky. And Chevrolet is a car or truck."

"Car?"

"Like my truck." He gestured to the parking area. "Only smaller. A *car*. And you don't say Chevro-*let*. It's Chevro-*lay*. *Mike Sweeney* is the owner of the car business."

She gazed at the stark white of her bare feet atop the grass and began to cry.

"Irene?"

"Ebb..."

She sniffled and cleared her throat. She tilted her head against his shoulder.

"Miss Irene, is there anything..?"

She took a long breath and lifted her head. "I'd like to tell you something. Would that be all right?"

"I guess."

"Do you have a handkerchief?"

Ebb reached around to his back pocket and pulled one out. He offered it to her.

Irene dabbed her eyes. "Thank you." She sniffled again. "I am sorry for being so emotional."

"Anybody would react the same way, I expect."

She took a long breath. "When I was small, I grew up in a lovely farmhouse that rested on the edge of a deep wood. I was forbidden to walk into that wood alone, ever, and my mother warned me in a stern voice, nearly every day."

"And your father?"

She folded her hands and rested them in her lap. "He was a soldier, Ebb, a hero killed in India while trying to save his men."

"Sorry to hear that."

"My mother was good and proper, and cared for me more than she cared for her own life, or for anything else, for that matter. One bright spring morning, she invited me for a walk in those woods to pick wildflowers for our supper table. We hadn't gone very far, when I turned and found my mother had disappeared. I dropped my empty basket and spun in all directions, but she was gone. *Just gone.* She had vanished without a sound and left me alone in the very place she had told me never to go without her."

"Sounds downright terrible."

"The fear started in the front of my eyes and spread to the back of my throat. Have you ever been so afraid, Ebb, you couldn't talk, couldn't breathe?"

"Irene—"

"And that's how I feel now. *Right now.* Imagine, Ebb, having no memory of your life, not knowing anything about yourself but your name, and there's nothing that says you can even be sure of *that.*" She wiped tears from her face with the handkerchief. "I'm sorry. I'll be fine in a minute."

"Listen to me."

She turned to him.

"It ain't as bad as you think." He smiled. "Your memory is *coming back.* You just *remembered* about your mama, where you grew up, the woods you were afraid of and all."

She stared at him.

"That's a good thing, Irene. Right?"

A smile started on her lips. She lightly patted his forearm. "You're right. That is a good thing."

"Good. Let's sit here for a while. Maybe it takes nothing more than a little peace and quiet, and before long your memory will come all the way back."

She gave him a small nod. "It would be worth a try." She exhaled and looked down at the grass. Why did I tell Ebb Cade the story about my parents, even though only part of the story was true? My father did serve in India, but was not killed there; he was found butchered into many pieces on the floor of our own kitchen. Must have struck my head harder than I thought. I was not thinking clearly, and that had to immediately improve. Of course, I had not revealed the full extent of the story, of how my father had taken an Indian woman into his military home for most of one year before being discovered, thus humiliating my mother for the rest of her life. And how I could not bring myself to forgive my father, even up until his last day on Earth.

***

Ebb stared at *The Chapel on the Hill;* a shiver touched the back of his neck. He had helped build that church, but he was forbidden to even walk in the door. The very idea started his blood to boil when he let himself think about it. He remembered his daddy never seemed to care about those things, as if he just accepted the way it was, since in parts of the South, nothing had ever really changed much, and there was little anybody could do about it.

But Ebb was smart, as his momma always told him, and what troubled him more than anything at this moment, even more than white folks still trying to keep down the black man in a time of war, was that he suddenly realized *Ida had been right.* Sometimes he forgot how smart Ida was; Ida realized something about this young woman didn't make much sense. And a few seconds ago, it all became clear; Irene Tennyson, had been lying to them from the start.

I myself believe that there will one day be time travel because when we find that something isn't forbidden by the over-arching laws of physics we usually eventually find a technological way of doing it. **David Deutsch**

Chapter 32: Lebanon, Ohio
Present Day

Jessie and Bell sat silently on front-porch rockers next to each other. Bell's scrapbook covered the top of his thighs.

The air was missing any trace of a breeze. The sun hovered straight overhead and had quickly heated the thick early-afternoon air. The two little dogs were sprawled in the shade beside each other on the edge of the porch, as if they had been friends forever.

"Do you want to start?" Jessie asked.

Bell glanced at her from the other rocker.

She said, "Is something wrong?"

He leaned forward. "I suddenly realize how insular I have been, Warren, my feelings kept inside, carefully guarded."

"Yeah. Sounds like someone else I know."

"Please explain, Warren, if you would like to."

She met his gaze. "Dating in my 20s was pretty ordinary, Bell, even boring, that is before I met...Billy. William Barlow Conger, star receiver for University of Louisville Cardinals football team for three years. They called him the *Electric Eel.* Quite a popular guy, and BMOC, if you know what I mean."

"BMOC?"

"Big Man on Campus. I didn't know him then, in his college days, but that is what his friends told me, later. His resume was pretty terrific. After he graduated and went to Chase Law School, he became an Assistant Hamilton County district attorney."

"An athlete and a professional man."

"Quite. We first met on several cases he prosecuted here. I was the police witness, and he would examine me in court. Later, we took to examining each other *out of court*. That wasn't so professional."

He blinked at her.

"The first six months with him were fantastic, special, like nothing I had ever experienced. We..." She scooted her rocker and faced him. "Billy actually lived up to his resume. And after six months of being treated like an absolute princess, I finally decided to bring Billy home."

"For an introduction to your parents."

"You see, Bell, being with Billy broke down all my emotional walls. I opened up to him, completely, and maybe for the first time in my life. It felt wonderful to have a partner that way, to totally trust him with my innermost thoughts and feelings." She stopped and looked down at her hands.

"You brought Mr. Conger to *The Golden Lamb*."

She shook her head. "He *met us* at the inn. Otherwise, if he had been in the car with us..."

"I understand."

"Billy was there for me afterward, right through the funerals, my surgery, for many months. But later, I pulled back from him, without thinking about it or planning to do so. Nothing changed. Billy didn't do anything wrong. It was just that—"

"You were afraid of becoming that close to anyone again."

"For fear of losing someone else, someone who I cared for greatly. I couldn't stand the thought of risking all the devastating heartbreak again."

"Understandable."

"So, for the past eighteen months, I've been closed off emotionally, just as you were saying before. I guess it has been a way of protecting myself. Because, Bell, when you've got nothing..?"

He nodded. "You ain't got nothin' to lose."

She gazed at him. "Bob Dylan. You."

"A favorite of Lester Brooks."

"You've surprised me again."

"That lyric sticks with me, Warren, although frankly, many other Dylan lyrics leave me puzzled."

"You and about 400 million other people."

He smiled. "Look, Warren, your reaction to the sudden loss of those dear to you is not of *unusual* concern. Your behavior is quite typical, if I might say."

"Perhaps. But, you know what? It feels good to be able to express my feelings to you now. I've pulled so far back from everyone else in my life, since..."

"Warren, I told you I understand."

She shook her head. "Go on, Bell. I'm sorry I interrupted you before. Tell me what you were thinking."

"Well then. For most of *my* adult life, I have been in the company of family: mother, father, one older brother, and later my wife and daughter. But even though I went to church, taught my classes at the Edinburgh medical school, and helped the Yard with more than a few supposedly unsolvable puzzles, while spending my life in Scotland I never had an actual *friendship* with anyone. Family members do not count in that regard. As you and I motored back here from the bank, it occurred to me that apparently, you and I have *developed* a *friendship*, even though we met quite recently."

"I know. Weird."

"That circumstance gladdens me."

She smiled at him. "Me, too."

Scooter padded to Bell and rested his chin on one of the doctor's knees near the scrapbook. Bell scratched the little dog's head. "I miss my Malcolm." He cleared his throat. "Many a time I had long conversations with that little beagle."

"Really?"

"Only when nobody else was around. It could be embarrassing for a grown man, and a surgical professor, to be caught speaking with his dog, late on a summer evening on the back porch, or on a cold winter night before a fire."

"Not at all. In the weeks Doc has been in my life, I've spoken with him more than all my conversations with everyone else all added together."

Bell looked down at his little wire-haired mutt. "This Scooter does have an understanding *expression*. But somehow, I believe all he ever thinks is either *Play with me* or *Time to eat.* Nevertheless, Scooter has been the recipient of many of my introspective monologues over the years." Bell rubbed Scooter's neck.

Jessie stared out at the front lawn and let the silence gather around them. She stretched her back and twisted her hip to work out a kink. "We've become an interesting pair."

"Yes. Quite interesting."

"There's something else I've been wondering about."

"What is that?"

"Fallon Dalmore."

"Oh?"

"She reminds you of someone. Your wife Elizabeth?"

Bell rubbed his temple. "Elizabeth's family name was Dalmore. And Fallon Dalmore bears a strong resemblance to Elizabeth. Both are tall, freckled, with long red hair. In a low light, one might even be mistaken for the other. Elizabeth and Miss Dalmore are also the same approximate age, at least they were when I last saw Elizabeth."

He looked at the porch floor.

She said, "Remind me to come back to the question of *your* age."

"Certainly."

She reached down and patted Doc's side. "Is it possible Fallon is descended from Elizabeth's family?"

"It is likely. And frankly, Warren..." He gazed out at the horizon and didn't say anything.

"What is it, Bell?"

He stood and shifted his weight on the weathered planks of the porch. "I've been in this world for ten years. A *decade*, Warren. And in all those years, I've had just two friends, before you. And *no* romance."

"Welcome to the club."

"Upon my landing here, at least for the first year or so, my heart was still full of my Elizabeth. I ached to see her, to hold her, to sense the fragrance of fresh soap behind her ears, each moment of every day. Even though my intellect told me I had little chance of ever seeing Elizabeth again, my *heart* refused to surrender that fight. But, even after the years progressed, and my love for Elizabeth faded softly like a summer breeze at sunset, I still refused to pursue any female companionship."

She nodded. "Because if you did, the truth about your *past* might complicate things."

"I wanted to take her hand, Warren, and run out the door with her. I wanted to take Fallon Dalmore's hand."

"But you couldn't."

He shook his head. "I could not, even though my heart instantly wished to do so."

"That's tough."

"Sometimes, Warren, I feel as though I've been sentenced to a time-travel purgatory."

"It's not as bad as all that."

He stared at her. "No. I suppose it is not."

Jessie took a breath and let it out. "Bell, last night I couldn't sleep much."

"It was a sleepless night for me, as well."

"I gave our time-travel discussion some thought...and I believe I found a *flaw* in your logic."

"Please. Tell me."

"You said one axiom of time travel is, the past is the past and cannot be changed."

"Correct." He moved the rocker and sat beside her. "By definition, the past has *already happened*. This was a driving theme in *Borrowed Time*. You and I have discussed this point."

"With that in mind, yesterday you spoke of my reasons for wanting to travel to the past and compared them with your own reasons."

"I wish to return to a few moments after I left July of 1892, but my mission would not be to *change* any circumstance, other than to remove myself from the storm's path. Then my life would proceed essentially as it would have proceeded, had I not vanished a few seconds in 1892. While you, Warren, wish to travel *twice* to the past, should you discover the means to do so. One journey would be to take Doc and go back to an instant *after* the little dog disappeared in a storm. You believe if Doc does not permanently vanish from his own time, your grandfather Paul does not become despondent, turn to heavy drink, and die at a young age."

"Yes. And secondly?"

"Your other journey would be to somehow prevent the automobile accident when you left *The Golden Lamb* several years ago, which resulted in your hip injury and...the death of your parents."

She blinked. "It hurts in the center of my chest whenever I let myself remember that night. Real pain, Bell. It never lets me forget."

"Guilt can have a physical effect on the body, Warren. The trick is to let yourself realize the loss of your parents was not your fault."

"I was behind the wheel. I should have reacted faster."

He stared at her. "From what you've told me about the incident, nothing you could have done would have made any difference."

Jessie sighed. "Yeah."

"But please go on, Warren, about the flaw in my logic?"

She waited a moment. "Clearly, you are the smartest person I have ever met. But you've missed something, Bell, Dr. Joseph Bell, the very real inspiration for Sherlock Holmes. You have failed to really consider your wife and daughter."

His eyes widened. "Good God."

"And now you've thought of it."

"Elizabeth. And my Polly..."

"Exactly. If you go back, and never disappear from their lives, your daughter probably does *not* become a famous painter, a painter who inspired many others, by the way. And even if she did start to paint, the *subject matter* of her paintings would likely be quite different." She let that sink in, then: "I did more research on Elizabeth."

He turned to Jessie. "You discovered her philanthropic work."

"She was a leader in Scotland for many years, bringing about positive changes to both hospitals and mental institutions."

"Elizabeth did not begin to devote her time to those causes until some eight months after I was swept out of her life, based upon the data I've been able to uncover over the years."

"And beyond her charitable efforts," Jessie went on, "she set an early positive example for the *women's* movement, even though there was no actual *movement* to speak of in Scotland back then."

He blinked. "So, you are saying just the act of going back would change everything else that happened *after* that point, along my natural timeline."

"And because of that fact, you *cannot* travel back, since..."

"Since the past cannot be changed. Of course. Polly *did* become a talented painter. Elizabeth *did* engage in extensive charitable work. And it is therefore inescapable that either I *cannot* find the manner and means of going back, or if I *do* manage to return, for whatever reasons, my efforts do not, or *did* not change anything, since you and I would not be having this conversation had I been successful on such a journey." His face paled. "Perhaps time travel to the past is not even possible?"

"Why do you say that?"

He fingered the scrapbook, still on his lap. "Two reasons. First, the inevitability of a disruptive paradox."

"You mean a *grandfather* paradox?

A smile crossed his lips. "Many stories have been written where the time traveler meets a version of him or herself on a journey to an *earlier* time. The question of an irresolvable paradox nearly always is a central plot point."

She showed him a questioning scowl. "If the traveler goes back and, say, does something that results in his grandfather never meeting his grandmother, then it would be impossible for the traveler to have been born. Thus, the paradox. If he was never born he could not have gone back in time."

"But second, and more importantly, Warren, as of this moment I am aware of one dog and just three people who have actually traveled through time."

"Three?"

"And all four were propelled into their future."

"Explain."

"Brody MacKay."

"The Dundee asylum attendant?"

"You saw him today."

"When?"

"The bank video."

Her jaw dropped. "And the woman in the wheelchair?"

"She identified herself as Catherine Eddowes."

"I heard. So?"

"Catherine Eddowes is the name of Jack the Ripper's fourth canonical victim. She was eviscerated on Mitre Square in Whitechapel on September 30, 1888."

Jessie stood and paced.

"The woman in the wheelchair," Bell said, "the third human time traveler, the woman who I believe to be the mastermind behind the murder of Timothy Timmons today, the murderess of one victim in Cleveland, one in Columbus, and one poor woman in Dayton, Ohio, earlier this year, was and is, Irene Thayer Lithgow."

The Grandfather Paradox...is not an issue. In a sense, time travel means that you're traveling both in time and into other universes. If you go back into the past, you'll go into another universe. As soon as you arrive at the past, you're making a choice and there'll be a split. Our universe will not be affected by what you do in your visit to the past. **Ronald Mallett**

Chapter 33: Hartwell, Ohio
December 31, 2009

It was clear to Bell from the first day with Hattie Brooks, the woman had little time left on this Earth.

While in Edinburgh, Bell had seen many patients afflicted with cancer of the lungs, and those people usually met a ghastly, inevitable end. In 2009, medical science had made great progress in the diagnosis and treatment of lung cancer and many other cancers. He spent an entire day reading about the subject on Hattie's Mac. Yet lung cancer had not been eradicated, and it still claimed its fair share of lives, even from those who had never smoked a cigarette or any other tobacco product.

The past months had been a whirlwind for Bell and his elderly companion. Sometimes she behaved as if she had energy enough for three people. And other occasions she barely had enough left at the end of an active day to climb the stairs to her bedroom. Bell asked her to slow down, but Hattie insisted, and the two of them were out and about, as Hattie frequently said, four or five nights per week.

One of their very first excursions was to *The Great American Ballpark* to watch a professional baseball game. Bell was somewhat familiar with the American game of baseball before arriving in 2009 Cincinnati, but he had no idea what the experience of attending a game might be like. He was instantly fascinated by the music, the incredible lights, and especially the giant rectangle that displayed immense pictures of the players. And even more amazing to Bell was the electronic technology that allowed the operators of the giant rectangle to show again something that had happened just seconds before. It was astonishing.

The people in attendance were fascinating, as well. They screamed, they yelled obscenities; they became intoxicated and fell on the concrete stairs, all in the name of supporting *The Reds*, which was the name of the Cincinnati team. Bell had not asked Hattie why this team was given the name, *The Reds*, but it was on his list of things to ask at some point; Hattie had so much fun at the game he did not wish to interrupt her enthusiasm.

"What is this, Hattie?" Bell had asked.

"A brat."

"A brat?"

"With mustard. Ballpark food."

Bell took one small bite at the end of the hotdog bun.

Hattie had taken Bell to four games that July and August, and after each trip to the ballpark, Hattie parked Lester's old Chevy Silverado at home, and the two of them walked with Scooter to what Hattie called, *The UDF*, where together they enjoyed ice cream. Bell had not ever tasted anything as delicious as a UDF ice cream sundae, and instead of just letting himself enjoy the flavors of vanilla, chocolate, and whipped cream all together, Bell could only imagine the expression on Polly's face as she might have sampled this extraordinary concoction.

On a September Sunday afternoon, Hattie took Bell to the Cincinnati Planetarium, and here, for the first time since he landed in 2009 months before, Bell felt nearly at home. The passage of time had not changed the planets, the solar system, and the universe, and Bell felt comforted by a familiar frame of reference.

In the middle of the month, Hattie called a taxicab to pick them up and drive downtown for the annual Octoberfest celebration. Here, Bell felt even more at home, since the entire event seemed a throwback to a time much closer to his own 1892 Edinburgh. He soon learned, after Hattie and he finished a second brimming pint of ale, why Hattie had chosen to commute back and forth in a hired vehicle.

Lane Cohen

Halloween fell on a Friday evening in 2009, and Bell enjoyed watching Hattie on her front porch, giving candy to tiny beggars. Hattie preferred the small chocolate bites of *Three Musketeers* wrapped in silver foil. Bell wondered how Alexander Dumas would have reacted to his name being associated with a candy treat. In the space of ninety minutes that evening, Bell became acquainted with many princesses, ghosts, three Luke Skywalkers, a flock of vampires, characters from something called *Pokeman*, Batmen, and Spidermen, of all shapes and sizes, a tiny witch who could not have been older than five, but who still threw an icy glare his way, and many girls of about twelve who were supposed to be something called *The Spice Girls*. Hattie refused to explain about *The Spice Girls* and told Bell he was better off not knowing.

It was one of the most fun evenings of Bell's life, except when he pictured how much fun Polly would be having if she somehow magically appeared beside him.

On one bitter-cold evening at the beginning of December, Hattie drove Bell to the Cincinnati Zoo for its annual Festival of Lights. As Bell soon discovered, The Festival of Lights was a yearly opportunity for parents to escort their children to the zoo in the coldest of nighttime weather to enjoy endless fantastic displays of colorful illumination and to blindly answer calls from their children for more hot cocoa. From the look on Hattie's face as they toured the hilly grounds reflected in blues, greens, and yellows, Bell knew at once that Hattie enjoyed the zoo and the lights even as much as did the endless stream of children.

On a relatively mild December evening, Hattie and Bell walked to the Wyoming Middle School, about a half-mile from her home, where they sat in the auditorium and listened to the school's annual Christmas concert.

"Hattie," Bell whispered.

She blinked at him from the next seat.

"I know this carol; Little Drummer Boy."

"A classic," Hattie said.

"The choir in my church sings it, as well."

Hattie patted his knee and smiled at him.

As the mixed choir sang the solemn, ghostly melody, Bell imagined himself back home, in church on a frigid winter night,

A Matter of Time

Polly and Elizabeth sitting on either side of him in the pew, as they all let the tunes of the holiday surround them with feelings of peace and good cheer.

Bell recognized at least half the other carols either sung by the various middle-school choirs or played by the concert orchestra. It was here Bell realized that no matter how far back or forward in time a person may travel, some things simply do not change.

On December 31st, Hattie insisted the two of them celebrate New Year's Eve by eating Chinese food at *Uncle Yip's* in Fairfield, a few miles north. She and Lester had long ago made *Uncle Yip's* their traditional place to welcome in a new year. It was relatively quiet, and generally free of nearby drunk drivers. After all, who goes drinking on New Year's Eve at or even near a small neighborhood Chinese restaurant?

"Are you enjoying your General Tsao's chicken?" Bell asked.

Hattie swallowed a small mouthful. "Fine. Just fine. But I should not have had so many of the crab Rangoon. I can barely finish half of the chicken."

"Who is this General Tsao?" He pointed at her plate.

"Oh," Hattie said, "he was the Chinese general who organized the building of The Great Wall of China."

Bell stared at her. "Hattie, if you don't know the answer, there is no need to invent one."

"I was joking, silly."

"Then you could at least chuckle next time."

He smiled. "Do you know what I'm thinking?"

"You wish somehow you went *poof* from 1892 and showed up in 1955 in Marilyn Monroe's bedroom?"

Bell considered. "You refer to the blonde female in that film we watched last month, where the two men *dress* as women to hide from the criminals?"

She shook her head. "*Blonde female*? You talk like a cop."

"I do?"

"*Some Like It Hot*. Yes."

"You think that sort of woman might appeal to me?"

"Well, I gotta tell you, Joseph, I would start to worry about you if she didn't."

"Worry?"

"Lester was gaga over Marilyn. He tried to keep it to himself, but I could see lust plastered all over his face whenever she appeared on the silver screen."

"No, Hattie. I was not thinking about Marilyn Monroe, even though I realized you were joking again."

"Gotcha."

He shrugged. "I made it a point with my family this time of year, to have us sit together in my parlor in front of a fire and speak to each other about our blessings."

"Sounds nice."

"Too often I find people complain of the negatives they see around them, when instead, I feel they should consider all for which they have to be thankful. Our God-given blessings."

Hattie gazed at him. "And just before, you were thinking about your own blessings?"

He leaned forward and took one of her hands in his own. "Six months ago, there is no place or time on this planet I would have rather awakened, than face-down in the 2009 garden of Hattie Brooks."

She had enough time to smile before a deep cough rattled from the center of her chest. Hattie edged her hand away and raised a napkin to her mouth. "Joseph, maybe we should go home."

Bell took a breath. "Hattie..?"

"Just take me home, Joseph. I think you should drive."

"I?"

She nodded. "You'll be fine. Cars nowadays practically drive themselves." She reached into her purse and dropped several bills on the table. "Let's go, Joseph. I need to lie down. And I need my little friend Scooter beside me."

Bell felt small tears start in the corners of his eyes as he stood and stepped across to Hattie, pulled her chair back, and gently gripped her arm as she struggled to stand.

Time travel is usually only possible in one direction; plodding ever-forward at the pace of a ticking second hand on a clock. **James Altucher**

Chapter 34: Oak Ridge, Tennessee
June 16, 1944

Ida Cade stood beside her kitchen sink and chopped onions to add to the chili she was preparing for dinner. Her brain spun about her new houseguest. Ebb asked her to have patience and give it a few more days, until he could decide what to do. And after all, the poor woman was alone and obviously confused, even if she wasn't being entirely truthful. Ida shook her head. She would do as Ebb asked, since she loved her husband and trusted his judgment. But something in her stomach told her Irene Tennyson was keeping a whole basketful of secrets, and secrets in a time of war, and in Oak Ridge, Tennessee, could turn out to be very dangerous.

Ida heard a floorboard creak. She turned her head and watched her visitor step barefoot into the kitchen; she almost disappeared inside Ida's old terrycloth robe, and the young woman's hair was tousled as if she just got out of bed.

"Hello, Miss," Ida said.

"Good morning."

"It is nearly afternoon."

Irene squinted at her. "Pardon?"

"Half-past 11:00."

"Gracious. I have not slept so long in all my life."

"You must have needed it. Would you like some eggs, some toast with jam?"

Irene eased down onto a wooden chair at the small kitchen table. "I shall not forget your kindness, Ida, or your husband's. I believe the both of you have saved my life."

Ida set a paring knife on the wooden countertop, stepped around, and sat in a chair on the other side of the table. "It is Christian to give help to those in need. The Bible says an act of kindness is repaid ten-fold."

Irene smiled. "Allow me to begin that repayment now by preparing food for both of us."

"That is not necessary."

"Yes, it is, Ida. It is most necessary, and only the beginning of my repayment, if I can find the proper manner in which to do so."

Ida pointed to the icebox. "Eggs and fixings are where they ought to be. The pans are below the stove."

"Very well." She stood. "I prided myself on the meals I prepared for my husband. And after he vanished, I cooked for myself nearly every day. This is not new for me."

Ida decided to save questions about Irene's vanished husband until later. But at least it showed the woman's memory was returning.

Irene padded a few steps to the icebox door. "Thank you for supplying the periodicals yesterday."

"Periodicals?"

"The many editions of *The Saturday Evening Post*."

"We rarely toss out a copy. Ebb likes to look at the cover paintings over and over."

"I spent much of yesterday on your comfortable sofa. I read much of perhaps ten editions."

"Anything interest you?"

Irene took an egg carton and set it on the counter. "America and Britain, at war with Germany."

"And Italy."

"Italy?"

"Yes."

"I've always wanted to travel there."

"Not now."

"Who is Italy fighting?"

"Us. The Japanese are fighting us, too."

She nodded. "I read about the attack at Pearl Harbor."

"One of the worst days ever on this Earth."

"A *sneak attack*, the writers said."

"They flew planes at us while their people were in Washington talking peace."

"Planes?"

"Hundreds of them."

Irene nodded. "Disgraceful."

"Honor has its place, even in times of war."

"Where is Pearl Harbor?"

"Hawaii."

"Where is that?"

"The Pacific."

"That is a long way from Tennessee." Irene started the flame on one burner of the gas stove. "In the periodical, they named this war *World War Two*. Does that mean there was a World War one?"

"Around 1917. Went on for a couple years."

"Who was fighting then?"

"About the same as now. America and Britain against Germany. Italy and Japan were not involved in that one."

"That saddens me, Ida, all the fighting, the killing. And for what?"

"Seems there's always some lunatic trying to take what's not his."

The frying pan sizzled. "Ida? Looks like you are getting ready to bake a cake?" Irene gestured at a bowl filled with white flour.

"It is my Ebb's birthday. I am making him a special dinner for when he comes home from work, his favorite chili, and a gooey two-layer chocolate cake."

"I hope you don't mind me asking, but Ebb seems quite a bit older than you appear to be. I would guess he's around 60. Is that right?"

Ida took a breath. "My Ebb is 37 today. Same as me."

"Oh. I am sorry. I meant no insult. But from his white hair, his missing teeth, and..."

Ida bit her bottom lip, then: "Before Ebb went to work for Clifton Construction, he was big and strong and twice as good-looking as the handsomest man you ever..." Her words choked at the back of her throat.

"That's all right, Ida. No need to go on. I was just curious."

She edged a wooden spatula into the fry pan and flipped the eggs.

Ida shook her head. "I'm not sure if all this is a secret, but could you promise me to never repeat any of it?"

Irene brought two small plates of eggs, set them on the table and sat beside Ida. "I promise."

Ida looked at her plate. "Up until a few months ago, my Ebb's teeth were healthy and strong, and his hair was dark as night."

Irene blinked. "What happened?"

Ida folded her hands tightly atop the table. She glanced to each side, almost as if to spot anyone who might be watching. "Some crazy kid from town crashed into him when Ebb was driving his work truck. Ebb wasn't hurt too bad, broken wrist was the worst. But when he got to the hospital, after the doctors fixed his bones, that's when the *scientist's* showed up. What they did then? Can't say much about them, their names and all."

"I don't understand."

"Miss Irene, they told him *it was for the war.* They told him it would save the lives of our soldiers."

Ida's hands began to tremble, and Irene placed one hand atop them. "Now, now."

"I'm all right." She smiled. "You know, Irene, I wasn't sure about you at first. But you have a kind heart. Your past might be a mystery, but whoever you were before your memory blacked out, I'm certain you were a good person."

"Thank you. That is quite kind."

"You're welcome."

"Ida, do you know what the scientists meant about saving lives?"

She poked a fork at her eggs. "I shouldn't say."

"Did the scientists do something to Ebb?"

"They did *something*, all right. Pumped some vile concoction into his blood. Filled him full of *hellfire*, made him sick for weeks."

"I'm sorry to hear that. Try your eggs."

Ida absently raised a forkful of eggs to her lips. "This is good."

"Extra butter is the trick."

A Matter of Time

Ida stirred her fork though the scrambled eggs. "Miss Irene, about those scientists...what goes on here in Oak Ridge. If I don't talk about it to somebody, I swear it might just drive me mad. I can trust you, right?"

Irene gazed straight into Ida's dark brown eyes. "We are friends, Ida, you and I. Friends help each other, trust each other." She smiled. "Besides, as I said before, you and Ebb saved my life."

Ida stared at her. "I know this is going to be hard to believe, but they're making...a bomb...that can blow up a whole city, or so they say."

Such a thing cannot be possible."

"God in Heaven knows what the soldiers will do, once the scientists are through with it."

Irene set down her fork. "Tell me more."

One may never get to know how fast time travels till the one gets in that position to race against time. **Neel Preet**

Chapter 35: Cleveland, Ohio
January 29, 2019 – 12:30am

The driver fumbled with the switch that controlled the windshield wipers on the black Lincoln MKX. The air swirled with cold fog, and he could barely see the white markings on the street. Ice streaked the windshield despite the wipers; the exact workings of the vehicle's heat system were still somewhat of a mystery to him. The driver carefully guided the vehicle into a parking area connected to a market of some kind; *Kroger's,* the bright sign read. He stopped beside a group of automobiles parked near the street, and then glanced over his shoulder at his back-seat passenger.

"This good?" he asked.

The woman in back pulled her dark coat collar tighter against her neck then stared out her window. "Bitter cold tonight. Reminds me of many cruel places I've been in my lifetime."

"You and me both, yeah?"

She watched University students mill about on the nearby concrete pathway lined with small taverns and restaurants. Some of the students had found their way across the street to this parking area where they had left their automobiles while they had enjoyed the nearby frivolities of the night. While many things changed with the passage of time, some remained constant, and public intoxication seemed to be one of those constants. Even though it was a night filled with a cold fog, the young men and women stumbled against each other and laughed together as they entered and exited the many alcohol establishments, apparently oblivious of the natural elements.

Without a word, the driver pushed open his door and

stepped around to the back of the car. He wore a black coat and a black knit hat. He gripped the handle of the rear door and pulled.

She stepped out onto the frosted blacktop and steadied herself. The driver did not offer to assist. The woman pulled the hood of her coat up around her head, and covered most of her short dark hair. "Wait for me here."

The driver studied her face through the night mist. Streetlights reflected in the woman's metallic green eyes. "Whatever you say." A chill touched the back of his neck as he walked around and dropped back into the Lincoln.

The woman turned and quietly took a few steps toward a shadowed corner. She stopped near the side of the market, where the large building protected the parking area from the hideous overhead lights. She glided her bare hands into the pockets of her coat, focused on the many young people cavorting across the street, and waited.

***

Ashleigh Compton weaved between the crowd of college students inside Moe's Bar and Grill. It was hard to see clearly with all the thick smoke.

Where is Madyson?

Last time she saw her roommate, she was playing pool with two guys from an apartment across campus. In the midst of all the smoke and tequila, she and Madyson got separated. Nothing to worry about. They had driven the four blocks in Ashleigh's Prius, and if Madyson expected a ride back to the dorm, she would have to find the car, sooner or later.

Maybe Madyson had stepped outside to get a breath of fresh, icy air. If nothing else, Ashleigh could use the reprieve to clear some of the alcohol-induced fog from her brain.

At Moe's entrance, the cold stung her face and cut through her denim jacket, which provided little warmth on such a cold night, but she looked cute in it, and that was what mattered. She shivered and wrapped her arms across her middle.

No Madyson.

Stuffing her hands in her jacket pockets provided little warmth. The chill of a downtown Cleveland winter night made her wish for the warmth of Carolina Beach, back home.

She decided to cross the street, find her car, and sit inside with the engine running and the heater cranked to the max. Madyson would eventually come back to the Prius.

She angled to the street where she looked both ways, stepped over a snowplow berm onto the frozen blacktop, and made a beeline to the Kroger's lot directly across from Moe's. There, her Prius was covered with frost and parked close to a row of dumpsters. She reached into a front pocket of her jeans for her key fob, but since her fingers were cold and clumsy, the fob tumbled to the blacktop. She bent to retrieve it and straightened.

Seemingly out of nowhere, a short woman in a long black coat with a hood around her face stepped up beside her.

"Oh, crap." Ashleigh's heart suddenly pumped hard.

"Pardon me," the woman said with an English accent. "It was not my intention to startle you."

"You scared the shit out of me, lady."

"It looked as though you might need assistance. You appear unsteady."

"Yeah? I've been drinking." She wiped cold tears from her cheek. "What's it to you?"

"Miss, are you certain you are sober enough to pilot your vehicle?"

"Pilot? No, it's a Prius."

"Your words are slurred."

"I'm going to sit a while, anyway, and wait for my friend to show up."

The woman just stood there, smiling.

Ashleigh squinted at her. "What are you doing out in this parking lot? I mean, it's late, it's cold, you're alone."

"I have a driver." She tilted her head in the direction of a long black Lincoln. Exhaust vapor puffed from the tailpipe and a man sat behind the wheel.

"You should go back to your car...where it's warm."

The woman chuckled. "I suppose it does not matter."

"Well, look, nice talking with you and all, but my butt is freezing off." She pressed her key fob and the Prius door locks clicked. "I gotta get in—"

The woman lunged at her.

A Matter of Time

Ashleigh stiffened. Her key fob dropped to the pavement.

"Life brims with random chances," the woman whispered in Ashleigh's ear. "Tonight you are the victim of one of those random chances." She jerked her hand upward, driving cold steel deeper.

A guttural moan escaped Ashleigh's throat as a throbbing heat burned at the center of her chest. She suddenly realized this was the warmest she had felt since she'd moved to Cleveland, not so very long ago.

Even if it turns out that time travel is impossible, it is important we understand why it is impossible. **Stephen Hawking**

Chapter 36: Lebanon, Ohio
Present Day

B ell tapped one finger on the scrapbook cover. "Shortly after Hattie Brooks left this world, it suddenly occurred to me how *careless* I had become."

"Careless how?" Jessie asked.

"Remember, Warren, the tornado tore the roof from the asylum and snatched me into the air. Two other people were in that room. Irene and Brody MacKay."

"So?"

"For the few months after, I was so immersed in my own predicament, and in my new life with Hattie Brooks, I failed to consider what should have been an immediate and inevitable conclusion."

"What became of Irene and Brody? Oh my God."

"When I finally focused on the problem, it was my distinct suspicion both Irene Lithgow and Brody MacKay might have also been propelled into 2009, just as I was."

Jessie glanced at the scrapbook in Bell's hands. "What did you do?"

"Hattie had instructed me quite well as to the workings of her *Mac*. It was a fairly intuitive process and was easier than I expected. One of the first things I researched after Hattie was gone was the location of shops that sold theatrical makeup supplies. Two such establishments were right across the river, in northern Kentucky."

"You're right. Not what I expected."

"You see, Warren, unfortunately, in 1892 I had many

weeks to learn the twisted nature of Irene Lithgow's persona. I believe today, in this time, psychiatrists might diagnose Miss Lithgow as a sociopath."

"And...and you were afraid if Irene showed up here, she might..?"

"People are motivated by many things, Warren. And these motivations serve as the impetus for action and behavior. After all, why does anyone do *anything*?"

She locked eyes with him.

"Almost everything in life is a result of cause and effect, Warren. *Emotions* are strong motivators. Jealousy. Revenge. Love can motivate the instigation of a romantic relationship, as can just pure physical attraction. Combine strong emotions and a physical attraction with *mental illness*, and the result might be a powerful motivating force."

"Bell, I don't know what you're getting at."

"During our sessions at Dundee, Irene considered me as many things: a confidant, a therapist, a wistful romantic interest. I believe she might have convinced herself she was in love with me."

"Stockholm Syndrome, probably."

He took a breath. "At the heart of it, Warren, I believe Irene considered me an *intellectual opponent*."

"Opponent how?"

He ran a hand through his short hair. "Beyond any attraction Irene may have held for me, she saw it as an intellectual *battle* between she and I. This was clear to me."

"How did you know?"

"I saw it in her eyes, Warren. She *favored* our sessions, as if they were an opportunity for her to share her true thoughts and feelings. And there was something else: even more than desiring release from Dundee, I believe Irene *enjoyed* taunting me."

"Such as dropping hints she killed her two husbands?"

He blinked several times. "I am certain."

Jessie stood. "All right, I'll accept that for the sake of argument. So, you're saying if Irene showed up in 2009, you believed she would go on a search and, what, try to reestablish a relationship with you?"

"At first."

She stared at him. "And then try to *kill* you."

"No."

"Then...what?"

"While she found herself attracted to me, while she desperately wanted to be set free from Dundee, possibly even more than anything, she also wanted to best me in a test of wits. Perhaps this was her misguided attempt to prove herself somehow worthy of my affection, as she occasionally hinted."

Jessie scowled. "Play a chess-like game for a while, toy with you, and then..?"

He opened the scrapbook. "At first I did not venture into the public eye without a full disguise. I kept this routine in place for over a year. Then, without any trace of Irene and Brody, I determined they must have traveled together to a different time altogether, or perhaps a different location."

Jessie pursed her lips. "I'm not sure I buy all of this, but do I get to see inside the *McGuffin* now?"

"Bring your chair closer."

Jessie lifted her rocker and placed it down closer beside him. She sat. "Show me."

Bell's fingers trembled as he turned the black cover of the large scrapbook. "Read the headline on this first page."

Jessie looked down at a copy of the front page of the Cleveland Plain Dealer. She read: "*Co-ed Butchered Near Campus.*" She glanced up at him. "The date of this paper is January of this year."

"Yes."

"January 30. Of *2019*, not 2009."

"Yes."

She tilted her head down toward the newspaper again. "Ashleigh Compton. She was from South Carolina, a freshman at Cleveland State, on the basketball team. And...oh my God."

"Read further."

"Parts of her body were..."

She brought her eyes up and stared at him.

Bell said, "The editorial staff saw fit to save the public from most of the gore."

"What I read was sickening enough. I don't blame them for leaving stuff out."

"It is as understandable now as it was then."

"Then?"

"Keep reading."

She focused on the page. "It says nobody could identify any possible suspect. The girl apparently had no enemies."

"My deduction is Miss Compton was, as they say, in the wrong place at the wrong time."

"She was discovered around 1:30am behind a Kroger's dumpster not far from campus."

"The area is riddled with taverns."

"I'm trying to make sense of this. You obviously think it was Irene who killed this woman?"

"There is no doubt, Warren."

"You're saying Irene Lithgow was swept through time, to *2009* as you were, but *waited ten years*, and *then* sliced up a student in downtown Cleveland, Ohio, 200 miles from Hartwell, where *you* landed?"

"That is one possible conclusion."

"I don't follow."

He turned the scrapbook page. "Look here."

She did. "Columbus Dispatch. February 28, this year." Her words stopped at the back of her throat. She shifted her eyes up at him. "Another killing."

"Yes."

Her words came slowly as she read: "*Capital University Student Found Murdered.*" She took a breath. "This happened late at night behind a bakery in the German Village. I *know* that bakery. My mom and dad took me there a few times. We went to Columbus for the zoo, and a couple concerts. That bakery was one of our stops."

"I have visited the German Village as well. Many taverns line those streets."

She looked at the page again. "Her organs..."

"Yes."

"A few were discovered a block away, atop the hood of a car. Some were never found."

"Grisly matters."

"Her liver, her lungs."

She felt bile rising and she choked it back.

Bell said, "Do you follow, Warren?"

"No. I don't."

He turned the page. She stared at him.

"You must follow this path to its end," he said. "Read this next article."

Her eyes widened at the newsprint. "Dayton Daily News. May 30, 2019."

"A few months past."

She glanced at him and then kept reading. *"UD Law Professor Stabbed 37 Times."*

"A third victim in just a few months. This one occurred on a street where university students gather to frequent the many taverns."

Jessie shook her head. "Irene Lithgow killed a girl in Cleveland, then another in Columbus, and a third in Dayton?"

"And this third killing was the most brutal and violent of the three."

Jessie scanned the news article. "This Dayton reporter connects the three killings, same methods, similar victims."

"Eventually a journalist will compare these three modern murders to the Ripper, from my time. I am sure of it."

"But, but *why*? For what unholy purpose would Irene Lithgow kill three perfect strangers?"

"Understand, Warren. The body of the third victim, 48-year-old Prof. Gwynn Price, was *eviscerated*. Her face and body were so disfigured her husband was only able to identify her by the jewelry she was wearing."

"God."

"Her *reproductive organs* were deposited blocks away, on the step of the rear entrance to the local police station."

She squinted at him. "You think she's coming for you now."

"Not exactly."

Her eyes widened. "By starting north in Cleveland, she has drawn a line south *with the locations* of her killings; Cleveland, Columbus, Dayton. And now *Cincinnati*, with the killing in the bank vault."

"That is my conclusion."

"If this is true, I understand why you looked for places to

buy makeup."

"*Costume* shops, meant for theatrical usage."

She considered. "Full costumes?"

"*Disguises*, Warren. I needed to immediately curtail any public exposure, if Miss Lithgow were here and sought to track me down."

"Out of self-defense."

"Partially, yes."

"Because you assumed if she were here, she would come for you. Eventually."

"As I said, I wore full disguises for a period of time after Hattie Brooks passed away. I inherited her house in Hartwell, kept mostly to myself except for short ventures out in public for marketing and such. I diligently studied all matters of media for any trace of Irene and MacKay. But nothing. Nothing at all. And my ultimate conclusion was either Irene and Brody were in 2009, 2010, but effectively in hiding, or they had actually been swept by the winds to another time and place altogether. Eventually, I dispensed with any disguises and attempted to continue along the path of a relatively normal life, that is, normal for a man who found himself in my situation. But once these Ohio killings occurred, I realized Irene Lithgow had a different plan than I had suspected."

"Tell me."

"She was not searching for me. Somehow, she had learned of my approximate location, both in time and space. By leaving her bloody trail, by imitating the methods of the Ripper, she knew I would recognize what she was doing."

"Which was?"

"Leaving a pathway for *me* to follow, so that *I might find her*, rather than the other way around. Or, at least, she was sending me a message that she was here, right here with me in this time. She does not wish to harm me, Warren. She could have accomplished that easily if that were her purpose, no matter what efforts I made to conceal myself. Once again, she wishes to impress me with her intellect, and shifted the burden to me, so that I applied my mind in a search for her, should I choose to do so."

Jessie gazed at him but didn't say anything.

He nodded and closed the scrapbook even though Jessie could see the book contained pages Bell had not shown her. "Nevertheless, I stayed close to home, studied history, read modern literature."

Jessie stood. "That explains why you remained out of touch after you started to write, why you never granted interviews, why you were never photographed."

"Partially, yes. But even after several years of living mostly in the shadows and finding no indication Irene Lithgow was here with me in this time, I minimally ventured out in society. I still attempted to stay out of the public eye, just as a precaution."

Jessie stood and walked the few steps to the end of the porch. "Bell."

"Yes, Warren?"

"Please explain how you've lived about 50 actual years, but you don't look one day over 40."

She turned to him and waited.

"That, Warren, is difficult to explain."

"I heard I'm supposed to be smart."

He smiled. "Yes, I heard that, too."

"Then..?"

Bell blinked and considered how to begin.

In Einstein's equation, time is a river. It speeds up, meanders, and slows down. The new wrinkle is that it can have whirlpools and fork into two rivers. So, if the river of time can be bent into a pretzel, create whirlpools and fork into two rivers, then time travel cannot be ruled out. **Michio Kaku**

Chapter 37: Hartwell, Ohio
January 23, 2011

B ell read aloud the last few sentences from a chapter of The Shining and stopped. He shifted in his chair and set the book on a small table beside the bed. Hattie squinted up at him from under her thick flowered quilt.

"Keep going," Hattie said. "I could hear a little more."

"I must say, Hattie, this is a most truly frightening work of fiction."

"You should see the movie."

"I have read Bierce, much of Poe, and yet this story is so disquieting I have strong mixed-feelings about continuing."

"Joseph, could you get my water, please?"

He took a glass from the table and handed it to her. "The real dilemma is attempting to determine if the dangers in *The Overlook* hotel are real, or whether the actual horrors are those that lurk somewhere within the darkness of Jack Torrence's brain. It is brilliant, really."

"We went to Colorado once, Lester and I."

"Oh?"

"We visited the Stanley Hotel in Estes Park, which Stephen King said was his inspiration for the story when he stayed there with his wife, Tabitha. Lester and I took the haunted hotel tour."

Bell lifted the book as evidence. "This is a strange choice, Hattie, to read before bed. How do you ever manage to fall asleep after these bloody visions?"

Lane Cohen

She pulled one hand from under the covers and placed it atop the back of Bell's hand. "This was for you, Joseph."

"I don't understand."

"King is my favorite author. Lester's favorite, too. I always thought it funny Lester read all of King's books, even though I don't think Lester ever read even one book all the way through before, even in high school. He always bought the Cliff Notes. Me too, back then."

"Cliff Notes?"

"They're brief summaries of novels. I remember picking up *Moby Dick* in 11th grade and knew I had to race to the college bookstore over at Xavier and buy the Cliff Notes version. It was only 55 pages long. Saved my life, Joseph. I think if I had been forced to read the two thousand pages of the actual book, I would have died."

He chuckled. "Mr. Melville might have taken offense at that comment."

"Yeah, well, I'm sure the tale of a crippled sea captain chasing a white whale around is a great story, but I think all the metaphors are well beyond me. Personally, and I wrote this for Mr. Hendricks in my essay about the book, I felt *sorry* for that whale. After all, you wouldn't be mad at a lion for eating meat."

"Uh, no, Hattie. I would not."

"Anyway, after I'm gone, and you start looking for something to read, I don't want you to forget about Stephen King. He is often overlooked when the great modern authors are named." She grinned.

"Is something funny, Hattie?"

"I think I just said a pun. Overlooked? *The Overlook* hotel?"

He squeezed her hand. "I'm not sure that's a pun, Hattie, but it is funny."

She closed her eyes and coughed once. "Joseph, where's my Scooter?"

"I believe he is downstairs on the carpet near the sofa."

"Could you bring him to me, Joseph? I want to feel him on my chest and rub his ears as I fall asleep."

Bell took a breath. "Is there...anything else I can get for you?"

"Just Scooter."

He waited a moment. "Hattie, if you don't mind, I'd like to tell you—"

"No. Joseph. There's no need to tell me anything. Now, I'm tired. Please go get Scooter for me."

"Of course."

He stood, felt uncontrollable tears building behind his eyes, turned his head from her, and stepped slowly to the bedroom door.

Time travel is possible. For example, an object traveling at high speeds ages more slowly than a stationary object. This means that if you were to travel into outer space and return, moving close to light speed, you could travel thousands of years into the Earth's future. **Martin Ringbauer**

Chapter 38: Oak Ridge, Tennessee
June 16, 1944

Ebb Cade angled his fork and scraped the last of the chocolate icing from his plate. "Best ever, Ida." He licked his lips and set his fork on the edge of the plate.

Ida smiled from across the table. "Glad you enjoyed it"

"Yes, Ida," Irene added. "I have not tasted better."

"You are both too kind."

Ida stood.

Ebb said, "Sit a while. Dishes can wait."

She eased back onto the chair. "They surely can."

Irene said, "Ebb, tell us of your workday."

"One day pouring cement is much like every other." Ebb blinked and looked away.

"Cement?"

"Uh huh."

"Exactly what is it you do?"

Ida said, "He's foreman of the concrete work." She smiled at Ebb, reached over and patted his forearm. "Got more than thirty men working for him."

"They're not working for *me*, Ida. *Clifton* is the company they work for. All of us."

"My Ebb's been doing concrete most of his life."

"Ida, Miss Irene's not interested in concrete."

"Oh, yes I am, Ebb. Please. Go on. I'd like to hear."

"He supervises the concrete trucks, measures out the floors, the walls. Sticks to the plans they give him, makes sure all his men follow the rules." She thought for a moment. "I would think most all the construction work is done by now."

"No, we will be starting on a new building next week. Saw the plans real quick, and it looked like some kind of warehouse. Big."

"Sounds fascinating," Irene said. "What is to be stored in the warehouse, once it is completed?"

"The *Clifton* folks don't tell us that. We just build them. What the Army uses them for is their business."

"Army?"

Ebb shook his head and leaned back in his chair. "You saw them around yesterday, all suited up, rifles in their arms, grenades clipped to their belts."

Irene frowned. "I saw a few of them."

It was quiet for a moment.

Ida jumped in. "Well, I need to get up before light. Early shift at the clinic."

Ebb said, "Ida's a nurse down there, in charge of a whole floor. Her momma would be downright proud of her."

Ida pushed back her chair and stood. "I surely hope she would." She stared at Ebb and blinked. "Don't stay up much longer. Miss Irene should turn in. I truly believe she needs rest more than anything."

"Don't worry about me, Ida. I'll be fine. And I will take care of the dishes before I retire."

"Irene—"

"I insist."

Ida pushed her chair closer to the table, leaned over and kissed Ebb on his forehead. "Happy birthday, my Ebb." She smiled at Irene then stepped quietly from the room.

Irene touched the edge of a cloth napkin to her lips. "Your wife is devoted to you. I see it in the way she looks your way, even when you are not looking back."

"We been together a long time." He took a breath and let it out slowly.

"That's nice, Ebb. I admire a couple who is faithful to each other."

"Ida's birthday is in two months." He sniffed. "Ida and me

is the same age. Thirty-seven."

"She told me."

"Wouldn't know it to look at us. At *me*."

"Ebb, Ida and I had a little heart-to-heart. She told me things, like what the scientists did to you."

He shook his head. "Ida shouldn't have said nothing."

"Worry not. Any secret either of you has is a secret of mine as well."

He lowered his voice. "Even though me and Ida been married a while, I have secrets of my own."

"Oh?"

"I ain't never told nobody this, but...I can see in the dark, like a *cat*."

Irene leaned forward. "You couldn't do that *before* the scientists came to you?"

"There's more." He pointed to his mouth. "This mouth used to be full of strong teeth, Miss Irene. A few weeks after those scientists got through with me, the front ones started falling out, a few here, a few there. Now all I got left is about three molars on each side." He huffed. "Makes me look like a country hick."

"Nonsense. Besides, Ida knows about the scientists and how your teeth fell out after those injections."

"Not what I'm talking about. Not my better eyes, neither. Ida knows about that, too, but this is a secret Ida *don't* know." He leaned forward, a bit closer to her and pointed to his hair. "That poison in my blood got nothing to do with my hair turning white as a ghost, didn't wrinkle my face, neither. Those things didn't happen until right after..."

He stopped talking and gazed at her.

"What is it, Ebb?"

"Miss Irene, I was wondering. How did you drop straight out of the sky?"

"I don't remember, Ebb. Wish I did."

"Ida is the religious one. I go to church with her and all, say the prayers like I'm supposed to, but I lived all these years and never truly believed in God or much else...until a few days ago."

She stared at him. "Just come out and say what you're

trying to say."

He took a breath. "I wished a prayer last night, outside in the yard, right before I turned in. I looked up at the sky and prayed to Jesus in heaven, thanking him for *sending* you to me. Cause that's the answer. The only way to explain it truly is you're an *angel from above*, sent down to us from Jesus himself."

"Well, I'm flattered, but—"

"Miss Irene, it must be you was *sent down* to help me, in my time of need."

She blinked at him. "Ebb, I'm certainly no angel, but I think it's time you explained about that secret."

He rested one elbow on the table and straightened his arm. He extended his index finger and pointed it straight down at the table. "I can't chance doing this for any more than a few seconds. If I do, well, my face might just wrinkle even worse."

Ebb lowered his finger, and Irene's eyes widened as she watched Ebb's fingertip and first knuckle disappear through the solid wood top of the kitchen table.

Don't time travel into the past. You can't change it. Today it starts all over again. Every tomorrow is determined by every day. **Serena Yates**

Chapter 39: Oak Ridge, Tennessee
June 17, 1944

E instein set his soup bowl on the commissary table, pulled out a metal chair and sat. He was unexpectedly hungry, and the lima bean soup smelled good, even though it was army food, and most army food was terrible. He dipped his spoon into the soup and raised it to his lips.

This soup was as tasty as he remembered, just like last week, the weeks before, and for all the months he had been here. For whatever reason, the army cook in *the facility* commissary had a talent for good soup, which was apparently the extent of his cooking talent. Einstein licked his lips and smiled. This one taste of soup was better than any meal he had for the last few years he had spent in Germany. Decent food and drink was scarce in his homeland back then, and when people were hungry, they would tend to follow any leader who promised to end that hunger.

"Dr. Einstein?"

He looked up. A man in his late 30s stood beside the table, holding a small notebook.

"Dr. Braddock," Einstein said.

"I...I finished the research you asked me to do."

Einstein gestured at the long metal table. "Please."

Dexter Braddock smiled uneasily, and then sat. He folded his hands atop his notebook. "I just passed Dr. Oppenheimer and Dr. Fermi."

"Oh?"

"They asked I tell you they would like your presence in Dr.

Oppenheimer's office. Something important."

Einstein looked at his spoon. "It is always something important."

"I supposed that's true, these days."

"You have conveyed their message. Thank you."

Braddock shifted on his chair. "This was not the type of research project I am used to."

"An advanced physics professor at Princeton should be capable of most anything."

"But I must say, Dr. Einstein, the research turned out to be *interesting.*"

"Research often is."

"Not so much about MacKay and Lithgow, but..."

"What did you find?"

"I contacted a colleague in Scotland. After that, the pathways were not that difficult."

"Go on."

"First, Brody MacKay. We discovered his birth record without much trouble. Born Brody Amos MacKay in Islay, Scotland, 1868. Died July 17, 1892. Buried in Islay without the body. He worked as a docks-man, and as an attendant at the Dundee Lunatic Asylum, in Dundee, Scotland. The obituary we found in the weekly Islay Chronicle called Brody MacKay," he looked at his notebook, "*a fine young lad who used his earnings to provide for his ailing parents.* Apparently, it says here, the parents had been stricken with *the consumption.* The obituary states MacKay was killed in a windstorm while he was on duty at the asylum."

Einstein didn't say anything.

Braddock continued. "Next, Irene Lithgow, actually Irene *Thayer Tennyson* Lithgow. Nothing about her in *Scottish* birth records, but I decided to become creative, and I instructed my contact to look beyond just Scotland. In short order, he found Miss Lithgow, born Irene Thayer Tennyson, in 1861 Bedfordshire, England, to Samuel Kenyon Tennyson and his wife, Martha. Irene was married, apparently twice, the second time to a fisherman in Edinburgh, Adrian Lithgow. We couldn't find much else about Irene. But—"

"Joseph Bell?"

Braddock cleared his throat. "Dr. Einstein, before I answer, may I ask you something?"

"Ask."

"You knew what I would find about Dr. Bell before you instructed me to research his name. Isn't that right?"

Einstein exhaled and stood. He gazed at Braddock for a moment, turned away and started across the gray concrete floor. "I appreciate your assistance, Dr. Braddock."

Braddock remained silent, glanced down at a bowl of half-finished soup, and then watched the stooped man in the rumpled gray suit shuffle to the commissary exit.

Know that love is truly timeless. **Mary M. Ricksen**

Chapter 40: Lebanon, Ohio
Present Day

" **A** ll the theories that address movement through time involve traveling at incredible speeds," Bell said. "Do you follow?"

Jessie glared at him from her rocker on the porch. "Seriously?"

"I apologize, Warren. It is not my intent to speak to you in a professorial tone."

"If I don't understand something, Bell, I will ask."

He shrugged. "My point is not to highlight how quickly a solid body can be propelled through time, but to illustrate how the *very molecules* of such solid matter are also so proportionately affected."

"I don't understand."

He allowed a brief smile. "As an example, the molecules of water typically change along with the ambient temperature. When water boils, the molecules race. When water freezes, the molecules move much more slowly. In fact, they slow to a near standstill, but, as you must know, the temperature of water molecules cannot sink as low as *Absolute Zero*, or negative 273.15 Centigrade."

"So, there's a limit to how cold something can get?"

"Not just something, Warren. Anything. *Absolute Zero* is a *theoretical* temperature, since that temperature has never been demonstrated as reachable."

"Okay. I'll ask. Why is that?"

"It is the *motion* of the molecules within the fabric of any solid object which *holds together* the molecules, thus forming the shape of that solid object, as we perceive it." He took his pipe from a side table and held it out in front of him. "Without the molecules in constant motion, as the molecules that make up this pipe, for example, any entity, or thing, would dematerialize, or cease to exist as a formed, solid object."

"Your point?"

"I believe, Warren, my transport though time has somehow *slowed* the activity of the molecules that make up, well, *me*." He waited for her response.

She winced. "Why did traveling through time not *speed up* your molecules rather than slow them?"

"Unknown."

"Okay. I think I get what you're saying."

"Back to your original question. Time travel is accomplished, by definition, either by moving faster than the speed of light, or by moving through a black hole, which is essentially the same thing. Traveling through a black hole *happens* faster than the speed of light. Because of those principles, I believe my time here since arriving is measured differently. Since the slowing of my molecules, one year for me living in the 21st century, equals approximately *one month* of time as you see it, and as you live within it."

She stared at him. "Like the movie, *Interstellar*, from a few years ago. There was a scene where characters were on a planet that existed within a different gravitational reference. One minute spent on that planet for those characters equaled, or amounted to months on Earth, or something like that. I was confused when I watched it, but I think that was the gist."

"Correct. I did see *Interstellar*. I make it a point to study all films that involve elements of time travel." He took a breath. "To continue, as best I can determine, I have physically aged approximately ten actual months since my arrival here ten years ago."

"Just ten months?"

"Yes."

"How can you tell?"

"The growth of my hair and nails, primarily. I have trimmed my hair and nails only four times in the last ten years."

She scoffed. "Reverse dog years."

"In a manner of speaking."

"Then how do you explain how Irene Lithgow appears to have aged about forty years since her arrival from 1892?"

"And oddly, how Brody MacKay, another traveler from 1892, appears not to have aged even one day?"

"Exactly."

"Warren, you will be disappointed in my answer."

"Try me."

He locked eyes with her. "Either Mrs. Lithgow applied convincing stage makeup today to portray advanced age, or...I have no idea."

When we see the shadow on our images, are we seeing the time 11 minutes ago on Mars? Or are we seeing the time on Mars as observed from Earth now? It's like time travel problems in science fiction. When is now, when was then? **Bill Nye**

Chapter 41: Oak Ridge, Tennessee
February - 1944

He didn't usually dream much, but when he did, he forgot all about it even before he got out of bed and stumbled to the bathroom.

However, recently he dreamed most every night, in bright colors, and he remembered everything. In fact, he enjoyed his new dreams and wished they would never stop.

Back when he was a kid growing up in Macon, the family dog was Sammy Boy, a droopy-eyed basset hound. Sammy Boy had chosen him right away as his best friend and would rarely be more than inches away from his side. The dog with huge ears that dragged along the ground was his constant companion. The two of them spent endless summer days playing by the edge of the fishpond near the vegetable garden. And sometimes they would fall asleep together, huddled close in the tall grass.

He had dreamed of Sammy Boy and their days back on the family homestead nearly every night since he got that needle poked into his arm and the fires of a hundred burning suns coursed through his veins each second of the day for weeks after. Then, as his teeth came loose and his eyesight sharpened, the new dreams began. A Hollywood movie played inside his skull the instant his head hit the pillow, and he remembered each detail when he awakened. The dreams became even longer, and more intense soon after.

Sammy Boy was indeed *full of lard*, as his momma often said, but nobody could call the hound slow. If he spotted a mouse or a rabbit, the dog would race after it as if just shot out of a cannon at ankle level. And in dreams, the two of them often ran together, speeding through pastureland, jumping high over fences and tree stumps, which, of course, neither the hound nor he could ever have really done. It was fun. These dreams became the best part of his life, and he looked forward to his dreamland movies more than anything else.

In one dream a few weeks ago, he dashed with Sammy Boy across a pure white snowfall. They put on even more speed, and quickly neared the side of their ramshackle barn, but instead of slowing down, the basset sprinted even faster, straight ahead, right at the side of barn's weathered wood planks, and...

He awakened outside on the cold ground. He sat up, shook his head, blinked a few times and tried to make sense of it. He shivered and crossed his arms across his chest. He knew he had fallen asleep right beside Ida, as always. But now..?

***

Ebb stared at Irene.

She stared back.

"The front door was locked when I got up to go back inside. Had to knock hard to wake Ida. She came to the door with a look in her eyes I ain't never seen coming from nobody."

Irene exhaled slowly. "What do you believe happened?"

He placed his palms flat on the kitchen table. "Only one answer. I went *through* the bedroom wall, Miss Irene, like a ghost, right on *through* without making a hole or leaving a mark. Ended up outside, flat on the ground at 2am. No other way to explain it." He waited for Irene to say something, but when she didn't, he continued. "Went for my robe, and Ida made us some coffee. We sat here in the kitchen, right at this table and looked at each other, s*tared,* with our mouths closed. Nobody knew what to say. After a while she shrugged, got up and went back to bed. Guess she figured there was no point in just sitting here."

"Are you certain it all wasn't part of one of those vivid dreams you were having? Perhaps you had been sleepwalking."

"Nah. Told you. Front door was locked from the inside, with a chain."

She nodded.

"Miss Irene, I was so shook I couldn't even think about getting back into that bed and falling asleep. I was scared it might happen another time."

"I understand."

"Sat on the sofa the rest of the night and stared out the front window. Could see the patrol Jeep pass down our street, once every fifteen minutes, like clockwork."

"Ebb, has it happened again?"

He shook his head. "Those dreams stopped after I started practicing."

"Oh?"

"I knew I wasn't crazy, Miss Irene. I thought about it and figured the only possible answer. The poison they put into my veins caused everything, my teeth, eyes, and now I could pass my body right straight through solid objects. The day after that first time, I left the jobsite at my lunch break and drove my truck into the nearby woods. Miss Irene, I stopped near a small tree, thought about it, rolled up my sleeve and pushed my fingers, my hand, and then half my arm though the bark of a young maple. I thought real hard, *and it was a snap.* I stared at my arm, still attached to my body, but half on one side of the tree, and half on the other. It was easy as pie."

Irene stared at him, speechless.

"At first, I was scared. Then, after a few more tries I started to laugh. Maybe those scientists had done me a favor. They *made me special.* I never thought I was anything too special, Miss Irene. But when I drove back to work, I looked at everybody a little different. You know what I mean?"

She rested her hand atop his. "Maybe there is some good in this after all."

His eyes focused on Irene's hand. Despite the coolness of her skin, he felt no reason to pull away. "The problem was, when I looked at the mirror in the barracks washroom at the end of the day, that's when I realized there might be a *price* for being special."

"Price?"

"Gray up here." He touched a finger to one temple. "And I looked tired, like I had just woke up from a month-long sleep."

"You're saying the injection the scientists gave you was

not responsible for your hair, and your aging? It was only when you used your special ability?"

"The docs gave me a good going over and told me I looked like I had aged a bunch since they last time they saw me. I didn't feel no different, Miss Irene, but I sure looked like I had been scared silly by a whole graveyard of goblins. And the docs had no reason for it, my hair and skin. They supposed it was because of the *pluto*nium they put into my blood. But I knew different."

She gazed at him. "That is quite a secret, Ebb. And I am flattered you decided to trust me with it."

He whispered, "There's more."

"Oh?"

"I'm glad I got you to talk to about this. I've kept lots bottled up inside 'til it almost *hurts*."

"Then tell me, Ebb." She wrapped her fingers around his.

"I heard some things at the compound." He leaned forward. "Those same scientists? They're feeling *bad* about what's been going on here."

"About the bomb?"

He took a quick breath. "Ida told you."

"She needed somebody to talk with, too."

"What I been hearing is mostly crazy talk."

"Crazy, how?"

"The oldest of the bunch, Dr. Einstein, he said he built...*a time machine*."

She stared at him.

"He said their idea was to go backward through time, back two years, and kill the scientist *Oppenheimer*. That way, their bomb would never have the chance to happen."

"Why would he want to do that?"

"I hear their bomb can wipe out thousands with one big explosion. The bunch of them said they didn't want to be remembered for killing innocent women and children."

Irene swallowed. "I suppose not."

"I been spending some of my breaks lately, listening through the walls of different places in the compound, like where they keep prisoners. Soldiers captured a man they found outside the laboratories, in the open, flat on the ground. Happened the other day, same time I found you."

"A man?"

"Young fella, wearing some old hospital clothes."

Irene gasped and stood. "The young man's name. Did you hear it?"

Ebb nodded. "He said his name real clear, Miss Irene, like he was proud of it. It was MacKay, Miss Irene. Brody Amos MacKay."

Time is too slow for those who wait, too swift for those who fear, too long for those who grieve, too short for those who rejoice, but for those who love, time is eternity. **Henry Van Dyke**

Chapter 42: Spring Grove Cemetery
Present Day

J essie remained quiet on their drive to Kroger's grocery. A light shower started just before they left the farmhouse. Raindrops pelted the canvas roof, and the Jeep's wipers streaked across the windshield. Traffic was sparse at 6am on a Wednesday, and after a short ride, Jessie guided her Jeep into the nearly deserted parking lot and switched off the engine.

Bell glanced at her. "I shall not be long." He stepped out of the Wrangler and pushed the door closed.

She tapped her fingers on the steering wheel and watched him push his gray Fedora tighter against his head as he gripped his cane and begin his walk toward the store.

They had talked and talked yesterday and well into the night. She'd opened a bottle of red table wine, made some real popcorn on the gas range, and they sat shoeless and cross-legged facing each other on either side of the sofa like old college roommates home for a reunion. She could sense Bell's internal barriers coming down little by little. She even caught him smile once or twice.

However, she soon realized it must have been difficult for him to feel much joy or happiness about anything when the irretrievable loss of his wife and young daughter pressed against his heart nearly every second. She tried to distract him with comments about the chaotic state of the world today, or with funny stories of the weird things criminals do sometimes, but nothing seemed to divert him for long. A somber pall would slowly return and shroud his expression.

She exhaled a long breath and smiled. It was strange. She had known him for less than a week, and yet she felt closer to him than to any man she had ever known. He was handsome, brilliant, and *funny* in an odd, quirky way. He was clearly a man with high moral values, devoted to a family he would probably never see again. And, of course, he liked dogs. Such a combination was rare. A man like this—

She halted her brain in mid-thought. How could she even consider..?

She looked out the window, saw Bell approaching the Jeep. He held a small bundle of flowers in one hand.

He opened the door and dropped into the front passenger seat.

"Pretty." Jessie flicked a glance at the flowers.

Bell closed the door and slipped his arm through the shoulder harness. "I'm ready."

Jessie turned the key, and the Jeep's engine rumbled to life. She guided the battered SUV out of the lot and toward the I-75 interchange.

***

It had been years since Jessie visited Spring Grove Cemetery, and nearing the stone entranceway brought a smile to her lips. The cemetery was one of Cincinnati's hidden treasures and appeared suddenly amid the concrete streets as a startling, verdant oasis. Endless trees lined carefully manicured pathways around thousands of gravesites and mausoleums. Many famous people were buried here, pioneers, Civil War generals, even a few senators and congressman. Jessie remembered a fieldtrip to Spring Grove she'd taken in middle school. The project was to collect fallen leaves from as many varieties of trees as possible and identify the leaves correctly. She smiled as the distant memories sharpened behind her eyes. That was the fieldtrip where Brian Collins put his arm around her on the bus on their way back to school. That image was as clear to her as if it happened just yesterday.

"You can park here," Bell said.

Jessie slowed the Wrangler to a halt in a small gravel pull-off. "The rain has almost stopped."

"I shouldn't be more than a quarter of an hour." He unfastened his seatbelt and pushed his door open.

"Can I come with you?"

"It is not necessary, Warren."

"I know."

"Then...certainly."

Jessie stepped around the other side of the car and stopped beside him. She pulled the hood of her blue windbreaker over her head. He turned and started a slow walk on a blacktopped path up a slight incline.

"It's as beautiful as I remember," Jessie said. "And so quiet. We are surrounded by urban sprawl, and this is like a secret island paradise."

"The lush grounds remind me of Scotland. Sunday was my favorite day of the week. When the weather allowed, Elizabeth, Polly, and I would walk to our church on the outskirts of town. We would attend the service, and then retrieve a basket of food and cold tea we left beside a tree near the church door. Then, like giddy children we would stroll to the nearby open pastureland, find a shady spot, and enjoy a picnic lunch."

"Sounds wonderful."

"And *this* place, this jewel of a memorial park, reminds me so much of the bucolic tranquility of home. I came here with Hattie many times when she visited Lester."

"There's history here. In an odd way, it's a fascinating place."

He glanced at her. "Thank you for walking with me."

"You would do the same for me."

"Yes. I would."

"I know what you must be feeling, Bell."

"Oh?"

"My family was close when I was growing up, and really, all my life. I miss my parents every second of every day."

"I know you do, Warren. It is a constant subtext of your personality."

"You make it sound so clinical."

A minute later, Bell stopped beside a gravesite. Jessie studied the two headstones and read aloud: "Nadine Hattie

Brooks. And Lester Alphonse Brooks."

"They were devoted to each other. I never met Lester, and yet Hattie spoke of him so often I feel as though I knew him."

Bell stepped forward, bent low and placed the small, colorful flowers against Hattie's headstone. "She loved working in her garden. Bright flowers made her smile."

Jessie let the silence surround her.

"Scooter misses you," Bell whispered to the grass. "He remembers his friend. I see him looking for you sometimes, hoping you will appear around the next corner."

Jessie felt tears touch her skin just under her eyes.

"I tell the little fellow you are fine, just fine, at peace." He bowed his head and pictured Hattie and him talking, with Scooter on her lap. She would sit and chat away about politics, baseball, the weather, and any topic to keep the conversation going. Hattie had lived alone for so long, Bell knew she treasured his unexpected company even if just to have someone to talk to.

Jessie watched him and sensed an incredible sadness. Bell was not here simply to pay his respects, out of routine loyalty. He came here regularly to maintain some sort of *connection* with a friend who meant the world to him, as minimal as that connection might now be. She couldn't remember seeing any grown man so overcome with visible grief.

Bell remained still a few more minutes and exhaled. He took one step back from the gravesite. "Next week, Hattie Brooks. I will come visit with you next week, as always."

Bell started to turn. Jessie suddenly moved close and wrapped her arms around him. She pressed the side of her face against his chest. Bell lifted his arms and rested them around the top of her back.

"You two were lucky to have found each other," Jessie said. She turned her head and looked up at him.

Bell gazed down into Jessie's iridescent blue eyes. He tried to think of something, *anything* to say to her. He eased back. Jessie released her grip.

They both stared at each other for a moment.

"You okay?" Jessie asked.

"Yes. I..."

Bell flashed a half-smile at her, turned and stepped away toward the blacktopped pathway.

***

Jessie remained still in the driver's seat and did not start the engine. Bell sat beside her and stared straight out the windshield.

"I'm sorry, Bell. I shouldn't have hugged you."

"Nonsense."

"Sometimes a good hug can lessen any sadness, at least for a few moments."

"Why should you be sorry?"

"No reason. I don't know. But you seemed..."

"You surprised me, Warren. That's all."

"Oh?"

"Visiting Hattie is emotional for me. I feel quite vulnerable here. I should apologize for reacting poorly."

She took a breath and let it out. "Bell?"

"Yes?"

"We were enjoying our conversation so much last night, and with the wine, we skipped over something important. I don't know, maybe we did that purposefully?"

"Subject?"

"Where we go from here, especially considering our two visitors from 1892 are lurking about somewhere."

Bell smiled. "The wine was quite good."

"And only $3.00 a bottle."

"You are correct, Warren. I think we were avoiding our circumstances last evening, perhaps only to momentarily relieve the stress. We should devise a plan. I have been considering our proper direction." He shifted in his seat. "It is reasonable to conclude Irene Lithgow and Brody MacKay arrived here in the same manner as I."

"The windstorm."

"And they arrived in 2009, just as I."

She stared at him. "Those two have been here, in my time, for the past ten years?"

"Or they both arrived in January of this year."

"Really?"

Lane Cohen

"It is a possibility. Whenever they appeared, it is reasonable to conclude they have no mechanism or manner with which to return to their own time...our own time. They are both here. I know a bit of Brody MacKay's family. He lived with his parents and supported them with money he earned from working the docks and his position at Dundee. If nothing else, I am sure Brody MacKay has desperately wanted to return home ever since he arrived here. But Irene Lithgow..?"

Jessie squinted at him. "She has less of a reason to go back, faced prison, or worse."

"Correct. So, even if Irene, as brilliant as she is, discovered or devised a manner to travel back to 1892 Scotland, I doubt she would decide to do so."

"Makes sense."

"The point is, finding them now would therefore solve nothing for you and me, Warren. Our respective reasons for traveling to the past would remain unresolved, even should we search and find Irene Lithgow and Brody MacKay."

Jessie took a deep breath and let it out. "We still have other reasons to find them. Right?"

He blinked, as if a thought just occurred to him. "May I accompany you today, to the police station?"

"Instead of dropping you off in Mt. Adams?"

"I shall keep to myself and not create any disturbance."

"I'm not worried about you, Bell."

"I will spend the day giving thought to our situation." Bell stared straight forward through the windshield again, as if avoiding eye contact with her.

"Detective Ebsen is on his honeymoon," Jessie said. "In Hawaii, the lucky stiff. You can use his office, his computer."

"That should suffice." A thought made him frown. "Are you certain our dogs will be fine?"

"The yard is fenced, they have cover on the back porch, and I filled two water bowls before we left. They'll be okay. Besides, I think they like being together. They are good company for each other...like us."

Bell furrowed his brow at her.

Jessie took her eyes from him and turned the ignition key.

Choices create circumstances; decisions determine your future. **John Croyle**

Chapter 43: Oak Ridge, Tennessee
June 18, 1944

Ebb Cade's fingers felt sweaty on the steering wheel of his truck. He guided the big Chevy around the last corner and glanced at the woman in his front passenger seat. Irene gazed out the window as she had from the minute they left his house. Ebb had become much less nervous about Miss Irene Tennyson, but the sight of the pale woman dressed in Ida's spare nurse's outfit unexpectedly made his flesh crawl. From the second he saw her step out into the morning daylight, wearing the powder blue uniform, the shivers at the back of his neck had returned in full force. He slowed the truck to a stop about a hundred feet from the military compound. "You sure about this?"

Irene smiled at him. "I should not be long, if all goes well. Are you able to wait for me?"

He nodded.

She reached over and patted his right thigh. "You saved my life, Ebb. You know that."

He huffed. "My mamma wouldn't be too proud of a son who ignored a stranger who needed help."

"Your mother would be quite proud."

"Thanks."

"All right. I shall return soon."

She turned from him, pushed open the door, and stepped out onto the gravel parking area.

***

"Hey, MacKay."

He was sure it was the voice of Pvt. Elza Gate, the soldier most often outside the windowless door to the room where he was locked up. Gate and he had talked off and on the past few days.

MacKay closed the book by Jules Verne. When they offered him something to read, he had asked for anything by Jules Verne or H.G. Wells, since *Mysterious Island* and *The Invisible Man* were the only books he had ever read all the way through. This one was *Journey to the Center of the Earth*, by Verne. Reading this adventure tale was the one pleasant thing about being shut in this strange place. He couldn't wait to find out what the explorers would find hidden beneath the very ground they walked upon.

"MacKay?"

"What?"

"You got a visitor."

MacKay swung his legs from his cot and touched his shoes to the floor. "Einstein, again?"

MacKay heard a chuckle on the other side of the door.

"Not even close."

MacKay stood and faced the closed door. He heard the lock click. The door pulled outward. Two figures stood in the glare of the hallway lights.

Gate said, "Lots better looking than that old boy Einstein, yeah?"

MacKay held his breath.

"This is Nurse Stride, from England. They send some of their nurses and docs here, and we send some of ours over there. That's what she said, anyway."

"Hello, Mr. MacKay," the nurse said. "I am Elizabeth Stride."

She extended her hand.

MacKay's throat tightened. He backed a step.

"Dr. Einstein wants you examined." Gate grinned. "And I guess Nurse Stride drew the short straw."

MacKay had no idea what to say, or if he should say anything at all. Not only was he trapped here with soldiers all around, and with a German man who asked ridiculous questions, but now he was faced again with the *Hellspawn* from Dundee.

A Matter of Time

"This will be painless, Mr. MacKay." Irene dropped her hand.

Mackay shook his head at the short woman in the nurse's outfit. Her hair was brushed back, neat and in place. She held a small square of papers in one hand.

"Anyhow," Gate said, "I'll leave you to your business. Knock when you're finished, Nurse."

The door clicked shut.

"Holy Jesus," MacKay whispered. He backed around until he was even with his cot.

Irene cocked her head. "Have you not missed me?"

"Like I missed getting struck with the fevers."

She chuckled. "Now, now. No need for that."

"Yeah, well..."

"I am not here to do harm. Quite the opposite, in fact."

MacKay edged farther back to his cot. He sat on the military-issue brown blanket near his pillow. "You ain't no nurse, last I knew."

"A necessary subterfuge." She stepped toward him and gestured with one hand at the cot. "Mind if I sit?"

MacKay turned his head away from her. Irene eased down and perched on the blanket at the foot of the cot. She set her small stack of papers beside her.

"Do you know where we are, Brody?"

"I sure as hell don't."

"But, do you recall how you came to be here?"

"Soldiers grabbed me."

"Before that?"

"Blacked out after that storm. Woke up on the ground outside here."

"And then?"

"And then, *nothing*, 'cept one person or another comes in here and asks questions."

"Who asks you questions?"

"Sergeant Gleason is one. Might be in charge of the soldiers around here. Not sure. He don't say much other than ask me stuff. There's Elza Gate, the soldier who brought you in here. And a doctor came to talk with me three, four times. Dr. Einstein."

"Albert Einstein?"

"From Germany. Ain't so easy to understand him. The way he talks."

Irene looked down at her hands folded in her lap. "Funny how fate works sometimes. Somehow, and for some reason, we are apparently meant to be together."

He lifted his face and stared into her shimmering green eyes. "I ain't no fool, Miss Lithgow, Miss *Irene* Lithgow. And I ain't stupid."

"I never thought you were, Brody."

"Somehow you tracked me down, sneaked your way into here by pretending to be a nurse, which you *ain't*. So just be straight out and tell me why you went to all this trouble."

Irene nodded. "I believe I can remove you from your current imprisonment."

"Remove me?"

"Yes."

"How?"

"That does not matter."

"Bloody hell."

"It will happen within the next few days."

"And then what?"

She took a deep breath and let it out slowly. "Brody, do you realize what has happened to you? To us?"

He chewed on his bottom lip. "I got nothing to do but sit in this place and think, Miss Lithgow."

"Irene."

"*Irene.* I got one book and no windows. So, yeah. I got an idea what's happened."

"Tell me."

He reached to his side and touched the cover of *Journey to the Center of the Earth.* "I like to read. You know? I like the *fantastic* stories. And that's the only thing makes sense to me, the strange soldiers, their rifles, the lights in this place, things Einstein talks about, *Dr.* Einstein. He's careful with his words, I can tell. But he's given away more than he's wanted."

"Your conclusions?"

"Something about that *wind*, that Dundee storm, something about it sent me, sent *us*, someplace *into the future*, fantastic story or not."

"It would take a keen mind to accept that probability."

"Like I said, I ain't had nothing but time to sit in here and think." He chuckled. "Nothing but *time*. Kinda funny."

"It is, in a way. So, Brody, do we have an agreement?"

"About you busting me out of this jailhouse?"

"Precisely."

"I thought you wanted to watch me *suffer and die*. You looked me right in the eye and said that. Seems like just the other day."

"I was not in a clear state of mind, being imprisoned in that horrible asylum for weeks on end."

"I should just forget you said all that?"

"We're two of a kind, Brody, whether we like it or not. Our journey will continue *together*. I came here to *help* you. Can you understand that?"

"Maybe, maybe not. But before I agree to anything, mind answering one question for me?"

"You may ask."

"How far into the future did that storm send us?"

"We are currently inhabiting the year 1944."

He swallowed. "I guess that explains most things."

"I was confused as well, at first."

"How did we end up in America?"

"That still puzzles me. I intend to spend some time in the library to attempt to find that answer." She looked down at her hands folded in her lap. "And, I have something else I need to research." She waited a moment. "And so, my question?"

He ran his hands back through his hair and lifted his eyes to her. "When do we get the holy hell out of here?"

The properties of quantum particles are fuzzy or uncertain to start with. This gives them enough wiggle room to avoid inconsistent time travel situations. Our study provides insights into where and how nature might behave differently from what our theories predict. **Brian Greene**

Chapter 44: Hyde Park, Ohio
Present Day

Jessie's office at the Hype Park precinct was little more than a long table and one chair. Other than a small photo of her parents and her all bundled in their warmest winter clothing amid the crowd during the Lebanon holiday carriage parade from about 20 years ago, the table held her computer monitor, a wireless mouse, a corded telephone, one fresh legal pad, and a solitary pen. She kept her worktable free of other papers, files, and random office supplies. When working on a case, her habit was to bring that one file into her office so that it received her complete attention, with no distractions.

Without a file on her table, for the past hour or so she had either stared blankly at the screen-saver of a full moon in a starry sky, or wrote on a legal pad until one sheet of yellow paper was completely filled. Her brain strayed to the man in Sergeant Ebsen's office, just down the hall. She had left him there with a desktop computer and a mug of hot tea. He had nodded to her and smiled as she stepped away.

His smile was so wise and understanding...

"Hey, Jessie."

She glanced up. Keaton leaned one shoulder through the doorway into her office.

"Buster?"

"Want to hear about your cousin?"

"Cousin?" She folded the sheet of yellow legal paper and

slipped it into her blazer's inside breast pocket.

He shook his head. "Cousin. *Cousin.*"

"Oh."

"Good God. You need more sleep."

"Sorry." She gestured at her monitor. "I was involved. What about my *cousin?*"

"I saw him in Ebsen's office, apparently with nothing to do, and I thought, hey, what the hell. I grabbed the Ormond file."

"Ormond who?"

"The girl who was murdered in that Indian Hill park, Haley Ormond. That case always bothered me."

She recalled the case. "Yeah, Haley Ormond-Musgrave. Her parents owned Ormond's Department Store."

"Yep."

"That's from four, five years ago?"

He nodded. "Haley Ormond, just two months shy of 28, who lived with her husband near here, over on Paxton, was found in her jogging clothes by the side of Blue Bird Trail walking path in Indian Hill on one cold January morning. Strangled. She was a housewife, a fitness guru, had plenty of friends, was liked by most everybody, no obvious enemies, no sign of robbery since all she carried on her were her car keys anyway, had two dogs with her, English Spaniels, I think. They sat by her body, remaining to protect their owner."

"Yeah, I remember seeing the photos. Cute dogs. They were wearing thick doggie sweaters."

"Husband, Cory Musgrave, was a real estate agent, out of town in Athens near the OU campus when it happened. Airtight alibi, no motive anybody could figure. Of course, he inherited the wife's enormous estate from the Ormond stores and remarried two months later, Kelli Jo Watters, former Bengals cheerleader. The fact the guy married a Bengals cheerleader so soon after his wife's murder, well..."

She leaned back in her chair. "You gave the Ormond file to my cousin."

"Correcto. And, what do you think?"

She smiled. "I think my cousin Wallace had that file for about fifteen minutes before he came back to you."

"Ten minutes."

She chuckled. "Told you. He's a criminologist."

"He's a damn *magician*. Saw right though the holes in the husband's alibi. Seemed simple enough after he explained it."

"I know what you mean."

Keaton gazed at her. "He's a cool guy. I could almost see the wheels turning inside his skull."

"It's unnerving sometimes."

He nodded and took a breath. "Well, I'm going to call the Indian Hill Rangers. I think they'll be real interested." He stepped away.

***

Bell's eyes were trained on the monitor when Jessie stepped into Ebsen's office.

"This precinct of the Cincinnati PD, and the Indian Hill Rangers had months, no *years*, to gather and examine the evidence. And you know what they came up with?"

He exhaled. "I assumed you would not mind if I assisted Detective Keaton."

She chuckled. "Buster had nothing to do with that investigation. You weren't helping him. The Ormond case has gathered dust for years. He was curious about *you,* but you knew that already."

"Perhaps."

She smiled. "Buster's had, well, a *thing* for me since we started working together. He's kept any flirting barely beneath the surface, but a girl can tell about those things."

Bell put his hands behind his head and leaned back in Ebsen's desk chair.

"Buster's pretty smart, and I think he doubts my *cousin Wallace* story."

He tilted his head at her. "Why would he doubt such a well-crafted tale? Why would he doubt I am your cousin, a man from *Scotland*, where you have no apparent association? There is nothing in your known heritage to suggest any Scottish connections, especially with a family who has lived exclusively in Lebanon, Ohio, since the 1950s. Why would he discount the authenticity of a story of a man whom you have never mentioned, a man who is unmarried and living *with you* at your farmhouse?"

"*Sarcasm*, Bell? I thought you might be above such things."

"Oh?"

"Look, I was pressed to think of a story that might make sense. Sometimes the bigger the lie, the easier it is to believe. Sorry it didn't meet your expectations."

"And so, you concluded Detective Keaton is somewhat jealous of a possible competitor for your affections, and he decided to, as they say, check me out?"

"Yeah, probably." She glanced over her shoulder out into the hall. "What did you tell him about the Ormond case?"

"The husband murdered the wife."

"That was the first thought, since in most murders, the primary suspect is a close family member."

"And that is where I directed my analysis."

"But that theory was dismissed right away. The husband, Cory Musgrave, was in Athens, Ohio, at the time. He was attending a conference of some kind."

"Yes. *Commercial Real Estate in Transition* I believe was the title of the two-day seminar, according to the file. His office, ReMax, paid for the excursion." He paused to look around. "Is it permissible to smoke in here?"

"Of course not."

"I thought perhaps in a police station, the smoking rules might be bent?"

"No. They aren't. You can't smoke inside."

He huffed. "In any event, the body was found by two female walkers just off the Blue Bird walking trail, at the farthest point from the entrance to the park, by the way, at approximately 9:15am. It was quite cold that morning, six degrees positive on the Fahrenheit scale, and according to the reports, the use of the Blue Bird trail, which is asphalt, incidentally, was sparse that morning. It is uncomfortable for anyone to walk or jog in weather that cold, no matter how prepared."

"Okay. Body found at 9:15. It was cold."

"No sign of any struggle, no off-trail footprints, no disturbance of any greenery and such. One photo revealed a single track of an agricultural cart of some kind in the remnants of snow to the side of the trail, a few feet from the body. Autopsy concluded the young woman had been strangled without a rope, scarf, or other implement. The killer used his own hands."

"His?"

"Incidents of one woman strangling another with her own bare hands are extremely rare. When a woman decides to murder in that fashion, she will almost always choose a rope or garrote of some kind to accomplish the task."

"Bell, where are you getting this stuff?"

"I explained to you earlier. In Edinburgh I had occasion to assist the Yard, and because of that, I focused some of my spare time to the study of criminal behavior."

"All right. You're a regular Sherlock Holmes."

He raised an eyebrow at her. "The file indicates Mrs. Ormond-*Musgrave* often drove to Rheinstrom Park and jogged at least six times around the Blue Bird trail, the length of which is eight-tenths of one mile. This trail was one of several she would choose at random, depending upon the day, and her mood. That is what the interviews with the victim's husband, and a few of the victim's friends, uncovered. She participated in half-marathons and used trails like Blue Bird for training. Apparently, she ran with her dogs at least five days each week and alternated the locations from French Park in Amberley Village, Glenwood Gardens in Woodlawn, and the Blue Bird trail in Rheinstrom Park in Indian Hill."

"She jogged. She was fit."

"The point here, Warren, is running outside in cold weather was a regular activity for Miss Ormond."

"Apparently. So?"

He opened the file on Ebsen's desk. "I asked Detective Keaton if I could examine these documents for a while longer." He spread photos out on the desk. "Come look."

Jessie inched closer and gazed down at the photos.

"What do you see?"

She spread the photos on the desk. "What am I looking for?"

"Look. Study."

Only ten seconds passed before the breath caught in her

throat. "Jesus."

"You've seen it."

She fixed her eyes on his. "Haley Ormond did not go to that park to jog that morning. She was strangled elsewhere else and dumped on the trail at Rheinstrom Park."

"Accurate."

Her breaths came faster. "The pics from the scene and from the photos in the morgue show the body, dressed as it was found, and individual photos of Haley's possessions and other articles of clothing."

"What is missing in the photos?"

"Bell, I swear, if you keep talking to me as if I'm a student in one of your classes..?"

"I apologize, Warren. Please. Continue your analysis."

"*Flannel socks*, Bell, the kind I wear to bed sometimes."

"Yes."

"No gloves. No hat."

Bell said, "Mrs. Ormond-Musgrave would not have gone to run outside on a cold morning without such implements, and not in flannel socks."

"*Meaning*, someone killed her *elsewhere*, dressed the body in running attire and a warm jacket, but neglected to provide the hat and gloves that any runner surely would have worn that day. And the flannel socks were probably what she wore when she went to bed. The killer neglected to change them. No real runner wears flannel socks to go jogging, even in the winter."

"My conclusions as well."

Jessie sat on the corner of the desk. "But how do we know the husband did it?"

"It was indeed the husband, Warren."

"But his alibi?"

"It would have been a simple matter for the husband to murder his wife while she slept, dress the body, transport her to the park, and drop her by the side of the trail."

"Wait a second. A *simple matter*? He was in Athens, at a conference."

"Witnesses place the husband at the Athens College Inn the day before the body was found. That evening, at the same motel, he was involved in an altercation with a bartender concerning the tab for his drinks and an order of buffalo wings. Several conference attendees broke up the argument at 10:00pm, before serious blows were thrown, and escorted Mr. Musgrave to his room. They left him atop his bedcovers nearly unconscious from alcohol consumption. That is what the witnesses reported to authorities."

She realized she was staring at him. "I'm listening."

"Witnesses also stated they saw Musgrave in attendance at the conference breakfast as early as 7:30 the next morning. They were quite certain."

Jessie's eyes widened. "He *faked* being drunk, and *purposely* caused the fight with the bartender."

"To cement his whereabouts the evening before the murder."

"I'm not positive, but from here to OU takes about two hours by car."

"The distance is almost exactly 150 miles, and the time to traverse that distance using the most direct route is estimated at two hours, forty-one minutes."

Jessie straightened up and faced him. "So, Musgrave could have driven home from Athens in the middle of the night, sneaked into his house unnoticed, since his wife would most likely have been sleeping, *strangled* her, struggled to dress her in running clothes, didn't bother with changing her socks, or searching for her gloves and hat, since he probably didn't consider that, carried her to his car, and drove to Indian Hill."

"With Bonnie and Clyde."

"Who?"

"The dogs. The English Spaniels."

"Oh. Right."

"Musgrave had to take the dogs along, since his wife never jogged without them."

"Makes sense."

Bell leaned forward in his chair and rested his elbows on the desk. "Even if we ignore the lack of hat and gloves, the flannel socks, and the tire track in the snow, *the two dogs* tell the tale more than anything else."

She squinted at him. "Of course. Who would attack a jogger in that park when she had two large dogs with her at the time? That would never happen."

He clicked his fingers. "And since there was no sign of any struggle or disturbance otherwise, the dogs must have *known* the person who transported them all to the park. My conclusion is Musgrave separated the dogs from the bedroom before he strangled his wife. Then as if it were a normal, daily activity, he stowed the corpse in the back of their Chevy Tahoe, loaded the dogs, and proceeded calmly to the park."

She blinked at him. "And the one tire track in the snow?"

"Most likely from a garden cart of some sort. You see, Musgrave planned to place the body a good distance from the start of the trail to delay its discovery. Transporting her that far would have been a significant effort. So, he took his garden cart, and used it to push his dead wife along the blacktopped trail."

She considered for a moment. "Her car."

"Pardon?"

"Her car was in the Bluebird Trail parking lot."

Bell nodded. "Mr. Musgrave would have needed an accomplice."

"The cheerleader?"

"Most likely."

She gazed at the pictures. "It's a great theory, Bell. It all makes perfect sense, I grant you that. But *proving* that theory is another matter. The fact that Musgrave had the opportunity, and probable motive, the cheerleader I guess, who was probably his co-conspirator, does not by itself prove anything. We still have the witnesses at the conference and nothing but conjecture."

"You may be correct, Warren. But, the last thing I told Detective Keaton was my research revealed the road most likely used in driving from Athens, Ohio, to Hyde Park, Ohio, to the Musgrave home on Paxton, quite near here, is partially on US 50."

She thought that could be right. "Go on."

"The section of US 50 connecting downtown Cincinnati to just before Portsmouth, Ohio, is a toll road."

Jessie's eyes popped wide.

Bell grinned. "Musgrave either had a toll transponder in the Tahoe, or, if he did not, a photo of the Tahoe license plate would have been taken as the Tahoe traversed the toll road, both to and from."

"My God."

"Records of highway usage are kept by the state agency in charge of such things. I suggested Detective Keaton submit a request to that agency, *ExpressToll* it is called, for their records for travel along US 50 on the appropriate date and time. I believe such records are sustained indefinitely."

"How did Buster react when you explained this theory?"

Bell furrowed his brow at her. "He stared at me for a moment, said 'Thanks,' and stepped away."

She chuckled. "You freaked him out."

"Oh?"

"He doubted my story about you, including the criminologist part. When you came up with your analysis in less than ten minutes, it not only shocked him that *anyone* could perform such a magical feat, but it also confirmed, at least partially, my story about you."

"You may be correct."

She took a breath. "Impressive. Truly."

"Simple deduction."

She shook her head. "Look, if you're finished solving long forgotten cold cases for the day, want to get lunch?"

"Yes."

"Because I might need to tell you...something."

He stood. "Might?"

"Can't decide."

"Subject matter?"

"Just *stuff*."

"Mysterious, Warren."

"What does your deductive reasoning tell you?"

"Nothing, other than what you want to tell me is not meant for the ears of your colleagues."

"I'll let Buster know we'll be gone for a while."

"I will be here when you return."

She turned and halted when Keaton rushed around the hall corner and blocked Jessie's exit.

"Buster?" Jessie said.

Keaton didn't say anything. His face had gone pale. He looked from Jessie to Bell and back again.

"What is it, Buster?" Jessie asked.

"A body...in the back of the yarn shop down the street."

Bell bolted upright. "Yarn shop, Detective?"

"Yeah. *Knot Right*, on Observatory. One of the owners opened the parking lot dumpster this morning. She was hysterical and got admitted right away into Jewish. She's under heavy sedation."

Jessie gazed at Bell thoughtfully then touched Keaton's forearm. "Who is the victim?"

Bell cleared his throat. "Laurie Markwell."

Jessie said, "Who?"

"Markwell," Keaton said. "She worked there." He turned and locked eyes with Bell. "How did you..?"

Bell shook his head. "We need to inspect the scene immediately." He moved around the desk and stepped quickly past Jessie and Keaton and out into the hall.

The basic idea if you're very, very optimistic, is that if you fiddle with the wormhole openings, you can make it not only a shortcut from a point in space to another point in space, but a shortcut from one moment in time to another moment in time.
Brian Greene

Chapter 45: Oak Ridge, Tennessee
June 17, 1944

Ebb waited to turn the ignition key as the woman got in the front passenger seat of the Chevy truck. The nurse's outfit she wore still made him edgy because it was Ida's outfit, and it seemed oddly out of place on Irene. She stared down at her hands, folded atop her knees, and gripped her fingers tightly together.

"Everything okay, Miss Irene?"

"Ebb, Oak Ridge has a library, yes?"

Ebb squinted at her. "Down on Maple. Been inside three, four times."

"Would you mind taking me there?"

"Now?"

"If it would not be too much trouble. Perhaps you could come back for me around, say noon?"

"Sure, Miss Irene. Why do you want to go there?"

"I thought if I researched some of my memories, it might help bring all of them back. A library seemed like a good place to try."

Ebb turned the ignition key. The big truck engine rumbled to life. "Should take five minutes or so to get there."

"Thank you, Ebb. You are so kind to me."

"Hope it does some good."

Irene stared out the pitted front glass at the gravel road before them.

A Matter of Time

***

After asking for some basic operational instruction from a library employee, it took Irene little time to acclimate to the techniques needed to research the library's newspaper archives. She stared at the illuminated screen as days and months of pages flew by. She started with the Oak Ridge Gazette, and then moved on to the New York Times. Dr. Joseph Bell did not appear in either of these dailies.

She changed her strategy and researched his name generally, outside of the newspapers. Dr. Joseph Bell - she found information straightaway. There was his photo. Dr. Joseph Bell had disappeared in a windstorm in 1892 at the Dundee Asylum. And the articles listed Dr. Bell as Conan Doyle's inspiration for the Sherlock Holmes character in *The Strand*. But if Dr. Joseph Bell had materialized in 1944 Oak Ridge, Tennessee, as she and Brody MacKay had appeared, so far the general public had taken no notice of his presence here.

Irene shook her head at the screen and considered where and how to begin a general study of Cincinnati, Ohio, in this library filled with endless shelves of books and marvelous electronic devices.

***

Irene settled into the hard truck seat and then angled her eyes toward Ebb. "Thank you, for allowing time for me at the library."

"Did it help with anything?"

"Perhaps some."

"That's good, Miss Irene."

She gazed down at her lap. "It's time I shared a few things with you, Ebb."

"Things?" He shifted the truck into gear and motored down Maple away from the library.

"I apologize for not being completely forthcoming."

"No need for that."

"Well...as you have no doubt observed, my *memory* may not be so impaired as I let on. I am truly sorry for such deceit."

"Might be I did notice something."

Her lips pulled into the hint of a smile. "I thank you for not saying anything, for trusting me."

"You got a good heart, Miss Irene. I knew that from the beginning. I think Ida saw that, too."

"You and Ida are good people. I shall always be grateful."

Ebb waited at a stop sign.

"You told me about a man the soldiers found outside here, a man they were holding prisoner."

"Yeah. Brody MacKay."

"I visited him this morning, before you escorted me to the library."

"Pretty much what I thought."

"You see, Ebb, I am acquainted with that gentleman."

"You are?"

"This might be difficult to accept, but Mr. MacKay and I are from the same place."

"Where?"

"Scotland. He was an attendant at a *hospital*. He *assisted* with some of the unruly patients."

"You worked at the hospital?"

She shook her head. "I was a patient."

He studied her. "You were sick?"

"It is hard to explain."

"I'm catching on to that." He slowed to a stop at an intersection, glanced at Irene, and started forward again.

"In any event, while Mr. MacKay and I were in the same room, the hospital was struck by a tremendous windstorm."

"Like a tornado?"

"Yes. We blacked out. And when we awoke, the both of us found ourselves in this place, in Oak Ridge, Tennessee."

He grimaced in thought. "That's *something*. The tornado lifted you...and then what?"

"I'm not sure."

"You were in Scotland, and then you got to Tennessee?"

"Yes."

"But why make believe to lose your memory, Miss Irene? You got nothing to hide, seems to me."

"There's more." She gathered her thoughts. "It is not only that Mr. MacKay and I were transported from Scotland to

America. We also were transported here from, well, a different *time.*"

Ebb raised one eyebrow. "I ain't surprised."

"No?"

"Explains lots of your questions."

"Again, I apologize for being less than fully truthful."

"When, Miss Irene? When did you leave Scotland?"

She waited a moment. "2019. I'm from the *future*, Ebb. So is Mr. MacKay."

"The *future*? What's it like there?"

"Different."

"Guess it would be."

"My friends, my family, *my very life* exists more than 70 years ahead."

He slowed the Chevy truck and eased to a stop by the curb. The homes on either side of the suburban street were small but neat and well-tended. Large trees supplied plenty of shade. Ebb reached over and gently rested the palm of one hand on Irene's forearm. "Sorry, Miss Irene. I'm sorry for you. But you got friends here. No need to worry about that."

She shifted her body toward him. "I suppose you must have a question or two for me."

"Question?"

"Perhaps about the war."

Ebb lifted his hand from her arm. "The war? You know what happens?"

"This will be hard for you, well, for *anybody* to believe."

"Considering what's been happening lately, I ain't so sure about that."

She brought her eyes up to his gaze. "The war never happened, Ebb."

"Never..?"

"The Germans did not attack anybody. Neither did the Japanese."

His face was blank. "How?"

"In the history I come from, Ebb, in the year 1937, the villain you know of as Adolph Hitler was *murdered* in Berlin, Germany, assassinated by two unidentified persons, a man and a woman. And because of that, the war never began."

His eyes widened. "What about the Japs?"

Irene shook her head. "They did not fly their airplanes to Pearl Harbor."

"They didn't?"

"So, Dr. Fermi did not use their time machine to go back and stop Dr. Oppenheimer, Ebb, since the army did not even *think* to build that bomb. There was no reason for it."

"Huh. That's...something."

Irene took a breath. "The *something* that *did* happen, Ebb, what *really* happened, is that Brody MacKay and I magically appeared here in 1944, and because of what we are now to do, *the world changes*, and millions of lives are saved."

"Because of you?"

"It seems so, but there's more."

"Miss Irene, tell me the rest."

"I will tell you, Ebb, but I must ask of you a tremendous favor, a favor with more than one purpose. I need you to get me that time machine."

Ebb took a breath. "You want me to walk through the walls of their office, get into the safe, and steal Dr. Einstein's time-machine box?"

"You are a smart man, Ebb."

"Don't know about that."

A tear started in Irene's eye. "I told you, Ebb. My life is *there*, decades from now. I do not belong anywhere else."

"And you want to go home."

"Yes. Of course. But first we have something important to do for the world."

"And this other, well, *purpose..*?"

She wiped a finger across her eyes. "I want you to go back in time with me...to shoot...to shoot—"

"Hitler?"

"Yes. Before he can even start his evil plans. Don't you see, Ebb? We would be that couple, that man and woman I told you about. That has to be the answer. And I cannot do it alone, Ebb. Besides, the history books from my time in the future say we did that together, that unidentified man and woman. They didn't know we stopped any war before it could begin."

Ebb stared at her. "I was right about you, Irene."

"Oh?"

"You are an angel sent down to this Earth itself. But, Miss Irene, you weren't sent down here to help me. You were sent to stop millions of innocent people from being murdered in a terrible war. And if this is all part of heaven's plan, well, the least I can do is help you...with all the strength I got left."

Irene smiled and patted the back of Ebb's hand. "Then let's get started."

People like us who believe in physics, know that the distinction between past, present and future is only a stubbornly persistent illusion. **Albert Einstein**

Chapter 46: Hyde Park, Ohio
Present Day

Jessie and Bell rushed out on foot. The yarn shop was a few blocks from the station. It was well before noon, but steamy hot already. Jessie felt droplets of sweat pop out on her forehead as she stepped hurriedly on the Hyde Park sidewalk beside Keaton and Dr. Joseph Bell.

Her new confidant had not said a word since they started out together. He was visibly startled when Buster had announced the murder of Laurie Markwell. Bell must either have known the victim, or the killing being so close to their current location set off some other kind of internal alarm. The answer was just a few more steps away, but whatever the explanation, Jessie suspected *Irene Lithgow* was somehow involved.

Knot Right came up quickly. The store specialized in alpaca yarn. They kept detailed records so customers could request shearings from the alpacas they preferred. Jessie had been inside the shop about six months ago to investigate a report of repeated shopliftings. She remembered the interior being upscale, meant to appeal to the generally privileged Hyde Park clientele. Back then she fought the impulse to remove her street shoes when she walked in and the thick creamy carpeting and overwhelmingly pristine décor surrounded her. She couldn't recall the names of the employees she had interviewed back then, but she didn't think Laurie Markwell was one of them.

They halted in a rear corner of the parking lot. Yellow police tape was strung about twenty feet from the dark green dumpster. The metal lid was propped open. A uniformed officer stepped toward them. He was about twenty-eight, with short dark hair mostly obscured by his police cap. Sweat trickled down his cheeks.

Keaton asked the officer. "What do you got?"

He wobbled to one side, removed his cap, and wiped his temples with his fingertips. "No class at the academy prepares you for things like this."

"Tell us what happened."

Bell said, "I will tell you, Detective."

Keaton glanced back to Bell. "Really?"

Bell stared off into space as if searching for a distant memory. "The ugly metal container in the corner of this parking area contains the remains of a remarkably likeable woman of sixty-five years, Mrs. Laurie Markwell. And one of the saddest parts of this crime scene, Detective Keaton, is Mrs. Markwell survived breast cancer, was dealing with severe grief from the sudden death of her only child, 32-year-old Clare Markwell who perished in a vehicle accident several months ago. And now, after all that, Laurie Markwell, wife of forty happy years to Geoffrey Markwell, a local barrister, has met an unfortunate and unnecessary end of her life due to no fault of her own."

Keaton stared at Bell. "I'm almost afraid to ask."

Jessie said, "My cousin knits sweaters for Scooter, his dog."

"Yes," Bell said. "Mrs. Markwell has been a friend for the last several years. I often frequented her shop. And I greatly enjoyed our conversations. She was highly educated in the arts. We avidly discussed painters of the 19th century. Her analysis of their many works was truly illuminating. Mrs. Markwell and I shared ice cream together on Hyde Park Square on numerous occasions."

Keaton focused his stare at Bell and gestured with the thumb of one hand over his shoulder at the dumpster. "But how did you know?

Jessie said, "We can talk about that later. For now, officer, what have we got?"

He cleared his throat. "One of the owners, Kathleen Meeker, carried trash out this morning. She opened the dumpster lid and then collapsed on the blacktop. When she came to, she called 911."

"And you got here first?"

"I called for the ME two seconds after I arrived. I found a big kitchen knife on the ground by the dumpster, in plain sight. Guess the killer wanted us to see it, or didn't care, one way or the other. And I did a quick check for prints. The black handle was covered in them."

"Is Dalmore on her way?" Jessie asked.

"Yeah. Not much for an ME to really do, except figure out the time of death. There's no mystery to what happened. The vic's throat was slashed, almost all the way around."

Bell took Jessie by her forearm. "May we speak privately?"

"Sure." Jessie threw a glance at Keaton. "Be right back."

Bell and Jessie stepped about twenty feet away until they were covered by the shade of a huge maple tree.

Jessie said, "It's Irene Lithgow's doing, isn't it?"

"I knew Irene was on the loose in Ohio since the beginning of the year. The clues were unmistakable. And yet I did nothing to specifically find her. Nor did I alert local authorities. Perhaps, had I acted properly, my friend Laurie Markwell might still be inside this shop. And I don't have many friends, Warren, as you might suspect."

Jessie's focus was taken by the ME van pulling into the lot. "Fallon Dalmore is here."

Bell took in a long breath. "If it is all the same to you, I am going to walk over to the Square."

"Now?"

"Walking stimulates the brain. I must decide how to approach...this."

She gazed up at him. "Okay, I guess."

"Anticipate some uncomfortable questions from Miss Dalmore."

"Uncomfortable *how*?"

"Do not be surprised by what she might ask you."

"And if you walk away now, she won't be asking *you* these questions, she'll be asking me?"

"I will be at the M5, a coffee and tea shop on the corner." He stepped away without waiting for a response.

*I myself believe that there will one day be time travel when
we find that something isn't forbidden by the over-arching laws
of physics we usually eventually find a technological way of
doing it.* **David Deutch**

Chapter 47: Oak Ridge, Tennessee
June 27, 1944

Albert Einstein shuffled across the compound through the
thick night air. The steady downpour had stopped about
an hour ago, but moisture still crowded every inch of the
glistening darkness. Humidity settled into his rumpled gray suit
as he walked to Oppenheimer's office.

Fermi and Oppenheimer nodded at him as he pulled open
the door, stepped inside, and clicked the door lock behind him.
Fermi was dressed in a black suit and olive-green topcoat. A
grey Fedora topped his head. Oppenheimer was coatless, wore a
white dress shirt and his inevitable thin black tie.

Oppenheimer waited until Einstein stopped beside them.
Then, after one deep breath, Oppenheimer turned behind his
desk, swung the hinged oil painting of Gen. Robert E. Lee
mounted atop his warhorse Traveller away from the wall, and
exposed the gray metal face of their safe.

Einstein felt slightly numb and watched transfixed. Almost
no sleep had come to him for the last few nights. Usually, no
matter what problems with which he had been wrestling, he had
a particular talent at night for partitioning incredibly complicated
thoughts from his daylight hours into a back corner of his brain.
He could then settle beneath his covers for a refreshing six-hour
rest. But these past few weeks the opposite had been true. No
matter what he did, no matter how hard he tried, he found
himself flat on his back, eyes open, staring straight overhead at
the dark wooden blades of a constantly moving ceiling fan.

Their problem initially seemed unsolvable. Developing a
method to harness the atom, *the very substance of all matter,*

initially stimulated him with an exhilaration he had rarely felt. But the closer he and his companions neared the ultimate conclusion of their experiments, the more dread crept up his spine. Was advancement in science always worth it, if just for the sake of advancement itself, or should scientists also be shouldered with the burden of studying the *possible consequences* of such advancements?

Oppenheimer finished turning the black combination dial and swung open the door. He inched forward and peered inside, remained still for about five seconds, and then he turned to his companions.

"What is it?" Fermi asked.

"Gone," Oppenheimer said.

"What do you mean?"

"We have been betrayed. The safe is empty, Enrico. *Empty.*"

"But...how?"

"I am the only person we entrusted with the combination," Oppenheimer said. "Someone must have discovered it, perhaps by spying on us." Oppenheimer moved around the desk chair. He exhaled and perched on the edge of the leather seat.

"Evidently, our security was flawed," Fermi said.

Einstein sank into a chair in front of the desk. "This is catastrophic."

"Yes," Oppenheimer said. "We have neither sufficient time or materials to fashion another device."

Einstein shook his head. "That is not what I mean."

"No?"

"There is now something potentially *much worse* than the bomb reaching completion."

Oppenheimer's eyes widened. He stood and placed his palms on the smooth surface of his desk. "Your device. M*y God.*"

"Yes," Einstein said.

"Whoever removed it..."

"Could attempt to alter history."

Fermi cleared his throat. "And perhaps in a much less benevolent way than the three of us intended."

"If you could travel back through time," Einstein began,

"motivated by greed, or with thoughts of great political advantage, what would you choose to do?"

Oppenheimer said, "Or perhaps one could travel to the *future*, and gain knowledge that would be dangerous here in the hands of those who might seek power or destruction."

"Robert, do you appreciate the irony of it?"

Oppenheimer grumped. "In our efforts to prevent the creation of immense destructive power, we have devised a different machine, but this one with potentially *more* destructive power than the other."

"Gentlemen," Einstein said, "we must regain the device, at all costs, and with immediate speed."

Oppenheimer shook his head. "How, Albert? How? Access to this office is restricted to us. Only us. There are no windows. I can spot no sign of a broken door, nothing out of place, the safe was properly closed and locked. Whoever did this not only had knowledge of the existence of your machine, but also possessed the means to gain entry to this room and to the wall safe without being detected by the military guards who patrol every inch of this facility. We have not a clue as to the whereabouts of the device."

Einstein pushed himself up from his chair and faced his startled companions. "I have an idea."

***

Ebb hobbled through the grass toward his truck. He held the small metal box against his side with one arm as he reached for the door handle. *Christ.* The box was just a little bigger than a cigar box but felt heavier than two bowling balls. It almost slipped away, but he caught it just in time.

His hand froze on the truck handle as he caught his reflection in the door window. His hair was now chalk white. And thick wrinkles encircled his eyes; he appeared to have aged ten years in a matter of minutes.

He dropped into the truck, started the engine and guided the slate-gray vehicle back into town.

If time travel were possible, the future would have already taught the present to teach the past how to do it. **Atom Tate**

Chapter 48: Hyde Park Square
Present Day

M5 Espresso sat in the middle section of the eastern side of the square, separated from the clamor that accompanied most of the specialty shops and crowded restaurants.

Bell liked the *M5*. He met Laurie Markwell here at least once per month over the last year.

Bell's fingers trembled as he raised a teacup to his lips. *Homeward Bound,* by Simon and Garfunkel floated in the air amid the scent of strong coffee. His vision blurred and he pictured how he and Laurie Markwell had watched the seasons change through the front window while they spoke with each other in quiet, civilized tones about art, music, and the state of the world. He liked Laurie Markwell's company quite a bit, and greatly looked forward to their monthly encounters.

Now she was dead.

And it was entirely his fault.

He shook his head; he desperately craved stronger drink than tea.

Bell focused on the street through the front window and watched Dr. Fallon Dalmore lean out of the police van she had had parked at an angle. She remained still for a moment, looked behind and over her shoulder then faced forward and gazed up at the *M5* sign on the cafe's window. She glanced quickly over her shoulder again, and then stepped toward the M5 entry door.

Bell set the teacup on the small cafe table and gathered his thoughts. He watched the tall woman as she opened the entrance door and walked inside. Her similarities to Elizabeth were unmistakable: their flowing red hair and scattering of freckles on equally fair skin. Dalmore stopped near him and set the van keys on the table.

"From the complete lack of expression on your face," she said, "you must have been expecting me."

He stood. "I presumed you would arrive before long."

She watched him. "I am sorry I didn't show up this morning as I said I would."

"Was there a problem?"

She shrugged. "Not really. A strange feeling I've had for a couple days. I came in a little later, after it passed."

Bell swept his open hand to the vacant chair at his table. "Please join me."

She blinked once and pulled the chair out. "There's a quote from Sherlock Holmes." She sat. "It goes something like, *when you have eliminated the impossible, whatever remains, however improbable, must be the truth.*"

Bell sat. "That is one of Sir Arthur's most recognizable lines given to his consulting detective."

"Yes."

Tears started to brim on Bell's eyelids.

"Hey, are you okay?"

He cleared his throat. "No, Miss Dalmore. I am not."

"I'm willing to listen, if you want to talk."

He wiped away a few tears with one index finger. "Intelligence is pointless if not used to fashion proper and effective choices."

"Did Conan Doyle say that as well?"

Bell stared. "Your resemblance..."

"To Elizabeth?"

His eyes widened.

Dalmore tapped one finger on table top. "My mother gave a photo scrapbook to me when I turned twenty-one. Her mother gave it to her when she had reached twenty-one, as well. The book has been handed down to the first daughter to turn twenty-one in each family since, well, the middle 1800s."

Bell held his breath for a moment. "Elizabeth Dal..."

"Yes."

"She appears on a photograph inside the book?"

"And the expression you *now* have on your face confirms everything."

He took a breath. "I suppose it must."

Dalmore blinked and then turned her eyes to the front window of the café.

"Is something wrong?" Bell asked.

She shifted back to him. "Just that weird feeling again."

"Déjà vu?"

"Perhaps." She swallowed. "Was Conan Doyle right?"

"He was right."

"And now must I accept the reality that traveling through time is actually possible?"

"It is no longer theoretical, but rather is proven to be factual."

She squirmed in her chair. "The instant I saw you in the vault, it all came rushing back. I remembered you from that scrapbook, the picture all gray and faded, but your face was unmistakable."

"I surmised you were descended from Elizabeth's family when I first saw you. As I said, the resemblance is striking."

She studied him and tilted her head to one side. "My mother and grandmother told me stories about the photos in our book. The legend went that Elizabeth Dalmore's husband, Dr. Joseph Bell, disappeared in a horrific windstorm while working at a hospital in the Dundee highlands. Am I to conclude, then, that Wallace Brewster and Dr. Joseph Bell are one and the same?"

He chuckled.

"What's funny?"

"I have kept that secret close for ten years, yet you are the second to whom I have recently admitted the truth."

"Jessie?"

"Yes."

"She told me you moved in with her."

"In a manner of speaking."

"That sounds like an interesting story."

"It is a temporary arrangement."

She shook her head. "As far as I know, Jessie Warren hasn't dated anyone in, well, a long time."

"Warren and I are not connected romantically."

She raised one eyebrow. "No?" A hint of a smile touched

her lips. She lowered her voice. "So, I have the honor of sitting here with a real-life time traveler."

"And I suspect you and I meeting in this manner rises to much more than a simple coincidence."

"Oh?"

"The concept of time moving as a flowing river, or of time being pushed through the ages as a relentless and mono-directional wind, might be very true."

She gazed at him. "If you say so."

Bell noticed the reflection of the overhead lights in Dalmore's deep brown eyes. "Miss Dalmore—"

"Fallon."

He inhaled. "As I started to say earlier, intelligence is wasted if not put to efficient and proper use."

"That is an odd thing for you to say to me at this particular moment."

"How do you mean?"

"I resemble your Elizabeth, in the space of less than a minute you have admitted your secret identity to me and the fact you are currently living with a young and beautiful detective whom I know quite well, with no romantic connection, by the way, and you now want to talk with me about your intelligence? Doesn't sound quite normal, if you don't mind me saying."

Bell studied her. "Can you come to the precinct tomorrow morning, say 7:30?"

"I suppose. Why?"

"We could share thoughts about times from long ago."

"Intriguing."

"Please bring your photos."

Dalmore nodded. "7:30, tomorrow morning, then."

"I ask that you please excuse me now." He stood. "I must somehow gather my thoughts on this case."

She took a breath. "They told me you knew the victim over at *Knot Right*."

Bell remained silent.

She stood. "Tomorrow."

Bell watched the tall woman as she turned and stepped into the glare of the light streaming in through the large panes of glass that faced the street.

Time travel is complicated, or so we think, since we have not yet managed to actually figure out how to do it. **Serena Yates**

Chapter 49: Hyde Park Square
Present Day

Bell felt the sweat cool across his forehead as he pulled open the street door and stepped into Teller's subdued lobby. The restaurant started as a bank in the 60s and had recently been repurposed as an upscale neighborhood tavern offering top-shelf food and beverages. Today, just after Teller's late-morning opening, only a few of the typical weekday lunch crowd had arrived.

Bell strode to the bar and pulled out a tall metal chair. He eased down on the wooden seat and leaned his arms on the mahogany bartop. He gripped his hands tightly together. From behind the bar, a young woman of about twenty-eight, with dirty blond hair, stepped toward him. She wore black slacks and a black sleeveless top. "Hi."

"Good morning," Bell said.

"Hot out there already?"

"Indeed."

She raised an eyebrow. "You okay?" She tilted her head down at his clasped hands.

Bell chuckled. "A popular question."

"What's the answer?"

"I'm fine."

"Meaning, you are *far* from okay."

He regarded her almond-brown eyes as they studied him then allowed a brief smile. "Miss...Miss..?"

"Jennifer. Most call me Jenn."

"You are correct, Jenn."

"That's what I thought."

"I suppose you have grown adept at observing people, from

both tending bar and from your position as a lifeguard, and then drawing conclusions from those observations."

She squinted at him. "Have you seen me somewhere before?"

"No. Your face and forearms are quite tan and freckled from many hours in the sun, yet the areas on your nose and around your eyes are not as dark, as if protected from the sun by sunglasses and the white sun-protectant worn typically by those employed as lifeguards. Plus, your shoulders are quite muscular, in the manner of a committed swimmer."

She glanced down at one bare shoulder, then blinked at him and rested her palms on the bartop. "I guess I'm not the only one who can make keen observations."

"Perhaps not."

"Scottish accent?"

"Yes, like the guy on Star Trek, I know. Now, Jenn, I believe I see a bottle of Johnnie Walker *Blue Label* on your top shelf."

She glanced behind her. "That bottle's been up there unopened, collecting dust since I started here."

"I would like a double, please."

"At eleven-fifteen AM?"

"With one cube of ice."

"That's thirty-two bucks a shot."

"I understand."

She leaned closer to him from across the bar. "I have to say, Scotty, you've got that look."

"Look?"

"Faraway pain." She studied him. "I think I've seen you in here before."

"Could be."

She pointed at a table across the room. "You sat over there...with a woman from the yarn shop. Laurie, I think."

Bell sniffled. "Dinner with a friend."

Jennifer patted the bartop. "She's been in a few times with some of her coworkers. I've bought some yarn from her before." Her eyes shifted to the front of the bar. "You expecting company?"

Bell glanced toward the glare at the door as Jessie stepped

in. "It is inevitable."

Jennifer drummed the fingers of one hand on the bar. "She's pretty."

"You are correct about that, as well."

She backed up, turned, and reached high for a bottle on the top shelf. She set the bottle on the bar and wiped the smoky glass with a white cloth. After unscrewing the cap from the bottle, she tilted the lip to a cocktail glass. Then, with tongs, she took one ice cube from a silver bucket and dropped it into the glass. Satisfied with perfection, she nudged it across the mahogany to Bell. "On the house."

"That is not necessary."

She glanced at the door again. "I'll come back in a few."

She turned, stepped quickly behind the bar, and out of sight.

Bell raised the glass to his lips and took a small sip.

"Coffee and tea house," Jessie said from just beside him. "Teller's is not a coffee or a tea house."

"Excellent deduction, Warren." He took another sip.

Jessie pulled out a barstool and sat. "Scotch?"

"I must admit, I cannot recall drinking any better spirit. This Johnnie Walker distills a wonderful beverage."

She faced the bar and leaned her arms on it. "The barista across the street told me you headed over here."

"I expected as much."

"Do you, uh, want to talk about it?"

"It?"

"Yes, Bell. *It*. The reason or reasons you left the yarn shop, came here and ordered a double of expensive Scotch, if I saw that bottle clearly."

"I am not sure if a discussion about this topic would help anything at all, at this point."

"Well, give it a try anyway, and let's see what happens."

He glanced at her, and then back down at the bar. He shook his head. "It is totally without explanation, Warren."

"What?"

"The ease that I can openly share my feelings with *you*. As I explained before, typically I am not the most open person, emotionally speaking."

"So I've noticed."

"The good citizens of Edinburgh, most of my surgical students, and even familiar neighbors of mine in the countryside, all of their conclusions about me were entirely incorrect."

Jessie fidgeted on the barstool beside him.

He gazed at his hands. "You have already deduced exactly to what I refer."

She pursed her lips. "Holmes."

"Yes."

"I bet after those first stories, most everybody totally identified you with Holmes...and they expected you to look, behave, and essentially carry yourself as Holmes would."

"Please remember, Warren, Conan Doyle had just started selling his Holmes novels in 1892. Only two of them were published at the time of my fateful day in Dundee, but Holmes' popularity had already begun, almost instantaneously, after his short stories, such as *A Scandal in Bohemia,* which appeared in *The Strand* in 1891. Sales of *The Strand*, by the way, tripled practically overnight."

"And once your connection to Conan Doyle was revealed," Jessie said, "most people expected you to act like Holmes, since, after all—"

"To them, I *was* Holmes. We were considered one and the same. My helping the Yard from time to time did not help matters in that regard, even though I attempted to keep such assistance from public notice. But Warren, believe me, besides our common trait of using deductive reasoning in our lives, Holmes and I bear little to no resemblance of personality."

"I get it, Bell. I get it. Through no fault of your own, you found yourself expected to live up to the reputation of a heroic fictional character."

Bell took a sip of Johnnie Walker. "It began to suffocate me, Warren. I could hardly step inside any tavern, market, my church, or even appear before my students without someone asking about various mysteries of their own, or how deductive reasoning actually works." He raised the glass of Scotch. "But I am not a heroic and mysteriously flawed consulting detective. I think and reason in a particular manner, yes, but bringing real criminals to justice is not my forte." He squeezed his eyes closed.

"Bell?"

"They expected *infallibility*, Warren." He opened his eyes and stared blankly at the bartop. "They were thrilled they lived around a real-life fictional character, one who could solve the unsolvable in a matter of seconds, seemingly without expending much effort at all."

"Holmes is a tough act to follow."

Jennifer stepped to the bar and smiled at Jessie. "Get you something?"

"Do you have Willett?"

"We do."

"A double, please. Neat."

Bell looked at her oddly. "Willett?"

"A Kentucky bourbon. Local favorite."

"Are you not still on duty?"

She set her handbag on the bar. "I'm here, with you, and I will not allow you to drink alone."

Bell gave her a quiet smile.

Jennifer glanced at Jessie. "So, the Willett?"

"Yes."

"Coming up." Jennifer turned to the back-bar and the shelves of bottles.

Jessie scooted her barstool a few inches closer to Bell. "My dad was a cop, Bell, the local small-town sheriff. The people *loved* him. For almost twenty years." She turned her head from him.

"Warren?"

She took a breath and turned back. "He was a hero, Bell. Not fictional, but a *real* hero. There seemed to be another story every few months of my dad saving a kid who fell through the ice in a pond, or one time he ran into a burning house just to save a family cat. I was so proud to tell all my friends at school that the sheriff was my dad. It made me feel special, as if I were somehow a better person just because—"

"Willett. Neat." Jennifer placed a cocktail glass on the bar, glanced at Bell then stepped away.

Jessie gazed into his eyes. "He was *the reason* I became a cop, so maybe I could be just like him. I wanted that since I was old enough to reason it through." She examined her glass of Willett. "Lebanon PD sponsored me for the academy, and it took less than six months from when I started with them after graduation before I realized I had to leave. No matter what I did, Bell, no matter how well I performed my duties, I knew I could never live up to my dad's legend. And, of course, everyone expected me to act as he did, be just like him. But I knew almost instinctively, and right away, that I would never be the kind of hometown cop my dad was. Never. That person just wasn't me and would never be."

"You are saying your dad was a tough act to follow."

"You got it, Bell." She lifted the glass of Kentucky bourbon.

He lifted his glass, as well. "A toast to your father, Warren. May his memory ever live within your heart."

She touched her glass to Bell's. "It does, Bell. I think about him and mom each day of my life."

They both took a long swallow.

Bell smiled. "Warren, do you fully appreciate the irony with which we now find ourselves?"

She raised one eyebrow. "I think I do."

"Tell me."

"Our circumstances have now pushed you into becoming the consulting detective you never considered yourself to be."

"And due to a time-traveling dog, along with your sudden connection with me, you are also now presented with facing our difficult circumstances while unintentionally becoming a heroic law enforcement officer in the image of your own father."

Jessie felt her temples pulse with each heartbeat. She stared into Bell's sky-blue eyes. "Bell. Here's what we're going to do. Buster is running lead on, well, the murder of your friend at the yarn shop. I need to get back there at some point and check in with him, but before I leave here, you and I are going to finish our drinks and have lunch together."

"Unnecessary, Warren."

"I insist."

"All right, then. I find it difficult to argue with you."

"Good." She straightened, flexed her back, and stood from the bar-chair. "I need to go wash up. Order something for us.

Teller's is known for their wings." She chuckled. "I'd like to use deductive reasoning to determine if you even *like* wings, Bell, but I lack enough information." She flashed a smile at him and stepped away before Bell had a chance to answer.

Jennifer walked from the other end of the bar and stopped in front of Bell. "Sorry. I overheard some of that."

Bell gazed at her.

"And I've got to tell you something, Scotty. That woman is in love with you."

Bell downed the last of the Johnnie Walker. "Warren?"

"There's no question."

"Jenn—"

"It's in her *eyes*. Trust me."

"Does this come from your talent of keen observation?"

"No, Scotty. This is just me being a woman." She patted the top of his hand and stepped away.

***

The early afternoon sunlight struck Jessie as she stepped out onto the sidewalk. She squinted and raised her sunglasses to her face, angled to the corner of the square, and felt the tears building behind her eyes. She crossed at Edwards and quickened her pace. She needed to get back to the precinct. She needed some sanity back in her life. Now.

It was irresponsible and entirely unlike her to have abandoned the crime scene so quickly. Keaton knew something was up, but she had ignored him and walked away with barely a goodbye. Craziness. *She just left.*

And headed straight for Bell.

They had shared good whiskey, a plate of wings, and they actually laughed together a few times.

It was nice.

Jessie halted. She couldn't go back yet and face Keaton with any sense of composure. She needed a few more minutes to gather her thoughts and calm herself.

She abruptly turned toward the lush grass at the square's center. A few people sat either on the ground or on the scattered few benches. She found the last empty bench near a young couple who were sprawled on a blanket with their little Maltese terrier, and she collapsed down onto the broad strips of wood. She needed to clear her mind and think. She had to think...

Jessie's shoulders trembled as her mind spun in endless circles, making cognitive thought impossible.

A soft moan escaped her lips. The smiling faces of her mom and dad when they were happy and thriving floated in the air in front of her. She saw Doc's brown eyes and toothy smile, his three legs. She knew how his disappearance haunted her grandfather and greatly shortened his life.

If only she had the power to...

She leaned forward and caught her head in her hands as tears suddenly flooded from her eyes, through her fingers, and fell silently into the grass.

It's a weird fact that the worst sceptics of time travel are science fiction writers who tell the stories. **James Gleick**

Chapter 50: Lebanon, Ohio
Present Day

B ell pulled on his pajama bottoms, sat on the edge of the bed in Jessie Warren's spare room, and gently rested his over-sized book atop his knees.

Scooter jumped on the bed and stretched his body against Bell's leg.

He reached down and scratched Scooter's neck. "God bless America, Scooter. You are not permitted on the furniture."

Scooter yawned and settled in.

It had been a long and difficult day. Warren had retrieved him from Teller's in the last of the afternoon, and they had spent hours back at the precinct, along with Detective Keaton, discussing the murder of Laurie Markwell. Bell had remained silent for most of the conversation; there was little he could have said without revealing secrets better kept.

Bell smiled down at Scooter and opened his book of newspaper clippings. He flipped the pages and stopped at the photos of Elizabeth and Polly as he had done for years each night before he retired. He had collected the photos from studious research he'd conducted shortly after Hattie Brooks passed away. He stared at the photos, and the images unfalteringly stared back at him. His wife and daughter had been taken from his life for the past ten years, and yet his memories and these photos remained. Visions of his family with their life together in Edinburgh sometimes also visited him in vivid dreams, and when those images came to him, it was without question the best part of his day.

He placed the open book face-down atop the bedspread.

His wife and daughter had been gone from his life for a decade, but they had never really been far away. Bell smiled. That was a good thing.

Bell's nightly routine usually included reading for a short while. Immersing himself in a world of fictional characters generally allowed the chance to ease his mind from the troubles of the day, and tonight he had chosen a work by Stephen King, *Dr. Sleep,* which he had brought with him from home. He understood *Dr. Sleep* was the sequel to *The Shining*, and he had postponed reading this story since it raised strong emotions within him just to hold the volume in his hands and scan the author's name. Nevertheless, *The Shining* had been Hattie's favorite, and it was about time he read the sequel; Hattie would have favored it.

He adjusted his bed-pillow to allow for a better reclined position. The movement of the pillow revealed a folded sheet of yellow paper beneath. Bell stared at the paper for a moment, and then took its edge with two fingers. He studied the paper more closely; from outward appearances it was nothing more than a sheet of ordinary lined legal paper. He unfolded the paper and found it covered in script, written with dark blue ink.

He began to read:

Crazy, the Patsy Cline song goes. Crazy.

That's my life for these recent days. I'm not sure exactly why all this has happened, but what I know for certain is that everything turned upside-down for me the instant Doc appeared out of thin air amid a lightning strike behind my farmhouse, and later when I found Wallace Brewster sitting peacefully at Evangeline's Tea House. He was enjoying a lovely Sunday morning, having tea, reading newspapers, and not suspecting that Jessie Warren would storm into his life and toss it all spinning out of control.

As we grew to know each other, you were quick to spot the absolute grief which, as you put it, underscored all my days since my mom and dad were taken from this Earth. I think that's mostly how you described it. After you said that, I not only realized your observation to be true, but I felt instantly ridiculous for not understanding the impact of that reality before.

So, I've thought a lot, about how I've pulled back from or completely avoided nearly any close personal relationship I could have had for the past eighteen months, maybe as a way of eliminating the chance of any additional pain. I guess that was one of my ways of coping, as you noted, plus trying every way possible not to even think about it. Occasionally, especially on cold, lonely evenings I've considered how to deal with it by moving on and trying to start new relationships. I really have. But how is it even possible to cope with an ever-present grief while, at the same time, attempting to start along a new path, and to find new relationships? The whole idea makes no sense to me. I'm not sure it's even possible.

I don't really know.

What I do know is that I am a coward. Only a coward would put these thoughts in writing and sneak them under your pillow, rather than face the pressure of telling you face-to-face.

So, now that you understand the depth of my cowardice...

I love you, Bell.

I fell in love with you within minutes of our first meeting. I know that's not possible either, but haven't you and I been dealing with the seemingly impossible lately?

I know what I should do. I—

Three raps at the door startled him.

"Bell?" Jessie's voice was soft on the other side of the door. "Bell, are you awake?"

"I am. Yes."

"Can we come in?"

"We?"

"Doc is with me."

"Certainly." He glanced around for the top to his pajamas. Nothing. He gathered himself and just sat there.

The door whispered inward.

Jessie stepped barefoot into the room. She wore red plaid boxers and an oversized black University of Cincinnati jersey. Doc trotted in, jumped on the bed, and sprawled out behind Scooter.

"Am I disturbing you?" Her eyes glanced at the sheet of legal paper in his hands. "Oh."

Bell tilted his head toward the foot of the bed. "Please."

She moved to the bed and sat. Her feet dangled just above the area rug. Bell turned to her, the legal paper still in his hands. "Warren, I—"

"No. Before you say anything, I'm sorry."

"For what?"

"I don't know, Bell. Everything."

"You have nothing to be sorry for."

She glanced down at the yellow paper. "I was hoping you hadn't found it yet and maybe I could take it back before you had a chance to..." She shook her head. "And you know what? I also shouldn't have come in here to begin with."

She started to edge her legs off the bed.

He touched her elbow. "I'd like you to stay."

She stopped. "The letter was a terrible idea."

"Please stop apologizing. Tell me what's troubling you."

She eyed the paper in his hands. "You know that already."

"Do I?"

"Use those powers of deductive reasoning you're famous for. You had to know everything I was feeling even before you read my insane scribbling." She pointed at the letter.

"You're wrong about that, Warren."

She placed one hand on his forearm. "Please, Bell. Please. Just this one night could you call me *Jessie*? When you call me Warren it feels, I don't know, somehow cold."

"That is not my intention."

"Even so."

He raised an eyebrow at her. "*Jessie*, I certainly knew you were fond of me, but for the rest..."

She huffed. "You mean my body-language, eye contact and everything else didn't give it away?"

"Correctly reading a woman's thoughts is a rare talent." He smiled.

Jessie smiled back. "You must be right."

With one quick movement she shifted over, straddled him, and sat across his lap face to face, her hands on his shoulders. "If you could read a woman's thoughts, you would have known I was going to do this."

"Uh..."

"But you didn't."

"No."

"That's okay. Neither did I."

"Warren, *Jessie*—"

"Please be quiet and listen to me, Bell. I'm not the only one dealing with grief. Your wife and daughter have been out of your life for ten years, and you still haven't found a way to let them go." She gazed into his eyes. "Just like me, you haven't tried to move on either."

Bell was shaken. He also suddenly realized this was the closest he had physically been to a woman since... "I have considered this, Jessie. Quite often, in fact."

"Good. Then you should know I'm right."

"I do not doubt it."

She looked down and then back into his eyes. "Remember the theory we talked about, of how time might flow like a river?"

"I sense the fragrance of lavender."

"Don't change the subject, Bell."

"Joseph. Or Joe, if it is all the same to you."

She grinned. "Joe?"

"Yes."

"All right, Joe. And the river of time..?"

"I remember."

"Do you suppose the two of us have somehow been swept together along the same current, as though our meeting was far from accidental?"

Doc inched across the bedspread and rested his chin on Jessie's thigh. Jessie smiled, reached down and patted his head.

"I think this little guy loves me, Bell...*Joe*. And we just met a month ago." She blinked. "How about that?"

Bell raised his arms and placed his hands on Jessie's back. "Jessie, I—"

She put a finger against his lips. "Here's what I'd like to do, Joe."

"You have my attention."

"I might be legitimately crazy, but I am not crazy enough to rush into this, and maybe ruin, well, everything."

He noticed how the blue was darker toward the center of her eyes. "Your suggestion?"

She took a breath and let it out slowly. "Can we spend this

night together...just *hold* each other, to be close, for the real human contact? I don't know if that makes any sense, but damn it, Joe, I ache to rest the side of my face on your chest and feel your arms around me, cradling me, *cradling each other*, and remain silent together until at least an hour after the sun rises." She smiled. "Or maybe a little later."

A few tears started on Bell's eyelids.

"My God," Jessie said. "You're crying."

Bell moved one hand from behind Jessie and wiped his eyes. "You might find this difficult to believe, Jessie, but I find your suggestion as appealing as you do."

"No, Joe. I don't find that difficult to believe at all."

"Then it's settled." He glanced around. "Let me find a shirt."

She shook her head. "No, sir, if you don't mind. You're fine just as you are." She moved to the side and sat on the bed.

Bell turned and adjusted his pillow again then leaned back against it.

"So, we're really going to do this," Jessie said, halfway to herself.

Bell moved one arm out to his side. "I believe Einstein might agree with you, Jessie."

"About?"

"How the river of time might be sweeping the two of us inexorably together."

"You think?"

"And if Einstein were right, there might be absolutely nothing we can do about it."

Jessie's mind spun. "Einstein is one of history's smartest humans. So, who are either one of us to say he was wrong?"

Jessie felt the breath catch in her throat. She stared at Bell, her eyes lost focus and then closed as she felt herself lean forward, and then sink slowly down into his open and welcoming arms.

Lane Cohen

A seminar on time travel will be held two weeks ago. **Geoff Tibballs**

Chapter 51: Hyde Park, Ohio
Present Day

Detective A.J. *Buster* Keaton shuffled down the precinct hallway toward Jessie Warren's office. He lightly rapped the knuckles of one hand along the smudged paint of the wall as he angled slowly forward; his legs were a little numb. It was hard to figure exactly why his legs had apparently vanished from his body since his brain was spinning as if strapped inside a working centrifuge; he could focus on practically nothing.

He tilted his left wrist and glanced at the old Casio watch that had belonged to his dad who had worn the ancient digital device for as long as Keaton could remember. The Casio was one of his dad's familiar trademarks, and it comforted Keaton to stare at and study the battered watch even when he could have cared less about the time of day. Looking at the Casio usually centered him. But not today. Not now.

Jessie Warren, a woman he admired more than he cared to admit to himself, had been huddled in her office with *Cousin Wallace* for the past few hours this morning, since about 7:30. *Cousin Wallace.* Right. That man was no more Jessie's cousin than Sidney Rosenberg, the old guy who worked the register and owned The Echo Cafe around the corner. Something was being purposefully obscured about Brewster and his true relationship with Jessie, but sooner or later the truth about Wallace Brewster would float to the surface for all to see, just like how the skeletons of bodies tossed into the Ohio River by random Newport gangsters in the 20s inevitably found their way out of the water and back up into daylight.

Keaton had caught a glimpse of Jessie and Brewster a few

~236~

times that morning through the hallway window glass. They sat beside each other, staring at whatever they saw on Jessie's computer monitor. Neither of them looked very happy. But that was somehow fitting; at this moment, Keaton wasn't feeling very happy either.

***

Jessie was oddly calm on their drive to the precinct. Usually her mind was full of details of the day ahead while she also avoided the inevitable traffic problems. But today, her mind was occupied by something else.

They held each other until Jessie was awakened by the chirping of the many bird families who called the Warren place their home. She opened her eyes and realized she was in the same position as when she had fallen asleep; her head still rested against Bell's chest.

No. Joe's chest.

When she stepped out the bathroom, her hair completely tousled and her make-up nonexistent, he was sitting on the edge of the bed dressed in his khakis and a plain white shirt. He reached for his wire-rimmed glasses, placed them on his nose and around his ears, and smiled at her. Joe did. Joe smiled at her. He was handsome, calm, and still here.

She supposed that was a good sign.

They did not speak much on the drive to Hyde Park, and they had remained quiet since they sat down together at Jessie's desk and focused on the computer monitor. Their plan was to search for clues concerning Irene Lithgow's whereabouts, but they had yet to begin.

"I suppose one of us should say something," Jessie said. "I volunteer."

Bell shook his head. "No, Jessie. I will begin the conversation." He paused for a breath. "I need to address a few topics with you."

"Address a few topics? Sounds like I'm in a meeting with my accountant."

"I apologize."

"For what?"

"My personal conversations over the last decade have been

severely limited and my manner of speaking has become inartful. Truthfully, after Hattie Brooks passed from us, other than a few words to a waitress, waiter, a barkeep, or taxicab driver here and there, an occasional conversation with Laurie Markwell, I have spoken to practically no other person." He gazed into her blue eyes. "Other than long talks with Scooter, of course. And now...with you."

She smiled.

Bell focused on the time signature on the computer.

"What is it?" Jessie said.

"Fallon. Fallon Dalmore."

"What about her?"

"It is presently 8:30. I asked Dr. Dalmore to meet us here at 7:30."

"You did?"

"I asked her yesterday at the tea cafe."

"Fallon's reliable. She will turn up."

Bell collected his thoughts. "Jessie, I was never adept at expressing my innermost feelings, well, verbally."

She squinted at him. "And you would like to do that?"

"Yes. Yes, I would. Before Fallon arrives."

"Okay."

"It is difficult for me, perhaps for anyone, to open up emotionally, and risk—"

"Heartache?"

"Rejection, I suppose. Or a fear of committing emotionally to someone, and then—"

"Losing them?" She shook her head. "Sorry for finishing your sentences."

He chuckled. "We share similar thoughts."

"We do."

"Of course, Jessie, I spoke of this fear to you before. I am sorry to be repetitive."

Jessie sighed. "You can trust me, Bell. *Joe.* The last thing I would ever do is hurt you."

He took a breath. "I know. I do trust you."

"And I have no intention of leaving this world any time soon."

"I know that as well."

"Then..?"

He looked down at the floor and then back up, straight into Jessie's eyes. "You were right. It has been long enough. I need to let go of the past and move on with a life here."

Jessie felt her heart thump against the front of her chest. "I'm listening."

"No matter what becomes of Irene Lithgow's appearance in 2019, it is probable she was transported just as I was, that is, due to a natural phenomenon that we cannot conceivably duplicate. Because of that, even should we find and stop Irene and Brody MacKay from their murderous spree, their capture or elimination is not likely to reveal any method for me to return to 1892 Edinburgh."

"Probably right."

"And because of that..." He took a breath. "As I lay awake last night while we held each other, it occurred to me that perhaps... Perhaps you and I might spend more *personal* time together. In the future."

Tears started under Jessie's eyelids. "Personal time? In the future?" She chuckled.

"It was not my intention to be humorous."

She smiled at him. "I know that, Joe. That's what makes it funny."

He smiled back at her.

"Yes, Joe. I would like that. Spending *personal* time with you sounds right."

"Jessie, I am hesitant to reveal something else to you, but I must do so before you and I go any further along this path."

"I know. Something's wrong with you, physically. Is that it?"

"You could not help but to observe."

"You've been *shaky*, your cane, balance a little off, since the first morning we met."

"Unless we do find Irene, and unless she can somehow reveal a method for returning to the past, I am afraid the days I would have to spend nurturing a relationship with you might be, well, quite limited."

She stared at him and tried to make sense of what he was trying to say, when Keaton halted at Jessie's door, rapped twice, and pushed it inward.

"Hey."

Jessie was startled and looked up at him. "What's...up, Buster?"

"I've got an old man in the interview room."

Jessie squinted. "Who?"

"He had a military ID. An old one. He said he tracked someone here, someone who was *different*...as though the person *didn't quite belong*. That's how he put it." Keaton's eyes settled upon Bell.

Jessie scooted her chair back and stood. "Buster, did he tell you his name?"

"You might recognize it. *Albert Einstein. Dr.* Albert Einstein, he said."

Bell stood.

Jessie stopped breathing.

Keaton grinned. "Yep. That's right. Maybe it's time you two were straight with me."

Jessie glanced at Bell and moved toward the door. She stopped a few feet from Keaton. "Maybe you're right."

Keaton huffed. "I'll hold you to it. Now, let's go have a conversation with the good doctor."

***

Jessie edged ahead and led the way down the hall to the interview room. *Albert Einstein.* That made no sense. Who in the world would show up here and identify himself as Albert Einstein? Jessie shook her head as she neared the door. That made no sense at all.

But somehow, considering all the recent impossible events in her life, it might make all the sense in the world.

She peered into the room through the door's upper glass partition. An older man sat completely still on a metal chair. He stared straight ahead. His hands were folded and propped in front of him on the table. He appeared to be in his 60s, his hair silver-gray and cut short. A neatly trimmed moustache of matching color covered his upper lip. He wore a conservative charcoal suit, a white shirt, and a dark blue tie with angular light-blue stripes.

"Jesus," Jessie said.

"Told you," Keaton said.

Jessie pulled open the door and stepped inside. Bell and Keaton followed. Keaton pulled the door closed behind him. The click of the door latch echoed off the bare walls of the interview room.

Einstein eyed his visitors and smiled. "Ah."

He pushed himself to his feet, extended one hand toward Bell and cleared his throat. "I am Albert Einstein, Dr. Bell." His words were coated in a thick German accent.

Keaton said, "Who's Bell?"

Bell glanced at Jessie and moved closer to Einstein. He took the old man's hand. "I am please to make your acquaintance."

"Jesus," Jessie said again.

"I must say, Dr. Bell, from the two photographs of you I was able to find, you now appear a bit younger than I was expecting."

"Perhaps that is something *you* can fully explain to *us*, Doctor," Bell said.

Einstein furrowed his brows at him.

Keaton leaned forward. "Uh, guys?"

Jessie took another step toward the table and stopped. "I am Jessie, Dr. Einstein." She flashed a nervous smile and extended her hand. "Jessie Warren."

Einstein clasped her hand in his smooth fingers. "It is my pleasure, Miss."

She broke away from Einstein's gaze. "Oh, and you've already met my partner, Detective Keaton."

Keaton placed one elbow on the table, raised his hand and waved it once. "Whatever."

"We call him Buster."

Einstein grinned. His mustache pulled back from his cheeks. "*Buster* Keaton?"

"Yeah, sure," Keaton said.

"One of my favorite film funnymen," Einstein said. "He and Stan Laurel never fail to bring laughs to me."

They were silently astonished.

Einstein said, "Perhaps we should all sit."

Without taking their eyes from Einstein, Bell and Jessie found chairs and sat.

"I imagine you have many questions," Einstein said.

"One or two," Keaton said.

"Miss Warren," Einstein said, "I must say, it is refreshing to meet a *female* police officer."

"Oh?"

"Such a thing was practically unheard of 75 years ago."

"Things change with the passage of time, Dr. Einstein, but I guess I don't have to tell *you* that."

He jostled his mustache. "And time is a commodity we might have little to spare, as it has turned out. But before we face that problem, other questions may be answered by doing a search on your telephonic device."

She shrugged. "Search?"

Bell said, "He wants us to discover what history has to say about Albert Einstein."

Jessie pulled her phone from her jacket pocket. "Oh my God. What if history..?"

Keaton chuckled. "Is this where you two are going to be straight with me?"

"Detective Keaton should know," Bell said.

Jessie stared at her phone screen. "This...this can't be."

Einstein said, "I conducted a similar electronic search some days ago at a library in Oak Ridge, Tennessee. You will find the records of history state I expired of an abdominal aortic aneurysm on April 18, 1955."

Jessie set her phone on the table. "At Princeton Hospital."

"But if you are here now, that can't..." Keaton stood up, leaned forward, and pressed his palms on the table. "Now wait a second." He shifted his incredulous gaze to Jessie, Bell, and then back to Jessie. "Do you mean to tell me..?"

"Yes, Detective Keaton," Bell said, "from the facts as we know them, your undeniable suspicion is correct."

"Facts?" Keaton shouted at Bell. "What facts? I have no such undeniable suspicion. *You* conclude since the man here in the room with us *resembles* Albert Einstein, and has a fake German accent, he therefore must be the *real* Albert Einstein. Seriously?"

Einstein grumped. "My accent is not fake, Detective."

"The *fact* is, Mr. Brewster, or Dr. Bell, or whoever, the only significant *facts* I can consider are the sentences about Albert Einstein that have filled the pages of our history books for the last 90 years."

Einstein nodded. "I believe I can offer some additional information which might aid in your analysis. And these particular facts would not, I presume, appear in your historical narratives."

Jessie took a breath. "We would like to hear them."

Einstein smiled at her. "I shall attempt to be brief."

Jessie, Bell and Keaton stared at Einstein as he reached down to the floor beside him and hefted a scratched leather valise onto the table.

...depending upon breakthroughs, technology, and funding,
I believe that human time travel could happen in this century.
Douglas Adams

Chapter 52: Oak Ridge, Tennessee
June, 1944

Rudolph Avram Skurow had heard rumors about the famous Jewish scientist from Germany living in Oak Ridge, but he had never seen the man until today when he walked into his shop on Maple, right in the center of Oak Ridge's small downtown business district.

Skurow was not accustomed to meeting anyone famous, and the unexpected appearance of *Albert Einstein* in *Skurow's Stamp and Coin* set Skurow's nerves on edge. In fact, these days *any* stranger who approached his door would instantly raise his worst suspicions, but this was not a jackbooted thug dressed in black. This was *Albert Einstein*. What could the most intelligent man in the world *possibly want* inside his humble shop?

"Mr. Skurow?" Einstein smiled from across the glass case filled with displays of gleaming coins and rare stamps.

Skurow extended his twisted fingers across the counter. "If you are who I believe you are," Skurow said in a thick Polish accent, "it is indeed an honor, sir."

Einstein took his hand. "When I consider your recent history, sir, as it has been related to me, the honor is truly mine."

Skurow released Einstein's hand. "Please. I prefer *Rudy*."

Einstein nodded. "Certainly."

"Dr. Einstein, I believe our one true God assisted my young son Moses and me from the shadows each second we scraped the dirt away from under that barricade." He took a breath. "I wish I could say my sister and her boys were as fortunate that day."

A Matter of Time

Einstein examined the glittering coins. "I appreciate your feelings, Rudy. I was lucky myself, to have left before..."

Skurow shook his head. "By the time many of us realized what was to happen, it was far too late. If only we could have spied into our own futures back then, Dr. Einstein. How much easier life might have been, for many."

Einstein gazed at Skurow to judge his age. His body was that of a man of perhaps 50, but his eyes were a hundred years old. "Perhaps I should not have raised the subject."

"No, no. Perfectly fine. Perfectly fine. Please, please, sit." He gestured to a wooden chair with a mottled cloth seat. "How may I assist you?"

A boy of perhaps six years old appeared from behind the counter and leaned against Skurow. The older man placed one arm on the boy's shoulder. "This is my son, Dr. Einstein."

"How do you do, young man?"

The boy did not react.

"Dr. Einstein, if you would permit, I have a working camera in the back. Would you allow a photo of you, with my boy. I want him to look at the image years from now and remember how he met a truly great man. It might be the one and only time in his life."

"Certainly, Rudy. Certainly. I would be proud to pose for such a photograph."

The boy turned his eyes from Einstein and pressed his face into the sleeve of Skurow's wrinkled shirt.

Einstein sat up straight. "When we complete the photo, we will have business to discuss." He reached into the inside breast pocket of his gray jacket, pulled out folded green cash at least three inches thick.

Skurow squinted at the cash, balanced one elbow against a metal cabinet, and waited for Einstein to begin speaking.

***

Marley's Barber Shop stood on the corner of Main and Oak for the last 30 years, and it would probably remain there for as long as Toby Marley could hold his clippers steady enough to cut a man's hair. And right at this moment his hands needed to be as steady as they could possibly be as he watched the long, silver clumps tumble off the old man's shoulders and onto the well-worn wooden floor of his barber shop.

Marley remembered about two years ago a *general* sat in this very chair, a *general* with just wisps of hair, but with more stars on his shoulders than those that filled the night sky. Marley didn't read the daily papers much; his nephew Frankie had been killed somewhere in the Pacific a year before, and even thinking about the war depressed him. He found no joy in reading story after story about how many lives continued to be lost. But Marley's customers talked in the shop, and Toby realized how important this general was to winning the war.

Marley recognized *the general* back then. It was impossible not to. They said Dwight Eisenhower, or *Ike* as the radio news reporters called him, might be in charge of the whole war, and there he was, right in the middle of Oak Ridge.

In all his years, he had never cut the hair of, or even heard of anybody named *Dwight*. But times were different. Not only was tiny Oak Ridge, Tennessee, suddenly the center of hundreds of military personnel, with trucks and planes that never stopped roaring by, but now *Albert Einstein* was in his barber chair having most of his moustache and well-known wild silver hair trimmed short.

***

Einstein admired the clean lines of the new white church as he took a few last steps through the light gravel. He gripped his bulky valise close to his chest and he eased down onto a plain bench beside a children's play area. He took a deep breath and gazed across the thick green lawn at the sprawling military complex below. It was relatively quiet down there at 5:30am, but in a short while the soldiers would resume their marching about, patrolling the entire perimeter and keeping a close eye open for anything or anyone who might threaten the security of *The Project*.

He turned to one side and set his battered valise on the seat of the bench. As he stared at the familiar carrying-case, a smile crossed his lips. He pictured the moment, ages ago, when a room packed with Princeton students presented him with this gift of appreciation. Their grateful applause when he opened the package still echoed somewhere in the back of his brain.

He reached inside the valise with both hands until the tips of his fingers touched the cold metal of the compact box. His smile vanished. He hefted the heavy object out into the thick morning air, then set his prototype on the wood slats beside him and stared at the numbers that glowed from the face of the machine.

2019.

Last evening when he ran the calculations of the tracking mechanism, the year 2019 appeared, just as it did now; *four* distinct disturbances within the quantum field. There could be no mistake; the thief, or thieves somehow stole the primary device from Oppenheimer's safe and adjusted the controls to propel a traveler forward in time, forward all the way to 2019. Why Irene Lithgow and her companion Brody MacKay would choose that year, or why they would not desire to return to their familiar surroundings of 1892 was a mystery, at least for the moment. One of the other disturbances was almost certainly caused by Dr. Joseph Bell. The fourth was a complete mystery to him.

Einstein focused his eyes on the metal bracings of the children's swings. He told Fermi and Oppenheimer he had no choice but to travel forward, retrieve the device, and return to 1944, a moment after he originally left. They stared at him but remained silent; they knew he was right. Einstein's machine must be recovered from anyone who might attempt to affect the flow of time in a manner that may prove destructive.

Einstein hoped the church and the adjoining play area remained unchanged in 2019. If not, his plan might be defeated even before it began. But, there was no way to know.

The aging physicist touched the first dial on the machine and nudged it forward. The numbers on the face of the mechanism spun and flashed until they abruptly halted: July 24, 2019, 8am.

Einstein took the machine with both hands and stood. He stepped a few yards to the swings, wrapped one arm around one of the metal braces, and pressed his thumb against a single toggle switch. A roar descended from the heavens and a million stars filled his eyes as Einstein's hand and arm held onto the swing bracing with all the strength he had left.

Today, we know that time travel need not be confined to myth, science fiction, Hollywood movies, or even speculation by theoretical physicists. Time travel is possible. **Martin Ringbauer**

Chapter 53: Oak Ridge, Tennessee
July, 2019

The thick moist air instantly attacked his nose and the back of his throat, as had happened nearly each day since he relocated to Tennessee, for what seemed like ages ago.

He cracked open his eyes to a sharp morning sun that glinted through low-hanging clouds. After releasing his one-handed grip on the swing bracing, he gathered his wits and glanced around.

The white church was right there, *still there*, just as he had seen it as he pushed the quantum toggle switch forward just a few seconds ago. And the children's swings beside him were also there, but appeared painted a new shade of white. The surrounding lawns were freshly trimmed.

He blinked. The gravel parking areas had been paved, covered in a flat, black surface. And instead of the completely empty parking areas when he had arrived at the church early this morning, metal vehicles of many shapes and sizes were lined in neat rows, filling almost all the spaces marked by painted lines.

He let out a long breath and grinned.

It worked.

His prototype device had worked, and his theory about utilizing a spatial anchor had also been accurate; the metal bracing of the children's swings had proven to be effectual. The plutonian energies had indeed propelled him through time, but not, apparently, to a different geographic locality. He was still in Oak Ridge, right at the spot from where his time-traveling journey began.

Einstein gripped his heavy valise with both hands, and willed his legs to inch forward, toward the church. His head pounded with an insistent ferocity as he struggled to focus. He titled his eyes upward and took note of the sun's position in the sky. It was mid-morning, perhaps, and from the gathering of motorized vehicles in the parking areas to the sides of the church, he concluded it must be Sunday morning. It would be a rare event for a church to be so well attended on a morning other than Sunday.

He continued to walk forward in his new suit, and angled toward the corner of two main streets that lined the front of the church. Downtown Oak Ridge would be a short walk from there. If his luck held out, *Skurow's Stamp and Coin* would still be in business in 2019, but there was certainly no guaranty that would be true. If it was not still here, then he would attempt an alternate plan.

He managed to slightly quicken his pace and tried to ignore the throbbing pain that pressed against the center of his forehead. His mission remained, and he could not fail. The idea of what might occur should one of his machines be used for evil intent was too horrendous to contemplate.

He didn't bother to wipe the sweat that already trickled through his newly trimmed hair and down the sides of his face as he stepped steadily toward where he hoped the downtown library existed.

***

He stopped on the street and stared at the old storefront then let out a long breath and struggled to shift his valise to his other arm.

The *Skurow's* sign was battered from changing weather and just plain age, but *Skurow's Stamp and Coin* shop remained, nearly the same as when he had last observed the store many years before.

It was somehow comforting to know that some things from his past had not changed to any great degree despite the nearly inevitable effects of the passage of time.

He pulled open the metal screen door and stepped into a

shadowed entryway. Squinting, he could spot no customers. A man of perhaps eighty years was using a white cloth to polish the glass top of a display case.

"Hello," the man behind the counter said without looking up.

Einstein remained still. "Good morning, sir."

"Pardon me, but I just opened my shop. I seem to be opening later and later these days." He glanced at his wristwatch. "Five past 11:00. I have not even switched on the music from my CD player. I usually find it much too quiet in here, alone with my own thoughts. The silence can drive a person nearly crazy sometimes."

"I understand."

"Well then, Sinatra? Big Band?"

"Pardon me?"

"Do you care for Big Band?"

"That would be fine."

"Good. That is the last CD I inserted into the player, and I have not been able to locate the rest of my collection since then. Must have moved them to a drawer somewhere."

The man turned and reached to the device behind him. He touched a button, and *In the Mood* instantly piped into the air.

"There we go." The man shifted his eyes to Einstein. "My father adored Big Band music, and he played their records nearly all the time." He closed his eyes and opened them. "Excuse me, sir. I am Moses Skurow. Do you have something to sell inside that classic valise you carry?"

Einstein took a few steps forward and halted at the edge of a sunbeam that streamed in through the storefront windows. He scanned several framed photos on the wall behind the counter. "Moses Skurow. Of course. Your father was Rudolph, uh, *Rudy* if I recall."

Skurow studied Einstein more closely, and any trace of a smile vanished. "God in heaven." He paled, stumbled back a few steps, and sat on a hard wooden chair.

Einstein moved to him. "Are you unwell, Mr. Skurow?"

Moses Skurow glanced up and behind him at the framed black-and-white photos mounted on the wall.

"It is you." Skurow squinted hard.

"You are correct, sir."

"Pardon, please pardon me." Skurow pushed up out of the chair and took two careful steps to a cluttered desk. He found a teacup and raised it to his lips. He sipped from the cup as he gazed at Einstein. "You may not believe this, sir. I certainly do not expect that you would. But even though I may not remember many details of my early childhood, I most certainly do still remember that day." He gestured up and behind him at one of the photos on the wall.

Einstein focused on the photo. "I recall."

Skurow pulled a wooden stool to the glass case and sat on it. "I assume if you explain how this came to be, I probably would not really understand." He took his teacup with trembling fingers and set it back down.

"You have lived a long life, Mr. Skurow, and have already seen many wonders from today, which people from fifty years ago would have no doubt found astonishing."

Moses Skurow blinked several times. "Well, then, please tell me what brings you to honor this shop again, Dr. Einstein."

"Gold coins."

"Gold..?"

"Yes. I would like to exchange a few gold coins for local currency."

Skurow raised his brows inquisitively. "Please allow me to see these coins."

Einstein reached inside his jacket breast pocket. He then placed five gleaming coins on the glass.

Skurow inspected the coins. "These are quite valuable, Dr. Einstein, above the value of the metal alone."

Einstein grinned. "I concluded as much. Gold has retained its value throughout recorded history."

Skurow took a magnifying glass with a heavy brass handle and placed the lens over the coins. "1943. These coins are from 1943 and 1944."

"I am aware."

"I have recently purchased a number of silver coins, from those same years, and earlier."

"Oh?"

Skurow placed the lens down on the countertop. "Dr.

Einstein, is it possible this is not the first time these fine gold coins have graced this shop?"

"I have recently accepted the fact that most things are possible."

"I see." He cleared his throat. "Allow me to consult a few books I have in the back. Then, I shall return, and I look forward to hearing that explanation you promised."

"That sounds fine, sir."

Skurow eased up from the stool. He took another look at Einstein. With *In the Mood* still resonating in the air, Skurow shuffled behind the counter, smiled over his shoulder, and pushed open the door.

Time is precious – spend it wisely. **Anonymous**

Chapter 54: Oak Ridge, Tennessee
June, 1944

The morning sunlight beamed into the house through the window and glinted across the silver coins on the kitchen table.

Every so often Ebb took the three old cigar boxes full of coins from the hallway closet, removed his treasures from inside, stacked the coins in neat rows, and gazed at them for an hour or so. He would picture his pa's smiling face back in Macon when he gave Ebb another silver U.S. dollar. Each Christmas morning, Easter Sunday, and on Ebb's birthday, his pa would reach into a shirt pocket, pull out another big coin, and place it into Ebb's waiting hands.

His pa was always good about saving a little extra from his pay each week, for something special now and then, and to keep some money in the house in case of any emergencies. His pa didn't trust the banks anyhow; the war between the North and the South may have been over for more than 60 years, but things had been slow to change in every place he could see.

Not once did Ebb ever think of spending the special gifts from his pa, even when the money ran short from time to time. Keeping the coins and looking at them now and then brought pictures of his close family back to his mind, and those memories might have been the happiest times of his life. He smiled. Ida would understand. *He had to do this*, and if it worked, Ida would be overjoyed when he returned home. But just in case something happened to him, he knew Ida could barely pay the bills if he was gone for too long.

He took the pencil into his calloused hand and began to write on the small sheet of white paper.

When we see the shadow on our images, are we seeing the time 11 minutes ago on Mars? Or are we seeing the time as observed from Earth now? It's like time travel problems in science fiction. When is now; when was then? **Bill Nye**

Chapter 55: Lebanon, Ohio
Present Day

B rody MacKay sat in the mechanical carriage with his hands gripped to a black wheel. He had always been good with mechanical contraptions, and it hadn't really taken that long to master driving the massive wheeled vehicle that Irene had managed to acquire from that poor fellow she met in that tavern. Still, he drove slow and careful, since there was plenty he still did not know about driving *anything* in this time and place.

He glanced to his right; Irene Lithgow sat beside him, as peacefully as if she were sitting in a church pew on Sunday morning. Her hands were folded on her lap, her thumbs rubbing against her palms, over and over. Even looking like a peaceful parishioner, and after all their months together, the very sight of this *Hellspawn* from Dundee still froze him to the bone.

"Please remain here, Brody," Irene said, breaking the silence.

"Yeah, look. I don't mind sitting out here waiting for you again like always, but can you tell me, I mean, how long will—"

"I know." She abruptly turned toward him. "Soon, Brody. Soon."

"You promised before."

"This is different. I am here just to visit."

"Yeah?"

She blinked at him. "A peaceful conversation will be all that happens."

"Is this about that girl in the tunnel?"

"Just conversation today, Brody. Do not fret."

"I told you I wasn't going to be part of these things any more. They ain't right, since the beginning. And *I told you*, about my ma and pa, what I owe to them both. You said you understood."

She let out a long breath. "Yes. I did say that, Brody. I remember. This visit today should be our final task before we return."

He frowned. "I don't want to wait much longer."

Irene stared at him. "I believe I am right, Brody, when I tell you that when we go back, we will arrive mere minutes after we were swept out of 1892 in the first place. For us, and for everyone in Dundee, it will be as though we never left."

MacKay started to say something but stopped before he uttered a word.

Irene opened the door of the black Lincoln and stepped out onto the dirt driveway of the old farmhouse.

The properties of quantum particles are fuzzy or uncertain to begin with. This gives them enough wiggle room to avoid inconsistent time travel situations. Our study provides insights into where and how nature might behave differently from what our theories predict. **Tim Ralph**

Chapter 56: Hyde Park, Ohio
Present Day

K eaton stared across the long table and wondered if he had never actually awakened this morning from a weird dream.

For the last few moments, as the man who called himself Albert Einstein spun the most far-fetched tale of time travel and, *Lord help him*, a 1944 *secret plan* to sabotage the Manhattan Project, Keaton turned to one side and ran a search on his phone. When the Google results appeared, Keaton felt what little breath he had left stick at the back of his throat. "Sherlock Holmes," he mumbled. "*Sherlock Holmes.*"

Einstein stopped speaking.

Bell shifted his gaze to Keaton. "Pardon?"

Keaton shook his head. "Yeah. It makes sense. *It totally makes sense.*"

"Buster?" Jessie said.

"No, Jessie. *I get it.* I do."

"What?"

Keaton smiled and leaned his elbows forward on the table. "When I was a kid, my dad took me to the Rossville theatre downtown on Main. Remember that place? It's been torn down now for years, but back then, on Saturday mornings they showed really cheezy sci-fi films for $1.50. If you watched those movies now, you would think them awfully bad, but not me, not then. Dad bought the two of us SnoCaps, and we had the best time.

You know? Dad and son together, just being pals." He chuckled. "Mom didn't like it. She thought those movies were too grown up for me, and that I would have nightmares."

"Was she right?" Jessie asked.

"I had my share of sleepless nights, afraid some creature might come up from the basement, or walk through my walls, and get me while I was defenseless and alone."

A few tears clung to his eyelids. "Dad's favorites were the movies about time travel. When we walked home together after those, he always asked me what I would do if I could travel through time, and maybe change history."

Jessie nodded at him. "We had already decided to tell you, Buster."

"Tell me?"

"Everything."

Keaton nodded. "Let *me* tell *you*."

Jessie shrugged. "Whatever you want."

Keaton stood and faced them. "Mr. Brewster, here, or should I say *Dr. Joseph Bell*, has been somehow transported from 1892, and probably from Edinburgh, Scotland, although God knows how he accomplished that."

Einstein cleared his throat. "You are correct, my boy. Of that I am certain."

Bell gazed at Einstein.

"And I suppose since Dr. Bell's time-travel trip actually happened," Keaton continued, "then I cannot eliminate the possibility that this other gentleman sitting here with us, is truthfully Albert Einstein, as he claims."

"I do not *claim* it," Einstein said. "I *am* Einstein, as certain as the moon will rise and fill the heavens this evening."

Keaton eased down onto his chair. "Would someone then care to explain to me how you, Dr. Bell, and you, Dr. Einstein, came to be sitting across from us in 2019 Hyde Park, Ohio, this fine morning? And to take things one step further, exactly *why* are you both here?"

"I will." Jessie glanced at Bell.

He gave her a go-ahead nod.

"As far as Joe, uh, *Dr. Bell* is concerned, he was propelled from 1892 Dundee, Scotland, into his future by a tornado that ripped an opening in the time-space continuum. It was, in other words, *a force of nature*, unexpected and unplanned."

"Yes." Bell stared directly into Jessie's eyes. "A force of nature, indeed."

Keaton watched Bell and Jessie gaze at each other. "Yeah. Got it." He shifted his gaze to Einstein. "And you, sir?"

Einstein took a long breath and gripped the heavy metal object within his valise. He pulled out the box and placed it in front of him on the table. "Since my arrival in this time less than one week ago, I have studied the historical accounts of..."

Jessie edged closer to Einstein and placed her hand upon his forearm jacket sleeve. "You are among friends here."

He cleared his throat. "Hiroshima."

"Oh." Jessie lifted her hand from Einstein's sleeve.

"And Nagasaki," Einstein added, his voice ragged. "Thousands upon *thousands*. Incinerated." He stared across the room.

Keaton studied the old man in the new gray suit and new short haircut. "Those explosions essentially ended what was turning out to be an endless war with Japan, Dr. Einstein. Hundreds of thousands had already been killed one way or another. They say those two bombings saved the lives of countless soldiers."

Einstein raised his eyes. "It is one thing to face an armed enemy on the battlefield, sir. It is a far different matter to murder helpless civilians, women and children, instantly burned alive." He squeezed his eyes shut, and then opened them and focused on Bell. "But my journey here, and the historical records of this time, reveal something else entirely."

Jessie balanced her elbows on the table and leaned forward. Albert Einstein. It was incredible. She was sitting right here in the precinct, listening to *Albert Einstein* lecture about time-travel. Unbelievable.

"The theories of different time streams and alternative realities appear to be proven facts," Einstein said. "Since your recorded history, Detective Keaton, remains unchanged since I appeared here, since according to your records I passed from this life more than 60 years ago, and yet I am *not* dead, but instead am sitting here now, very much alive. My arrival in 2019 must have created another *different* time stream, an alternate or parallel universe, as it were."

Bell said, "Of course."

"And it follows, therefore," Einstein went on, "that no matter what I do here in this time, the history from my own past reality will not be altered in any way."

Bell studied the rectangular metal object on the table. "Dr. Einstein, you devised a time-travel mechanism."

Einstein acknowledged that with a smile.

"For the purpose of...what?"

"The Manhattan Project had to be *halted* so the bomb would never come to be."

Jessie's face turned pallid. "Why? The war would have gone on forever."

"*We* thought...Enrico, Robert and I...if we could prevent the atomic explosion, then the three of us would not be counted among the most monstrous murders in history."

Keaton said, "You mean *Fermi* and *Oppenheimer*?"

"Yes."

Bell considered. "You believed you could prevent the massive explosions by *traveling to the past*?"

Einstein remained still. "To stop the project in its infancy, but before we could launch our plot, the *unthinkable* happened."

"What was that?" Keaton asked.

Einstein settled his eyes on Keaton. "The fact that instead of traveling into my past, I am sitting here now, more than six decades into the future and following four separate time-stream trails that should reveal the answer to your question."

"Four?"

"Yes. Dr. Bell is one, of course, and two from 1944."

"And the fourth?" Jessie asked.

"Doc," Bell said.

"Doc?" Einstein said.

"A dog," Jessie said. "Doc was brought here via a lightning strike."

"Ah," Einstein said. "That certainly provides the answer to a question I had."

Bell's eyes suddenly widened. He stood. "Good God. This metal box is *not the only device* you constructed. Am I correct?"

Einstein tapped the fingers of one hand on the metal surface of the box. "This mechanism here was my prototype. The actual device Dr. Fermi was to use to travel into our past time was stolen from our safe."

Bell paced. "Fermi planned to travel into your past to stop the project, but how would he do that, Dr. Einstein?"

Einstein shifted his position and leaned his elbows on the table. "Dr. Fermi was to attempt to convince Robert, Dr. Oppenheimer, to abandon the project before it had a chance for eventual completion."

"Convince him, how?" Jessie asked.

Einstein shook his head. "The details of our scheme do not matter now. Once we discovered that Pauline had been taken from us—"

"Pauline?" Keaton asked.

Einstein sniffed. "My name for the second device...my mother's name."

Jessie gestured at the metal box on the table. "And this device?"

"Hermann. The prototype is named after my father."

Bell's eyes suddenly widened. He stopped breathing.

"Bell, Joe, what is it?" Jessie said.

Jessie, Einstein and Keaton stared at him.

Bell took a breath. "Dr. Einstein, you purposely traveled forward to 2019 in order to retrieve Pauline."

Einstein nodded.

"Well, then, I've got two questions," Keaton said.

Einstein focused on Keaton.

"Am I correct that your prototype time machine must somehow have the capability to *track* your time traveling thief?"

"Quantum particles leave a distinct trail," Einstein said. "The principles first advanced by Hans Geiger led to a quite effective device capable of detecting types of radiation. I modified that technique and incorporated a method of detecting quantum particles into Pauline and Hermann, in case tracking time-travelers, or their machines was somehow needed."

"And so," Keaton continued, "you came here, to 2019 Cincinnati, not to track Dr. Bell. You were chasing after the person or persons who stole *the other time machine* from your

Oak Ridge facility."

Einstein stared at him. "The machine did detect the remnants of the quantum particles disturbed by Dr. Bell. That is why I am sitting here in this room with you now. But you are correct. My mission here was to find Pauline." He took a breath. "And your second question?"

"Who stole the second time machine? Who are you chasing?"

Bell stood and locked eyes with Jessie. "I believe I can answer that question."

Jessie stood and faced Bell. "God no."

Bell nodded at her, as the horrendous realization suddenly washed over both of them.

Looking, backward, we recall our ancestry. Looking forward, we confront our destiny. Looking backward, we reflect on our origins. Looking forward, we choose our path. Remembering that we are a tree of life, not letting go, holding on, and holding to, we walk into an unknown, beckoning future, with our past beside us . **Harold Schulweis**

Chapter 57: Lebanon, Ohio
Present Day

The small black-and-white dog settled immediately across Irene's lap as if they were old friends. She gazed down at the mutt and stroked the top of his head with the tips of her fingers. The dog seemed contented and looked up at her. Irene smiled.

Her family never had a dog when she was growing up. Most of the other children with whom she was acquainted back then did have pets of one kind or another, usually a dog or a cat, sometimes more than one. Irene remembered being jealous of those children, and how special they must have been to deserve having four-legged friends to accompany them through their undoubtedly rigid and lonely lives.

She read the name inscribed on the dog's collar tag: *Doc*. She smiled again. Doc was a cute name for a dog. She wondered how Doc had lost his left rear leg. Perhaps he was attacked by a wolf, or maybe his leg had been caught in a hunter's trap. Whatever happened to him, Doc did not seem to be hobbled at all by the missing limb. Once she freed him and his small and scruffy companion from the fenced enclosure outside the rear of the house, they both had happily followed by her side as she walked around to the front porch. Then without difficulty at all, Doc jumped up into her lap as soon as she sat in the rocker and called to him.

A Matter of Time

What a *good, good* doggie.

***

MacKay relaxed back into the comfortable seat, closed his eyes, and sighed once at the serenity of the invisible orchestra. The sounds came from everywhere, all at once. He didn't know the name of this music or who wrote it, but he did know how wonderful listening to music could be in the year 2019. So far, and especially compared to everything else he had experienced, when he was left alone in this vehicle with the music surrounding him, it was by far the most enjoyable part of any day.

He pushed another switch, and the vehicle windows magically disappeared. A soft breeze drifted inside and touched his cheeks and bare forearms. MacKay gazed outside the vehicle. Pastureland and fields of crops stretched in every direction. It reminded him of home, the house and big barn where his ma and pa still lived, barely holding on.

The last few years had been tough for his family. Since his brothers had moved away, one to Dublin and one to London, and Pa was stricken with the consumption, the big man struggled to even hold the reins of his horses anymore, and he could barely take a pain-free breath. Their fields were left halfway unplowed, sparsely seeded, and little by little his boyhood home was slipping through his family's fingers.

He stared out the front glass. He had accepted the truth that the sudden, fierce wind had somehow tossed both him and Irene *through time itself*, into the year 1944, and also somehow flew them across the Atlantic Ocean all the way to America. It was beyond their control, a pure act of Mother Nature, like a blizzard or flood. But now for the moment he was somewhat safe in the year 2019, and at least had some choices he could make. For reasons unclear to himself, he had decided to believe Irene Lithgow's promise to return him back to his family in 1892 Scotland, in exchange for his help. He shook his head and squeezed his eyes shut. How in holy *Hell* could he have put his trust in Irene Lithgow, the accursed witch who threatened to torture and kill him not so very long ago?

...When he opened his eyes, he still tightly gripped the metal pole that supported the children's swings, as Irene Lithgow had instructed him to do.

He gingerly uncurled his fingers and tried to blink away the fierce pounding at the center of his forehead. Christ, that was painful.

He shifted his eyes all around. Irene Lithgow was beside him just as she had stood a few moments ago. She rubbed her temples with fingers from both hands. Her breathing puffed small clouds of mist into the air; somehow, it must have changed from summer to winter, and in just seconds.

He spotted the church off to one side; it was still there, but certainly had been freshly painted a more brilliant white than he had seen shortly before. The metal swing poles had also been painted a matching white instead of a dull gray.

"It worked." Irene chuckled.

MacKay inhaled a breath. "Yeah?"

Irene took a few steps through the crunchy sand around the swings then grabbed one of MacKay's hands. "Brody..."

"This ain't Dundee, Irene. It ain't, and there's no fooling me about that. We are supposed to be—"

"Brody, listen. There's something we must do, something we have to do before we travel back to Scotland."

MacKay pushed her hand away. "Bloody Hell with that."

"It concerns your friend Dr. Bell."

He squinted at her. "What about him?"

"He also traveled through time, Brody, just as we have."

He looked from side to side. "This place is the same, but...different."

"We are now further in our future than even before."

"And the seasons changed."

"We simply arrived here in a different month."

He stared at her. "Dr. Bell has something to do with all this?"

"He is here, Brody, somewhere in 2019."

Brody gasped. "2019? Holy Christ, you mean to say—"

"It does not matter why or how. What only matters is that we have to find him."

He wrapped his arms around his middle for the warmth. "Dr. Bell was always decent to me and all."

Irene faced MacKay. "It will be fine, Brody. Fine. With your assistance, we will locate Dr. Joseph Bell the best way I can conceive to do so. And after, we will use the mechanism from Dr. Einstein to take one more trip, through time itself, back to Dundee. And you will then be reunited with your family."

MacKay took a breath and tried to determine if the woman beside him was being truthful...or possibly just insane. But at this point, it made little difference; she had the time mechanism and knew its workings. He certainly could overpower her at almost any moment, but without the knowledge of the function of the magical device, he was at her mercy if he ever had any realistic hope of returning home.

MacKay nodded at her. "Tell me what we're going to do."

***

MacKay blinked. He was not going to sit here and let Irene Lithgow lie to him, right to his face, ever again. He needed to take control of his own life, and the time to do that was now.

He pressed a button under the dashboard, pushed open the car door, stepped outside then hurried around to the back of the car. The trunk lid was open, exposing the contents inside. He spotted a black-handled knife with a black sheath covering its blade. He gripped the knife, slipped it through the belt around his trousers to his right side, adjuster his light jacket, and pushed the trunk lid closed.

Time, like an ever-rolling stream, Bears all its sons away; they fly forgotten as a dream dies at the opening day. **Isaac Watts**

Chapter 58: Lebanon, Ohio
Present Day

J essie guided her Wrangler onto the I-75 off-ramp and slowed to the stop sign. She glanced in her rearview mirror and spotted the Cincinnati cruiser with Buster at the wheel. She grinned. Buster had insisted on taking Albert Einstein as his passenger on their way to Lebanon. She could not possibly imagine the conversation between those two on the forty-minute drive from the precinct, and she chuckled to herself at the thought of its awkwardness.

After Einstein had finished speaking, they had all stared at each other around the table in the interview room. After a few silent moments, they decided nearly all at once it would be best to leave. Jessie suggested they gather at her farm, since it certainly would be better for more intensive discussions. They would have privacy and be free from the inevitable distractions typical of a police station; they would need to focus their full mental energies on Einstein's time-traveling box, the best use for it, and how to discover the whereabouts of Irene Lithgow who undoubtedly possessed Einstein's second device.

They stood. In less than two minutes Bell sat beside Jessie in her Jeep, and Einstein carefully eased into the cruiser. The drivers started their engines, shifted into gear, and rolled out onto the quiet Hyde Park street.

***

Irene grinned at the small brown-and-white mutt as he hopped up onto the seat of the rocker beside her. The dog sat at attention, staring at Doc who was curled up in Irene's lap, perhaps wondering about whatever dogs might wonder. She had not taken the time to read the name on the tag that hung from the dog's collar, but she imagined *Buddy* to be a good name for the little canine. Buddy and Doc. At least for the present, these fellows were her friends and companions.

It was nice, *peaceful*, sitting out here on the porch with the two dogs and the scene of the farmland across the way. It might be a fine place to live out her years, of course with a companion worthy of her attentions. Yes. She was correct; a lovely spot in the countryside, somewhere like this, would be ideal.

It was not so very long ago that she and Brody MacKay found themselves sharing a new and strange landscape together, with nothing certain about what was to come. The time-travelling machine invented by Dr. Einstein had the means to power perhaps only two journeys through time, as Ebb Cade had reported to her after he had listened to Dr. Einstein through the walls of their office, and she had quickly decided to spend one of those trips to fly herself and MacKay to 2019 where she hoped Dr. Joseph Bell had been spirited through time by the Dundee tornado. She took a long breath as she remembered how little thought she had put into that decision; she felt it was what she was supposed to do, and she simply went about doing it, whether it was the correct decision or not.

***

...It was only a moment or so after appearing in 2019 Oak Ridge outside The Chapel on the Hill, that Irene realized she had not considered a few of the inevitable realities of attempting to live in a time that was not her own. She had entrusted MacKay to carry the heavy satchel she had brought along, which contained all the unexpected coins they had quickly scooped from the Cade kitchen table. It was a shame about the good-natured Ebb Cade; he had meant only the best for her, and had, indeed, possibly saved her life. Nevertheless, after Ebb passed through the walls of Dr. Oppenheimer's office and obtained the time device at her request and instruction, he had aged so quickly there was nothing she could do for the poor man except to return him to his small residence. She owed him that, at least. They eased him down, and he crumpled on his back to the scuffed tile floor of his kitchen. He stared up at her and Brody MacKay with the most vacant expression she had ever experienced. She could not imagine what he must have been feeling at that moment. All at once she felt a twinge of regret for Ebb's devoted wife Ida when she would return home at the end of her day only to find him dead.

The walk to downtown Oak Ridge seem to take no time at all. It was impossible to know if Skurow's Stamp and Coin still existed in this time, but she had always considered herself somewhat lucky, and hopefully, her luck would not abandon her in this future time.

After twenty minutes or so, she and Brody MacKay reached downtown. Other than a few unfamiliar large business establishments, such as Walgreens, and PNC Bank, much of 1944 Oak Ridge remained seemingly unchanged. Freddie Merchant's Furniture and Poppa Rick's Soda Fountain looked out on Maple Street, just as before.

They stopped in front of Skurow's. Irene let out a long breath. There it was, still operating after more than seventy years, seven decades since she had last seen the small stamp and coin business she had discovered on one of her several 1944 scouting trips around Oak Ridge.

"Give the parcel to me, Brody," Irene said.

He obeyed. "What are we doing at this place?"

"Just wait for me out here. I should not be long."

"Yeah." He looked at the ground. "Fine."

Irene pulled open the door.

***

The old man turned around when he heard the metal street door of his business squeak open. He gently set a tray of glittering watches down on the top of a glass case and squinted into the glare. A woman stepped toward him. She pressed a canvas satchel against her side with one elbow. He caught the flash of green from her eyes as she stopped across from him.

"Hello, ma'am. How might I help you this morning?"

"Hello, sir. My name is Irene. Irene Lithgow."

He took a small breath and extended one hand to her. "I am

Moses Skurow."

Irene shook his hand. "It is my pleasure." She eased the satchel from her shoulder and onto the glass case. "I have items I would like to sell."

Moses Skurow gazed at her. "Of course. My customers buy or sell, sometimes both. It is the way the business of collectables works."

Irene flipped open the canvas flap on the satchel and gripped a handful of the silver coins. She placed them carefully on the glass of the countertop.

Skurow blinked away from her gaze and tilted his eyes downward. He studied the coins through his wire-framed glasses for a few seconds without reaching to touch any of them. Then he looked back across at Irene and gestured at the satchel. "This bag is full of coins like these?"

Irene smiled.

"Some of these could be quite attractive to collectors, over and above the value of the silver content."

"I am in somewhat of a hurry, Mr. Skurow."

Skurow bent his head down at the coins again. "Are you British?"

"Originally, sir, yes."

"If you don't mind me asking, from where does this treasure of silver coins come?"

Irene frowned. "You wish to determine if these coins have been stolen?"

"You might expect, ma'am, uh, Irene, that since I took over operation of this shop from my father decades ago, I am often approached with merchandise possessed not by its rightful owner."

"I certainly understand. No, Mr. Skurow. These fine silver coins have been in my family for generations. My papa was a soldier, sent to India and other faraway places, and he collected silver coins from all over the world. He passed away, and after my mama left this Earth, leaving me quite alone, these coins became solely mine, since I have no siblings."

"I suppose then, Ms. Lithgow, you wish for me to appraise and then purchase these items?"

"For American dollars, please."

Skurow felt a disturbing pressure at the center of his chest. He had no idea what made him feel that way. Perhaps it was this stranger's comment about a British soldier being sent to India. The last time that would have happened was... "It will require a number of hours to properly appraise this number of coins."

"As I said, Mr. Skurow, my time is limited."

He took a breath. "The same could be said for any of us."

She caught something painful at the center of his gray eyes. "Mr. Skurow, you have already determined these silver coins have significant value, yes?"

"Yes."

"Then, perhaps, I could leave the coins with you, and you can then appraise them at your convenience."

"You would leave them here?"

She nodded. "All I require would be an advancement of your final payment to me."

Skurow furrowed his eyebrows at her. "An advancement of how much?"

"Several thousand, perhaps two thousand, two thousand American dollars."

"I must tell you, Irene, that I have already seen one or two of these coins that alone might be worth that sum."

"Then, you should have no difficulty with such an advancement."

Skurow studied the young woman for a moment. "Truth be told, you have no real idea of the total value of these coins, is that correct?"

She nodded. "Correct."

"And just so that I am clear, you wish for me to, well, give you several thousand dollars, after which you will leave all the coins in my possession without any official inventory or accounting, since, as they say, you have little time to waste."

"Yes."

He chuckled. "You are more trusting, Irene, than most customers with whom I have come into contact in my recent past."

"I rely upon your reputation for honesty."

"I appreciate that, Irene. My father opened this shop long ago, in a time of war, and when trust was a rare commodity."

"I understand perfectly."

Moses Skurow gestured at a black-and-white framed photograph mounted on the wall behind him. The faces of an older man and a small boy gazed down at him. "This was my poppa, Rudolph, and me. The photo was taken in the late 40s."

Irene looked up. The man in the picture smiled directly at the camera. His arm was perched upon the boy's shoulder. "Rudolph, your father, appears proud of his son."

Moses Skurow smiled. "Everyone called my poppa Rudy. He insisted." He blinked at the picture. "And it was I, and everyone in Oak Ridge at the time, who were proud of him."

"Oh?"

"He escaped the worst horror this world has ever known, and he managed to rescue me at the same time. By all that is holy, my poppa should not have lived long enough to have even been included in this photograph."

Irene groaned. "Mr. Skurow, as I said, I have a schedule I must keep."

"Please excuse me while I retrieve your cash and a receipt for the coins from the back of the shop. I shall return in a few minutes."

"Your fair dealing is appreciated. I will stay right here." She gazed over his shoulder at a different photo of the same young boy posing to the camera beside an older man with silver hair and a matching mustache.

Skurow tried to ignore that lingering pressure at the center of his chest as he turned from Irene and stepped away...

If the universe came to an end every time there was some uncertainty about what had happened in it, it would never had got beyond the first picosecond. It's like a human body, you see. A few cuts and bruises here and there don't hurt it. Not even major surgery if it's done properly. Paradoxes are just the scar issue. Time and space heal themselves up around them and people simply remember version of events which makes as much sense as they require it to make. **Douglas Adams**

Chapter 59: Cincinnati, Ohio
2019

The sights that flew by outside the dirty and streaked bus window were both amazing and disquieting. Some images were familiar, but others were almost beyond all imagination. Her former captor, the perverted Brody MacKay, stared out the glass as though he had been suddenly transported to Alice's Wonderland, although she was certain MacKay had never heard of Alice's literary adventures.

It had been a simple matter to find and hire a hansom vehicle to transport them through Oak Ridge to the local bus terminal. The displays of schedules and destinations were clear and easy to follow. She found a ticket seller and paid the fees for their journey to Cincinnati. The entire trip seemed to take no time at all, and she even found a few moments to relax and doze off after they had been riding for less than an hour.

***

"What are we doing here, Irene, if you don't mind me asking?" MacKay glanced at the huge metal vehicles that rolled all around him in the transportation terminal.

Irene said, "We will hire another hansom."

"Where are we going?"

"There is a large university in the vicinity."

"Why there?"

Irene looked off into space. "I would expect men of greater than average intelligence frequent that area."

MacKay stared at her. "I don't understand."

"If we are to accomplish our task, if we are to be successful, we will need guidance from someone who lives in this time, someone familiar with the local customs, the city itself. Hopefully, we can locate Dr. Bell and complete our business here."

MacKay took a breath and let it out. "Look, Irene, all I can think of is my Ma and Pa. All right? I said I would come with you into this future, and you would then take us back to 1892. We don't belong in this time, Irene. I can feel that it's wrong. Can't you? Besides, in this time, you and I have nothing. All our friends, all our family have turned to dust long ago. I don't think I care to live out my days in a place where I would be nothing more than a ghost to everyone around me."

"Yes, Brody. I understand. And I agree. Let us hire a hansom cab and visit the area around the university as soon as possible. I am certain we will find taverns and inns there in plentiful numbers."

"I ain't really hungry, Irene. Rolling in that huge metal carriage unsettled my midsection some."

She shook her head. "We will not be searching for food and drink, Brody."

"Then, why the hell are we going there?"

She smiled at him. "Let us find a hansom. I will explain on the way."

He closed his eyes, having little choice but to cooperate with whatever Irene Lithgow had within her twisted mind. "Can we just get on with it?"

Irene glanced around for any trace of a hansom cab for hire.

***

"This here is one of the best spots," the taxi driver said. "Always crowded with students and teachers from UC." He stood on the curb and opened the rear door.

Irene and MacKay leaned out of the bright yellow vehicle and stepped onto the concrete street. A brief cool breeze wafted across her face, and she pulled the gray hood attached to her wrap-around cloak up around her head.

"That's be twenty-two fifty," the driver said.

Irene studied the driver. He was short, just a few inches taller than she was, with copper-brown skin, black hair, and a thick black beard. She judged him to be of perhaps Indian descent. Irene fished in her small bag and pulled out a few green bills. She held them out to the driver.

He took the cash and stuffed it in his front pocket. "Change?"

Irene shook her head as if she had done this hundreds of times. "Would you please direct us to a popular tavern or inn, where my friend and I might enjoy a meal and spirits?" She adjusted the hood around her head.

The driver pointed across the street. "Right over there. Ladder 19. Best burgers in Corryville. And they got about four hundred beers on tap."

"Thank you, sir."

He stepped around to the driver's door. "You folks have a great day." He climbed inside the yellow vehicle and started the engine.

***

MacKay stood outside the *Ladder 19* tavern and gazed at the people on the walkway and the motorized traffic in the street. It was terribly crowded, loud, and confusing. If this was his future, he was sure he would not like it very much.

Irene Lithgow had asked him to remain outside the *Ladder 19* while she entered the tavern. She said she would not be inside very long, if fortune followed her. So far, Irene had been gone for about twenty minutes, and despite what he had told her before, his stomach was starting to gurgle with hunger. Perhaps he should have insisted on going inside with Irene and ordering a pint or two.

He looked down at the gray pavement and shoved his hands into his trouser pockets. He barely understood why Irene Lithgow did *anything*. But he would wait out here and observe the present time of 2019 until Irene decided her task inside was finished. He had little choice. He just hoped it would not be very long.

***

It took only a minute or so, after her eyes adjusted to the dim surroundings, that she spotted an appropriate candidate for her purposes. She chuckled. *An appropriate candidate.* That made it sound as though she was searching for an upstanding citizen to participate in a public election for a seat on the town council. She chuckled again; nothing could be further from the truth.

***

Nestor Martelli glanced once again at the sea of papers on the table in front of him and squeezed his eyes shut. Another semester nearly gone and another tsunami of essays to grade. The very thought of diving into the random and generally non-sensical thoughts of his sophomores in Classic English Literature nearly paralyzed him into a block of solid granite. Well, that was nothing new. It happened twice every year, and he supposed he should be used to it by now, after eleven years of teaching the same class. The same authors, the same lessons, the same thoughts exchanged, the same *Catcher in the Rye* impassioned speeches, and the same generally confused complaints about *Beowulf*, and, of course, *Huckleberry Finn, Moby Dick*, etc. all endlessly the same. Only the faces of the students changed, and he was not certain anymore if even that was the case. Wouldn't it be a strange twist if all his students were actually the same people, each and every year, playing some mystical prank on him? It may as well be true; nothing at all was ever different, and it was practically enough to drive a rational person to complete insanity.

He opened his eyes and spotted a thick glass mug of Christian Moerlein draft beer. A waitress must have placed it down on the table while his eyes were closed, or perhaps he had dozed off in boredom or utter despair. Who knew for how long? It was still a little early in the day for beer, especially since he needed to return to the university in an hour or so, but what the hell? He was entitled to break some of the rules from time to time. Besides, if he had to guess, probably eighty percent of his students were intoxicated in class, high from one substance or another. Maybe ninety percent. These days, it was almost the norm. Why should he be any different? Times had, indeed, changed, and why should he not change with them?

He reached for the mug and raised it to his lips. He caught a figure reflected in the glass, approaching his table like a watercolor in the rain, as a singer in some old song once said. He gazed ahead and blinked. His eyes must be entirely filled with tears, because he could not be seeing this clearly. A woman glided to a stop and stood at the edge of his table. The glare from the front windows obscured her precise features shadowed by a gray hood she wore over her head. Only a few wisps of dark hair peeked out from the front of the hood. A flash of metallic green from her eyes pierced the air and struck him at his core. His breath caught at the back of his throat.

"Hello," the woman said.

Martelli blinked again. "Uh, Hello." He stood and stumbled a bit backward as his chair caught on one of his shoes.

"Excuse me, sir, but you seem alone. I am a stranger here, and practically alone as well. My younger brother is with me today, and he does not favor public usage of alcohol, so he resists entering establishments such as this one." She glanced at the mess on the table. "I wondered if you would care for a companion to share a pint?" She gestured at the vacant chair. "Oh, if I am disturbing your important work, please pardon me."

Martelli's jaw dropped open but no words came out.

"Sir?"

"Oh, yes, sorry. Please join me. Yes. Please do." He offered her a chair

Irene smiled. The man was medium height, with ordinary features, not handsome, not ugly. His front hairline had somewhat receded, and he wore eyeglasses with dark frames. Irene moved to the chair and sat without taking her eyes from him. "Allow me to introduce myself, sir. I am Elizabeth. Most call me Lizzie."

Martelli swallowed. "Lizzie? Are you British?"

A Matter of Time

"Yes. And you are..?"

"Nestor. Nestor Martelli." He held an open hand out to her.

"It is my pleasure, sir." Irene took his hand for a brief moment and released it.

"Mine, too, Elizabeth."

"Please. Lizzie. I am unfamiliar with the name Nestor."

"It is Greek, Lizzie. It suggests a person who travels, or better said, a person who returns from a long journey."

"I have never traveled to Greece, and now that I think about it, I have not traveled practically anywhere outside the confines of my family home in England, and to Oak Ridge, Tennessee. Now, I have traveled here."

"I am nearly forty-three years old, Lizzie, and I am sorry to admit to myself that I have never traveled to Britain, France, or *anywhere* in Europe. The farthest I have been from Cincinnati, where I was born, by the way, is to Cancun. My parents took the family there as a celebration of my college graduation. I think my little sister is still sunburned from that trip."

"Are you employed? You appear to be a professional man, from what I can observe."

"I teach across the way at UC. Classic English Literature."

She raised one eyebrow at him. "I always found the time to tuck myself away somewhere with a great story written by a great author, to pass my time when I was still a young girl."

He scooted his chair a bit forward. "Do you have any favorites?"

She smiled. "The Moonstone."

He stared at her. "By Wilkie Collins?"

"I have read and re-read that story. I think I began to actually think of myself as Rachel Verinder, the unexpected detective of the story."

"I...I..."

"Nestor?"

He shook his head. "I am truly sorry, but in all my years of teaching, I have never had a single student mention that book, which is, as you might know a true classic for several reasons."

"Well, all I know is that I enjoyed the story immensely. And, of course, the works of Jane Austen. *Pride and Prejudice* is another favorite of mine."

Nestor Martelli began to feel as if he had suddenly been transported to an old black-and-white *Twilight Zone* episode. How else could he possibly explain how, completely out of the blue, a woman dressed in an old-fashioned cloak, a woman named *Lizzie*, with green eyes that could paralyze a man instantly with their stunning beauty, would walk up to him uninvited as if he were actually attractive? And when he considered her interest in classic literature, well...

"You know," he said, "Lizzie is the name of the heroine from *Pride and Prejudice*."

"Oh, yes. I do know."

"Of course. Of course." He raised the mug and took a sip of beer. "Oak Ridge, Tennessee? You mentioned you traveled to Oak Ridge. Why there, of all places?"

"Oh, I lived there only briefly."

He studied her face. "I can't remember why that place sounds so familiar."

"Just another small American town, Nestor. Not much to speak of." She lowered her eyes and stared at her hands folded on the table.

Martelli asked, "Is something wrong?"

"No."

"Would you like to order something?"

"Perhaps a pint. Yes. As I suggested before, we could share a pint, together."

"Sounds good. I will get the waitress."

She looked up at him. "Nestor, could I impose upon you for some small assistance?"

"Depends, I suppose."

"You have kind eyes, Nestor."

"Lizzie, you have fine eyes, if I may say so. With what do you need help?"

"It is really both my brother and I. We are searching... Our *eldest* brother has vanished from our lives. We have only a few pieces of evidence with which to use to find him. And so far, our efforts have not revealed his current location."

"Vanished?"

She nodded.

"What evidence do you have?"

"Several old photographs. They are not so clear, I'm afraid. We also have reason to believe he resides somewhere in the Cincinnati area, but is probably utilizing an assumed name."

"I might be able to help you, Lizzie. It would be best, however, that I use the computer at home. It is more efficient in this regard than my phone."

"I understand. Is your home far from here?"

"I could practically walk there."

"*We* could walk there. I will ask my brother to wait here for us. Perhaps he will become hungry enough to overcome his opposition to being inside."

"That would be fine."

Irene stood from her chair. "Please wait for me, Nestor. I should not be more than a few minutes. Then, I will make sure my brother is properly situated, and then you and I can walk to your nearby residence."

Nestor Martelli stood. "I will be right here, Lizzie."

She strode away into the glare of the windows at the front of the café.

*** *** ***

The first thing Irene noticed in Nestor Martelli's residence were the shelves completely filled with hundreds of books. She grinned when she recognized many of the titles. Classic books have apparently survived the passage of time, and she was pleased to consider that notion.

She glanced around at the many framed photographs and paintings on all the walls, as if they were attempting to conceal the very surface of the walls themselves. The images were almost entirely seascapes. Apparently, Nestor Martelli liked oceans and beaches.

Irene glanced around again as Martelli sat at a desk and began to push buttons in front of his computer screen. She spotted no photographs of a woman with whom he might be romantically connected. She also saw no photographs of any family members. Perhaps Mr. Martelli was just as alone as she was in this time and place.

"Let me see those pictures, Lizzie."

Irene stepped to him and reached inside her cloak. She

pulled out two photographs she had been able to print from the library at Oak Ridge. Martelli took the photos and studied them. Irene moved, stood behind him, and placed one hand on his shoulder.

"These are old, Lizzie. I mean, these are really old."

"Will that present a problem for you?"

"Uh, well, no, not exactly, but you say the man in these two photos is your brother?"

Irene took a long breath and sniffled. "Please, Nestor."

He placed the first photograph on his scanner. A moment later, he scanned the second photo. "There we go."

"Are you making progress?"

"Just need to sign into Facebook. They have some underlying facial recognition software embedded within its system. I've accessed it a few times before."

"I see."

He stared at the screen. "There. Got it. Found a posting by a lady in Hartwell, a Susie Palmisano. She says the picture is of her neighbor, Hattie Brooks, and her friend Wallace. Here. Come look and see. Is this a picture of your brother Wallace?"

Irene studied the picture on the glowing screen. The image was indeed that of the eminent Dr. Joseph Bell.

"Yes," Irene said. "That is indeed my brother."

"I have the address in Hartwell where this posting was from. It should lead you right to your brother, if he is still there." He pushed his chair back, stood, and faced her.

"Thank you, Nestor. I have so little in my life. You have helped me, a complete stranger, immensely. You could have turned me away and left me to flounder in my search with almost nothing to go on."

She reached up slowly with both hands and touched the sides of his face. "Nestor..."

As if some invisible force surrounded and pressured him, he lowered his mouth to her and closed his eyes. He tasted her lips and sensed the fragrance of fresh soap. He suddenly considered Molly Renfro who was the last woman he had kissed. When was that, exactly? A year ago? Maybe more than that? He thought about Molly just as he felt an incredibly sharp pain stab at the very center of his chest.

Sometimes I wish I could go back in time, sit down with myself and explain that things were going to be okay, that everybody loses ground sometimes and it doesn't mean anything. It's the way life works. This is hard to understand in the moment. You get to thinking about the girl who rejected you, the job you got fired from, the test you failed, and you lose sight of the big picture – the fact that life has a beautiful way of remaking itself every few weeks. **Donald Miller**

Chapter 60: Lebanon, Ohio
Present Day

Jessie spotted the long black sedan nearly a hundred yards before she reached the end of the farmhouse driveway. "Jesus." She gunned the Wrangler's engine; it growled in protest.

Bell glanced around. "What is it?"

The tires kicked up clouds of dust from the dirt driveway. Jessie jammed her foot on the brakes and the Jeep slid to a stop. Jessie shoved open her door and jumped out. She sprinted to the farmhouse.

***

Keaton brought the cruiser to a quick stop behind the Jeep. He watched Jessie hop out of the car and dash away through dust-filled air. He had no idea what had suddenly provoked her, but if Jessie needed his help...

The young detective shoved open the cruiser door and stepped out into the soft dirt of the farmhouse driveway.

***

Jessie raced to her front porch in less than twenty seconds.

She leaped up the steps and halted; the vision that struck her eyes punched every trace of breath from her lungs.

Oh my God...

Doc.

She had Doc in her lap.

Jessie's right hand shifted to her side. She jerked out her pistol, balanced the weapon with her other hand and pointed it straight at the woman who was seated on one of her rockers. "Listen to me." Her words were soft but commanding. "Very gently, place my dog on the floor. Now."

Irene studied Jessie for a moment then chuckled. "And we have not yet been introduced."

"I know who you are."

She tilted her head. "Has Joseph been talking about me?"

"I swear to God, if you so much as pinch that little dog..."

"You are mistaken, Miss Warren, if you believe—"

"Now!" Jessie yelled. "Put him down, on the porch. I won't ask again."

Irene shrugged just as Bell, Keaton, and Einstein stepped up and stopped behind Jessie.

"Irene," Bell said under his breath.

"Ah. Joseph." Irene grinned. "It was only a matter of time before we were reunited."

Keaton touched Jessie's shoulder from close beside her. "Holster your weapon, Jessie. Think about it. Whatever's going on here, we can figure it out, and without the use of firearms. Jessie? Please. Focus. Think about it."

Jessie gritted her teeth. Her Beretta 92 remained aimed directly at Irene's face. "Buster, you don't know what's really happening."

"Jessie, come on. Breathe. Calm down. She's unarmed."

"She's dangerous, Buster. You have no idea."

Irene draped both arms around Doc and pulled him close to her middle. She rested her chin on the top of his head and gazed at Jessie. "In the short time this little dog and I have known each other, we have grown quite close. When I found him, it appeared you had abandoned the little mutt, leaving him with nothing to do within his enclosure but to dig and dig, as dogs do. Idle hands, you know, but in this case, idle paws. Well, you understand. Do you not? Had I not rescued him, by this time he and his brown-and-white friend might have engineered an entire series of underground tunnels. And his water bowl was bone dry, Miss Warren. In the future, perhaps you should use some of your energy and mental focus toward the construction of aqueducts, such as the Romans did many years ago. The Romans were known throughout the ancient world for their engineering prowess, designing and constructing viaducts and aqueducts, thus bringing some civilization to a practically uncivilized world. Your small friends would never want for fresh water if you set your energies properly to it."

Jessie stared at her. "The dogs have plenty of water. You're rambling about nothing, and you're still holding my dog."

Scooter hopped off the other rocker, trotted over to Bell and sat on the wooden planks of the porch near Bell's right ankle. Bell scooped up the dog with one hand.

Einstein took one step closer. He studied the heavy metal box in his hands and then looked over at Irene. "She is one of the travelers from 1944," Einstein said. "Definitely. And according to my readings, the other traveler is a short distance away, perhaps in the vehicle we passed at the end of the driveway."

Irene gasped. "Albert Einstein?"

"Yes. I am Einstein."

"I have read much about you."

"Then you have me at a disadvantage."

"From what I've read, intellectually speaking, that is most unlikely."

"You and your nearby companion somehow managed to slip unnoticed into a guarded military building, a locked office within that building, into a safe controlled by a combination lock, and removed my other device, all apparently with an ease I am unable to explain."

"Dr. Einstein, if I explained how I accomplished that supposedly magical feat, you would undoubtedly be less impressed than you might now believe." Irene took Doc in both hands, bent forward and set him on the porch floor in front of her.

Doc immediately padded over to Jessie and pushed the top of his head against her shin.

Irene eased back in the rocker and gazed at Bell. "It has been quite some time, Joseph."

"In more ways than one, Irene."

She smiled. "Perhaps since I have now obeyed Miss Warren's commands, please ask her to not point that weapon at me."

Bell glanced at Jessie. She remained still.

"Jessie," Keaton said. "I'm right here...with you. Please."

Her eyes remained focused at Irene Lithgow. "Don't be mistaken, Buster. If we don't end this now, and I mean right now, what do you suppose will happen later?"

"What do you mean?"

"She deserves to die, Buster, for the murders she committed, both in our time and in her own time, back in Scotland. And if you take her in, she will never be convicted of anything. You asked me to think about it? You think about it, Buster. She will be a Jane Doe, unidentified, no prints, no history in our systems at all. What do you think will happen? I should shoot her, now, before we let this go any further."

"No, Jessie," Keaton said. "Calm yourself. Let the law take its course. She won't get away with murder."

Jessie noticed her hands tremble as she lowered the gun. She slid it back into the holster at her belt and let out a long breath. "There's a lot you don't know, Buster."

"Fair enough."

Jessie turned her gaze to Irene. "Well then, since we're all settled now, please explain to us, Irene Lithgow, why you have appeared uninvited here at my home? And please keep in mind, if you so much as take one step toward my dog again—"

"Miss Warren," Irene said, "you know exactly why I am here. Does she not, Joseph?"

"Jessie can speak for herself."

Irene nodded. "To save all of us some time, I will come right to the point. No reason to waste any more of the limited moments God in heaven gave to us."

"You came for Joe," Jessie said. "That's obvious."

Irene stared at her. "Miss Warren, your friend Dr. Joseph Bell formed a close relationship with me while I was a helpless captive in Dundee."

Bell grumped. "*Helpless* is not a word I would ever use to describe you, Irene."

She smirked. "Even so, I have always felt that Joseph and I were fated to become connected in life...and possibly beyond. This adventure we are all experiencing should serve to convince you of that, Miss Warren. Joseph and I have travelled unimaginable distances, and have somehow ended up here, within a few yards of each other, in both time and space. It is far more than merely a coincidence."

Jessie huffed. "Coincidence? Of course not. You engineered this, Irene. Your actions were purposeful, for you to find and be with Joseph at the end of things. This is as far from a coincidence as it could be."

Irene studied her. "Middletown, Ohio."

"Sorry?"

"I have recently spent some hours reading on a computer about small rural villages in America. Middletown, Ohio, not that far from our present location, by the way, is such a place. In the late 1940s, years after the war, Middletown was quiet, mostly farmland, and as free from crime and strife as a town might be. It seemed nearly the perfect time and place."

Jessie glanced over at Bell. "You thought Bell would voluntarily vanish into time with you, back to the 40s, and, and what?"

"My intention was always to demonstrate to Joseph exactly how much I am worthy of his attentions. And...his affections."

Bell said, "Irene, I am standing right here. There is no purpose in speaking as though I cannot hear you."

"Worthy, Irene?" Jessie glanced to her side at Bell. "Worthy how?"

"Miss Warren, you might believe you know Joseph quite well, but as he has no doubt recounted for you, Joseph and I spent countless hours talking with each other, sharing our most innermost secrets and feelings. We gained an intimate awareness of each other during those times, and Joseph knows exactly to what I refer. His talents utilizing the deductive reasoning for which he his renowned should serve him well as far as this analysis is concerned."

"You allow me too much credit," Bell said. "Deductive

reasoning is only viable when facts are utilized, and as far as you are concerned, Irene, I am uncertain of any such facts, since your emotional composition is typically motivated by reasons that essentially lack any fragment of sanity."

"To speak your mind plainly, then, Joseph, you therefore believe me to be insane. Is that a correct analysis?"

"More or less."

"I see. I see. Well then, I suppose I must do even more than I have already done to show you, Dr. Joseph Bell, that my intellect and cleverness display that I am truly worthy of a man of your superior quality and intelligence."

Bell glared at her. "You truly believed I would be motivated to spend my life with you because I would somehow be impressed with the methods you have used to go about murdering strangers?"

She shrugged. "In reality, Joseph, just as The Ripper chose his victims in our own time, those women were trollops, quite willing to consume alcohol and either sell their bodies for profit, or just give away their virtue with no arrangement for payment at all. Besides," she leveled her eyes at him, "not all of them were strangers. Were they?"

Bell edged forward. Jessie took one hand and pressed back against his shoulder. "Joe."

"This, this person killed my friend Laurie Markwell," Bell said, "for no reason that makes any sense at all."

"Joseph, you spoke before of motivation," Irene said.

Keaton said, "We'll take her in and make a case. She won't be hurting anyone again, in this time or in any—"

Bell put his hand up, silencing Keaton. "Irene, in spite of the friendships and relationships I have established here in this time, I do not belong here. My place is in Edinburgh in 1892 with my wife and daughter."

Irene let out a long breath. "From the photographs I have been able to find, it is amazing how much Fallon Dalmore resembles your wife Elizabeth, from 1892 Scotland."

"Photographs? I doubt it." Bell shifted his eyes to Jessie. "I asked Dr. Dalmore to meet us this morning." Bell turned to Irene. "What have you done to Dr. Dalmore, Irene?"

"Joe," Jessie said, "What makes you think she's done

anything to Fallon?"

"Now that you mention it," Keaton said, "Fallon was supposed to check in with me about the Markwell matter first thing. She never showed up."

"The human body can do without food for quite some time," Irene said. "But as far as the lack of water is concerned, well..."

Jessie lunged at Irene and grabbed her shoulders. "What have you done?"

"Miss Warren, your grip is quite strong, almost manly. Women of my day were rarely so muscular."

"Damn it, if you don't want to see what these muscles can really do, then you better tell us, and I mean right now."

Irene smiled. "But I already have."

"What?"

"I have already told you what I have done, and where I have done it. You have all the facts you should need, right now, at your complete disposal. All you really need in addition to what I have given you is a keen mind to analyze that information."

Jessie released Irene's shoulders and turned back to Bell. "Do you have any idea what she is talking about?"

Bell shook his head. "I am afraid I do not."

"Perhaps I might be of assistance?" Einstein said.

"Yes, of course," Jessie said. "We have the world's greatest mind here to help us. Please, Dr. Einstein. What do you know?"

Einstein nodded. "Detective Keaton, how long have you lived within the general area?"

"My whole life. I was born in Western Hills, went to school there, and then went to Xavier. Moved around a little, but never went far from where I was born."

"Excellent," Einstein said. "Then you are quite familiar with the city of Cincinnati, its history and surroundings. Is that a correct statement?"

"I guess. So what?"

"Detective, I am now going at ask you a few questions. Your answers to those questions will lead us to the information we seek."

"Uh, okay?"

"Where might we find a working viaduct? It is a raised bridge or other structure which is constructed to carry traffic across a valley, or other low ground."

Keaton's eyes widened. "There's one in Western Hills, been there forever. Takes traffic across I-75."

"Was the construction of the bridge somehow, oh, abandoned at some point during its construction?"

"Abandoned? I don't think so... But, now that you mention it...ages ago, I'm not sure maybe in the 30s, 40s? The city started to build a subway system that started *under* that viaduct, but it never got finished. Some people say it's haunted, or something. I think the entrance to that tunnel, the beginning to the subway, is still there, right under the bridge, but it's all boarded over."

Einstein nodded. "Thank you, Detective. That is quite helpful."

Jessie stared at Einstein. "You think Irene kidnapped Fallon Dalmore and concealed her within that abandoned subway?"

"I come to that conclusion based upon the words Miss Lithgow shared with us previously within her impromptu lecture about Roman engineering."

Jessie straightened her shoulders. "Buster, get on the radio. Tell them to break into that tunnel below the Western Hills Viaduct. Tell them we believe a kidnap victim is being held inside."

"I'll be right back." He strode quickly off the porch and onto the driveway toward his cruiser.

"Congratulations, Dr. Einstein," Irene said. "Your reputation is well deserved."

Einstein gazed at her.

"Irene," Bell said, "if these demonstrations of your intellectual strategy are meant to impress me, they have done the opposite. Inflicting harm to innocent people impresses me less than your overwhelming sociopathic tendencies."

"I believe you will think otherwise, Joseph, once you are alone and able to give this your full mental attention. And when that happens, I want you to imagine how it might be like to live your remaining days in a peaceful, bucolic town with a companion with whom you can share endless intellectual discoveries."

"Well now," a male voice from the end of the porch said, "ain't that interesting."

Bell, Einstein and Jessie all turned to see Brody MacKay at the edge of the porch. His right hand pointed a long gleaming knife straight at Irene Lithgow.

"Ah." Einstein looked down at the metal box he held in his hands. "Hello, Mr. MacKay. Welcome. You are our other traveler from 1944." He chuckled. "It seems like years since you and I have seen each other."

MacKay focused his eyes on Einstein. "Albert? What are you doing here? Last I saw you was in that jailhouse."

"I am attempting to see that things are set right."

"You look different, your hair, that new suit."

Einstein pressed a hand on his lapel. "I wanted to appear less conspicuous in this time, Mr. MacKay."

"I recall a promise you made me, Albert."

"Transporting you home to Scotland, yes, I recall."

"It looks like you could not manage a way to do that. I did not expect that you would."

"Mr. MacKay, I had the best of intentions in that regard."

MacKay came up the porch steps and moved toward Irene, the knife pointed straight at her. Keaton ran up the steps from behind MacKay, quickly shifted over and blocked him. He raised both hands out in front of him. "Hold on, buddy," Keaton said. "And put that knife down."

"Brody MacKay?" Jessie said.

"That's right." Brody had not lowered the knife.

"Jesus, Bell. He looks just like Timmons."

"I believe that was their idea, Jessie," Bell said.

"You are correct, Joseph." Irene cackled. "It took numerous trips to numerous financial establishments before we found a suitable double."

"And you were obviously, then, wearing convincing makeup that day."

"True."

"And my pen?"

"Just another signal sent straight to you, Joseph."

"Look," MacKay said, "you got no idea the lies this, this witch has told to me."

"Put down the knife and tell *us*, Mr. MacKay," Keaton said.

"It was supposed to be the two of us going back to Scotland, and just us, Irene Lithgow and me. I was listening, and now she sits here and invites Dr. Bell on some other trip through time, when we all know the time machine she's got can travel only one more journey. Can't say why I ever trusted her, but let me tell you, those days are over."

"Where did you get that knife?" Jessie asked.

"She keeps it and others like it in the back of our car. That's also where—"

"Brody, no," Irene blurted out.

Jessie said, "Mr. MacKay, is the time box in the trunk of that black car at the end of the driveway?"

MacKay nodded.

"Then let's go get it," Jessie said. "Okay?"

"I don't know about that. I still need to get back to my own time, yeah? And without that box..."

"Brody," Bell said, "how long were you listening to our conversation?"

"Long enough."

"Then you understand Irene Lithgow has no intention of traveling back to 1892."

"Yeah. I do understand that."

"But also understand this Brody. I knew if I ever discovered a method for returning to my 1892 Scotland, it has always been my intention to follow that path, back to my own time and place."

Jessie stared at Bell. She started to say something but stopped herself.

Bell would not let his eyes shift to Jessie. "And as Dr. Einstein has explained to us, the machine has the capability of transporting more than one person."

MacKay considered. "You mean, you mean you would take me with you?"

Bell nodded. "It seems only right, Brody. And I know your parents have probably suffered in your absence."

"Dreams like that, about my ma and pa suffering, have visited me almost every night, Dr. Bell."

Jessie tried to catch her breath and focus. "Okay, then, Mr. MacKay. Shall you and I go retrieve that box from your car?"

"Brody, don't do it," Irene said. "You don't know these people. How can you trust them? I promised to return you to 1892, and I certainly will do just that."

MacKay chuckled. "You ask me how I can trust them? Remember, Irene Lithgow, Dr. Joseph Bell is not a stranger. Also, I should never have trusted you from our first day together. Maybe that's a lesson I was supposed to learn. But, if I have to choose between trusting Dr. Bell and trusting you, well...you lose."

Jessie nodded at MacKay, and they both began to walk across the porch toward the dirt driveway.

Perhaps it's true you can't go back in time, but you can return to the scene of a love, of a crime, of happiness, and of a fateful decision; the places are what remain, are what you can possess, are what is immortal. – **Eric Weiner**

Chapter 61: The Farmhouse
Present Day

"Two time machines," Keaton said. "Power enough for one last trip, each box."

"Correct, Detective." Einstein stood at the edge of the porch, about ten yards from Irene Lithgow, with the rest of their group, Jessie, Bell, MacKay, and Keaton, just beside him. Jessie cradled the second time box against her midsection.

Keaton stared at the metal box Einstein held with both hands.

Jessie bit down hard on her bottom lip as a whirlwind of images streaked inside her brain. Joe was leaving. That was certain, if the box did its work. How could this be fair, by any sense of that word? They had just found each other, both physically and emotionally; their connection was undeniable.

She could encourage him to take her along, back to 1892, but that was crazy; it wouldn't work. First, he promised Brody MacKay that he would take Brody back as well. And as Dr. Einstein had instructed, the machine had power enough to transport two people at most, and he was not entirely sure of even that maximum capability.

Secondly, Joe had never truly let go of Elizabeth, and his life with her in Scotland. It would only make sense that the right thing for him to do would be to return there, even if it created some kind of alternate time stream.

But when she really considered all the possibilities, she knew that not only was she not destined to return to Scotland with Joe, but she was to take a different time-travel trip altogether.

"I'm curious, Dr. Einstein," MacKay said.

"Curiosity is the beginning of most scientific discoveries."

"Have you considered what you might do now, to where in time you might travel?"

"I have given the matter some thought."

"Please. Tell us."

"My answer might surprise you."

Keaton shook his head. "There's not going to be much that could surprise me any longer, Dr. Einstein."

Einstein took a breath. "My research has revealed another Dr. Einstein living in this time."

"Another?" Jessie said.

"Thomas Martin Einstein."

"A descendent."

"Yes," Einstein said. "My great-great grandson."

"Wow," Keaton said. "Where is he living?"

"Santa Monica, California. He is a physician, practicing at a university medical center."

"And so, you plan to show up there and, and..?"

"And introduce myself to my fifty-nine-year-old great-great grandson." A smile started at the corners of his mouth.

"Wow. And then what?"

"An excellent question, Detective, and I have given the matter some serious thought."

"Please explain," Bell interjected.

"I have conducted considerable study as to the problems facing this current time."

"What problems?" Keaton said.

"The issue I see published most often is the general concern about climate change."

"Yes," Jessie put in. "That topic of imminent global climate disaster is hot right now."

Einstein pulled his mustache. "If your news reporters are correct, not only is the climate of the Earth unnaturally warming, but mankind is contributing to that effect."

"That is one of the current theories," Jessie said.

"Then, if that is accurate, perhaps my scientific

investigatory talents might be well spent attempting to reverse that oncoming ecological disaster."

They all stared at him.

Jessie ventured to speculate. "Albert Einstein, here with us in this time, trying to fix climate change. Unbelievable. Just the very thought of that—"

"And you, Jessie?" Keaton jumped in.

"Me?"

"From the little I've overheard, are you going to use the second box to travel...where?"

She scanned all of them. "Yes. I am. If I did not, my life would remain haunted and I could never be really happy."

"Tell us," Keaton said.

Bell stepped closer to Jessie, stopped and faced her. He took a breath, began to speak, but no words formed on his lips.

"Bell?" Jessie said. "Joe?"

"Jessie, I..."

She moved closer. "What is it?"

"May we speak privately?"

She glanced at Buster and Einstein, took Bell's hand and led him away to the far end of the porch. "You look terrible."

"It mirrors how I feel at this particular moment. Joy and sorrow, both at once."

She studied his face. "I know. It's clear to me already. You've decided to return to 1892 Scotland."

"I have."

"And without me."

"I wish this could end differently, Jessie. For you and me, together. Good God. We just found each other. It seems...hardly fair."

He released her hand and turned away.

"Joe?" Jessie moved in front of him. She saw quiet tears glisten on his cheeks. "We've got the ability to time-travel. Think about it. With that power, we should be able to figure a way for this to end well for both of us. Christ, we've got Albert Einstein here to help us if we can't figure it out for ourselves."

"I do know that...but you think, Jessie..." He cleared his throat. "Think through the emotion of it and face the undeniable facts."

She moved a few steps to her side and leaned back on the porch railing. "Our ability to time-travel is limited. Right? Einstein said each of the devices has power enough for one further trip through time."

"And that is why, Jessie, despite the great power we possess, to actually travel through time but once, makes our decisions incredibly harder than they might have seemed at first."

She glanced across the porch at Einstein. "The fact that Einstein is here among us has changed everything, hasn't it?"

Bell stepped around and faced her. "You know that it has."

She gestured with both hands. "Einstein spoke to us of alternate, parallel universes, rivers branching out into smaller streams. That would explain how when Einstein traveled into our 2019, he instigated a new path, a concurrent timeline, which had no effect on what might have happened before in this present, or in any other stream of time."

Bell touched her shoulder. "And so, as opposed to what you and I deduced before, should I travel back to 1892, perhaps one hour or so after I initially was swept away, I would begin yet another stream, without changing anything in any other timeline."

She smiled through the tears that pooled in her eyes. "Meaning, you, you could return to Elizabeth and Polly, without affecting anything in their other concurrent existence, the one in which you would remain lost."

"Yes. That is what it means."

"Of course. Of course, you're right. If you have a chance to regain your life, your family, then you must. You must do that Joe. You have no other choice, really."

He stepped closer. "Jessie, when I thought I had no possible way to return to my Scotland, I let myself become closer to you than—"

"No, Joe. No. Enough of that. I understand. So let's put that behind us, and I mean right now, and figure out what comes next."

Bell sniffed and stared at her. He knew she was pretending not to be terribly effected by this unexpected turn of events, but he knew her well enough to realize that was far from the truth.

"Two machines. One time-trip each."

"Yes."

"Dr. Einstein has already decided to forgo one of those journeys, not return to 1944, and instead, attempt some kind of, well, 2019 family reunion with his great-grandson in California."

"I would give anything to be there when Einstein's great-grandson opens that front door."

He nodded. "Jessie, it is my intention to arrive in Dundee about an hour after the tornado struck the asylum, and I plan to bring along Brody MacKay, as I promised to him. MacKay will be able to rejoin his family. They will not even be aware that anything irregular had happened."

"That sounds like a good plan, Joe. A good plan. Things should work out well for both you and MacKay."

He moved closer to her and took one of her hands. "I think it only right that you use the second device for its one remaining time-stream journey."

Jessie squeezed her eyes shut. "Where the hell am I to go?"

"I am sorry, but this is a decision you must make alone."

She stared at him.

"You will have to be at peace with that decision, to live on with the outcome and aftermath for the rest of your life. You must be certain."

"How, Joe? How am I supposed to know..?"

"It is not a matter of intellect, Jessie. You must listen to the voices deep in the center of your heart that have counseled you along the pathways throughout your life up until now. Those inner voices will guide you, as they always have."

Jessie gazed at him, her eyes bright with a sudden realization. She slowly reached up and took his cheeks in both hands then stood on her tiptoes, tilted her lips up, and kissed him quickly. "You're right," she said, an inch from his mouth. "And I know exactly what I'm going to do."

Go back. Go back in time. Everyone's life is a chain of memories. In each chain there are shining links, happenings where this element of wonder...was very strong. Why don't you reach out and relive some of those memories? If you work at it, remembering the wonder can revive your ability to live life as it should be lived. **Arthur Gordon Webster.**

Chapter 62: Lebanon, Ohio
Present Day

K eaton clicked one cuff on Irene's wrist and the other cuff around the arm of a metal glider that hung from the inside ceiling of the porch. He straightened up, stepped to one side, and faced the slender woman who stared at him with a flash of metallic green.

"You're damn lucky I was here," Keaton said to her. "Jessie had blood in her eyes, and that's something I've never seen from her. She was like a different person."

Irene smiled. "What is to become of me, Detective Keaton?"

"I'm going to take you back, hold you until I can figure something out."

She shrugged. "That might be more difficult than you could imagine."

"Oh yeah?"

"How can you hold onto a ghost, Detective Keaton? Because that is what I am, a ghost of an autumn breeze, cast astray within the ages of time."

Keaton scoffed. "That's real poetic, Miss Lithgow. But from what was left of the body of Laurie Markwell I saw tossed away in a dumpster like another day's disposable trash, it might not be as hard as you might think. Besides, from what Jessie and Dr. Bell told us, Laurie Markwell is not the only recently dead body you're responsible for. With some digging, and with the stuff Jessie found in the trunk of your car, modern law enforcement techniques will find what we need."

Irene glared at him. Keaton felt a chill touch the skin on the back of his neck.

"I'll be right back." He turned from her and walked to the porch steps.

***

Detective Keaton," Einstein said.

"Yeah?"

"Later in this day, might I impose upon you for some assistance?"

"Uh, yeah. Sure. What do you need?"

"Perhaps you could advise me regarding transportation to California."

"Yeah, I could do that."

"I thank you."

"In fact, maybe you would like to drive across the country, with me. I could take you in my car."

"Again, I am grateful for whatever you can provide."

Keaton chuckled. "Wow. A road trip with Albert Einstein."

"I will most likely nap along the way."

"Yeah, well, even so. It might be a story for me to tell my kids about, if, uh, I ever have kids."

Einstein reached out his hand to Keaton. They shook hands once, and nodded to each other.

Bell said, "And while we are on the topic of transportation, Detective Keaton, might I impose upon you as well regarding transportation for Mr. MacKay and myself?"

Keaton squinted at him. "To where?"

"Scotland. But while I have proper identification, and can travel abroad unimpeded, the same cannot be said for Mr. MacKay. Somehow, those security barriers must be overcome."

"Yeah. I can work on that, Dr. Bell. We'll make it happen."

Bell smiled at him.

***

A Matter of Time

Jessie, Bell, MacKay, Einstein, and Keaton gathered about twenty yards from the porch at an old flagpole. The state flag of Ohio hung limply against the gray metal.

"I thought this flagpole might work as the quantum anchor you spoke of, Dr. Einstein," Jessie said. She glanced at Bell. He closed his eyes.

Einstein nodded. "This metal pole existed in the 1960s?"

"Yes. My grandparents installed it when they first built the farmhouse." She looked at Keaton. "Buster, are you still wearing that old Casio watch?"

Keaton glanced at his wrist. "Yeah. So?"

"Does it still keep good time?"

"It's like the Conestoga Wagon of digital watches, but it is always accurate, as long as I change the battery regularly."

"What time do you have?"

He looked at his watch. "Uh, five after one."

Jessie nodded. "Buster, would you do me a favor?"

Keaton studied her. "Jessie, are you sure about this?"

She let out a long breath. "No."

"Then..?"

"I don't really know, Buster. I'm just going with what my heart tells me, as I have done since this whole thing started." She glanced over at Bell.

"I mean, if you disappear," Keaton said, "gone to another time, I don't know, Jessie. I mean..."

She moved toward him and touched his forearm. "You mean you'll miss me. I know that, because I will miss you, too."

Keaton smiled through a few tears that started on his eyelids. "I can't imagine what it will be like here without seeing you at the precinct every morning, Jessie. It won't seem right."

Jessie gathered herself. "That favor, Buster?"

"Yeah, Jessie. Of course. What can I do?"

"Irene Lithgow is cuffed to my glider, and safe from any escape, at least for now."

"I don't see how she could break free."

"Okay. Fine. But don't take anything about Irene Lithgow for granted. She is not only a vicious killer, but she is also brilliant, and if there is any way for her to escape, she will figure out how to do it."

"Okay. Okay, got it."

"No, Buster. Listen. Really listen." She moved close to him and lowered her voice to a whisper. "She is evil and deserves to die."

He inched back a step and stared at her. "Deserves to die? Where's this coming from? Think about it, Jessie. You've never talked like this."

"I am afraid, Buster, either that witch will somehow find a way to escape her confinement, or she will eventually be acquitted of any crime, simply because it might be impossible to convict a person with no identity."

"I won't let that happen, Jessie. Trust me."

She nodded. "I do trust you, Buster."

"Good. And that favor?"

"Yeah. The favor. Okay, it is about ten past one now, right?"

Keaton nodded.

"I'm going to use the time box in a few minutes, if I don't chicken out. After I do that, I want you to stay here. Do not leave right away."

"Not leave?"

"No. Just stick around for, oh, an hour. At exactly ten minutes past two, please go back up to the porch and rap on the front door."

He stared at her. "Just, just knock on the door?"

"Yes."

"And then what?"

"I'm not sure. Maybe something, maybe nothing."

Keaton shrugged. "That's not much of a favor."

Jessie waited a moment, and then moved close to Keaton and hugged him. "Thanks, Buster. Thanks. I mean it. You've been a good friend."

Keaton felt tears begin again in his eyes as he returned Jessie's hug, and he instantly ached for this one single moment to last a lifetime.

That's the thing about Time Travel; you're always moving forward, even when you go back.

Chapter 63: The Farmhouse
Present Day

Jessie wrapped one arm tightly around the flagpole. The cold gray metal sent a chill across her skin, right through her shirtsleeve. She took a long breath and let it out.

She was really going to do this. Just the thought the implications of her decision nearly made her dizzy.

Doc was nestled against her chest, his front paws drooped over her free arm. The little dog had been her constant friend since she first found him behind the house in the sudden rainstorm, not far from where she was now standing. She owed Doc quite a bit just for his companionship; she was not about to let him down.

Einstein said, "Remember, Miss Warren. The device is fully prepared, and is set for August 17, 1962, according to your wishes. The time calculations are quite precise. When you are ready, simply push the single switch on the far left of the front of the machine."

Jessie gave a small nod and did not raise her eyes. She was aware of Bell, Brody MacKay, Buster, and Einstein watching her, but she hated goodbyes and had always avoided any dramatic farewells whenever she could. And this was definitely the worst goodbye of all.

"Go with God, my friends."

Jessie gritted her teeth, held her breath, and touched the switch with one finger.

***

Jessie noticed the freshness of the air even before she

opened her eyes. A light rain pelted her skin and the top of her head.

She tried to focus in the darkness. The flagpole, the nearby barn, the surrounding trees, all appeared the same, the best she could tell. The pounding in the front of her head didn't make it any easier to see clearly. Maybe in the morning, when the sun rose over the valley, and her headache was gone, things would look different.

A few lights glinted from the farmhouse, about a hundred paces away. She hugged Doc closer. He stared up at her, perhaps searching for a clue as to what might come next.

"Okay, Doc," Jessie said. "Shall we go?"

She exhaled and started forward. Her shoes scuffed the gravel in the path. She gazed ahead; the farmhouse was right there, her house, and it looked as it always had, just as she remembered.

A shadow moved on the porch and she halted. A sudden pressure started in the center of her chest.

A terrible thought suddenly occurred to her. Einstein theorized about time being like a river, ever-flowing in one direction and splitting into separate streams, which perhaps represented alternate universes or concurrent time-streams. Einstein felt that traveling to the past would not change the traveler's own time-stream, but would rather create a new and separate timeline.

But maybe by just going up on that porch she could start some kind of *butterfly effect*, like the one Bradbury wrote about. What if Bradbury was right and Einstein was wrong? The repercussions could be catastrophic.

She shook her head; too late to worry about that. Much too late. Her decision and its consequences were determined as soon as she had pressed that switch. Nothing she would do now could change what was destined to happen.

Jessie stepped closer.

"Who's that?" a male voice called from the porch.

"Hel...hello," Jessie said.

"What are you doing out there?"

"Sir, I..." She walked on, but still could see only a vague shadow on the porch.

"Are you hurt?"

"No. No, I don't think so."

"Hold on a few seconds."

The shadow moved to the end of the porch and down the steps into the grass. Jessie watched the figure step toward her.

"Doc," the man shouted gleefully. He stopped on the path a few yards from Jessie. "Oh my gosh, you found Doc."

The black-and-white dog squirmed out of Jessie's arms and dropped to the ground. He took two steps and jumped straight up into the man's arms.

"Hey, hey, little guy," the man said. "You've been out in the rain for almost an hour. I was starting to worry." He cradled the dog against his chest. "Funny thing...you should be soaked."

Jessie felt her face flush. There he was, right in front of her, Grandpa Paul, as a young man. He had died before she had been born, and it was a truly strange rush to actually meet him in this lifetime, especially when he was young and healthy.

"Hey, hey, I'm sorry, Miss. Come up on the porch with us," Paul said to her.

"No. Oh, no. I'll be on my way."

"Nonsense. It's still raining a little. Come on. I'll fetch us some coffee. Or maybe a beer."

"Yeah. Coffee sounds good."

They reached the steps and walked together up onto the porch. The ceiling shielded them from the last of the rain.

"Where did you find him?" Paul asked.

"Oh, the path behind the farmhouse."

Paul wiped raindrops from his forehead and eyebrows. "Doc likes it back there. Must be some good smells, or maybe some rabbits to chase. If there's one thing this little fellow likes more than anything, it's chasing rabbits."

"Yeah."

"Oh, Hell, excuse me. My momma taught me better manners than this. "I'm Paul. Paul Warren."

He extended his hand. Jessie flushed again. *The Grandfather Paradox*; what did Bell say about *The Grandfather Paradox*?

"Hi." Jessie took his hand and released it, then glanced around. No paradox. No obvious changes, at least not yet.

"And what is your name, miss?"

Jessie thought quickly back to what she had planned to say should this moment actually happen. She frowned as she suddenly realized none of those alternatives seemed right, now that she found herself standing across from her grandfather.

Jessie said, "Uh, I don't know."

"Don't know your name?"

"Or much else, really. Can't seem to remember. I must have gone for a walk on the path, the storm came up quickly, I remember lightning striking nearby, and, and after that..?"

"Hey, now. Listen. You look pretty shook up." He gestured across the porch. "Why don't you have a seat on this glider, rest for a few minutes? Try to breathe and calm yourself."

She moved to the glider and eased down onto the dark wooden seat.

Paul said, "Good. Look, sit tight. I'll be right back."

He turned away and stepped into the house.

She told him she couldn't remember her name. Exactly how did she come up with that one? If a criminal suspect told her that story, she would consider it pretty flimsy, but it was all she could think of to say.

And what did she really expect would happen once she brought Doc back to his own time? No real plan had ever occurred to her; she knew only a primary objective. Primary? It was her only objective. She had to bring Doc back to her grandfather, changing Grandpa Paul's life, *extending* his life so that he does not spend his days dying of an unrelenting despair.

But now..?

"Oh, hello," a female voice said.

Jessie brought her eyes up. Grandpa Paul stood beside a young woman.

"Hello," Jessie said. She started to stand.

"Oh, no," the woman said. "Sit."

Jessie edged back.

"I'm Nancy."

Jessie just stared. This was Grandma Nancy, as a very young woman. Incredible. She suddenly considered: why do science-fiction writers never talk about the grandmother paradox? It made no sense. She would have to ask Bell about it, if she was destined to ever see him again.

"Pleased to meet you," Jessie said.

"I hear you rescued our Doc from the storm."

"Yeah, I suppose I did."

Nancy studied her. "May I ask you something?"

"Sure."

Nancy took the back of a chair and pulled it closer to the glider then settled onto the chair. "It stormed for nearly an hour...just let up a few minutes ago."

"Uh huh."

"And you found Doc on the path behind the house?"

"Guess I did."

"Well then, Miss, unless my vision has completely failed me, you look barely damp. Truth be told, by all rights you should be dripping wet."

Jessie bit her bottom lip. "Sorry, uh, *Nancy*, but I can't explain it. Maybe after I found Doc, we discovered some cover."

"Cover?"

"Shelter. Could have been. I'm really not sure."

"Miss, did you fall and hit your head?"

"Wish I knew. Last thing I remember was this tremendous blast of lightning. It sounded like four hundred cannons firing all at once."

Nancy squinted at her. "Cannons?"

"It was really loud."

Paul said, "Nancy, she's obviously been hurt somehow. I'm sure with a little time, she will come to her senses."

"With a little time?" Jessie chuckled.

"Yes," Paul said. "Is that funny somehow?"

"A little."

Paul frowned. "In the meantime, while you settle and get your thoughts together—"

"In the meantime what?" Nancy gazed at her husband.

Paul looked at Jessie. "We were about to have supper. Please join us. It is the very least we can do for bringing our friend Doc back to us."

"No, I—"

"Please. I insist."

Jessie pondered the invitation. "If you don't mind me

asking, since we're strangers and all, will it be just the three of us?"

"Three of us?"

"Having supper."

"Why do you ask?"

"I just wondered if you had any kids inside."

Nancy shook her head. "No children have yet graced us."

A smile found its way to Jessie's lips. "All right. Sure. I'd love to have supper with you. With both of you."

Paul smiled. "Good." He rubbed his chin. "There's just one thing, though."

"Yes?"

"We will have to call you something until your memory returns."

"Oh. Yeah."

"How about Mary Lou?"

Nancy said, "Where did you come up with that name?"

"You know, like that Ricky Nelson song." He sang, "Hello, Mary Lou, goodbye heart."

"Sure, Paul. I suppose Mary Lou is as fine as any other name. Just stop the singing. That sounded terrible."

Paul ignored her slight. "Let's get to the table, then. Potatoes are getting cold."

Paul and Nancy Warren watched their unexpected visitor ease up gingerly from the glider. Then the three of them walked inside.

Time present and time past are both perhaps present in time future. And time future contained in time past. **T.S. Eliot**

Chapter 64: Scotland
Present Day

If Brody Mackay had already been surprised and amazed by what he had experienced while in 2019, that was all nothing compared to gazing at the clouds outside the window of the enormous metal bird as it soared through the heavens.

How could such a thing be possible? Even in his own time of 1892, the scientists were hard at work inventing one contraption or another. But this was different. This was practically magical.

The airplane landed and the two of them found their way through the mass of people in the airport terminal. Where were all these people going, and just how many of these winged-machines were all in the air at the same time? It was truly a time of great scientific achievement, but why did it seem that everyone and everything were in such a hurry?

After Dr. Bell hired a hansom cab, and as the city flashed by the windows, MacKay was suddenly grateful that he was about to return to his own time, a much quieter and less crowded place. He knew he did not belong in a world of noisy streets, a world where the meaning of the words peace and quiet had apparently been forgotten.

***

The hansom rolled to a slow stop on a deserted one-lane road. Fields of lush green covered most everything in all directions. Bell and MacKay glanced at each other, relieved they'd arrived at their destination.

"You folks sure this is where you want to go?" The

hansom driver looked at their reflections in his rearview mirror.

Bell reached into his jacket and pulled out his wallet. "Sir, what is the fare?"

"Twenty and eight."

Bell handed the driver some cash over the back of the driver's seat. "Thank you."

The driver took the cash, glanced at it, and nodded. "Come to pay your respects, then?"

"Respects?" Bell pushed his door open, wrestled with a heavy valise he was carrying, stepped out of the hansom and onto the grass.

"Place out here used to be a looney bin, sir, back in the day. It's where they shut away the crazies."

"Oh?" Bell gazed at something that jutted up from the ground in the middle of a field. He pointed toward it with his free hand. "Is that the marker, over there?"

"Sure is, sir. And that one was fixed up a couple years ago. Old marker faded with the weather and all. They placed the marker right beside the old brick column, which is all that remains of the original building."

"I see."

"Seems there's folk that lost family in the great storm back then, the wind that tore the place down and killed about two dozen. Some of the families of those that got killed pay to keep the marker and that column right there. If you're from around here, you know the story."

"I know some of it."

"Hey, Dr. Bell," MacKay said. "Can we get to it?"

The driver gazed at MacKay. "Dr. Bell, you say?"

"Uh, yeah." MacKay shrugged.

"Funny. The original Sherlock Holmes, Dr. Joseph Bell, was one of the Dundee staff killed that day."

Bell squinted at the driver. "I was not part of the Dundee staff, sir. I just performed a psychological rotation out of the Edinburgh medical school."

"What's that?"

"And there was no real Sherlock Holmes, sir. He was a fictional character."

"Yeah, well, I knew that."

"Pardon me, sir. Pardon me. It has been a long journey. Thank you, sir, for the transportation and the historical information." He closed the passenger door and stepped back. MacKay followed him.

The driver leaned to the passenger window. "You don't want me to wait for you?"

"That will not be necessary, sir."

"Best of luck to both of you, then." The driver engaged the transmission, and the drab vehicle sped away.

Bell and MacKay turned and walked to the jagged object they had spotted out in the field. They stopped and stared at the old column with horse hitches still nailed into the bricks. Beside the column, they saw a gray stone rectangle. MacKay read, "Here on July 17, 1892, at least twenty-four souls were taken by the Forces of Nature."

"It's all that remains." Bell took a long breath and looked at MacKay. "And it is fortunate for us that it is still here." He tucked the time-travel box under one arm and studied the crumbled brick column.

That's the thing about time travel; you're always moving forward, even when you go back. **James A. Owen**

Chapter 65: The Farmhouse
Present Day

K eaton looked at his wrist, glanced over at Irene Lithgow, still handcuffed to the glider, and then back at his watch; 2:08.

Two minutes to go. Two minutes before he performed the favor Jessie asked him to do.

He tried to think of any reason that made sense for him to wait an hour, walk over a few steps and knock on the front door, especially since the house was not occupied. Jessie disappeared in a flash of colored lights about an hour ago, and as far as he knew, she lived here alone.

It made no sense at all.

"Can I at least obtain a glass of water, Detective Keaton? Even the worst criminals in history were not denied water."

Keaton shook his head. "I'm not sure that's true, actually. We'll be getting out of here in a couple minutes. I've got a few water bottles in the cruiser."

Irene stared at him. Her green eyes projected a cold shimmer.

Keaton glanced at his watch once more. "All right, then."

He took a few steps to his left and raised a fist toward the door. He waited a moment, and then rapped his knuckles four times on the hard wood.

"Nobody's home," Irene said flatly.

Keaton shoved his hands into his front pockets and waited. He didn't know what he possibly could be waiting for, but it seemed right that he wait a few seconds or so. He flinched back as the front door pulled suddenly inward. He squinted into the glare. An elderly woman stood in the doorway. The afternoon sun glinted across her short silver hair.

"Uh, hi," Keaton managed.

The woman stepped forward onto the porch. She was short, and had luminous blue eyes.

Keaton blinked, looked away from her face, and then spotted the black Beretta 92 in her right hand, hanging down at her side.

"Hello, Buster," the old woman said and smiled. "You haven't changed at all."

Keaton's breath caught in his throat. "Jessie?"

She shook her head. "I'm Mary Lou. Mary Lou Warren."

"No you're not. I'd recognize your blue eyes anywhere."

"Then I want you to know that I've thought about it, Buster, just like you said." She gritted her teeth, raised the pistol, and aimed it straight at Irene Lithgow. "I've thought about it for a long, long time."

The quiet night was shattered by four sharp gun blasts.

Keaton stood frozen as the strong odor of cordite floated all around him.

The parallel universes approach that we suggest says there are different parallel universes where things are roughly the same, and each one is mathematically on a separate space-time manifold. You can go between those manifolds when you travel back in time. **Barak Shoshany**

Chapter 66: Santa Monica, California
Present Day

Thomas Einstein found his desk chair and slumped onto it. He pulled open a bottom desk drawer and gazed down at a dark brown bottle of Maker's Mark, sealed with its signature coating of red wax. He sighed and closed the drawer. He was not about to start that again.

Another day, another two surgeries. Nothing out of the ordinary. Maybe that was the point; fatigue closely followed boredom, he once heard it said, and whoever came up with that saying was probably right.

Lately, and for the last two years or so, his never-changing routine was beginning to drive him close to falling off a cliff into despair, as he had tried to find a way to make his life feel more like he was actually accomplishing something important rather than just keeping to his teaching and rotation schedules, moving ever-closer to retirement. It didn't seem like much of a true goal in life, and he was about fed up with it. Was this really all his life had boiled down to? No great achievements, no chorus of voices rising up and singing his praises at some random awards ceremony. One day, he would really like to hear those people call out and sing his name, if only once, as egotistical as that must have sounded. But instead, his life was relegated to a day-to-day routine, always, and never changing.

With his family name, he had a great deal to live up to, and it saddened him to think he would never come close to fulfilling that legacy.

His desk phone buzzed and startled him. He pressed the speakerphone button. "Yes, Cosette?"

His office receptionist was a nice enough girl, a talented graduate student in her very early twenties, whose parents no doubt met in a community theatre production of *Les Miserables.*

"I think...I think you should come out here."

"Cosette, you sound a bit frazzled. Why I should come out there. I have no patients or consults on my schedule today. Perhaps you've been on your own out there for too long."

"Dr. Einstein..." she lowered her voice to a whisper. "The second he walked in I thought I might be dreaming, but I'm wide awake and looking straight at him right now.""

Thomas Einstein stared at the desk phone. "Dreaming?"

"He's sitting in one of the chairs, just smiling at me. And he's holding a bouquet of flowers...pretty flowers."

Thomas Einstein groaned. "Okay, Cosette. Be there in a second." He pushed out of his chair and started out his office door, smiling to himself as he stepped into the hallway. *Flowers?* It appeared today might not be as routine as he had first expected. He approached reception from behind Cosette; she was standing behind the counter, looking out into the lobby. He took another few steps and stopped. An elderly man who held a bouquet of flowers stood from his chair and grinned.

His heart thumped in his chest.

She was right. Cosette was right.

"Thomas?" The man held the bouquet in front of him as if displaying a trophy.

And at that very instant, Thomas Martin Einstein's breathing stopped, his vision blurred, he heard symphonic music and a chorus of voices rise up from all around him, and he was certain, at that precise moment, all traces of any boredom had completely vanished, and he most definitely could hear the people sing.

People think of time travel as fiction...and we tend to think it's not possible because we don't actually do it. But mathematically, it is possible. **Ben Tippett**

Chapter 67: Dundee, Scotland
Summer, 1892

E lizabeth Dalmore Bell sat in the grass with her chin on her knees and gazed about ten yards down a small hill at the rubble of the Dundee Asylum.

A few droplets of rain cooled the heat she felt on her cheeks and forehead. She shifted, folded her legs underneath her, tilted her head and stared at the ground. Tears began to pool in her eyes.

The facts are never fair, Joseph had said to her from time to time. *The facts are just the facts, and once established, cannot be disputed. Fairness has nothing to do with it.*

She wiped her eyes with a cuff of her blouse. Of course, Joseph was right. Very little in life was fair, if anything at all, but that realization didn't make this heartbreak any easier.

She looked back over her shoulder and watched little Polly about twenty yards away. She crouched down and took one of Malcolm's front paws in each hand. Elizabeth could not hear her words, but Polly was talking non-stop to that hound, as always. Lord knew what Polly was saying, but Malcolm perked his droopy ears and tilted his face at her, as if he understood every single word.

Elizabeth turned her head back around, and she stared once again at the debris in the center of the field. Up until a short time ago, her life was headed in a straight, unfaltering course, a life that included a successful, devoted husband, and a happy, loving daughter who was truly the shining star of her life. Now, in less time than it took to prepare a morning breakfast, her life had been broken into a thousand jagged pieces, and it was impossible to predict what path her life might now take. But whatever happened, whatever she did now, her life would continue without Joseph, and that kind of life would not be as fulfilling as it might have been, but for the uninvited intervention of Mother Nature.

Elizabeth stood and again glanced back at Polly. Oddly, the little girl was running toward her with her arms waving wildly into the air.

***

Brody MacKay coughed as he tried to clear his throat from the dust and grit. His head pounded over his eyes, just the way it did when he woke up on the ground in Tennessee.

"Brody," a voice said. A hand gripped his arm and pulled him to a sitting position. "Brody, it's me."

MacKay focused. "Dr. Bell?"

"Yes. Are you all right?"

MacKay blinked. "I think so."

"Good. Can you stand?"

MacKay nodded.

"Then let's get you to your feet. Take my hand."

Bell reached down, took one of MacKay's hands and pulled.

MacKay gained his feet, steadied himself, and looked around. "It worked. Holy Jesus, the time box worked."

"It appears so." He glanced around for his cane, and then noticed the tremble in his fingers had vanished. "There are people looking through the broken walls, Brody, like the storm just happened. We must have arrived ninety minutes or so after the fury of the storm ended, as we planned."

MacKay slapped dust from the front of his shirt and trousers. "Dr. Bell, I don't know how I will be able to repay you."

"It was the right thing to do, Brody. No thanks necessary."

"You are a man of your word, Dr. Bell. And there ain't many men I can truly say that about." His expression changed as he caught sight of something beyond Bell's right side. "Dr. Bell? There's a little girl running right this way."

A voice called, "Poppa."

"And a dog."

Bell turned just as Polly ran into him. She threw her arms around his middle. A second later, the hound leaped into the air. Bell reached both arms out at the last instant and caught the thick-bodied Beagle. "Malcolm."

The dog licked happily at Bell's face. A small dog on the ground barked and yapped up at both Bell and Malcolm. Bell bent and lowered Malcolm to the ground.

"Poppa, I knew you were fine. I knew it." They hugged each other again. "Who is this other dog?"

Bell was about to answer when Elizabeth stepped up, hugged him, and let out a long breath. She kissed the side of his face and pulled back a step. "I was concerned, Dr. Bell."

"No need, Elizabeth." They studied each other.

"Ah, excuse me, and all," MacKay said. "But I should be on my way."

"Oh, Brody, Elizabeth, this is Brody MacKay. He works, uh, worked at the asylum."

"Pleased to meet you, Mr. MacKay."

"Poppa," Polly said, "who is this cute dog?"

"This little fellow has been my friend for quite some time...at the asylum. He lived there, I believe. His name is Scooter. I'm sure I must have mentioned him to you, Polly."

The little girl scooped up Scooter and held him in both arms. "But where is Scooter going to live now, Poppa?"

Bell looked at both Polly and Elizabeth. "If it's all right with both of you, I thought he could come home with us."

"Truly, Poppa?"

"Malcolm seems to like him."

Elizabeth raised one eyebrow at him. "Certainly, Joseph. Scooter is welcome."

MacKay said, "Dr. Bell, my horse Thunder is gone. Looks like he tore down the hitching post and galloped away. The storm must have spooked him something fierce."

Bell hugged Elizabeth tightly. "You are welcome to spend the night with us, Brody. I will come back here with you at first light. I am sure we will find your horse. There is plenty for him to eat here; he has no reason to wander far."

"That's real friendly of you, but my ma and pa will worry if I don't come home. I can hike around the moor and make it there in less than thirty minutes if I put my legs into it."

Bell nodded. "Then I will meet you back here at 7:00am, if you would like. We will find Thunder."

"All right. Well, goodbye to you for the night, Dr. Bell. And a pleasure to meet you fine ladies, as well." MacKay tipped his hat to Elizabeth and Polly, even though he wasn't wearing a hat. He turned and strode quickly away along the dirt path that led to the edge of the woods.

Elizabeth smiled at the sight of Polly sitting in the grass, the two dogs with her and with each other. After a few moments, she stepped back from Bell inquisitively. "You are wearing some peculiar and unfamiliar clothes, Joseph. These are not the clothes you wore when you left home this morning."

"Oh?"

"Also, why have you not mentioned Scooter before? That is peculiar, as well."

"To what conclusions do these observations lead you, Elizabeth?"

"All is not as it seems. I cannot discern exactly what, but something is amiss."

"You've always been the smartest of our family, Elizabeth, but sometimes the facts you consider are not the facts at all."

"So, the facts can be disputed?"

"At times. Yes."

She stepped close to Bell. "There was not a single moment, Joseph, that I thought I had truly lost you. I knew, somehow, you would find a way to survive this."

He took her shoulders, pulled her even closer, and kissed her forehead. "As the Earth spins on its axis, as our planet revolves around the sun, and as our galaxy spins within our universe, I will love you forever, my Elizabeth, and there is nothing in space or time that will ever keep us apart."

Tears came quickly to her eyes. "Let's go home, Joseph."

He smiled as he took her hand. They began to walk back to what had been the front of the asylum, and to their horse-and-buggy. Polly saw where they were headed and ran to catch up, with Scooter and Malcolm close behind.

Whether you can go back in time is held in the grip of quantum gravity. We are several decades away from a definitive understanding, 20 or 30 years, but it could be sooner than that.
Kip Thorne

Epilogue: Spring Grove Cemetery
Morning: Present Day

Keaton glanced to his right at Mary Lou Warren as he guided his cruiser to a stop in the gravel pull-over. He considered how old she must be as he switched off the engine and remained still. Judging a person's age was never something he was good at, but if he was forced to make a guess, he would estimate this woman's age at somewhere in her late 70s. Whatever her age, his front seat passenger appeared in good shape, fit and alert.

He tried not to think about Mary Lou Warren's age any longer. It was early, far too many random thoughts were already spinning in his head, and he felt slightly dizzy. He trained his eyes straight ahead through the cruiser windshield; the cemetery was lush, green, and apparently deserted. He tried to gather his thoughts. "Is this right?"

"Fine. I have two spots to visit. They are close by, but are in slightly different directions from each other."

"Okay. I'll let you pay your respects alone, give you some peace. Is there anything else you want to say to me before you, uh, get out?"

She noticed that he avoided her eyes. "It would be nice if you would uncuff me."

He gave a quick chuckle. "Miss Warren, my mother was absolutely infatuated with Paul Newman. You know, the actor?"

"I know who Paul Newman is," Mary Lou said.

"Well, she liked his *blue eyes*. She often said that even

when Paul Newman grew pretty old, his blue eyes never changed. They were still dreamy even when he was in his 70s."

Mary Lou didn't say anything.

"Anyway, the county cruiser is just behind us, blocking the only road that leads to the exit. They're allowing us this time only as a favor to me. I called in a few cards."

"I appreciate that."

They both sat without moving for nearly a minute.

"Should I ask which gravesites you are here to visit?"

She shook her head. "It wouldn't make any difference to you."

"Then why not tell me?"

She smiled. "My grandparents are buried here...and a friend of a friend."

"Fair enough." He reached into a front pants pocket and pulled out a set of keys. "Give me your wrists."

She held the cuffs out to him.

Keaton noticed her hands appeared tan and strong; no arthritis had yet visited this lady's fingers. He inserted a key into the cuffs and unlocked them.

"Thank you."

"*Your* blue eyes, Miss Warren...are just as beautiful now as—"

"Buster, no." She reached over and placed one hand on Keaton's forearm.

He gazed down at her hand as tears began to form in his eyes. "This is Einstein's doing, isn't it?"

"To some degree."

Keaton wiped his tears from his cheeks with his free hand. "I won't see you again."

"Probably not."

"Do you, uh, have a plan?"

"I do."

"And I suppose you've developed this plan over a long period of time."

"Yes, although the phrase *a long period of time* could be interpreted in different ways."

He smiled at her. "Those county guys won't just sit out there forever."

"I know."

Keaton studied her face. "Goodbye, then...Jessie."

"Thanks, Buster. I will never forget your understanding."

"Yeah, well, Jessie, you know it's always been more than just my understanding."

"Goodbye, Buster." She pushed open the Cincinnati cruiser door and stepped out onto the early morning grass.

***

The gravesites of Paul and Nancy Warren remained carefully kept, just as the last time she had visited here several months ago. There they were, side by side and together now as they were for most of their lives. Jessie bowed her head and closed her eyes.

"It is unlikely that I shall return here, Grandpa Paul, Grandma Nancy," she whispered. "But that shouldn't matter. You both will stay alive, in my heart, and a constant part of my days, for all my remaining time on this Earth. Thank you for treating me as you would have treated your own daughter, should you ever had children." She took a long breath. "And if we are all fortunate, we shall again be with each other sometime later. I've never been very religious, but..." She wiped tears from just below her eyelids. "Whatever shall happen now, I owe both of you too much for me to adequately explain. Just know that I loved you always, and I'm thankful we were permitted to spend so much time together."

She nodded once at the grave markers, turned, and walked back to the pathway in the grass. Jessie stepped along slowly for about two minutes and stopped. She gazed down at a different headstone.

"Nadine 'Hattie' Brooks," Jessie read. She smiled. "You and I never met, Hattie, but Joseph spoke of you so often it feels as though we are far from strangers." She shook her head. "This will be the last time I visit here, Hattie, at least I expect it will be. Anyway, Joseph still loves you, and I'm sure that wherever he is, he still thinks about you all the time. Take care, Hattie, and know that you made a good, positive difference in the life of a man I care so very much about. And I suppose, making a positive difference in life is the best that any of us could possibly hope for."

She gazed at the ground, then turned and began a quick walk off the path to the back boundary of the cemetery where she hoped the battered old Corolla was still parked there, on the other side of the cemetery fence behind a neglected stand of trees.

***

She found the place easily. After a short walk through a light rain from the Edinburgh Waverley train station on the outskirts of Old Town, she found the cottage nestled amid a row of similar homes, all carefully tended with flowing shrubbery and tall thick hedgerows. She imagined that this neighborhood had probably not changed much in appearance for more than a hundred years, maybe longer, and that thought gave her some small comfort as she faced the front door of the cottage. She took the last few steps, faced the door, and raised her hand. The door opened before her knuckles touched the door.

"Oh, hello," a woman inside the doorway said.

"Hello."

"I, uh, wasn't sure you would actually show up."

"Neither was I."

"Well, please come in out of the weather. It is still sprinkling a bit." The woman was in her mid-forties, with long, curly brown hair and deep brown eyes. She pulled the door closed and faced her guest. "I'm Jessie," the woman said. "Jessie Dormer. Well, Jessie *Bell* Dormer, actually, but I suppose you knew that."

"Yes. My research uncovered your full name."

"I suppose it would have."

"I'm Mary Lou Warren." She extended her hand.

They shook hands. "Pleased to meet you, Ms. Warren."

"Likewise."

"Warren. Huh." She chuckled.

"Something funny?"

"No. Oh, no. Strange, is all."

"Ms. Dormer, the longer I live, the more I come to realize the world is truly filled with strange occurrences."

Jessie Dormer gazed at her and nodded. "May I offer you

tea? I have also prepared cucumber sandwiches. I did not know if you favored them or not, but I felt I needed to offer something."

"Yes. Of course. That would be fine."

"Please, make yourself comfortable. I shall return in a moment."

Mary Lou gazed around at the room as soon as her namesake had stepped away. The sitting room was ordinary enough, if a bit old-fashioned. But what drew her eyes immediately were the six or seven fairly large oil paintings, framed and mounted on each of the walls. She stepped closer to a painting of a sunny seascape, blue-green water lapping at the white beach. A man stood at the water's edge. He held the hand of a small girl who stood beside him. They both faced the water, as if admiring the horizon, enjoying a peaceful, glorious day together. A short brown dog was with them, sitting, and it stared at a nearby sea bird pecking in the sand.

A signature was written with blue paint in plain letters across the bottom right corner.

"Tea will be ready in a few," Jessie Dormer said as she walked back into the sitting room. She moved close to Mary Lou and gazed at the painting. "This is one of my favorites."

Mary Lou sniffed once. "I noticed the signature."

"Oh, that's my grandma Polly."

"Polly Bell."

Dormer sighed. "She began painting when she was just a little girl. She made a small studio here from one of the bedrooms. When I came to visit, she would take me in there and show me her works in progress. I inherited the cottage after she passed. I've kept it the same as always. Somehow I couldn't bear to change anything. I come here on weekends to just relax and remember."

"I understand. These paintings, these scenes, they are all so bright and happy."

"I know. Never even one dark cloud in the sky. I think that's why I liked them so much."

"They are lovely."

"I tried to convince Grandma Polly to get them into a gallery, or just sell them at a street fair, but she would not hear of it. She told me these images were for her, so that she could remember some of the happiest times in her life. She would never even consider these paintings being taken from her."

Mary Lou sniffled and blinked the beginning of tears away.

"Are you all right, Miss Warren?"

"Yes. I'm just moved, is all, very emotional."

Dormer studied her. "Since you have been doing research before you got here, for your book and all, you probably already know how I got my name?"

A soft whistle came from the next room.

"Oh," Dormer said. "The water is up. Come. Let's pour our cups and sit outside in the garden." She smiled and started away. Mary Lou followed her a few steps behind.

Mary Lou scanned the kitchen. It was equipped with modern appliances, but the countertops, the walls, and floor all appeared original, although they had to have been completely reconditioned. House plants and flowers filled the tiled windowsills, and fresh potted herbs crowded the counter tiles around the sink. The effect was quite charming.

"Let's take ourselves outside, yeah?" Dormer held a tray with two teacups and a plate of small sandwiches.

Mary Lou followed her out the back door and into the morning sunlight. She admired the brick flooring and the nearby garden. The entire area was enclosed by shoulder-high brick fencing.

Dormer set down the tray on a side table, took a dishcloth she had brought from inside and blotted the light rain from two garden chairs. "Come. Sit."

They sat. Dormer handed Mary Lou a cream-colored teacup.

"Thank you."

"As I was saying before, about my name."

"Oh, yes. Please. Tell me. I may have missed some important facts."

Dormer poured tea. "One of my favorite things about coming here to visit Grandma Polly were the stories she would tell me when it was time for bed. Grandma would sit on the edge of the covers and tell me the same tall tales her father, my great-grandpa Joseph, would tell her at bedtime."

Lane Cohen

Mary Lou felt her cheeks flush.

"They were stories of high flying, fantastic adventure. The heroine of each story was always the same, a strong-willed, beautiful woman with shiny auburn hair and deep blue eyes."

"Sounds exciting."

"I believe he must have modeled the stories after the Alan Quartermain tales, a literary character from great-grandpa Bell's day. When I was old enough, I read some of the Quartermain books."

Mary Lou sipped tea.

"The two characters were quite similar indeed, I did find out, in their complete lack of fear, and in an endless quest for adventure. The main difference, however, was that Alan Quartermain dealt with real-life places and situations, although somewhat exaggerated. Great-grandpa Bell's heroine was more sci-fi, since most of her stories involved some element of time-travel."

Mary Lou's throat tightened.

"Each tale he told my grandma Polly was filled with trips to other times and faraway places. His heroine visited with Napoleon, Blackbeard the Pirate, Tom-Tom, who was a real Tarzan-like character who could barely put together one coherent English sentence, and many others. She visited ancient Egypt, battlefields filled with Roman Legions, and other times and places too many to count. Sometimes, the stories even had a hint, just a *hint* of romance. And when I visited here with grandma, she told me the same stories, over and over. In fact, they were so exciting and so terribly long, that I had a hard time falling asleep after." She smiled. "Grandma told me that her father Joseph would have wanted her to tell me those same stories, to ensure that those adventures, and the characters who meant so much to us, managed to live on, at least in some regard."

Mary Lou set down her teacup and remained quiet.

"And the name Grandpa Bell gave to his heroine...it was Jessie. Jessie *Warren*."

"I...see."

"That is why I reacted oddly when I learned your surname was Warren."

"I suppose I can, uh, understand your reaction."

"And that is also the reason my mother and father named me *Jessie*, after great-grandpa Bell's heroine. You see, my parents knew how much those adventure stories meant to me, since they instantly reminded me of all the wonderful times I spent with Grandma Polly. That name, *Jessie*, and my middle name *Bell*, also served as a kind of memorial to Joseph Bell, who, as you no doubt are aware, is known to history for other reasons altogether." She waited a moment. "Ms. Warren?"

"Yes?"

"You said in your emails you are an author?"

"I did say that."

"Would I be familiar with anything you have written?"

Mary Lou shook her head. "Even though I have written ten novels over the years, I am still unpublished."

"Oh?"

"I always felt the stories were mine, private and for me only, not for the eyes of others. This latest book I am working on deals with your great-great grandfather."

"Yes. You told me."

"I decided to bring Dr. Bell to present-day Scotland, and to other places, to see how he might apply his renowned talents to modern problems."

"Interesting. I have considered the same, from time to time, I think just so I could imagine meeting him."

Mary Lou eased back in her chair and gazed up at the few clouds in the blue sky. "Ms. Dormer, how much time do you have to spend with me this lovely morning?"

"Plenty, I suppose. After your emails, I set aside the entire day, actually."

"Good. I wonder if you would like to hear some plot ideas for the story I'm writing about Joseph Bell, a story based somewhat on fact."

"Yes, I would. Certainly."

"This is a tale you might not have imagined."

Jessie Bell Dormer squinted at her. "Please, tell me."

She took a moment and settled herself. "It is a story...a story of people who loved each other, a story of great scientists who changed the world." She stopped to catch her breath. "Of course, we cannot leave out the stories of the dogs we loved, and who loved us, entirely and unconditionally. The dogs who changed our lives more than any of us can ever really explain."

Dormer's eyes pooled with tears as she stared at the elderly woman.

"And a story of one or two other...very important things."

"Yes?"

Mary Lou smiled and leaned forward. She waited until Dormer's eyes met her own. "Far-flung adventure stories of romance." She took a long breath. "And with, of course, a hint of time-travel."

A Matter of Time

Author's Note:

Obviously, some of the characters in the story were real people, such as Einstein, Oppenheimer, Fermi, and Dr. Joseph Bell, who is known for being Conan Doyle's original inspiration for Sherlock Holmes. Less obviously, the characters Ebb Cade and Pvt. Elza Gate were real people who worked and served at The Manhattan Project in Oak Ridge, Tennessee. Much of Oak Ridge is described accurately, such as The Chapel on the Hill, and the *hutments* that were constructed to house the hundreds of project workers. The doctors and scientists in Oak Ridge actually did inject Ebb Cade with a solution of plutonium so they could observe the effects of such exposure. Ebb Cade did experience many of the effects as described in the story, but as far as this author knows, Ebb did not acquire the ability to pass through solid objects. Thomas Martin Einstein was Albert Einstein's great-grandson, and he did work as a physician in Santa Monica, California. It is extremely doubtful that the two men ever actually met. And when you consider Thomas Einstein's life, it must have been tough for him to go through his years in the shadow of the smartest man on Earth.

LC

Lane Cohen

About the Author

Lane Cohen attended the University of Cincinnati, studied musical theater, and has appeared in West Side Story, Bye-Bye Birdie, Funny Girl, Footloose, Jekyll & Hyde, and more. His favorite authors are Robert B. Parker, Carl Hiaasen, and Stephen King. His favorite rule of writing: "Write drunk. Edit sober." - Ernest Hemingway. He's authored several short stories and novels, **A Matter of Time** being his third published book with TWB Press, plus **Protection**, the story of two brothers who face an ancient evil in Protection, Kansas, and **Below Par**, a comical tale of a brokenhearted romantic who immerses himself in learning the art of playing golf. A civil lawyer by day, he lives on a rural ranch in Parker, Colorado, with his wife, Barbara. Here he's pictured with his friend Leo, a dog who rescued him not long ago.

Other Books by Lane Cohen

The new owner of the old Darabont Estate in Protection, Kansas, has a problem. Hideous creatures live in the basement, the walls, and the shadows. So he calls on the town's Afghanistan war heroes, the Gates brothers, to help him rid the house of these tormentors so his family can live there in peace. The ensuing confrontation leads to the death of one of these monsters and sparks a war between the undead and the living, a conflict that will pit family values against family loyalties and determine the fate of everyone in this small town...monsters and humans alike.

www.twbpress.com/protection.html

Charley Davis, brokenhearted since his girlfriend dumped him, is living a dead-end life and working a mediocre job when his uncle offers him a path to a better future: "Quit your job and learn to play golf as good as the pros in only nine months." Charley, who has never played a round of golf, declines, but when his boss tries to make him a part of an illegal scheme, Charley quits his job and reluctantly accepts his uncle's challenge. Skeptical at first, Charley works with oddball trainers, a stray mutt befriends him, and without warning, his uncle brings in the ex-girlfriend to film his progress. Torn between past emotions and future love interests, Charley's journey to become a pro golfer is further complicated by an additional requirement. He has to do it all...blindfolded.

www.twbpress.com/belowpar.html

Lane Cohen

http://www.twbpress.com

Science Fiction – Horror – Supernatural – Thriller

www.ingramcontent.com/pod-product-compliance
Lightning Source LLC
Chambersburg PA
CBHW051136030726
47504CB00004B/893

* 9 7 8 1 9 4 4 0 4 5 7 0 8 *